Delores Fossen, a *USA Tod...* written over a hundred and fifty novels, with millions of copies of her books in print worldwide. She's received a Booksellers' Best Award and an RT Reviewers' Choice Best Book Award. She was also a finalist for a prestigious RITA Award. You can contact the author through her website at deloresfossen.com

Debra Webb is the award-winning, *USA Today* bestselling author of more than one hundred novels, including those in reader-favorite series Faces of Evil, the Colby Agency and Shades of Death. With more than four million books sold in numerous languages and countries, Debra has a love of storytelling that goes back to her childhood on a farm in Alabama. Visit Debra at debrawebb.com

DEPUTIES UNDER FIRE

DELORES FOSSEN

MEMORY OF MURDER

DEBRA WEBB

MILLS & BOON

First Published in Great Britain 2025
by Mills & Boon, an imprint of HarperCollins*Publishers* Ltd
1 London Bridge Street, London, SE1 9GF

www.harpercollins.co.uk

HarperCollins*Publishers*
Macken House, 39/40 Mayor Street Upper,
Dublin 1, D01 C9W8, Ireland

ISBN: 978-0-263-39726-0

0925

DEPUTIES UNDER FIRE

DELORES FOSSEN

Chapter One

It was like stepping into hell.

The memories immediately slammed into Deputy Eden Gallagher. The stench of the mold and decay in the barn. The dank chill crawling over her skin. The autumn wind moaning through the cracks in what was left of the walls.

And the still-dark stain on the cracked concrete floor.

Once, it'd been more than a stain.

It'd been fresh blood, and there had been a body, too.

"Mellie," she muttered, not able to suppress saying the name of the woman who'd been her mother in every single way that mattered.

Five months wasn't nearly long enough for the grief to have passed. Or for the memories of seeing Mellie's body not to cause a jolt inside her.

"You don't have to be here," her fellow deputy, Rory McClennan, insisted. "I can call in someone else."

Except he was more than her fellow deputy. A whole lot more. Rory was technically her boss at Renegade Canyon PD since he was the acting sheriff while Sheriff Grace Granger was on maternity leave.

Rory was also the father of her nine-month-old son, Tyler.

So, yes, a whole lot more.

Even though Rory and she weren't a couple any longer, and they hadn't been since before Tyler had been born, he wouldn't have any trouble realizing that she was far from okay. He was well aware this place held the hellish memories that were causing her breath to go thin and her heartbeat to race.

"It's my shift," she said, barely managing to get out the words. "I can do my job."

She hoped.

For Rory to call in someone else, it would mean a deputy would end up coming in on their night off. That was because only Rory, Bennie Whitt and she worked the swing shift, 4:00 p.m. to midnight, and Bennie was manning the office. She and Rory had opted for the swing shift so they could spend a good portion of the day with their son, and while those hours were generally quiet in their hometown, that hadn't been the case tonight.

A call had come in at nine thirty, forty minutes earlier, through Dispatch. A frantic ranch owner, Fran Cagel, had said her golden retriever had come home with blood on its feet and fur. According to Fran, the dog often came to the old barn since it was only a couple of acres away from her ranch.

Of course, it was entirely possible that the retriever had gone elsewhere since he'd been off-leash and roaming, as Fran had said was his routine. But after Rory and Eden had used a simple test to confirm it was indeed blood on the dog, they'd arranged for the sample to be picked up by the county lab to see if it was human. They had also contacted the town hospital in case someone injured showed up.

So far, nothing from the hospital, and while waiting for the lab results, they'd come here.

To hell.

To the place where Mellie had died. Or rather, where her body had been dumped.

Since they didn't know who'd killed her, or why, that only added to the nightmarish memories. It was bad enough when someone was murdered, but it was worse when there was no justice.

Especially when Eden was in the business of getting justice.

That failure had given her plenty of sleepless nights.

"Let's just get this done," Eden insisted, a reminder to herself to get her focus back on the job.

This should be a quick in-and-out, where they could determine if the blood had indeed come from here. If it hadn't, then they could search the surrounding area. But since it was already dark and the barn was out in the sticks, it'd be morning before a search team could start.

Stepping over the spot where Mellie had been found, she and Rory fanned their flashlights around the barn. It had probably once been impressive, with its massive arched top window above the entrance and the twelve stalls, six on each side. The glass was now broken, the remaining bits hanging on to the frame like loose, jagged teeth. And the rest of the place, well, there was nothing impressive about it.

"This should have been torn down years ago," Rory muttered.

Eden made a sound of agreement. If it had been, then Mellie wouldn't have been dumped here. Of course, that wouldn't have stopped her from dying, but at least she wouldn't have ended up here in this rot.

"I'll make another request," Eden assured him. Though her previous request had generated no results.

Seventy or so years ago, when the barn had first been built, the owner had stalled prize palominos here. After the owner had passed away, the land—and therefore, the barn and the nearby house—had gone to a distant relative, who apparently had no desire to sell or maintain the property. The house had had been struck by lightning and caught on fire when Eden had been thirteen, twenty years ago, and because of the sinister look to the place, some of the local teenagers had dubbed it the Devil's Hideout.

After Mellie's body had been discovered, Eden had requested that the barn be destroyed since it could be a hazard, but the owner's lawyers had come back with the argument that it was on private land with clearly posted No Trespassing signs. Added to that, it was nearly a mile from a main road, and the only way for someone to reach it was via a rugged ranch trail.

All of that was true, and she had firsthand knowledge of the trail's ruggedness since that's how she and Rory had gotten here. But Eden wished there wasn't such a hellish visual reminder of her foster mother's murder.

Trying to shove aside that thought, Eden walked several feet into the barn, and with Rory right by her side, they paused to listen for anyone or any sounds that shouldn't be there.

Nothing.

So they shifted, Rory aiming his flashlight to the left while she fanned hers to the right. The flashlights were solid, but they weren't creating nearly enough illumination for her to see what was in the shadows.

And there were plenty of shadows.

"I don't see any blood or dog tracks on the floor," Rory whispered.

Neither did she, but the wind wasn't cooperating with

their search. Along with creating those eerie whistling sounds, it was blowing around the dead leaves, dirt and other debris on the floor. There were fast-food bags, empty beer cans and even the remnants of what appeared to be a campfire in a banged-up metal bucket.

Judging from the talk she'd heard, the barn had become a ghoulish thrill for some teens. It was yet another reason to have it torn down.

Rory tipped his head toward the stalls. "We'll have to check them all."

Yes, they would, and there suddenly seemed like more than a dozen of them. Some still had stall doors. Others were just collapsed heaps of old wood. But each space needed to be searched, especially since there were enough large holes in the exterior walls, and the retriever could have gone in and out through one of those.

The two of them moved together, in a rhythm that came surprisingly easy considering they had only been work-ing together for five months. Before that, she'd been a de-tective in SVU at San Antonio PD, where the pace was a whole lot different than here in her hometown. Still, after Mellie's death, Eden had felt the need to come home. The need to be part of the police force that was investigating her murder.

Of course, Rory had played into that decision, too.

They weren't a couple, not any longer, but he was Ty-ler's father, and despite her turbulent past with Rory and his powerful, corrupt father, Eden hadn't wanted to deny her son a chance to be with his dad.

Something that she hadn't had growing up.

That, and her birth mother's untimely death, had been the reason Eden had ended up in foster care on the Horse-shoe Ranch in Renegade Canyon.

They kept moving. Kept looking. Kept listening. Still no sign of blood or a body. Eden froze, though, when she saw a heap in the corner of one of the stalls.

She didn't say anything, but Rory must have sensed something was wrong because he shifted in that direction, automatically aiming his flashlight at the pile...of something. Whatever it was, it'd been covered with what appeared to be a ratty sleeping bag.

Glancing around, they went closer, and using the toe of his boot, Rory moved the sleeping bag aside. The tightness in her chest eased up when she saw it was a couple of pillows. Apparently, someone had been camping out. Maybe a teen—

Eden gasped when her phone vibrated in her pocket. That reaction was proof of just how on edge her nerves were. She yanked out her cell and breathed a whole lot easier when she saw it was a picture from the live-in nanny, Leslie Darrington.

She turned her phone so that Rory could see the sweet photo of Tyler asleep in his crib.

Night, night, Mommy and Daddy, Leslie had texted.

Despite her surroundings, Eden smiled and touched her fingers to the image of that precious little face. She and Rory might be at odds with each other, but there was no doubt they both loved their little boy.

Rory smiled, too, and for just a second, their gazes met. And for that second, the old heat was there.

No. No. No.

When was that blasted attraction finally going to cool down? Eden had to consider the answer to that was never. After all, Rory and she had been on and off since high school, and while their *on* time had been amazing, his father, Ike, had always found a way to tear them apart, along with making Mellie's life a living hell. It was hard to try being happy with Rory when Mellie had been suffering.

Eden took one last look at the photo and put her phone away. Just then, Rory's phone dinged with a text. He looked at the screen and definitely didn't have the same smiling reaction that he'd had seeing Tyler's photo.

"It's from the county lab," he explained. "The blood on the dog is human."

Eden groaned and squeezed her eyes shut for a moment. That was not what she'd wanted to hear, even though the presence of blood didn't mean someone had been killed. She wanted to cling to the hope that someone, maybe the person who'd been camping out in that sleeping bag, had injured himself and left a blood trail for the dog to trample through.

"They'll run it through the database to see if they get a hit," Rory added a moment later.

Good. But Eden knew the limits of the database. The majority of people weren't even in it unless they'd committed a crime or worked in a job, like as a cop, that required a sample of their DNA to be on file. Still, it was possible they'd be able to get a match so they'd know whom they were looking for.

He slipped his phone back in his pocket, and they resumed the search. Eden got another jolt when a rat skittered across the floor right in front of them. She was silently cursing it when she heard something. A moan, maybe? Or maybe just the wind.

Rory must have heard it, too, because he stopped, and they both turned in the direction of where the sound had come from.

The very last stall.

They moved toward it, quickening their pace but still

making cursory glances inside the stalls they passed along the way.

The sound came again. Definitely not the wind, and it caused them to move even faster. When they reached the stall, they aimed their flashlights inside.

At first, Eden didn't see anything. Not until she directed the light over the far right corner.

Then, she spotted her.

A woman.

Oh, mercy. And she was covered with blood.

"I'll call for an ambulance," Rory said, snatching out his phone.

Eden hurried to the woman, and she stooped down so she could check for a pulse. It was weak, but she was alive. She had also obviously lost a lot of blood. It wasn't just on her face and clothes, but had pooled around her.

The woman lifted her eyelids, barely, moaned again and shivered. "Help me," she murmured, her voice barely audible.

"We will," Eden assured her. "Who are you?" she asked.

No response, and her eyelids drifted back down.

Eden studied her, taking in the long blond hair, what she could see of it, anyway. The torn black skirt, red top and heels. The clothing looked expensive.

And those stab wounds looked lethal.

Since adding pressure to the wounds could do more harm than good and potentially cause internal injuries, Eden focused on what little she could do. She yanked off her jacket and draped it over the woman to stave off what had to be a chill from the shock of the blood loss.

Behind her, she heard Rory finishing that 911 call for the ambulance, while she checked for any obstructions in the woman's airway. There weren't any. And the blood on her face and hair appeared to have come from a cut on the scalp. Maybe a sign of some kind of blunt-force trauma.

"An ambulance is on the way," Rory informed her, and he came into the stall, kneeling down beside the woman.

"Who did this to you?" Eden asked her, hoping this time she would get an answer.

But the woman made no sound.

However, Rory did. He groaned, causing Eden to snap back toward him.

"Hell," Rory muttered. "I know her."

There was something in his voice, in his stark expression, that had Eden dreading what he would say next.

"She's Brenda Watford," he added.

Eden repeated the name a couple of times, but she had to shake her head. It didn't ring any bells. "How do you know her?"

He swallowed hard. "She's, uh, my father's girlfriend. Ex-girlfriend," Rory amended. "And the last time I saw Brenda, Ike was threatening to kill her."

Chapter Two

Hell.

That was the one word that kept repeating through Rory's head. And he was certain it would keep repeating as the night dragged on.

A woman was now unconscious and barely clinging to life. His father's ex-girlfriend. Rory would need answers about that. Answers, too, as to why Brenda had been left here in this barn, where Mellie's body had been found.

Were the two attacks connected?

The odds were yes, they were. It was too much of a co-incidence for it to be otherwise. And that meant the connection would lead straight back to his father, Ike.

So, yeah.

That *hell* would be echoing in his head for a while.

With Eden right by his side, Rory kept watch around them as the EMTs eased Brenda into the ambulance. The moment they had her secured inside, they hit the sirens and started for the hospital.

Fast.

Because every second was going to count now. The woman was hanging on by a thread.

He and Eden hurried to the cruiser that they'd left off

the old ranch trail and jumped in so they could follow. If they got lucky, Brenda would regain consciousness and be able to tell them who'd attacked her and put her in the barn. If she named his father... But Rory stopped and decided he'd cross that bridge once he came to it.

For now, he drove toward the Renegade Canyon Hospital, glancing around to see if there were any indications of who'd brought Brenda here. The CSIs would arrive soon and do a thorough check, but the scene had already been disturbed, first with Eden's and his arrival, and then with the EMTs and ambulance. Maybe potential evidence hadn't been destroyed that would help them ID Brenda's attacker.

He glanced at Eden, who was pulling up some info on her phone, and he saw the slight tremble in her hands. A tremble she wouldn't want him to notice. She was a tough cop.

A damn good one, too.

But that didn't mean she could tamp down the basic human emotion of grief. She'd basically just relived one of her worst nightmares by walking into the barn and seeing another bleeding woman. At least this time the woman was alive. That hadn't been the case with Mellie.

"I figure you're about to ask me if I'm okay," Eden murmured while the cruiser bobbled over the seriously uneven surface of the ranch trail. "Please don't, and I won't ask you the same."

Good. Because neither of them was anywhere in the *okay* range right now. She was fighting those traumatic memories, and he was dealing with the firestorm he was about to face. He got started on that firestorm by giving the voice command to make a call to his father.

As usual, Rory had to steel himself for any kind of contact with his dad. Things hadn't been civil between them for a long time.

Rory supposed if he had to put his finger on when the rift started, it would have been when his mother transferred ownership of the ranch to Rory's older brother, Dutton, when he turned twenty-one. Rory had been just sixteen then, but he'd had no trouble choosing his brother's side over their father's.

Ike hadn't taken that well at all.

Of course, Rory had known that Ike could be a vindictive, mean-as-a-snake SOB. Those traits hadn't improved over the years, and they'd escalated big-time when Rory had become a cop. Then, Ike's venom had gone up even more when Rory's mom had died nearly a year ago.

And again, when Eden had given birth to Rory's baby.

Ike hadn't learned that news until the day Eden had given birth since neither Eden nor Rory had felt the need to tell him sooner. No way did Ike approve of Rory having a baby with one of Mellie's foster-home kids. Or "brats," as Ike was fond of calling them.

The call to his father connected, and it rang and rang and rang. Just when Rory thought it would go to voice mail, Ike finally answered. "What the hell do you want?" he snarled, obviously seeing Rory's number on his caller ID.

"I need you to come into the police station," Rory answered, making sure he sounded exactly like the cop that he was. "Be there in one hour."

That should give him enough time to check on Brenda, arrange for a reserve deputy to guard her, get a search warrant for Ike's house and vehicles and then prep for what would be the interview from hell.

Ike laughed, and it wasn't from humor. "And why would I do that?"

"Because someone tried to kill Brenda Watford. She's alive and talking." Yeah, the last part was a lie, but he wanted to rattle Ike. Or rather, it would rattle him if he'd been the one who had actually attacked her. "Be at the police station in one hour, or I'll be out to arrest you."

With that, Rory ended the call, figuring that Ike might just try to ring him right back. He didn't. So he was probably calling his lawyer instead or trying to find out anything he could about Brenda's condition.

"I'll text the hospital chief to put a lid on any and everything about Brenda's condition. Or anything she might say if she regains consciousness," Eden explained, already typing the message. "You know Ike will probably show up there."

"I know," he agreed.

No way would he let Ike get anywhere near Brenda, but it would mean a showdown of sorts at the hospital. Then again, just about every face-to-face meeting with his father qualified as a showdown.

Rory heard the swooshing sound to indicate she'd sent the text to the hospital, and Eden continued typing on her phone. Like him, she was also keeping check around them in case Brenda's attacker was still in the area.

But there were no signs of anyone or anything out of the ordinary.

"All right, here's the background on Brenda," Eden said, reading from the report she'd obviously just accessed. "Brenda Elise Watford, no police record. Owner of Watford Real Estate in San Antonio. Blond hair and blue eyes. Five-three, one hundred and twenty pounds, according to her driver's license. Divorced, no kids. Aged forty-one." She stopped, looked at him. "That's a big age difference between Ike and her. Ike's what...seventy?"

Rory nodded. "He will be in a few weeks."

But it was hard for him to think of Ike as a senior citizen since he was a big, imposing man who still had a lot of muscle on him. Ike was plenty strong enough to have lifted a woman Brenda's size and carried her into that barn. Then again, Brenda could have been lured there and attacked, which would have meant that no carrying had been involved.

"Ike's girlfriends are usually a lot younger than he is," Rory added on to that. "And, yes, he had those girlfriends even when he was married to my mom. His relationships don't last long, though, because the women seem to grasp his true colors soon enough and dump him."

She stayed quiet a moment. "You said the last time you saw Brenda that Ike threatened to kill her."

Rory had known this was coming, and what he had to add to that comment was going to make Ike look even guiltier. "About six weeks ago, I went to the ranch to visit Dutton."

No need for him to explain that while Dutton owned Towering Oaks, he didn't live in the main house. Dutton had had his own place built, and it was as far away from Ike as possible, while still remaining on the actual ranch.

"I have to drive past the main house to get to Dutton's," Rory went on, "and that day, I saw Ike and Brenda in the driveway. They were clearly arguing, and I stopped when I saw Brenda slap and push him."

That put some fresh alarm on Eden's face. "Did Ike slap and push her back?"

"Not that I saw. But I don't know exactly what went on before I arrived." He paused, gathered his breath. "Ike told me to get lost." Of course, his father had added a lot of profanity to go along with that barked order. "I stayed put and talked to Brenda. She was fuming and said that Ike was turning her clients against her, that he was doing a smear campaign to ruin her name and that he'd even leaked some risqué photos of her on the internet."

"Did he?" Eden asked.

"Someone did. Brenda was in her underwear, doing what I guess you'd call a drunken sexy dance. Maybe for Ike." Though Rory definitely didn't like to think about that. "Maybe for someone else. But Brenda was convinced Ike had been the one to post them. I didn't get the chance to question her more on that because Ike and she got into a shouting match with some name calling and threats."

"Threats?" Eden repeated. "Like Ike saying he would kill her?"

"That and other things. Brenda said she was going to start her own smear campaign and that when she was done with him, Ike would regret he'd ever met her." Rory recalled the rage he'd seen on the woman's face. Then again, there had been fury on Ike's face, too. "That's when Ike said she'd better back off or she'd end up dead."

Eden didn't seem the least bit surprised by that. Then again, she'd heard Ike issue similar threats to Mellie when they'd gotten into disputes, usually when Ike accused one of Mellie's *brats* of trespassing on the ranch. Of course, the irony was Ike didn't own the ranch, and Dutton would have never caved to file trespassing charges against anyone in the foster home.

"Did Brenda back off?" Eden asked.

"I'm not sure." Hopefully, that was something they'd soon find out from the woman herself.

They finally reached the end of the trail and got onto the main road. The ambulance was able to pick up some speed. So was Rory, and he knew it wouldn't be long now before they reached the hospital.

"All right," Eden said, typing on her phone. "I'll start a deep dive on Brenda and go through all her social media."

That was one of Eden's specialties—data mining to come up with info and insights into victims, suspects and persons of interest. She'd no doubt honed that skill while working as a detective at SAPD, but she'd also developed some solid investigative expertise there as well.

And she would go at Ike with both barrels loaded.

Not literally. Eden wouldn't get violent with him, but she would dig, and dig hard, to prove Ike was responsible for the attack on Brenda. Because if he had indeed done it, that might also lead to his arrest for Mellie's murder. Not being able to solve that had no doubt been a constant, painful thorn in her side.

In his, too.

There'd been no physical evidence to tie Ike or anyone else to her death. Ike had been home alone at the time so he had no alibi, but there was also no proof that he'd gone out that night. The CSIs hadn't been able to find squat to get justice for a good woman who'd devoted her life to helping kids.

So, yeah, a thorn in his side as well.

"I'm not seeing any photos or posts about Ike on Brenda's Facebook page," Eden muttered. "She probably deleted them, but once I'm back at the station, I'll see if I can recover anything useful."

Ike wasn't on social media, so Eden wouldn't have that available to her, and while the ranch was sometimes in the news for its prize horses, Ike wasn't usually included in those articles. His father had basically washed his hands of the ranch and his sons. But for reasons Rory would never understand, he continued to live there. So did Ike's much younger brother and his wife, Asher and Kitty, and their twelve-year-old adopted daughter, Jamie. Jamie was one of the few people who Ike actually seemed to like and vice versa.

Rory hoped like hell that she wasn't in danger.

He made a mental note to talk to Asher, Kitty and Jamie about maybe staying elsewhere until the dust had settled on this investigation. Rory didn't think they were in actual danger, but Ike was a bear to be around during the best of times. No way were the *best of times* happening with him currently as their number-one murder suspect.

Rory drove past the Welcome to Renegade Canyon sign and continued to follow the ambulance onto Main Street and then into the parking lot of the hospital. The EMTs had obviously already alerted the medical staff, because the moment the ambulance pulled to a stop, two nurses and a doctor came rushing out.

Since there were very few degrees of separation in a small town, Rory recognized all of them and knew they weren't a threat to Brenda's safety. They were fast and efficient in working with the EMTs to get Brenda out of the ambulance, and she was then rushed not toward a treatment room, but straight toward the critical-care area.

Rory took out his phone to text Dispatch to get a reserve deputy here, and he went to the hall to wait for the EMTs to return so he could question them. If Brenda had regained consciousness in the ambulance, he wanted to know everything she'd said. However, he saw someone who had him stopping cold. The tall brunette was making a beeline toward him.

His aunt, Helen Weatherford.

She was his late mother's younger sister, and while she'd

been raised in Renegade Canyon, she hadn't lived here since she left years ago for college. She now made her home in San Antonio.

Helen was wearing black jogging pants, a workout top and running shoes. As usual, she had her long hair pulled up into a ponytail. She looked like an AARP ad for a super fit fiftysomething-year-old woman.

"What are you doing here?" Rory asked, trying not to sound as if it was an accusation. Though that's exactly what it was.

Helen got closer and gave a rather frosty nonverbal greeting to him. Frosty because his aunt believed Ike, Dutton and he hadn't done enough to save her sister. And Rory had to admit he did feel some serious guilt about that. He simply hadn't realized just how serious his mother's illness was until it'd been too late.

"I was visiting an old friend. Sheila Mendoza," Helen said, her tone as icy as her expression. "She's recovering from an appendectomy."

Rory was sure he frowned. And that he looked confused. He didn't recall Helen being especially close friends with Sheila, and it was late. Well, late for hospital visits, anyway.

"Why are you here?" Helen asked, volleying glances at Eden and him. Her attention settled on the blood that was on Eden's shirt. "There's nothing wrong with your baby, is there?"

"No, Tyler's fine," Eden replied. "We're here on police business."

Helen made a sound that could have meant anything. "How's Dutton and his new baby?" she asked, but there didn't appear to be any real interest in her question. Dutton was clearly still on her bad side, too.

"They're good," Rory assured her.

Helen stared at him. "And Ike?" Her tone slid right from cool politeness to venomous.

With reason. Helen was no fan of Ike, and Ike felt the same way about her. She had plenty of disapproval for Dutton and him for her sister's death, but she downright hated Ike. In fact, it'd been Helen who'd talked her sister into signing over the ranch to Dutton. It had essentially cut Ike out of being a part of the ranch that he had run for several decades.

"I'm guessing Ike has a reason for being here," Helen commented. She glanced in the direction of the ER doors.

Rory heard the footsteps before he even turned to see Ike storming toward them, and judging from his expression, he was spoiling for a fight. Good. So was Rory, and he wasn't in the mood to take any flak off his father.

"Make one wrong move, and I'll arrest you," Rory snarled. He aimed his index fingers as a warning to Ike.

"One wrong move?" Ike howled, and he didn't stop until he was right in front of them. "I'd say you already did that by demanding I come in to be grilled." He spared Eden and Helen a narrow-eyed glance. "Did one of them convince you that I've done something to get me locked in a cage?"

"No, the evidence did that all on its own," Rory replied, firing right back at him. "Your ex-girlfriend, a woman you threatened right in front of me, was brutally assaulted. During the grilling, I'll expect you to give me a full, truthful account of what went on between Brenda and you."

Ike kept his glare on Rory a moment longer before he shifted to Helen. She seemed to be enjoying this moment a little too much.

"Did you try to kill your ex…again?" Helen asked. There was a taunt in her voice. "I mean, technically my sister wasn't your ex, and you didn't actually murder her, but you sure as hell contributed to her death."

Rory sighed. This certainly wasn't the first time he'd heard his aunt voice that particular theory. And she might even be right. When Rory's mom, Doreen, had been diagnosed with cancer and been told she had six months to live, Ike hadn't gotten her to receive traditional treatment, but instead had encouraged her to go to an experimental clinic in Mexico. She'd died within three weeks.

"Well?" Helen persisted. "Did you try to kill this woman, too?"

Ike took one menacing step toward his former sister-in-law. "At the moment, you're the only woman I'd like to see dead, Helen," he snarled, though he shot a glance at Eden to indicate she might be on this hit list, too.

"Enough of this," Rory snapped, and he moved between Ike and Helen. "Time for you to go home," he said to his aunt before shifting to his father. "And you need to go to the police station. I'll be there after I question Brenda."

Both Helen and Ike went silent, and Rory tried to figure out what the heck their expressions meant. Were those nerves he saw?

"Question her…" Helen murmured. "Good," she added a heartbeat later. "Maybe she'll remember everything Ike did to her."

Apparently, Helen decided that was a good thing to say before exiting, because then she turned and walked away.

Ike didn't. "What did Brenda say when you found her?" he asked.

Not spoken like a demand but rather…what? A plea? Maybe. But Rory could take that two ways. Either Ike genuinely cared about what had happened to Brenda, or else he was worried she'd rat him out. Rory didn't get the chance to find out because he saw the doctor, Amy Calvert, heading their way.

"Stay here," Rory warned Ike, and Eden and he went to the doctor so that Ike wouldn't be privy to whatever they said.

One look at Dr. Calvert's face, though, and Rory knew. Hell. He knew. That's why her words weren't a surprise. Still, they gave him a gut punch.

"I'm sorry," Dr. Calvert said, keeping her voice at a whisper. "But Brenda Watford is dead."

Chapter Three

Two unsolved murders.

That was the thought going through Eden's head as she dealt with the chaos of the morning. Unlike other kinds of chaos, though, most of this was thoroughly enjoyable.

Not the pressing worry about the murders, of course.

Not her continuing battle with the grief over losing Mellie, either.

But rather the hectic morning routine of being a mom to a nine-month-old baby. A baby who could crawl lightning-fast, babble nonstop and make a thorough mess of the blueberry oatmeal he was having for breakfast. Eden was mopping up some of that oatmeal on Tyler's face while he wiggled and tried to duck away from the washcloth.

She turned at the sound of the footsteps, already knowing who it was. Leslie and Rory. Eden had heard the nanny letting Rory inside, which meant he was right on time. He'd never missed an 8:00 a.m. visit since she and Tyler had moved back to Renegade Canyon.

"Dada Dada," Tyler squealed. He clapped his hands, flinging the oatmeal far and wide. Leslie laughed and hurried to get another wet cloth to help with the cleanup.

"Did he get any breakfast in his mouth?" Rory asked,

going to Tyler and giving him a kiss on the top of his head. Rory also ended up having to pick a fleck of oatmeal off his own lips.

"Not much," Eden muttered, looking up at Rory.

Their gazes met, and she saw what his smile couldn't hide. He hadn't slept well. With reason. They had another murder on their hands, and their prime suspect was his father.

Ike wasn't exactly cooperating, either. He'd given "no comment" to every question in their interview with him, and when his trio of lawyers had arrived, they'd insisted the interview be postponed until this morning. They'd had another demand, too. That any future questioning not be done by his son and his son's former partner.

Legally, it was a valid request since it was a conflict of interest, but that could be said of everyone in the entire police department. Ike knew every single one of them, and he didn't get along with any of them. Still, Ike didn't have a personal connection to Deputy Livvy Walsh, and since she was on the day shift, anyway, she would be the one to conduct the interview.

In the meantime, Ike hadn't been locked up because there hadn't been enough evidence to hold him. It hadn't been easy for Eden to watch him just walk out of the police station. It'd felt as if once again, she was letting Mellie down. But she'd had to remind herself that Ike might not have been Mellie's killer, and he might not have murdered Brenda, either.

"You okay?" Rory asked her, and he continued to study her. He was no doubt seeing the fatigue from the restless night she'd had.

"I'm fine," Eden said. "You?"

He nodded, and their gazes continued to hold. And there

it was. Along with the concern was the heat that neither of them wanted.

Really?

Now?

As she usually did, Eden silently cursed it and tore her attention from him. Sometimes, just looking at Rory fueled the attraction. Sometimes, it came no matter what she did or didn't do.

"I can take over if you two want to go ahead and leave," Leslie offered.

Their leaving definitely wasn't part of the morning routine. Usually, they spent several hours with Tyler in his playroom, or if the weather was good, they took him to the pasture to see the horse that Rory had given Tyler. But that routine would have to be broken today since they needed to make another trip to the crime scene. The CSIs were already there, and with some luck, they might have some info for them.

Eden nodded, stood and kissed her son. "Mama and Dada will be back," she said, purposely not adding a *soon* to that.

Because Eden had no idea how long the trip would take, and after that, she wanted to observe Ike's interview. Rory would no doubt want to do the same thing.

Rory gave their son a kiss, too, causing Tyler to beam a smile at him. That was usual as well. Tyler clearly loved his daddy, and while Eden couldn't say it was exactly comfortable having Rory around and in such close contact, she knew they were doing what was best for their son. They were putting aside their differences and co-parenting.

Coinvestigating, too.

Which meant that close contact with Rory would continue for a while.

That also meant dealing with the constant rounds of this attraction that just wouldn't go away.

Still silently cursing herself, they left the house, heading for his cruiser, which he'd parked in her driveway. "I talked to Dewey Galway on the drive to your place," he said, referring to the medical examiner, and Eden heard the dread in his voice. "He's still doing the postmortem, but he was able to tell me that the cause of Brenda's death was the blood loss from the stab wounds. There were six of them."

"Six," she muttered. "A lot."

"Yeah. Not what the ME would call a frenzy, and in fact, he thought the killer might have been trying to avoid any major organs. For instance, there were no wounds near the heart."

She gave that some thought as they stood outside the cruiser. "So the killer didn't want her dead right away. He wanted her to suffer?"

Rory shrugged. "Or the killer didn't know what he was doing." He shook his head. "It doesn't make sense. Why stab a woman six times and leave without making sure she's dead?"

Yes, that was puzzling. Unless the killer did indeed believe she was dead. Or perhaps he'd been interrupted and had had to flee. Though Eden couldn't imagine what kind of interruption would pull a murderer away from his prey when they were in such a remote location like the barn. Still, it was possible the dog had startled him or had become aggressive, causing him to run.

"Brenda had also been drugged," Rory went on. "She'd been roofied."

Eden silently groaned. Rohypnol was a fairly easy drug to obtain, and it was even easier to slip into a drink. So did that mean Brenda had been in close contact with her killer, close enough for the killer to have spiked her drink?

She continued to mull over that scenario while she told Rory about a call she'd gotten earlier from the sheriff. "Grace is champing at the bit to come back to work," she told him. "But thankfully, Dutton convinced her to stay put."

"Yeah, I talked to Dutton on the way over. The doctor won't clear Grace for duty yet."

Not a surprise, since she'd needed a C-section to deliver her son, Nash, only three weeks ago. Grace needed to recover and spend time with her newborn.

"I also got a call from SAPD this morning," Rory went on as they got in the cruiser and started the drive to the barn. "Brenda had a stalker. A guy named Carter Rooney. She had a restraining order against him."

That got Eden's attention. "An ex-boyfriend? And was there violence involved?"

"Not a boyfriend and no record of actual violence. Carter claims Brenda ruined him financially." Rory paused. "However, he has left threatening voice mails and texts for Brenda, and he doesn't have an alibi for last night. SAPD will be questioning him."

"Good." And since Eden still had plenty of contacts at SAPD, she shouldn't have any problem getting a recording and summary report of that interview. "We'll need to talk to Carter as well," she added.

"Yes. I'll set that up for later today. Depending on what comes out of his interview with SAPD, we might have to go to him."

She made a sound of agreement. There might not be enough compelling evidence to force Carter to come to

Renegade Canyon. Still, it would be worth the drive to talk to him in person.

Rory took the turn off the main road and onto the ranch trail. Where they immediately hit a huge pothole. The surface of the trail had gotten worse since their trip here the night before, no doubt from the influx of traffic. First the killer, then Rory and her, followed by the ambulance and now the CSIs.

They were still a good quarter of a mile from the barn when Rory's phone rang and Dispatch popped up on the dash screen. Rory answered it right away on speaker.

"Deputy McClennan, you have a call from a Diedre Bennington," the dispatcher said. "She wants to talk to you."

The name was vaguely familiar to Eden, but she couldn't quite recall who the woman was. Rory didn't seem to have that problem because he muttered some profanity under his breath.

"Put the call through," he instructed and glanced at her. "Diedre is another of my dad's ex-girlfriends. In fact, he was having an affair with her at the time my mother died."

Sweet heaven. Eden groaned. She had always known Ike was a jerk, but she hadn't known that he'd cheated on his dying wife.

"There's bad blood between Ike and Diedre?" she asked.

"Oh, yeah," Rory confirmed just as the woman's voice began to pour through the speakers.

"Rory," she said with a whole lot of rushed breath in just that simple greeting. "I heard about the dead woman. The second one. Both enemies of your father. Am I next?" Diedre blurted. "Is Ike coming after me?"

"There's no indication of that, Diedre," Rory commented, but there wasn't much assurance in his voice.

With good reason. Ike might be doing just that. Eliminating some old grudges.

Including the one he'd had with Mellie.

But as a cop, Eden had to look at the whole picture here. And set aside her personal hatred for Ike. A person didn't just start a killing spree unless there was some kind of trigger. She just wasn't seeing that.

Not yet, anyway.

But she made a mental note to look into Ike's finances and health. Getting bad news about those things could sometimes send a person over the edge. Also, with his seventieth birthday coming up, Ike could feel he was running out of time to settle some old scores.

"Have you arrested Ike?" Diedre asked.

"No." And Rory didn't add to that. "But if you're worried about your safety, you should take precautions. Is there a friend or relative you can stay with for a while?"

"Yes," she said on a sob. "But if you just arrest him, I'll be safe. All of his enemies will be safe. You have to know Ike's behind this. Don't let your family ties blind you to what Ike is."

Rory groaned and shook his head. If anyone was aware of the kind of man Ike was, it was Rory.

"I'll let you know if and when Ike is taken into custody," Rory told the woman. "And I have to go. If you have any immediate issues with a threat, you should contact SAPD since you're in their jurisdiction."

"But they can't arrest him," Diedre spluttered. "You can."

"Call SAPD if there's a threat," he repeated.

With that, Rory ended the call and dragged in a long, weary breath. Maybe because he hadn't wanted to deal with the woman who had possibly caused his mother some emotional pain. Of course, there could be many of Ike's ex-lovers who'd done that.

Rory immediately made a call to someone they knew. Detective Hailey Patterson at SAPD. Eden had worked with her, and he had met her several times when she and Rory had been in one of their on-again cycles.

Hailey's call went to voice mail, and Rory left a message to let the detective know about Diedre's concerns for her safety. There wasn't much SAPD could actually do in situations like this. Not even man power to provide personal security when there hadn't actually been an attempt to harm Diedre. Still, the woman would be on SAPD's radar in case something did happen.

"Even if Ike is the killer, I can't see him going after her," Eden muttered. "Not when there's this much attention focused on him." But then she stopped, and rethought that comment. "Unless he has some kind of urgency to rid the world of people on his bad side."

Rory didn't seem the least bit surprised by her last remark, which meant the same idea had likely already occurred to him. "I can't get access to his medical records, but I'll have a talk with the housekeepers and Jamie."

"Jamie," she repeated. Not a question.

She knew that was Rory's twelve-year-old cousin, who lived in the main house on the ranch with Ike and her parents. Rory had told her that because of the age difference, he'd always thought of Jamie as his niece, and they were fairly close. It was possible Jamie had seen or heard something that would shed some light on whether or not there'd been a trigger for Ike to start killing.

"Do you think you should try to encourage Jamie and her folks to stay elsewhere?" Eden asked.

"I advised them to do that this morning before I went to

your place. But Ike doesn't consider them enemies. They'd never crossed him. Never butted heads with him over something Ike wanted."

The way Ike had butted heads with Rory and her.

Good. She was glad the girl and her parents weren't having to face that kind of ugly wrath.

Eden looked up when the barn came into view and felt exactly what she'd been expecting. That overwhelming sense of dread. It didn't matter that the barn was no longer cloaked in darkness. Sunshine and a clear sky weren't going to diminish the eerie feel of the place or lessen her memories of what had gone on there.

As expected, the county CSI van was parked off the trail and in a small clearing beneath some trees, and she saw one of the CSI team, dressed in his white protective jumpsuit, boot covers and gloves. He was stooped down, looking at something on the right side of the barn, but he glanced in their direction when they got out of the cruiser. Eden figured there was at least one other CSI inside.

They made their way to the investigator outside, and as she got closer, she saw it was Lou Garcia, a fairly new CSI. But he had worked the same barn after Mellie's murder.

"Have you found anything?" Rory immediately asked him.

Lou motioned toward an even smaller trail on the far side of the barn. "We found tire tracks over there, but they were practically obliterated. Looks like some deer trampled over them. Still, I took a casting so we might come up with something."

Eden frowned when she turned toward the trail. She wished that they had looked there the night before, but it'd been too dark for them to see much of anything. Added to that, their focus had been on getting Brenda some help and talking to her to see if she could ID her attacker.

"That trail's even rougher than the one we used," Rory remarked.

"Yes, it is," Lou agreed. "If the killer came that way, he or she would have needed an off-road vehicle, and even that wouldn't have been a pleasant drive." He shifted and pointed toward the back of the barn. "There were drag marks there. Along with some of the victim's blood."

"So she was bleeding before he put her in the barn," Rory muttered. "That means whatever vehicle he used would have her blood, too. And there'd be blood at the location where she was attacked."

They were looking for another crime scene. SAPD had already ruled out Brenda's house and office, so the next step would be to search Ike's house.

Rory took out his phone and requested a warrant to have the CSIs examine all of Ike's vehicles and the main house. She was betting Ike and his lawyers would fight that, but it was a fight they'd lose. With Ike's motive and means, and with no verifiable alibi, that would be enough for a judge to issue a warrant.

Once he'd finished his call, the two of them started toward the front of the barn. "The attack happened elsewhere," he said as if spelling it all out for himself. "And the killer brought her here. Not an easy trip. And a risky one. Why take that risk?"

"To make some kind of statement," she mused. "To put her in the same place as Mellie."

Rory stopped in the entry of the barn and turned to her. "But he didn't put her in the same place. He put her at the back of the barn. And he didn't use the same trail to get here. He used one that's more visible from the main road."

True, and that caused Eden's mind to whirl with possibilities. "We didn't disclose the exact location of Mellie's body in any of the reports." She stopped, cursed. "And that means we could be dealing with a copycat."

"Bingo," he murmured, and she could see the worry in his eyes.

Two victims. Two killers. And if one of those killers wasn't his father, then someone was trying to set Ike up.

They were about to step inside when they heard the approaching vehicle. A motorcycle. They turned to see Rory's brother, Dutton, and he pulled his Harley to a stop behind the cruiser.

"A problem?" Rory immediately asked. "Is the baby all right?"

"He's fine," Dutton said, nodding a greeting to Eden. He walked closer, stopping next to them and staring at the barn. "I considered just calling you, but I decided this was a conversation best done in person."

Rory sighed. "You're here to tell me something that could get Ike arrested," he said, guessing.

"No. Not Ike," Dutton said. "Aunt Helen."

Eden didn't know who was more surprised by that, Rory or her. "What did she do?" Rory asked.

"It could be nothing, but it's been eating away at me all night." Dutton gathered his breath. "Two days ago, Helen came to the ranch. I know because I happened to be taking out one of the new horses for a ride, and I spotted her with Ike. They were on the back porch, arguing. About what, I couldn't tell, but as I rode closer, Helen whipped out a knife from her purse and seemed to threaten Ike with it."

Sweet heaven. "Neither one of them mentioned a word about this," Eden said.

"That doesn't surprise me," Dutton grumbled. "I got off

the horse and hurried to them, and when Helen looked in my direction, Ike knocked the knife from her hand. Then, he mocked her, saying she was nothing but a coward. Always had been, always would be. He continued to goad her until she burst into tears and ran off the porch. She got in her car and sped away."

Eden shook her head. "What was the argument about?"

"Ike wouldn't say. I called Aunt Helen, and she finally answered a couple of hours later. She said it was all a misunderstanding." Dutton shrugged. "Maybe it was. Ike and Helen have certainly had a lot of clashes over the years."

Rory made a sound of agreement. "But I've never known Helen to pull a knife on him. What did Ike say about the incident?"

"He laughed it off, insisted it was no big deal, that Helen had just gotten her dander up, and he added a few more clichés, like making a mountain out of a molehill."

It didn't sound like a molehill to her. "What did Ike do with the knife?" Eden asked.

Dutton shook his head. "I don't know. It wasn't on the porch by the time I got back there after I went to check on Helen." He paused. "Why? You think it was the murder weapon?"

"Well, we don't have the murder weapon so it's possible. What did the knife look like?" she persisted.

"It was one of those Swiss Army ones. Not a long blade. Maybe three inches," Dutton answered.

Rory took out his phone again. "I'm texting the ME to see if he can determine the depth of the stab wounds on Brenda's body." He finished the message and looked at his brother. "And I'll talk to Helen."

Dutton sighed. "Yeah, that'll be fun." He glanced

around. "I'll leave you to it. Let me know, though, what Helen says."

"I will," Rory assured him. They said their goodbyes and as Dutton headed back to his motorcycle, she and Rory went inside the barn.

Once again, she had to force her attention away from the stain of Mellie's blood. It was easier to do that today since she could focus on the two CSIs, Molly Hanks and David Barrow, who were working all the way at the back of the barn. There was enough light coming through the cracks that she could see they were examining something on the wall.

Rory must have noticed, too, because their pace quickened. Maybe the CSIs had found something they could use.

They stopped a few feet from the stall, and Rory opened his mouth, no doubt to question them. He didn't get the chance.

Because an explosion ripped through the barn.

Chapter Four

Rory heard the deafening blast. Felt it, too, when his body jolted and then lunged forward. He couldn't stop himself from being hurled into one of the stalls, and he landed, hard, on what was left of the hay-strewn floor.

The impact knocked the breath right out of him, and while fighting for air was a high priority, he was also trying to register what had happened.

Some kind of explosion had torn through the barn.

Debris was falling all around him, and there was the sound of someone moaning. Someone in pain.

Eden.

She was hurt, and he had to get to her. But he couldn't see her. The air was a cloud of dust, filled with bits of rubble and smoke.

Hell.

Was the barn on fire? He couldn't see or feel any flames, but at the moment the only things he could feel were the vise-like pressure in his chest and the all-consuming need to get to Eden so he could help her.

Grappling for air, Rory clutched his chest, and he managed to get to his feet. There were more of those moans, but he couldn't be sure if it was Eden or one of the CSIs. Someone was definitely hurt.

He caught on to what was left of the stable wall so he could try to propel himself forward. Thankfully, nothing in his body seemed to be broken, and he was slowly regaining his breath.

With the much-needed air filling his lungs, Rory had the strength to move, and he glanced around, picking through the heaps of wood and other junk that was scattered pretty much everywhere. He certainly couldn't see Eden or the CSIs, so he moved out even farther and continued glancing around.

Most of the barn wall directly ahead of him was gone. The blast had torn a huge chunk out of it, and the gaping hole was large enough to drive a vehicle through. His stomach dropped when he realized that was the area that the CSI, Lou Garcia, had been checking when he and Eden had arrived. Rory prayed the guy was all right, but he wasn't seeing any movement outside.

No movement inside, either.

But he heard that groan again.

"Eden?" he called out.

It seemed to take an eternity for her to answer. An eternity where Rory had to battle the worst-case scenarios to keep them out of his head. He couldn't lose Eden. He just couldn't.

"Here," she finally said. Like him, her breathing was labored, but he could pinpoint her location in the stall next to him.

The stall where Brenda had been left to die.

Rory used his hand to try to wave away some of the cloudy particles that were obstructing his vision. He stepped over some of the pieces of shattered wood and inched his way to the stall.

And he saw Eden.

Alive.

The relief flooded through him. But not for long, because while Eden was on her feet and staggering toward him, the CSIs, Molly and David, were still on the floor. Molly was moaning, and there was blood on her head. But David wasn't even moving. He was either unconscious or dead.

In the back of his mind, Rory realized the crime scene had literally been blown to hell and back, and that the killer was likely responsible. But he couldn't focus on that now. He went to Eden, and before he could stop himself, he pulled her into his arms.

She didn't resist. In fact, she hugged him right back.

"Are you hurt?" he asked.

She shook her head. "I don't think so. Just dazed. You?"

"Same." He hoped. The right side of his chest was throbbing like a bad tooth, so he might not actually be injury-free after all.

Rory wanted to keep her in his arms, but he knew that couldn't happen. He eased back, managed to take out his phone and called Dispatch to request an ambulance, backup and the county bomb squad. Heaven knew how long it would take them to get out here, but Rory wanted a thorough investigation on the cause of the explosion.

First, though, he had to tend to the wounded.

Eden was obviously on the same wavelength because she went to Molly, and Rory went to David. He checked for a pulse and found one. Weak, but the man was still alive. Rory wanted him to stay that way.

There were three ragged-edged boards on David's chest, and Rory gently pushed them aside so he could check for injuries. Beside him, Eden was doing the same thing to Molly, who was bleeding from what appeared to be a gash on her forehead. That wound in itself didn't look critical, but it was possible the woman had a severe concussion.

Once he had the boards off David, Rory spotted the blood. It was seeping through the top of the CSI jumpsuit. Not a lot of it, but enough for Rory to know David had been cut or injured by the flying debris. Thankfully, he was breathing on his own, but he still wasn't conscious, and he didn't react when Rory tapped his cheek.

"Lou," Molly muttered.

Rory looked at the woman to see if she had spotted her fellow CSI, but she hadn't. Instead, she was looking at that massive hole in the barn wall.

Eden's gaze met his, and he immediately saw the concern in her eyes. Rory was concerned, too, because it was possible Lou had been right on top of the explosive device when it went off.

"I'll check on him," Rory said.

Then, he had a debate what to do. He considered telling Eden to get Molly to the cruiser. But that came with risks.

Huge ones.

Because the killer could be out there, waiting for them to come rushing out of the barn. Added to that, it probably wasn't a good idea to leave David alone. If he stopped breathing, Eden would need to try to save him by starting CPR.

"Be careful," Eden told him as he moved away from her.

"You, too." And he gave her one last look before he started across the barn.

It wasn't a fast trek to go across the thirty or so feet of space, since there were more of those chunks of wood everywhere. Some of the pieces were now sticking up like giant splinters, and if he fell on one of those, he'd have more than aching ribs.

Rory had no choice but to step on some of the debris.

He wobbled a few times, regained his balance and kept moving. He tried not to think that there could be a second explosive device.

No. Best not to think of that.

While he walked, he tried to listen for any sounds to indicate the third CSI was alive. Any sounds of the killer, too, but the only thing he could hear was Eden murmuring something to Molly, and the breeze stirring the trees outside.

Rory finally made it to the hole so he could look out, and he saw yet more debris there as well. What he didn't see was the CSI. Not at first, anyway. Then, he spotted him about five yards away. Bloody and unmoving.

Hell.

Rory couldn't see any signs of life, and he started through the hole so he could hurry to him. The sound stopped him.

A sound he sure as hell hadn't wanted to hear.

It hadn't come from Eden or any of the CSIs, but rather from overhead. The barn roof creaked, and the sound soon turned into something much louder. Much worse.

The roof was caving in.

"Eden!" Rory shouted.

That was all he managed to get out before all hell broke loose. Wood and steel beams came down with a loud swoosh, crashing onto the floor and creating another of those clouds of debris.

"Eden," he called out again.

He couldn't see her. Couldn't hear her. If she was saying anything or even moving, the sound was muffled by more of the roof falling. From the sound of it, every board and beam of it was coming down, and Eden and the two CSIs would be trapped.

Rory had to rein in the overwhelming urge to run to

her. To try to cover Eden with his body and protect her. But he'd never make it to her. With all the wood and steel falling, he'd be crushed.

Or killed.

The roof surface and the support beams were slamming onto the ground, causing the sides of the barn to start shaking. Mercy. What was left of the walls could collapse on them as well.

He had to risk it. He had to get to Eden so he could try to get the CSIs and her to safety. Muttering a prayer, Rory took off, dodging the chunks and sheets of wood raining down around him.

When he was about ten feet away from the place where he'd last seen Eden, Rory finally spotted her. Eden and Molly were trying to get David through a large hole of the barn. They were struggling since they, too, were having to avoid getting hit by the falling debris. Added to that, David was still unconscious, so it would have been like moving dead weight.

Rory continued to move, keeping his attention fixed on Eden, and he was close enough for their gazes to meet when another chunk of the roof came down. He could do nothing to stop it. Rory could only watch as it fell, slamming down right on Eden and the CSIs.

The emotions tore through him. *Get to her now. Save her.* And he got the motherlode of adrenaline to fuel him forward. Rory figured the roof would continue to fall. Hell, the whole place would, and he might get hit, but for now, his focus was on getting to Eden.

Feeding off that adrenaline, Rory tore his way through the wood, trying to avoid the rusty nails sticking out from some of the pieces. He just kept tossing aside what he could until he saw something.

The lower half of a body.

It took him a second to realize it wasn't Eden. It was David, and while Eden and Molly had apparently managed to get him partially through the hole, they hadn't gotten him fully through.

And his legs had been crushed by one of the support beams.

Rory had no idea if the man was still alive, and he couldn't take the time to find out. Not when yet more of the roof slammed down directly behind him. Every second counted now, if he hoped to get out of this alive, so he flipped the beams over and pushed them aside. Normally, that would have been a much harder task, but it was obvious the wood was rotting.

The moment Rory had David free, he took hold of him and pushed him through the opening. He had some help because Eden and Molly were right there, and they grabbed on to David, sliding him the rest of the way out.

Rory followed him.

The moment he was outside, he lifted David into a fireman's carry, tossing him over his shoulder. Rory prayed that wasn't making the man's injuries even worse, but he had no choice. He had to get them away from here.

"Move," Rory told Eden and Molly.

They did. They turned and started running. Rory was right behind them, and not a second too soon.

The entire barn crashed to the ground.

Chapter Five

Eden winced as the nurse cleaned a small cut on her forehead. It was the fourth one, and there were still several more to go. Thankfully, none of them were serious. In fact, Eden could have tended them at home, but Rory had insisted she be examined after their ordeal at the barn.

Where they could have been killed.

Eden couldn't push that thought aside. Couldn't push away the memories of seeing the roof fall while Rory was still in the center of the barn. It was a miracle he hadn't been crushed when the roof caved in.

Lou hadn't been so lucky. He was dead, killed instantly by whatever explosive had been set off just outside the barn. Eden didn't have an official report on it yet, but she suspected Lou had been right by, or even on, the device. The young man hadn't stood a chance of surviving.

David hadn't come out of the ordeal unscathed, either. He was in surgery for internal injuries he'd sustained from the falling support beam. She did have an official report on him that'd come from one of the doctors. David was critical but was expected to live.

Like Rory and her, Molly's injuries were mostly superficial. Cuts, scrapes and bruises. Molly had been admitted to the hospital, though, for an overnight stay because of the hit she'd taken to the head. The doctors didn't think it was serious, but they wanted to keep an eye on her.

And speaking of keeping an eye on someone, that's exactly what Rory was doing to her.

He was sitting in the chair in the treatment room, talking on his phone and watching as her injuries were treated. He'd already gone through the process and was now sporting a butterfly bandage on his forehead and three Band-Aids on his left arm.

Eden knew this particular call Rory was making was to the nanny, to check on Tyler. But before that, there'd been one to Grace to update her. Then, several to the on-duty deputies. He hadn't put any of the calls on speaker, probably because medical staff were coming and going from the treatment room, but he'd managed to give her updates on the investigation when they'd gotten a moment or two to themselves.

Deputy Livvy Walsh was the senior officer in the squad room, so she was coordinating things with the bomb squad and the CSIs who'd been called in from another county. The explosion had put their own county's team out of commission, and the scene at the barn would have to be processed.

Eden wasn't holding out much hope the CSIs would find something to help them with Brenda's murder. The explosion would have likely destroyed any potential evidence. And that was no doubt the reason it'd been set.

By the killer.

It ate away at her to think the killer could have been there. Right there, where she and Rory could have caught him. Now more than ever she wanted this monster behind bars. And she wanted to know if he or she had also killed Mellie. That was a wound that wouldn't even start to heal until she'd gotten the woman the justice she deserved.

"What did Leslie say?" Eden asked him the moment he finished his call with the nanny.

"Tyler's fine," he assured her. "He's napping right now, but Leslie's going to take him outside to see the horse when he's awake."

Good. That was the routine that Eden and Rory had with Tyler, and Eden hadn't wanted him to miss out on one of his favorite activities. She wished she could be there, to see the enjoyment she knew Tyler would get from it, but they needed to stick with this investigation.

Because they had a possible serial killer on their hands.

Mellie, Brenda and now Lou. That was the magic number for the gut-twisting label of serial killer. And it was even harder to accept since it could be Rory's own father.

Or his aunt.

Eden certainly wasn't forgetting what Dutton had told them about Helen. It was hard for her to imagine Helen being enraged enough to kill and frame Ike, but she couldn't rule out that possibility. So, yes, she and Rory needed to press hard on this investigation, to put an end to the body count.

Rory stood and went closer, checking out the cut on her head as the nurse, Beatrice Garcia, put on the last of the bandages. Eden had known Beatrice for years, and the woman gave Eden a pat on the hand before she picked up her supplies.

"Wait here, and I'll get some paperwork you'll need to sign," Beatrice said. "Both of you," she added to Rory as she exited the area.

Rory moved even closer, leaning down and pulling her into a gentle hug. It wasn't exactly a professional response, but it was a welcome one. She needed him for just a moment so she could steady herself.

The hug didn't last long, and when Rory eased back from her, their gazes met. He said a single word of profanity. Then, he groaned.

She knew what that reaction was about. It was about the entire mess that was now their lives. They were in this together, and somehow they had to ID the killer and stop them.

"Ike's interview has been delayed," he said, checking his watch. "We've got about an hour. You think you're up to it, or would you rather just head home—"

"I'm up to it," Eden said, not able to say the words fast enough. "No way do I want to miss that."

Even though Rory and her wouldn't be the ones doling out the questions. Still, they'd be able to hear what the man had to say.

Rory nodded as if that'd been the exact answer he'd expected from her. "Ike's lawyers have told Livvy that he was with them during the time of the explosions," he went on. "So an alibi for that."

She shook her head. "That doesn't mean anything, right? The bomb could have been set before we even arrived at the barn or maybe even the night before, when Brenda was left there."

"Yes," he agreed. "That was in the preliminary report from the bomb squad." Rory glanced at his phone. "I got a text update from them while you were getting bandaged, and they said it was basically an IED that had likely been placed in a shallow hole. When Lou stepped on it, it went off."

Eden suppressed a shudder. Barely. That IED had cost a man his life, but it could have killed all of them had they been on that side of the barn.

Rory pulled up a photo. "The bomb guys believe the IED looked something like this."

She studied the tan-colored PCV pipe that had likely contained the explosive material. Along with that, there was wiring, a small battery and some kind of switch that she supposed was the detonator. It seemed small enough for a half dozen or more to fit into a backpack.

"What kind of expertise would it take to make something like that?" Eden asked, because she was having trouble picturing Ike putting together this dangerous device and then transporting it to the barn.

"Sadly, not much," Rory explained. "Instructions for that kind of stuff can be found on the internet. The bomb squad will gather all the parts of the IED and examine it." He paused. "It's possible that it wasn't homemade, that it was done by a pro."

Now, she could see Ike doing something like that. Despite not being the actual owner of the McClennan family ranch, the man still had money. Eden had learned that during the time she'd investigated him as a person of interest in Mellie's murder. When Ike and his wife had married, he'd sold his own ranch for nearly a million before moving to his wife's family place, and Ike had made some good investments with the cash from that sale. Added to that, Ike and his younger brother had split a ten-million-dollar estate when their parents had passed away.

So the bottom line was that Ike could afford the best. And if that's what he had done, then the best IED maker might be hard to catch since he or she would likely know how to cover their tracks. Still, the bomb squad might find something that would help them unravel this.

"I also got another call from Diedre," Rory continued a moment later. He was staying close to her, close enough that his left side was against her leg, and he had lowered his voice. No doubt so that no one passing by the treatment room would overhear them. "She offered to set herself up as bait for Ike to come after her."

Of all the things Eden had been expecting him to say, that wasn't one of them. "Bait? Last night she was terrified that Ike was going to kill her."

He nodded, and his expression conveyed his mixed feelings about that. "She could have been exaggerating. And if she was, then I have to speculate as to why. Did she think she could convince us to arrest Ike? Maybe," he concluded. "Or she could have just wanted to plant that seed in our minds."

"The seed was already there," Eden pointed out.

"Yeah, it was, but Diedre might have wanted to try to speed things up. She could be doing that with this bait idea, too."

Eden gave that some thought. And she saw how this could play out. "Diedre allows herself to be in a position where Ike could come after her, and then she somehow arranges for Ike to be there, too, before the cops run in to rescue her."

"That's what I figure she had in mind, as well. She could have even planned to goad Ike into attacking her so that it would add to the evidence against him." He looked her straight in the eyes. "I declined Diedre's offer."

Yes. Eden had known he would. Because for one thing it was dangerous. If Ike truly was the killer, he could murder Diedre before the cops could stop him. And if he was innocent and did little or nothing to the woman, Ike's lawyers could add that it was entrapment. Either way, a bait situation like that wouldn't end well for anyone.

"So is Diedre a suspect in the murders?" Eden asked.

Rory opened his mouth but didn't get a chance to answer because his phone rang. When he took it from his pocket, she saw Livvy's name on the screen and knew he had to take it right away.

"You're on speaker," he said after issuing a greeting. "Eden is here with me, and she's listening in."

"Good," Livvy said. "It'll save you from having to update her. Ike is here with his lawyers," she went on after gathering her breath. "I've put them in the interview room, but I'll wait until Eden and you are here before I start. Any idea when that'll be?"

"I'm guessing about fifteen or twenty minutes. We're just waiting on some paperwork."

"No rush," Livvy told him. "It might do Ike some good to stew a while. The more riled he is, the more likely he is to blurt something out."

"I agree," Rory and Eden said in unison.

"And besides, there's something we need to go over before the interview," Livvy continued. "I just got Brenda's phone records, and it includes copies of her texts for the past month."

That was routine in a criminal investigation, so Eden figured Livvy must have found something. Hopefully, something that would help them confirm who'd killed the woman.

"In the past two weeks Brenda sent a half-dozen texts to a number that the techs have identified as a pay-as-you-go, a burner," Livvy explained. She paused a heartbeat. "The messages are about Ike."

She felt Rory go stiff. "Read them to us," he insisted.

"All right. The first was sent exactly two weeks ago, and it seems to be a reply—'Yes, I believe Ike is behind Mellie's death.' There's no text or call from the unknown number or anyone else to tell us why Brenda sent that, but within five minutes, the unknown caller responds 'You bet your life he is.'"

So this would have been someone who knew Ike. And that led them back to Helen, or maybe Diedre.

"There's no name associated with the phone, and the phone is no longer in use," Livvy added.

That sent up a huge red flag for Eden. It must have for Rory, too, because he asked, "Any idea when the phone was discontinued?"

"I can narrow it down. Brenda sent a text to the number at three p.m. yesterday. According to the ME, that would have likely been only a couple of hours before she was attacked and left for dead. This morning when the techs tried the number, it was out of service."

So that could fit with…what? Eden had to mentally shake her head. Had this caller been connected to the killer? Or was the caller the actual killer?

"What do the rest of the texts say?" Rory asked.

"Text two again seems to be a reply with no corresponding text or phone call so it's possible it was in response to another conversation," Livvy explained. "It says 'Ike is cleaning house, and I believe you're right. He'll come after me.'"

Eden wished the woman had taken this to the cops, and they could have tried to protect her. And they might now have Mellie's killer in custody.

"The third text isn't until a week later, and it's a doozie," Livvy went on. "It says 'We need to find out who else is on Ike's hit list. Any ideas how we can do that?' The response came less than a minute later. 'I think I know someone who can bug his office and hack into his computer. Not sure he'd be careless enough to write something down, though.'"

Eden groaned. This had certainly escalated. "Was the listening device put in place?" she asked Livvy.

"Yes, according to the next text. That came two days later from the unknown number. 'Bugs have been planted in his office, truck and bedroom, and I'm listening. Will keep you posted.' To that, Brenda sent a response of 'Please do.'"

Eden met Rory's gaze, and she could see that all of this was as much of a surprise to him as it was to her.

"Request a warrant to have all three of those locations checked for listening devices," Rory stated.

"Already done. If the CSIs find them, they'll be brought in for testing. We might get prints off them. If they exist," Livvy concluded.

Yes, and that was an *if* they had to consider. Because if the unknown texter was the killer, or Ike, then all of this could be some kind of sick game the killer was playing with Brenda. There could be no listening devices.

"The fifth text also came the day Brenda was murdered," Livvy continued. "And the sender had this to say—'Overheard exactly what we suspected. Ike's cleaning house, and he named names in a meeting with a bomb expert he plans on using. Brenda, you're on the list.'"

"Hell," Rory snarled. "And what did Brenda say to that?"

"'Not surprised,'" Livvy said, continuing to read. "'Ike hates my guts. I'll be ready for him if he comes after me the way he did poor Mellie.'"

Eden felt as if someone had punched her. She'd always known Ike was a suspect, but it was a different thing to hear it all spelled out like this. Then again, the spelling out might be all lies.

"Several minutes later, Brenda sent the sixth text," Livvy continued. "And she asks 'Who else is Ike after?'"

Eden pulled in her breath, held it. Waited.

"'Me, of course,' the person texted back. 'Frank Mott, too.'"

That name was very familiar to Eden since he'd been questioned in Mellie's murder. There'd been no evidence against him, but like Ike, Frank wasn't in favor of Mellie running a foster home so close to his own ranch. He had spent years trying to get the place shut down.

But Frank also had an ongoing feud with Ike.

Eden knew that stemmed from rumors that Ike had had an affair with Frank's late wife, Miranda. There was zero evidence to support that, but Frank, like Helen, had always been vocal about Ike's cheating, and how that cheating had crushed Rory's mom, Doreen.

"There's another part to that sixth text," Livvy said, sighing. "Here it is verbatim. 'And because he wants to nip Mellie's murder investigation in the bud, Ike will be going after his son, Rory, and Deputy Eden Gallagher.'"

Chapter Six

Rory didn't know who the hell who had sent those texts to Brenda. And he couldn't even be sure they were true. But he still made the call to Sheriff Grace Granger.

"Tyler," Eden said, her breathing suddenly way too fast, and he saw the alarm all over his face.

Rory was sure he was showing some alarm, too. Not because Ike might be coming after Eden and him, but because their son might get caught in the crossfire.

Thankfully, Grace answered on the second ring, and while he hated to bother her on maternity leave, this was important.

"What's wrong?" Grace immediately asked.

"It's possible Eden and I are Ike's targets," Rory said. "Livvy has transcripts of Brenda's texts that she'll be sending you so you can see what I mean. This might be overkill, but I need Tyler protected. I'm thinking his nanny can bring him to stay with Dutton and you—"

"Absolutely," Grace interrupted. "Dutton and several of the ranch hands can go out to Eden's place and get them now."

Rory glanced at Eden to see if she was all right with that, and she gave him a quick nod while she was typing a text. No doubt to Leslie to let her know what was going on.

"Don't worry," Grace assured him. "Ike won't get near Tyler, and I'll have Dutton post some ranch hands around the house to keep guard."

That eased some of the worry inside him. Then, he cursed the fact that the threat was even a possibility. Eden and he were cops and had signed on for dangerous situations like these, but the danger shouldn't extend to their baby.

"Eden and you are welcome to stay here, too, for as long as you need," Grace went on. "How valid is the threat from Ike?"

"We don't know yet," he admitted. "We're about to leave the hospital and observe Ike's interview. He's lawyered up to his eyeballs, but if he's guilty, Livvy might be able to coax it out of him."

Grace paused. "You really think Ike's behind these murders? I want your gut feel, not only the circumstantial evidence against him."

Hell. That wasn't an easy question, but Rory did as she'd suggested and went with his gut. "I believe someone could be setting Ike up. And, no, I'm not saying that because he's my father. I'm saying it because if Ike wanted to eliminate his enemies, I doubt he'd choose to go about it this way."

Eden muttered an agreement. "Ike would have hidden the bodies better. He probably would have made the deaths seem like a botched robbery or suicide. Right now, everything points to him, and if he'd planned the murders, he should have had the evidence leading us to someone else."

"Yes, all of that makes sense. But I'll play devil's advocate. What if Ike intentionally made it seem as if he'd been set up? After all, even with a botched robbery and a suicide, he would have come under suspicion because of his bad blood with the victims. Ike could be playing a cat-

and-mouse game with the belief that if he is charged with anything, his lawyers can get him off."

Rory couldn't dispute a single word of that. Which was why Ike was still their top suspect.

"Even if Ike isn't the killer, the threat to Tyler is still there," Rory continued. "Because the person who responded to Brenda's text could be the killer. Along with setting up Ike, this person might indeed come after Eden and me."

"Yes," Grace confirmed. "And that's why the two of you will take precautions. FYI, Dutton heard what you said, and he's already heading to Eden's with the ranch hands. When Tyler and Leslie are safely here, I'll text and let you know. I'll also be watching Ike's interview through a live feed."

Good. The more eyes and ears on that interview, the better. If Ike was indeed trying to outsmart them with this sick plan, then he might give away a clue or two in something he said.

"Who else was named in those texts?" Grace asked.

"Frank Mott," Rory said. "And, of course, the person replying to Brenda's texts. No ID yet on who that is."

Grace stayed quiet a moment. "You want me to contact Frank and give him a heads-up?"

"I'll do that," Eden offered, probably to limit Grace's duties since she was on maternity leave. "And I'll ask him to come in for an interview."

"Good." Grace ended the call with a final "Be careful," and Rory stared at his phone a moment, hoping he'd done enough to protect Tyler.

Beside him, Eden located Frank's number, but the call went straight to voice mail. She left a message for the man to contact her ASAP.

As Eden put her phone away, Rory looked at her, ready

to try to reassure her that their son would be all right, that he would be safe with Dutton and Grace. Before he could say anything, though, Eden reached out and pulled him into her arms.

"God, Rory. We can't let the killer get to Tyler," she muttered.

"We won't," he promised.

It was probably a mistake, but he slid his arms around her as well and eased her even closer to him. Touching Eden was always risky. Because of the blasted heat between them. Because that heat could muddle his thoughts and cause him to lose focus. But in this case, it only helped him focus even more.

They had so much at risk.

But they were a united force in protecting their child. Even with the heat, they wouldn't lose sight of that.

Rory stepped away from her when Beatrice came back in the room. The nurse gave them a long glance and seemed to be on the verge of asking them if she was interrupting. Rory nipped that in the bud. He definitely didn't want to discuss anything going on between them.

"You have the paperwork for us to sign?" he asked.

Beatrice nodded, produced some forms and two pens. Eden and he glanced over them, signed and headed out. Because of that threat looming over them, they kept watch as they went to the cruiser, got inside and pulled out.

Rory hadn't even made it out of the parking lot, though, when his phone rang, and he saw the unfamiliar number on the screen. Still, with all the moving parts of the investigation, he figured he'd be getting lots of calls from people not in his contacts.

"Deputy McClennan," the person said when Rory answered. "I'm Rachel Sanchez from Caldwell County CSI.

I'm heading up the team that's been searching the residence of Ike McClennan."

Rory felt his chest tighten. "Did you find something?"

"We did. Three listening devices."

So it was true. "Where?" Rory queried.

"Two in his office and another in his bedroom. Do you know if Mr. McClennan planted the bugs himself?" Sanchez asked.

"No idea. Were they well hidden?" Rory continued.

"Two were. One was on a bookshelf. It was attached to the spine of a book. Once we found that one, we looked for others and did a thorough sweep of the house. We'll send them to the lab so they can be checked for prints or trace. They might be able to tell who was receiving the info from them."

That would be very useful information. Ditto for the prints, especially if they belonged to Ike.

"The lab will contact you if they find anything," the CSI added.

Rory hung up. And cursed.

"Yes," Eden muttered, and she expressed what had caused this latest round of frustration. "Ike will use this to say he was set up."

"He will," Rory confirmed.

And, heck, it was possible he had been.

The killer could have used the info gained from the bugs to determine where Ike would be, to ensure he didn't have solid alibis for the murders.

"Who would have had the opportunity to plant bugs?" Eden asked.

"Too many people," Rory replied. "All the cleaning staff and the cook have the entry codes. And just last week, Asher and Kitty had a group of friends over."

That meant getting that list of friends, along with any maintenance or repair people who'd been in the house… Rory stopped, groaned. Because the bugs could have been there for months. Whover had planned these murders could have started the process ages ago.

Even though Rory was nearly at the police station, he went ahead and called Livvy to let her know about the listening devices. She would have to bring them up during the interview if for no other reason than to get Ike's take on them. He might be able to pinpoint who could have planted them.

While gloating that the bugs "proved" his innocence.

Yeah, that's exactly how it would play out.

With that thought and this whole dangerous mess weighing down on him, Rory parked and, still keeping watch, they went inside the station.

Straight into the buzz of activity.

All of the day deputies were present, each of them on the phone. Their conversations clashed with the sounds of the printer spewing out pages and yet more phones ringing. In the middle of that bustle, the black cat came sauntering toward Eden.

Sherlock was the unofficial adopted mascot who only doled out attention to a handful of people. And Eden was one of them. The cat rubbed against her legs, and Eden leaned down to give him a scratch on the head. Apparently, that was all Sherlock intended to tolerate because he turned and headed in the direction of the breakroom, where his litterbox and food dish were located.

Rory glanced in Grace's office and saw Livvy. Not alone but with someone he recognized.

Frank Mott.

The man was in his midfifties with salt-and-pepper hair,

but he still sported the build of a wrestler that had apparently won him some state competitions. Photos of him were displayed in the gym at the high school.

Rory was glad the man was here so they wouldn't have to track him down. Good. They could alert him that he might be in danger.

When Livvy looked at them, Frank followed her gaze, and then he immediately started in their direction. "I just listened to your voice mail," he said, directing the comment at Eden. "I was just up the street at the hardware store and came right down."

Eden nodded, and she motioned for Frank to go back in the office. They followed, and Rory shut the door.

"Something has come to our attention," Rory began, "and it's possible you could be in danger."

Rory didn't add more. He just waited for Frank to let that sink in. Of course, it didn't sink in well.

"In danger from Ike," Frank muttered. Not in a tone of someone lashing out in anger but rather as if this was the exact news he expected to hear.

"We're not sure of that yet," Rory said, settling for caution.

Frank sighed. "It's Ike. You know it is."

Rory wished he did know for certain. But for now, he had to look at all potential suspects.

And that included Frank.

Like Helen and Diedre, there was no love lost between Ike and him, and that was the reason Rory had to ask Frank a few questions.

"Have you visited Ike at his home in the past couple of months?" he asked, figuring he already knew the answer.

"No." Yep, that was the answer Rory had expected all right, and there was still no anger in the man's voice or expression. "I haven't been to your family's ranch in years. Why? Ike didn't say I had, did he?"

Rory shook his head. "It's just a routine question." So was the next one, but Frank wasn't going to care much for it. "Where were you late yesterday afternoon and last night?"

Frank sighed again. "You want to know if I have an alibi for that woman's murder," he stated. "I don't. I was home alone, and before you ask, no one can verify that." He paused. "Don't you think if I was killing women as a vendetta against Ike, that I would have gone after his friends instead? I sure as hell wouldn't eliminate people who feel like I do about Ike."

Maybe. But murdering his friends wouldn't accomplish one important thing—setting Ike up.

"Have there been any recent altercations or arguments between the two of you?" Rory asked.

Frank laughed but not from humor. It was all sarcasm. "Ike is always getting in my face about something. As you well know, Ike and I are both on the town council, and we disagree on pretty much everything on the agenda. Last month, it was the rezoning of that land just to the east of your family's ranch. I didn't want it classified as farmland, and Ike did."

Rory knew about that. It was land Ike was trying to buy since he'd decided to get back in the ranching business. But Ike didn't want just that one section of land, he wanted Frank's place, too.

And the foster ranch that Mellie had run.

Because if Ike had all of that, the acreage would essentially coil around the McClennan family ranch, and Ike would control some of the water supply that Dutton needed for the livestock. Rory wasn't certain Ike would actually cut off that supply, but knowing Ike, it was a card he might play if the rotten mood suited him.

"Any other disputes?" Rory persisted.

Frank shrugged. "A couple of months ago, Ike undercut me on a horse I was trying to buy." Then, he paused. "And there was an, uh, incident at my wife's grave."

Rory knew about that as well. Frank's wife, Miranda, had died in a car accident about two decades ago when she was in her thirties. From all accounts, Frank had been deeply in love with her, but Miranda had cheated on him. With Ike.

And about six months ago, a fistfight had broken out between Frank and Ike at the cemetery where Miranda was buried. Neither man had fessed up to what the altercation had been about, and no charges had been filed. The only reason Rory was even aware of it was because someone had seen the fight and reported it.

"Look, Ike and I have been at odds for years," Frank added a moment later. "I don't have the time or breath to detail every run-in I've had with him. And if I'd wanted to start killing because of him, that killing would have started twenty years ago."

When his wife had died.

Yeah, Rory could see that. But sometimes people just snapped. Sometimes, all the little things build up into something huge.

That could have happened with Frank.

"One more thing," Rory went on, aware that the time was ticking down for Ike's interview to start. "When was the last time you were at the barn on the old Sanderson Ranch?"

Frank didn't react with anger, but rather resignation and maybe some frustration at being dragged into this. It was possible the frustration was warranted, but Rory still had to treat him like a person of interest.

"Aka, the Devil's Hideout," he said, using the nickname it'd been given. "Again, the answer is years ago. You're asking because I worked there a couple of summers when I was a teenager."

Rory did indeed recall that fact from the background check that had been run on Frank after Mellie's murder.

"Mellie worked there, too, mucking stalls and grooming the palominos," Frank added. "Hell, so did a lot of teenagers. And your aunt Helen used to come out there and ride the horses sometimes."

Now, Rory didn't remember that coming up in previous interviews. He shook his head. "Why would Helen have gone there to ride when she lived on a ranch with dozens of horses?"

Frank shifted uncomfortably, and he dodged Rory's gaze for a couple of seconds. "You'd have to ask Helen about that."

"I will. But I'm also asking you," Rory retorted.

"All right." Frank dragged in a long breath. "I believe Helen was there to see me."

"See you?" Eden repeated. "As in romantically?"

Rory heard the surprise in Eden's voice, and he thought he knew why. Helen had always had that to-the-manor-born vibe about her, and Frank had come from a blue-collar family. Yes, he'd earned enough to buy his own ranch and it was successful, but in those days, Frank wouldn't have been in Helen's economic circle.

"And did Helen and you see each other?" Eden asked.

"No, we did not because I was with someone else at the time," he insisted, and Frank looked Rory straight in the eyes. "I didn't kill those women," he repeated. "Ike did, and I hope you can do the right thing and arrest him. If not, there'll likely be another murder soon."

The man's gaze slid to Eden, and he didn't come out and say that he considered her a potential victim. While Frank's gaze wasn't accompanied with any intense emotion, it still felt like an unspoken threat.

"I'll watch my back," Frank added a moment later. "I hope everyone on Ike's bad side will do the same. Are we done here?" he asked.

"For now," Rory replied. "If I have any other questions, I'll be in touch."

Frank tipped his head in farewell, slipped on the white Stetson he'd been holding in front of him like a shield and walked out. Rory's and Eden's phones dinged with texts as they watched the man go, and Rory saw Grace's group message to both Eden and him on the screen.

Tyler and Leslie arrived at the ranch, Grace had texted. All is well. We'll keep them safe.

That helped ease some of the tension in his muscles, and he could see it had the same reaction for Eden. Tyler was their top priority, and with him safe, they could focus on their jobs.

Livvy got to her feet and began gathering her files. "Ready to start with Ike?"

Rory nodded, and he hoped the interview went a lot better than he was anticipating. It was possible as soon as those bugs were brought up that the lawyers would try to put a halt to the process by claiming it was something they needed to learn more about.

He and Eden followed Livvy down the hall, but then they peeled off, going into the observation area while Livvy continued into the interview room. Rory immediately spotted

Ike seated at the metal table, and he had two lawyers on each side of him.

Yeah, lawyered up to his eyeballs was right.

Livvy turned on the recording, adding the pertinent details of the date, time and the names of those present. She was in the process of repeating Ike's Miranda rights when Rory's phone rang.

"It's Detective Vernon from SAPD," he said to Eden.

No need for him to clarify who that was. He was the cop assigned to supervise the search of Brenda's house and office in San Antonio.

"Deputy McClennan," Rory said when he answered, "and you're on speaker with Deputy Eden Gallagher."

"Good. Because you'll both want to hear what turned up in Brenda's bedroom."

Rory silently groaned at the detective's tone, and he steeled himself for what he was certain was going to be bad news.

"The CSIs found a burner phone in a plastic bag," Vernon explained. "It was tucked away at the back of the top shelf. So, hidden from sight."

Rory's mind began to whirl with possibilities. And they weren't good possibilities, either. Some people did keep burners around for emergencies, but they didn't usually bother to hide them.

"The burner wasn't locked," the detective continued, "and there were some texts on it." He paused. "They match the replies on the messages on Brenda's other phone."

Hell in a handbasket.

"You understand what I'm saying, right?" Vernon asked.

"Oh, yeah." Rory understood all right. If the burner belonged to Brenda, then she had likely sent those texts to herself, and there was only one reason she would have done that.

To set Ike up.

"Are there any other messages on the burner, or was it used to make calls?" Rory queried.

"No. That was it, just those replies."

So the odds were Brenda had indeed planned on using those texts to try to frame Ike. Had the woman also murdered Mellie?

Maybe.

It was definitely something that needed to be investigated. In fact, it changed everything about how they needed to approach this case. And it left Rory with a huge question.

If Brenda had murdered Mellie, then who the hell had killed Brenda?

Chapter Seven

Eden was silently cursing right along with the profanity Rory was muttering. This wasn't just a setback to the case they were building against Ike, it could be the kiss the death.

She snapped back toward the observation window when she heard a phone ring. Not Rory's, but one of Ike's lawyers, Stephen Arnette. Livvy hadn't yet gotten started with the questions, but the lawyer took one look at his phone and stood.

"I need to take this," Arnette insisted. "So hold off on the interview until I get back." With that, he stepped out of the room.

It was tempting to try to listen in on the conversation, but Eden didn't want to do anything that Ike's lawyers could legally use against them, and Arnette could argue the call fell under the umbrella of client-attorney privilege. Instead, Rory used the time to text Livvy and let her know what was going on.

And, of course, Livvy's reaction wasn't good.

She tipped her eyes to the ceiling for a moment, and Eden figured she was doing some silent cursing as well.

It didn't take long—less than two minutes—before the

lawyer came back in the room. Arnette certainly hadn't bothered to plaster on a poker face, and unlike Livvy, he was practically gloating.

He sank back down into his chair, and the other lawyers and Ike huddled around Arnette while they had a brief, whispered conversation before he turned his attention back to Livvy.

"I demand my client's immediate release," Arnette said. "I've just learned information that proves his innocence."

Sweet heaven. Did Arnette know about the burner phone or the bugs? Or maybe he knew about both? If so, there was a serious leak at either SAPD or among the CSIs.

"Really?" Livvy asked in a discussing-the-weather tone. "And what info would that be?"

"Unless you're completely out of touch with this investigation, Deputy," Arnette stated, "then you're aware that someone planted three listening devices in his home." His tone was both scolding and condescending. "Clearly, the real killer did that to obtain knowledge of my client's whereabouts so he could then be set up to take the blame for those poor murdered women."

"Uh-huh," Livvy countered, managing some condescension of her own. "And how exactly did you come by this information?"

Arnette didn't quite smile, but it was close enough. "I got it through an anonymous tip."

"So you have no idea if the tip is true," Livvy retorted.

That wiped some of the smugness off Arnette's face. "It is. I have confirmation from someone I trust. And, no, I'm not required to give you that name."

There were some situations in which a lawyer could be compelled to do just that as long as it didn't violate the attorney-client privilege, but this wasn't a fight worth taking on. The cat was out of the bag, and they'd have to deal with it. That, and the burner phone that'd been found at Brenda's house. That phone implied she had been the one to create Ike's hit list of enemies.

Implied.

But Eden also knew it could have been planted. Perhaps by the same person who'd planted those listening devices at Ike's.

"You have no actual proof that I killed those women," Ike stated, leaning forward and looking Livvy straight in the eyes. "Because I didn't do it. Someone is playing you, Deputy Walsh." He fanned his hand around. "Playing you and the whole damn police force, and whoever it is, they're making you all look like fools."

Eden wished she could say for sure that wasn't happening, but there were certainly a lot of pieces that didn't fit.

"Is my client free to go?" Arnette snapped.

"Not quite yet. Just a few more questions." Livvy managed a relaxed pose despite this interview having been derailed. "When was the last time you were in Brenda Watford's house?"

"Eight months ago," Ike said without hesitation.

"Wow, you seem so sure," she commented, and she didn't wait for him or his lawyers to respond. "So if we study the traffic-cam feed in and around Brenda's office, we won't see you."

Ike pulled back his shoulders. "I might be on them. I often go to San Antonio to visit friends and to eat out."

"Were any of those friends or restaurants near Brenda's house?" she continued.

"I don't think so." Ike's eyes narrowed. "Why are you asking that?"

"Because it's possible something was planted inside her

house." Livvy slid a look at Arnette. "Guess your anonymous tipster didn't come through on that one for you. Or that person you rely on to confirm things." She shook her head, shifted her attention back to Ike. "Shoddy work on your lawyers' part. As much as you're paying this crew, you'd think they would be more on top of things."

Arnette muttered something under his breath that Eden didn't catch, but she figured he'd just cursed. He stood and went back into the hall, no doubt to make a call to find out what Livvy was talking about.

"Stephen Arnette exiting the interview," Livvy said for the benefit of the recording, and she shifted back to Ike. "What about your ex-lover, Diedre Bennington? When's the last time you've been to her place?"

"Months," Ike snapped. "Why? Did she lie and say I'd been there? Is she the one feeding you lies about me being a killer?"

Livvy shrugged. "She's indicated she might have some concerns about her safety when it comes to you."

Ike laughed, but there was no humor in it. "She's a liar. Hell hath no fury like a woman scorned."

"You scorned her?" Livvy asked.

Ike's mouth went tight. "I ended a relationship with her that I should have never started."

Livvy jumped right on that. "Because you were married at the time. And your wife was dying. Yes, probably not a good idea to spend time with your mistress rather than be by your wife's bedside."

Oh, Ike didn't care for that being thrown in his face. And she heard the slight shift in Rory's breathing. It had touched a nerve for him, too.

"Yeah," Ike growled. "And being with her was a mistake."

It was indeed, and that affair had been the final straw for Rory. Before that, he'd more or less tolerated his dad. But afterward, all civility was gone between them.

Ike shook his head in disgust. "Trust me," he went on, "I've paid over and over for that mistake. Diedre has hounded me for nearly a year, trying to make my life miserable, and she turned my wife's sister against me." He jabbed his index finger at Livvy. "Those are the two you should be questioning right now. Diedre and Helen. You can bet your bottom dollar they'd recently visited Brenda."

"Why?" Livvy ventured. "Did they form an I-hate-Ike's-guts club?"

"Something like that," Ike grumbled. "I saw the three of them together in a restaurant in San Antonio."

"When was that?" Livvy persisted.

Ike lifted his shoulder. "A couple of months back. Since you're so hell-bent, why don't you check traffic-camera feed for that? It was at the Elm, downtown. That's a reservations-only place so they might even have a record of it."

"Interesting," Eden muttered.

Rory muttered his agreement, and he took out his phone to text a question to Livvy. Ask Ike about the knife he took from Helen.

He watched as Livvy read the text, and then she turned her attention back to Ike. "I understand you were in an altercation with your former sister-in-law, Helen. Tell me about that."

"Altercation," Ike spluttered like it was a profanity. "More like all bark and no bite. Helen threatened me with a knife, and I knocked it out of her hand. I told her to leave or I'd call the cops and have her arrested for attempted assault with a deadly weapon. Not that you cops would have done anything about it," he grumbled. "But the threat worked. She tucked tail and got out of there fast."

"What did you argue about?" Livvy asked.

"Same ol', same ol'. You did my sister wrong. Boo-hoo. Helen hasn't learned how to shake off the past." But there was something in Ike's tone that made Eden believe Ike hadn't quite managed to shake it off, either.

"So you argued. Helen took out the knife, you grabbed it and she left," Livvy said, summarizing. "What happened then? What did you do with the knife?"

"I was going to throw it away, but then I thought maybe it'd sting for her to see it again. You know, a reminder that I bested her. So I put it in a plastic bag and had my assistant take it to her house. She wasn't home so he left it by her front door."

"Where anyone could have taken it," Eden muttered and then groaned.

"Your assistant will confirm he left it?" Livvy asked.

"Damn right, he will. He even got a picture of it, like delivery drivers do." Ike took out his phone, and after thumbing through his pictures, he pulled up the shot.

Eden couldn't see it from where she was standing, but judging from Livvy's expression, it was exactly what Ike had said it was.

"It was the damndest thing," Ike went on after Livvy requested that he forward the photo to her. "My assistant said as he was driving out of Helen's neighborhood he thought he saw Diedre. Not sure what she would have been doing there," he added in a mutter.

Eden looked at Rory, who was already taking out his phone. "I'm arranging a meeting with Diedre," he said. "I think it's time we chatted with her in person."

Eden thought so, too. Because if Ike was telling the

truth, then maybe the unthinkable had happened. Mercy. Had Diedre and Helen created an unholy alliance to go after a man they wanted to destroy?

When Rory finished his call, he turned to her. "Diedre says we can see her now. It'll take us about twenty-five minutes to get to her place. Are you game?"

"Absolutely." She glanced in the interview room. "Livvy will have to cut Ike loose soon, anyway, and I'd rather not be around for that."

Eden didn't mind having words with Ike, but it would be a waste of breath. Besides, she figured Arnette was on the verge of filing a complaint of police harassment, and it was better not to add any fuel to that.

The moment she and Rory were in the cruiser, Eden made a call to Leslie, putting it on speaker, and the nanny answered right away.

"We're all settled in," Leslie said. "And Tyler is having a blast with the toys in the playroom." As usual, the nanny sounded upbeat, but Eden still detected the worry. "Is everything okay with Rory and you?"

"We're on our way to interview a person of interest," Eden explained. "We just wanted to see how Tyler and you were doing."

"Listen for yourself," Leslie said, and she must have moved her phone closer to Tyler, because Eden could hear Tyler babbling. And laughing.

That did her heart good to hear her baby so happy. Thankfully, he was too young to understand what was going on.

"Grace and Dutton have been great," Leslie went on. "They've put Tyler in the nursery since baby Nash is still sleeping in their room. I'm in the guest suite directly across the hall from Tyler. I'll keep a close eye on him."

"Thank you," Eden and Rory said together.

It was Eden who continued, doling out the news that Leslie needed to know. "Ike will likely be released if he hasn't been already. We didn't have enough grounds to hold him."

Leslie stayed quiet a moment. "Dutton insisted his father wouldn't get near this place."

"And he won't." She hoped. "Just keep Tyler inside for a while, all right? Maybe it won't be long before we get all of this sorted out."

"Yes," Leslie muttered. "Stay safe," she added, and after saying their goodbyes, Eden ended the call.

Eden's sigh was a little louder than she'd intended, and Rory reached across the seat to take hold of her hand. Somehow, it seemed just as intimate as a kiss. And Eden welcomed it. Having their son in possible danger was bad enough, and she couldn't imagine going through this without Rory.

Since she had to get her mind off Tyler, Eden eased her hand from Rory's and used her phone to start getting some work done. She located the number for the Elm and called the restaurant.

It took her a couple of minutes to work her way up to the manager, but once she got through, it was confirmed that Diedre had indeed made reservations there. She got the info she needed from the manager, ended the call and then groaned.

"Five and a half months ago," she said to Rory. "That's when Diedre made a reservation for three at the Elm."

"Five and a half months," he repeated. He didn't groan. He cursed.

And she knew why. That was shortly before Mellie's murder.

It could be a coincidence. In fact, it probably was because she was still having a hard time imagining three of Ike's enemies plotting murder over a meal.

"I don't suppose the manager could recall anything about the lunch?"

Eden shook her head. "And they only keep security-cam feed for a week." She went to a search engine to see what she could find. "I'll look through social media to see if Diedre posted or was tagged in a photo of the lunch."

Though she was having a hard time imagining that as well. If this trio had been discussing anything remotely criminal, they likely wouldn't have wanted to document the occasion. And that's why Eden widened her search to anyone posting a photo from the Elm during the time and date of Diedre's reservation. Data mining could be a tedious process, but she'd gotten lucky a couple of times using this angle.

She looked up from her search and realized that Rory was firing glances in the rearview mirror. "Everything all right?" she asked, automatically turning to have a look.

"It's good. I'm just keeping an eye out," he assured her.

There were a couple of cars behind and in front of them now, but she couldn't see a threat. Then again, the threat could be there so she was glad Rory was staying vigilant. She did, too, while she continued her search.

"No photos or posts for the time of the reservation," she told Rory. "But Diedre is very active on social media. She has a lot of bad things to say about Ike." She continued to scan through the dozens of daily posts. "The woman documented most of her meals, the weather and even her schedule. She made it very easy for the killer to know exactly where she would be."

"Most meals," Rory repeated. "But not the one at the Elm."

No, she hadn't, and that in itself could be telling. However, it didn't make her a killer.

"More posts about Ike," she went on. And she reached the ones that would have been while Rory's mom was still alive.

Good grief. Diedre hadn't hidden the fact she was involved with a married man. She didn't specifically name him, but there were a few photos of her with Ike.

And that brought her back to her concerns about Rory.

"Are you okay with seeing Diedre?" she asked as he took the final turn toward her neighborhood.

"I'm never okay with it, but I can manage it," he insisted. "What I feel for Diedre is all rolled into the same ball with the grief over losing my mom."

His father's cheating was in the mix, too. Then again, Ike apparently did a lot of cheating over the years.

"I'm sorry," she said.

He shrugged. "Dealing with Diedre will be worth it if we get answers about the murders."

Yes, but that didn't mean this wouldn't put Rory through an emotional ringer. And that's the reason she gave his hand a squeeze as they drove into Quarry Heights, an upscale neighborhood on the far east edge of San Antonio. There was no security gate, though, so they were able to drive straight through to Diedre's. They got out, but before they even reached the front door, it opened, and a concerned-looking Diedre met them.

"I'm glad you came," she blurted, ushering them inside. "Please tell me you've arrested Ike."

"No," Rory answered.

Diedre groaned. "I was hoping you had good news. I thought that's why you wanted to see me."

Rory gave Diedre a glance before they followed her into

a living room that looked more like a showroom for expensive furnishings than an actual living space.

"No," he repeated. "We're here to ask you some questions. And before we start, I'm going to read you your rights."

That put some alarm in Diedre's eyes.

"It's for your protection," Rory informed her. He recited the Miranda warning. Then waited, no doubt to see if Diedre was going to demand a lawyer. When she didn't, he launched into the interview. "Tell us about the lunch you had at the Elm five and a half months ago."

Diedre had been in the process of sitting down on a silver leather sofa but that stopped her. She froze. Blinked. "Lunch at the Elm. Why would you want to know about that…?" She sank down onto the sofa and rolled her eyes. "Because Ike saw me there, and he told you. What did he say?"

"He recalled seeing you." That was all Rory admitted while Eden and he took the love seat across from Diedre. "Tell us about it," he repeated. "Who was there with you?"

Diedre took her time answering. "Helen and Brenda."

So she hadn't denied it, and Diedre still seemed confused as to why they would be questioning her about this.

"I'll be talking to Helen," Rory went on, "but could you tell me what the three of you discussed during the lunch?"

Diedre opened her mouth but didn't answer. Probably because of the sound of approaching footsteps. All of them turned in the direction of the arched entry, and Eden saw the woman step into view.

Helen.

What the heck was she doing there?

Rory's aunt didn't offer up any explanation. Or even any

kind of a greeting. The glances she gave Eden and him were laced with annoyance.

"So you two are friends now?" Rory asked Helen as she sat down on the sofa. Not right next to Diedre, but on the far end. "Because after Mom died, I recall you having some nasty things to say about Diedre."

"Rightfully so," Diedre murmured.

Helen shot the woman a glance and wasn't able to mask the venom that was still there. "I suppose you could say that Diedre and I have reached a truce because of our mutual hatred for Ike. He helped my sister into an early grave with the stress he put on her. And Ike has done his level best to destroy Diedre both personally and professionally."

"The enemy of my enemy is my friend," Diedre said. "I mean, it's the reason Mellie and I got close."

Eden had known that Diedre and Mellie sometimes talked, but she wasn't sure Mellie considered the woman an actual friend. She could be wrong about that, though, and Mellie and Diedre could have indeed bonded over Ike's mutual hatred for them and vice versa.

"And now Ike is trying to destroy me," Helen interjected. "Did he claim Diedre and I are setting him up for the murders?"

Neither Rory nor Eden responded to that, but Eden decided to backtrack a little, and she read Helen her rights just as Rory had done to Diedre. Helen didn't seem bothered by that, and she didn't request a lawyer. She just gave Eden a cool stare.

"Why was Brenda at the lunch with you two?" Eden asked once she'd finished with the Miranda.

"Another enemy of my enemy," Helen said quickly. "In fact, it was Brenda who wanted to meet with us. The lunch was all her idea."

"I made the reservation because I eat there often and already had the app on my phone," Diedre added. "But, yes, Brenda arranged it. She wanted to find out if there was a way to make Ike pay. Nothing criminal," she added.

"Then, what did she have in mind?" Rory replied.

Helen and Diedre exchanged a glance. "She wanted to hire someone, a PR expert, who could start a smear campaign. She had already tried to talk Mellie and Frank Mott into going along with it, too, but I think they both turned her down. That didn't stop Brenda, though." She paused. "Simply put, she wanted to ruin your father."

"And did you want that, too?" Rory asked.

"We did," Helen admitted.

"Yes," Diedre confirmed. "And we even tried a second time to encourage Mellie to join us." She turned her attention to Eden. "After all, Ike was horrible to her for years. But Mellie turned us down again."

Eden couldn't ask the question fast enough. "When was this?"

"A couple of days after the lunch," Helen offered. "Yes, the timing is terrible, isn't it? I mean with Mellie being murdered shortly thereafter."

The timing was indeed suspicious, and it made Eden wonder if Mellie had said something when she had turned them down. Something that had spooked Helen, Diedre or Brenda. If the three had brought up anything about framing Ike for a crime, no way would Mellie have gone along with that.

Had that been the reason Mellie was murdered?

Sweet heaven, it was possible.

"So why are you here now?" Rory asked, turning toward his aunt. "More planning on how to get back at Ike?"

Helen shook her head. "No, Diedre is worried about

being killed. It's obvious Ike is on a murder spree, and we're both in danger."

Eden wasn't so sure about Ike's involvement, but the spree part might be what was happening. Still, it didn't mean Ike was behind it. *The enemy of my enemy is my friend* didn't always pan out.

And that put Helen at the top of their suspect list.

"Tell me about the altercation you had with Ike," Rory said to his aunt. "The one that involved a knife."

Helen's mouth went tight. "Altercation? Is that what he called it?"

"No, a witness did," Rory replied.

"Dutton," Helen grumbled. "Well, if altercation is the label you want to put on it, fine, but it was just another round of Ike being Ike." She gathered her breath. "I stopped by the house to pick up a locket that I'd given my sister years ago. She'd given me an identical one, and I wanted the set as a memento. Ike started slinging insults at me, and when I felt threatened by him, I took out my knife."

"Threatened?" Eden asked. "How?"

"Getting in my face. Telling me I was a whiny brat." She paused. "And then he said my sister hated my guts, that she would make fun of me whenever I wasn't around."

Eden could see that the last insult had truly gotten to the woman. Even now, there was a mix of both anger and hurt on her face.

"My sister loved me, and I loved her," Helen went on, "and I was sick of Ike and his toxic ways. So I drew the knife, not intending to use it. For just a second, I wanted him to be afraid."

"And was he?" Eden persisted.

Helen shook her head, sighed. "No, he punched my hand,

and I dropped the knife. He picked it up, and I thought he was going to use it against me, so I left."

That meshed with the account Dutton had told them. Of course, Dutton hadn't known what Helen's actual motives were for pulling that knife. It was possible the woman had indeed planned on harming Ike.

"What happened to the knife?" Rory asked.

"I have no idea. You'd have to ask Ike about that." She stopped, the anger overtaking the hurt in her expression. "Is he using that knife to try to set me up?"

"As far as I know, there's no proof whatsoever that Ike or anyone else is trying to set you up," Rory told her.

That was true. No proof. But that didn't mean it wasn't happening.

Rory's phone dinged with a text, and when he glanced at it, he stood. "All right. If you recall anything else about that lunch or if Ike attempts to contact you, please let us know."

Helen didn't react to that, but Diedre seemed relieved that the questions were over. They were for now. But Eden figured they'd be talking to Helen and Diedre again very soon.

"That was a text from Sanchez, the CSI," Rory said once they were outside. "The bugs they found at Ike's were tapped into his Wi-Fi, and they've traced the output from the eavesdropping devices to an internet server."

"To Helen?" she asked.

He shook his head. "No, to Brenda."

Eden didn't bother to groan, and that meant the listening devices couldn't be used in the case against Ike.

Or Helen.

It was essentially a dead end, leaving them to speculate about what had possibly happened.

"So if we're to believe Helen and Diedre," Eden said as they got into the cruiser, "Brenda arranged that lunch to gain support to launch a smear campaign against Ike. She might or might not have gotten that support. Either way, she bought the burner and set up those fake texts that she was presumably going to make sure the police saw."

"She could have brought them in when asking for protection because she was in fear for her life," Rory suggested. "Then, she planted the bugs and waited until she was certain Ike didn't have an alibi, and she attacked Mellie."

Yes, Eden could see that playing out. Mellie wouldn't have been afraid of opening the door to Brenda.

"She waited for the cops to arrest Ike," Rory went on as he drove away from the house, "but when that didn't happen, she could have planned another attack on Helen or Diedre."

"But someone killed Brenda first," Eden said, finishing.

She would have said more had she not spotted the young blond-haired man by the subdivision gate. He was frantically trying to wave them down.

"Hell," Rory muttered. "I recognize him from his photo. That's the man who was stalking Brenda."

"Carter Rooney," Eden related. SAPD had interviewed him after Brenda's death, but Carter was also on the list of people they needed to see.

"Get your gun ready," Rory told her.

She did, and he pulled to a stop next to Carter, who immediately came closer. Rory didn't lower the window, and they both gave Carter a once-over. If he was carrying a weapon, he had it well hidden.

"Deputy McClennan?" he asked.

Rory nodded but still didn't put down the window.

"Good. Because I have something you need to see." The man took out his phone. "I believe I have proof that Diedre was the one who murdered Brenda."

Chapter Eight

Rory didn't look at the phone that Carter thrust at him. He kept his attention pinned to the man himself, waiting to see if this was a ruse to try to murder them.

After all, Carter was a person of interest in Brenda's murder. Had to be since there was a restraining order against him. But other than not having an alibi, SAPD hadn't found anything to hold him, and Rory hadn't gotten around to questioning him.

Well, he sure as heck had some questions now.

"Why are you here?" Rory demanded, and he lowered the window just a fraction so the man could hear him better, but not so wide that he could get the barrel of a gun through the opening.

"Oh," Carter said, suddenly not as eager as he had been just seconds earlier. "I've, uh, been keeping an eye on Diedre." He motioned toward a small pull-off area on the other side of the neighborhood sign. "I'm parked over there."

Since that explained exactly squat, Rory repeated the question. "Why are you here?"

Carter huffed and lowered his phone to the side of his leg. "Because I'm worried the cops might try to pin Brenda's murder on me. I didn't kill her," he added quickly, "but they asked me a bunch of questions, and they think I'm guilty. I could see it. It was all over their faces."

"They believe that because you were stalking Brenda," Rory pointed out. "Or do you deny that?"

The man took his time responding and finally shook his head. "No. I followed her around. I called her and left threatening messages."

"You stalked her," Eden snapped.

"Well, if I did, it was because she deserved it," he added without a pause. "She deserved worse. Brenda destroyed my business."

Rory had read all about that, and it was true. Well, it was mostly true, anyway. Because she had been friends with Carter's late mother, Brenda had loaned Carter about fifty grand to open a pub near the downtown River Walk. However, after Ike's antics had cost Brenda a good chunk of her income and customers, she had called in the loan. Carter had fought repaying it, but it was a fight he'd lost. And without any working revenue, the pub had gone belly up.

Yet another casualty of Ike's dirty dealings.

"I asked Brenda just to wait a couple more months, and then I could start repaying the loan," Carter went on. "But she wouldn't. She took me to court."

"Because she had no choice," Rory pointed out. "She was on the verge of having to declare bankruptcy."

"She had a choice," Carter practically shouted. "She could have gone into business with me. Then, we both would have had an income."

"Maybe," Eden said, "but that wasn't the decision Brenda made, and you stalked her because of it."

Carter looked ready to spew out some obscenities about Brenda, but he must have realized that wouldn't do him any good. He clearly had something he wanted them to see. Something on the phone he held in a white-knuckle grip.

"After I lost the pub," he went on, his voice and demeanor much calmer now, "I started following Brenda, looking for something I could use to have her arrested. I wanted her punished."

"You stalked her," Eden repeated, and it was obvious she had no sympathy for this guy. Neither did Rory.

"Yes, I've already admitted that," he said, still in the calm mode. "And after she got a restraining order, I kept my distance but continued to watch her through binoculars and the long-range lens of my camera." Now, he did pause. "I was watching her the night she was murdered. I think I saw when she was taken."

Everything inside Rory went on high alert. "You saw who took Brenda but didn't tell the cops?"

"No." Carter held up his hands in a stop gesture. "I didn't actually see the person. I saw a car speeding away from her place, and in hindsight I think she might have been in the vehicle. I'm not sure when she was attacked, but I believe the timing would fit. It was maybe around five p.m."

Yes, that *could* fit. Could. But Carter didn't seem at all certain of the time. Then again, he could be feigning uncertainty and knew the exact time that Brenda had been snatched or lured.

"Tell me what you saw," Rory demanded. "And then when you're done, I want you to cover both investigative bases by going first to SAPD and then to Renegade Canyon to give a full statement." SAPD would need to be involved since the possible abduction would have taken place in their jurisdiction.

Carter gave a shaky nod, and he didn't look at all sure

he would do that. Eden must have thought so, too, because Rory saw her send two texts. No doubt to someone at SAPD and at Renegade Canyon who'd make sure Carter showed up to tell them this latest information.

Or this lie.

Rory wasn't sure which.

"Like I said, I was watching Brenda's place," Carter explained, "but I must have fallen asleep because I didn't see the car go to her house. But I woke up when I heard an engine revving, and I saw it speed past me."

Rory huffed. "So you don't know if the vehicle was even at her place?"

"I think it was." There was more uncertainty, but then something lit up in his eyes. "But the car isn't what I wanted to tell you about." He dragged in a long breath. "I tried to follow the vehicle, but when I lost it, I decided to drive by here." He motioned to Diedre's house.

"Why?" Eden asked. She had finished her texts, put her phone on her lap and slid her hand back over the butt of her weapon in her holster.

"Because Brenda had been coming over here a lot, and I thought maybe the car was Diedre's." He lifted the phone again. "There was a car in her driveway. I'm not positive it was the same vehicle I saw leaving Brenda's, but I believe it could be."

Carter showed them the photo that he'd taken of a dark green Jeep. The heavily tinted windows made it impossible to see inside, but the man had gotten a shot of the license plate.

Eden immediately snatched up her phone again and ran a search on it. "The car's registered to Diedre."

Rory had to stop himself from rolling his eyes. "It's not a crime for a person to park their car in their own driveway."

"Yes, but I think a crime might have been committed. Look at this," Carter insisted, showing them another photo.

It was of a very harried-looking Diedre coming out of her house and heading back to the car. Her hair was scraped back in a messy ponytail, and she appeared to be fumbling with her keys.

"Notice what's she's wearing," Carter added.

Rory noted the woman's slim black pants and gray top. "So?"

"That wasn't the outfit she had on when she came home," Carter explained. "She was wearing this."

In the next photo he pulled up, Diedre was wearing baggy sweatpants and a T-shirt that looked like workout clothes. Again, there was no crime in someone changing clothes, but then Rory looked at the time stamp of the photo.

Eight p.m.

If Diedre had been the one to attack Brenda, that would have given her time to get to Renegade Canyon with Brenda, stab her and leave her in that barn to die.

Hell.

Had that happened?

Had Diedre taken this damn hit list so far that she'd murdered two women?

Rory not only didn't have answers for that, but he also had another question to add to it. "Why didn't you immediately take this to SAPD or to us?" he asked Carter.

"Because like I said, SAPD think I'm guilty. I don't want to go to them with anything. And when I saw your Renegade Canyon cruiser, I thought maybe you'd be more objective, that you'd believe in innocent until proven guilty. I'm not guilty," he added.

Maybe. Rory was going to hold out judgment on that.

Rory tipped his head to the man's phone. "Text us those photos," he instructed. "Then, show them to SAPD. It's possible these pictures can clear your name," Rory added when he saw the hesitancy in Carter's eyes. "The time stamps could show you weren't near Brenda when she was attacked."

Of course, it might show just the opposite, but Rory was going to keep that to himself.

He rattled off his phone number to Carter, and the man began forwarding the photos to Rory's phone. Rory passed his phone to Eden so she could have a closer look and send them to the county crime lab for analysis. Of course, SAPD would be doing the same thing, but it wouldn't hurt to have two sets of eyes on these.

"One more thing," Rory went on, aiming a hard stare at Carter. "If you don't show up at SAPD within the hour, they'll come looking for you, and it'd be best if that didn't happen."

Carter gave another of those unconvincing nods, and he'd just finished sending the pictures when his gaze whipped in the direction behind the cruiser. Rory looked in his side mirror and saw Diedre heading their way.

"I have to go," Carter blurted, and the man took off running toward his car.

Rory considered going after him, but with Diedre and Carter as suspects, he decided for now to leave Carter to SAPD. Renegade Canyon PD could get a crack at him later.

"I'll give SAPD a heads-up about the photos," Eden murmured, taking care of that while Diedre stepped up alongside the cruiser.

"What's going on?" Diedre demanded, stooping down and staring at them through the window. "Why are you still here, and who is that man?"

Rory debated how much to say, and he decided to see how Diedre would react to Carter's accusations. "It's come to my attention that there was some unusual activity at your house the night Brenda was attacked."

Diedre's frown deepened, and she glanced at Carter, who was now speeding away. "That man told you something about me? Who is he?"

Rory didn't intend to spill that since Diedre might go after him. "Was your Jeep parked in your driveway at any time in the past twenty-four hours?"

Diedre froze for a couple of moments. "Why?"

"Just answer the question," Rory ordered.

After a long hesitation, she nodded. "I believe it was."

"But you don't know for sure?" Rory persisted.

She made another glance at the spot where she'd seen Carter speeding away. "Yes, I parked in my driveway in the afternoon, maybe around four o'clock or a little later. I, uh, had left for the gym for a workout, but I realized I'd forgotten my membership card so I had to go back in my house to get it."

"And then what did you do?" Rory continued.

Diedre's forehead creased. "What did that man tell you?"

Rory ignored that and repeated his question, causing Diedre to huff.

"I went to the gym," she snapped. "I had a long workout."

"What's the name of your gym?" Eden asked.

The alarm went through Diedre's eyes again. "I didn't actually work out in the gym. I decided to use the outdoor track. I jogged about four miles, sat for a while and then walked some before I came home."

It was possible Diedre was telling them she'd done that

walking around to cover for time she was gone. Time when she could have been attacking Brenda.

"And you parked in your driveway again," Rory said. It wasn't a question.

Diedre nodded. "My garage-door app wasn't working so, yes, I left my car in the driveway. Why?" she asked.

"Just routine questions." Of course, that was a lie, and this entire conversation would have to be put in a report with a copy sent to SAPD. "Did you wear your workout clothes home from your walk?"

Again, Diedre took her time answering, and Rory didn't think it was his imagination that the woman was about to lawyer up. If so, that would put a quick end to his questions. "Yes," she finally said.

"When did you change? You said you didn't use the gym," he reminded her.

This time, it was more than concern in her eyes. It was anger. "I changed in my car," she growled, "and I left on my workout clothes because I'd spilled a sports drink on my other outfit."

"And what happened to that outfit?" Rory asked.

Diedre stepped back. "This conversation is over," she snarled, and she turned and headed back to her house.

"I'll make another call to SAPD," Eden said as they watched Diedre storm off. "I'll see if they can get a search warrant for her house."

It was a necessary step in the investigation, but it would likely be too late. If Diedre had stabbed Brenda while wearing those clothes, then the top and pants had probably been destroyed, or trashed. Still, SAPD might get lucky and find something else they could use to build the case against Diedre.

Against Carter, too.

Because it was possible he was the killer and had given them the photos to toss the blame onto someone else.

Rory raised his window and started driving back toward Renegade Canyon while Eden dealt with getting that search warrant. As expected, it wasn't a fast process, and they were nearly halfway home before she finished.

"Detective Vernon will get right on the warrant for both Diedre's house and Jeep," Eden informed him. "And he'll make sure Carter comes in. I'll go ahead and forward Vernon a copy of the photos just in case Carter decides to delay that visit."

"Good idea." Because Carter was spooked. Or else just guilty. Rory didn't know which.

He heard the swooshing sound of her phone to let him know the photos had gone out. "I went ahead and sent them to the lab, too," she added, and she began to study the pictures.

Rory glanced at her and saw she had enlarged the area around the Jeep windows, no doubt trying to see if anyone was inside. Judging from her sigh, she couldn't manage that.

"I'm not seeing any blood or tears on either set of clothes," Eden muttered. "Nothing to indicate she'd had these on during the attack." She stopped. "But if she managed to drug Brenda, maybe there was no actual struggle."

Yeah, Rory had gone there, too. "Since Brenda and Diedre had that semifriendship deal, they could have met. Diedre could have given her the drug, and then once it kicked in, she could have led Brenda to her Jeep. And even into the barn. No lifting required."

Though that did leave them with a huge question. One that Eden voiced.

"Then, if she had Brenda drugged and in her Jeep, why would Diedre have returned to her house around four p.m.?"

Rory could only speculate about that. "Maybe she hadn't drugged Brenda yet, and Diedre was on the way to meet Brenda when she remembered she had indeed forgotten something at her house."

Maybe the search warrant could give them something else to work with to confirm or dispel that theory. The search should include a check of Diedre's GPS so they could track where the woman had been.

Eden muttered an agreement and continued to look at the photos. Rory made occasional glances at her, but once he was off the highway and onto the rural road that led to Renegade Canyon, he had to keep watch around them. Eden and he had possibly rattled some cages today with Diedre, Helen and Carter, and that rattling could have made the killer desperate to silence them.

Not a comforting thought.

Eden made a sharp sound of surprise, causing Rory's attention to zoom in her direction. It wasn't something she spotted outside the cruiser but rather in one of the photos.

"It's Frank," Eden blurted.

She held up the photo that Carter had taken of Diedre's Jeep speeding away from her house. Eden had enlarged not the Jeep, but the area on the other side of the street. There, tucked in along a cluster of cedar trees, stood Frank.

What the hell was he doing there?

"Should I call him and see if he's home?" Eden asked. "We could stop by there and have a chat with him."

"Do that," Rory agreed even though it was a possibility the picture had been altered to add Frank's image. But that only led to another question.

Why would Carter have done that?

Frank was a potential victim, not a suspect. At least he hadn't been until Rory had seen this picture.

Yeah, he definitely wanted to talk to Frank, and then Detective Vernon could do the same with Carter.

"Frank's not answering his phone," Eden said, and then she left a voice mail for the man to contact them right away.

Rory would give him an hour, and then he intended to track Frank down. If the man had any connection to these murders, then Rory needed to know.

"I'll reach out to the lab and light a fire, see if they can get working on the photos sooner rather than later," Eden said, making that call.

Rory had to slow down as he approached a curve that had earned the nickname of Dead Man's Bend, since over the years, it had been the site of two fatal car crashes. He came out the steep curve and immediately spotted something on the road.

Hell.

It was a strip of metal spikes stretched across the asphalt. A strip meant to take out the tires of a vehicle and bring it to a stop.

It sure as hell shouldn't have been there.

Rory slammed on the brakes. But he was too late. He hit the strip, the spikes ripping through the tires and causing him to lose control. It was like having four blowouts at once. He had to fight the steering wheel just to stay on the road.

But even that became impossible.

Because of the second strip of spikes.

The cruiser ran over it, and this time there was the sound of the metal spikes gouging into the tire barrels and rims. The vehicle skidded and another jolt slung them around.

Finally, the cruiser came to a complete stop. And in that blink, Eden and he were now sitting ducks.

Rory drew his gun and waited for the attack.

Chapter Nine

Eden drew her gun, too, and she fired glances all around them. She expected gunfire, but she couldn't see a shooter, only the thick woods that were on both sides of the road.

Woods where a killer could hide and lie in wait.

No way had kids done this. A spike strip wasn't easy to come by, and she knew in her gut, this wasn't a prank. It was a way to pin them in place while someone moved in for the kill.

Not Diedre, or even Helen, since Rory had taken the shortest route possible for the return trip home, and neither woman could have gotten ahead of them. But either or both of the women could have hired someone to do this. The same could be said for their other suspects, Ike, Frank and even Carter.

Any one of them could be responsible.

"Siri, call police dispatch," Rory instructed his app, and the sound of his voice cut through the heavy silence that'd settled inside the cruiser. The dispatcher answered on the first ring.

"This is Deputy Rory McClennan," he said. "I'm requesting immediate backup to the Old Sawmill Road about a half mile from the east side of the bridge on Dead Man's

Bend. My cruiser has been disabled by two spike strips stretched across the road. Tell responding officers to approach with caution."

"I'll get someone out there right away," the dispatcher assured him, and Rory ended the call.

Eden knew it would probably take only about ten minutes for one of their fellow deputies to respond, but those minutes would feel like an eternity. Added to that, the only risk wasn't from a possible shooter.

No.

They were on the back end of Dead Man's Bend, which was essentially a steep, blind curve. The cruiser was straddling the center line of the road with no shoulder to speak of that could be used as an emergency lane. They could be hit by another vehicle, and delivery trucks used this route to bring supplies into town.

The cruiser was bullet-resistant, but it certainly wouldn't withstand a head-on collision with a semitruck.

Eden listened for any possible threat. An oncoming vehicle. A shooter. But she heard and saw nothing.

Maybe this was the attack, having them locked in place like this. If the attacker had done some research, then they might have learned if a truck was indeed heading their way. No more would need to be done to either seriously injure or kill them. And the attacker could simply just walk away.

"Open your door just a fraction," Rory instructed. He was not only glancing all around them, but he also had his head lifted and was listening. "Not enough so that a shot can get through. But keep it open in case we have to run from the cruiser."

That definitely wasn't something she wanted to do. Because a shooter could just gun them down. Still, they might not have a choice in the matter if they were about to be struck by another vehicle.

She opened her door less than an inch while he gave the voice command to the phone app again, making a second call to Dispatch.

"Alert responding officers and any and all traffic that my cruiser is disabled in the center of the road," Rory said the moment he was on the line.

The dispatcher would no doubt do her best to make that alert, but it would be next to impossible to get out the word to everyone.

"Also remind any responders that there could be a shooter or explosives in the area," Rory added.

"Explosives," she muttered.

Dreading what she might see, Eden looked out the window and down at the part of the spike strip and road that was in her line of sight.

And her heart sank.

She'd been so intent on checking the woods for an attacker or listening for a truck that she hadn't thought to look for a threat much closer to them.

"I think there's an IED on the spike strip just a couple of inches outside my door," she said to Rory.

He scrambled over the console to have a look. Rory was right in her face, so she had no trouble seeing the confirmation in his eyes. He immediately pulled away, scrambling back to his own side to gaze out his side.

And he cursed.

"There's one here, too," he said.

The adrenaline had already been slamming through her, but that bit of info gave her another round of it. Something she definitely didn't need. Her body was already in the fight-or-flight mode, and she couldn't do either.

"Are there explosives?" the dispatcher asked.

"Yes. Get the bomb squad out here now," Rory ordered, "and block off the road in both directions."

"Will do," the dispatcher said before ending the call.

Again, that was going to be a long shot to accomplish the roadblock. Things like that took precious time, and anyone who did respond to block it off could be walking straight into an ambush.

"I don't see a timer or detonator on the IED," Rory muttered.

"Neither do I," Eden acknowledged. "So maybe it's like the one at the barn. If we step on it, it goes off."

He made a sound of agreement and looked her in the eyes again. "If we have to get out, jump over the IED that's on your side of the cruiser, but watch where you step. There could be other devices."

She got another rush of adrenaline, and Eden had to try to stop the worst-case scenarios from playing out in her head. If she and Rory were both killed, Tyler would be an orphan. He could lose both of his parents in a blink.

And for what?

So a killer could throw chaos into the murder investigation? Or was this more personal than that?

She thought of their names being on Ike's hit list. A list that Brenda might have composed simply to set up Ike. But what if she hadn't done that? What if the killer had been the one to set her up?

If so, the list could be real.

With Rory and her the targets.

That thought was flashing through her head, but Eden forced herself to focus on a backup plan. Rory was clearly doing the same.

"If someone starts shooting at us," he said, "don't try to

return fire. Shut your door and get down. Because a bullet could set off the IED."

Definitely not something she wanted to happen.

As close as the IEDs were to them, the cruiser would be blown up. Maybe they would be, too. But at least there was a chance the cruiser would protect them enough so they could stay alive.

"If you hear an approaching vehicle," he went on, "try to get out and dive to the side of the road."

Again, not something she wanted to happen. Not with the threat of a shooter or more IEDs.

The seconds crawled by, and when her lungs started to ache, Eden had to remind herself to breathe. Had to try to settle her heartbeat, too, because it was thudding in her ears, blocking out too many sounds.

But she did hear one sound.

A welcome one.

It was a police siren, and it was coming from the direction of town. Seconds later, they got a call from Livvy.

"Are you two all right?" Livvy asked the moment Rory took the call on speaker.

"Been a whole lot better," Rory replied. "Are you solo?"

"No. Bennie's with me. We're about three minutes out. What will we be up against when we get to you?"

Rory huffed. "Not sure, but for certain there are two IEDs and two spike strips. Slow down well before you get to Dead Man's Bend."

Livvy muttered some profanity. "We're working on the roadblock," she explained. "But it's not in place yet."

Which meant the worst-case scenario could kick in.

"No sign of who did all this?" Bennie asked.

"None," Rory replied. "And I can't see a vehicle on either of the two trails that are visible from where we're stuck." He paused. "It's too risky for you to come close to us. You'll have to wait for the bomb squad."

"Understood," Livvy murmured, and there was a whole lot of regret about this in her voice. "But Bennie and I can help if there's gunfire."

"No, you can't," Rory said quickly. "All a shooter has to do is hit the IED with a bullet, and the whole area can blow up." He stopped, gathered his breath. "For now, just stop anyone from coming closer and plowing into us because that can detonate the IEDs, too."

Livvy cursed again. "All right," she said, and Eden didn't think it was her imagination that Livvy was trying to steady herself. "Once we have a visual on you, I stop and we wait." She paused. "ETA on the bomb squad is fifteen minutes."

Eden was surprised it was that short amount of time. The bomb squad was a county unit, and they were based in a town on the other side of Renegade Canyon.

"Sit tight. We'll be there soon," Livvy added before she ended the call.

The silence came again, but Eden had thankfully tamped down enough of her body's reactions so she could hear better. And she continued to keep watch since she didn't want a shooter darting out from the woods for a sneak attack. After all, the plan might not be to kill them here, but rather to take them elsewhere so their bodies could be staged like Mellie's and Brenda's.

With the barn gone and the CSIs still crawling all over the site, the killer might have to find a new location, though. But there were plenty of other barns that might be a good substitute.

Every muscle in her body went on alert when she heard something.

The sound of an engine.

"Hell, it's not Livvy and Bennie," Rory groaned.

No, it wasn't. This sound was coming from the opposite direction, and it didn't take long before the vehicle rounded the curve.

Sweet heaven.

It was a Mack truck.

"Move now," Rory shouted, and they reached for their doors at the same time.

Eden shoved open her door, hurdling over the IED and praying. She was doing so much praying. She dived to the ground on the side of the road. There was a steep slope, and she didn't have time to look for IEDs.

Or anything else, for that matter.

When she hit the ground, she just kept moving. Kept sliding down, down, down. So fast. And she couldn't stop before her arm slammed into a tree. The pain shot through her, from head to toe.

And her gun went flying.

So did plenty of other things.

Eden heard the sickening screech of tires. Heard the impact, too, of the Mack slamming into the cruiser. Metal crunching metal.

Then, the explosion.

The horrible blast tore through the air, shaking the very ground beneath her and knocking her into the tree again.

Her training kicked in. Her survival instincts, too, and she forced herself to get up so she could grab her gun. The thoughts and fears were slamming into her now.

So many thoughts.

So many fears.

For the driver of that truck. Of the possible IEDs that could be planted around her. Of a killer who could be waiting to strike. But there was one thought that stood out above all others, and it was screaming through her head.

Rory.

She had to get to Rory.

Keeping watch where she stepped, Eden scrambled back up the slope. Not easily. It was one step forward and two steps back in some places, but she finally made it up to the top.

And her heart went into overdrive.

It was a war zone. Parts of the truck and the cruiser were everywhere. The cab of the truck was still intact, though, thrown yards away from the collision, and she could see the driver, bleeding but still held in place by his seat belt.

He'd need medical attention right away, but Livvy and Bennie would be calling for an ambulance. They could deal with the driver. She had to get to Rory.

"Rory?" she called out, silently cursing when she realized her voice had almost no sound. Not enough breath.

Dodging the debris and hoping she didn't step on another IED, she made her way across to the other side of the road. Eden was about to make another attempt to call out to him…

But then she saw him.

There was blood on his head. On his arm, too. But he was alive and moving up the slope toward her.

Eden went to him, and she let relief claim every part of her body and soul. She pulled Rory into her arms and held on tight.

Chapter Ten

Rory sat in the back of the cruiser with Eden while Livvy drove them to his family's ranch. He figured it was going to be a long time before the tension in his muscles eased up. And it was going to be a hell of a lot longer than that before he'd feel comfortable letting Eden out of his sight.

Thankfully, she seemed to feel the same way, and once they'd been checked out at the hospital and done the nightmare of paperwork that came with something like this, she hadn't put up any argument about going to Dutton's with him.

Part of that was no doubt because she wanted to see Tyler. So did he. He desperately needed to be with their little boy and make sure for himself that he was okay. Again, Eden had to be of a like mind. But no matter what her reasoning, Rory would be able to keep an eye on both her and their son.

Even though it was already getting dark, there was enough dim light coming from the dash for him to see the fresh bruise on her chin. No stitches this time, but he'd heard the nurse say that Eden had bruises on her right arm and leg. He had some scrapes and bruises as well, but they were blessedly minor for both of them. It could have been much, much worse.

They'd come damn close to dying.

Again.

And once again the killer hadn't cared squat about their lives or any collateral damage from that IED blast. No one had died this time with this attack, but the driver of that Mack truck, Arlo Jenkins, had serious enough injuries that he'd had to be medevacked to a hospital in San Antonio. Arlo had simply been trying to do his job and make a delivery to a store in town when he'd driven over that IED.

Livvy pulled to a stop in front of Dutton's, and Rory spotted two ranch hands in a truck on the other side of the driveway. They were probably armed and ready in case the killer showed up here.

Dutton had taken other precautions, too. There had been two more hands in another truck positioned by the gated entrance, and two others were patrolling the grounds. The external security system was on as well, and while it wouldn't be impossible for someone to sneak onto the ranch, the sensors and motion-activated cameras would make it a little harder to approach undetected.

Livvy turned toward them, resting her left arm on top of the steering wheel, and she looked back at them through the metal grating that separated the front and back seats. "Damn," she muttered. "You two look like you lost a fight with a couple of heavyweight champions."

Close. They'd lost a fight with a killer. A killer who possibly had been long gone even before the cruiser ran over those spike strips. Added to that, they couldn't rule out any of their suspects as being responsible.

Livvy added a sigh. "Get some rest," she said as he and Eden got out of the cruiser.

Muscles that he didn't even know he had protested the simple movement. Not a searing pain, thank goodness, but both of them would likely have to deal with the soreness for a while. The impact of hitting those spike strips had been the equivalent of a collision. And then there'd been the falls down the slopes.

Yeah, there'd be lots and lots of discomfort.

Muttering their thanks and goodbyes to Livvy, they walked up the porch steps to Dutton's massive house, where seemingly every light was on. Dutton let them in, and the moment they stepped inside, they saw Grace standing to the side.

With Tyler.

Since it was past his bedtime, his son had sleepy eyes, but Rory was glad Grace and Dutton had kept him awake.

"Mama, Dada," Tyler babbled, lunging for Rory, who caught him and immediately adjusted his position so he could get hugs from both parents.

Just that hug eased a whole lot of the aches in his body. Relieved plenty of stress, too. Things had been touch and go during the attack, but Eden and he had had a lot to fight for. This. Their precious little boy.

"I've been reading the reports of what happened," Grace said. "But we can get into all of that in the morning. We can get into a lot of things tomorrow," she added. "There's lasagna in the fridge if you haven't had dinner."

"Thanks, but Livvy had some burgers brought from the diner while we were writing up our statements," Rory explained.

Not that Eden had eaten much. And he hadn't pressed her on that, either, since he figured her stomach was just as unsettled as his was.

Grace nodded. "All right, but if you get hungry, help yourself to anything in the kitchen. For now, I want you two to get some sleep. And that's an order," she said firmly, the concern all over her face and in her voice.

The concern was there from Dutton, too, and he used his phone to reset the security system while giving Rory the once-over. "We'll catch this—" He stopped, barely cutting off what would have been a word that Tyler shouldn't be hearing. "Person," Dutton said, finishing his thought.

"Yeah, we will," Rory responded, and he wasn't just blowing smoke. They *had* to catch the killer. There was no other choice. Because until they did, no one was safe.

Not even their baby.

"Tyler's been fed, bathed and he's ready for bed," Grace told them. "Leslie's in the guestroom, and she has the monitor. She said just to let her know when she should turn it on so you two can get some sleep."

Rory would be letting the nanny know that she wasn't on duty tonight because he would be staying with Tyler. He'd sacrifice a good night's sleep for the peace of mind that it'd give him to be in the room with his son.

"Nash is down for who knows how long so Dutton and I are going to catch some z's while we can," Grace added. She gave them gentle hugs before she and Dutton headed up the stairs toward the main bedroom.

Eden and Rory were right behind them, and Tyler leaned toward his mom so she could take him into her arms. She kissed the top of his head and held him close for several long moments. When they reached the nursery, she handed Tyler to Rory so he could do the same.

Since Tyler was rubbing his eyes now and fussing a little, Rory eased him into the crib, and he turned on his favorite mobile—horses—that someone had obviously brought over from Eden's. They both kissed Tyler again, and Rory texted Leslie to let her know there was no need for her to turn on the monitor.

Leslie quickly responded with a thumbs-up and a question. Are Eden and you all right?

No. They weren't. They were shaken to the core and nowhere closer to IDing the killer. But Rory went with a thumbs-up emoji of his own.

They stood by Tyler's crib until the boy drifted off to sleep. Even then, they didn't move. Maybe exhaustion was playing into that because Rory seemed frozen in place, and he might have just stood there all night had Eden not turned to him. In a blink, she pulled him into her arms.

"I thought you'd been blown up," she muttered, her voice cracking.

He'd thought the same about her, and Rory had experienced a mountain of relief when he had seen her coming down that slope toward him. And when she had dragged him into her arms, well, that'd been priceless.

Just as this hug was now.

Rory wasn't naive enough to believe that those hugs would erase all the barriers between them, but he couldn't help believing it was a start. They certainly felt like a unit. Like old times. And the old times escalated significantly when Eden eased back, and their gazes locked.

They stared at each other, and he saw her lips part as she sucked in a quick breath. He was doing some faster breathing, too, and his heart had revved up.

A lot of things had revved up.

And they just kept heading in that direction when they moved toward each other at the same time. Their mouths met, already desperate and hungry for what a kiss could give them.

And the kiss could give a whole lot.

Heat, comfort and oh, so much pleasure.

Rory dived right into the kiss. Right into the heat. And he let the taste and feel of her slide through him. Talk about a cure for all those aches and soreness. A cure for the nightmarish flashbacks, too. This kiss made him feel as if everything was right with the world.

It was temporary, of course. He knew that reality would soon set in. But for now, he just took everything Eden was offering him, and she was offering a hell of a lot.

She pressed her body against his. Her breasts to his chest. Center to center. He did some pressing, too, tightening his grip around her while staying mindful of her injuries. If she was feeling any pain, though, she wasn't showing it.

Eden made a sound of pleasure that he knew all too well, and it hiked up the heat even more. Rory notched it up further by deepening the kiss, by pressing even more against her.

Of course, the pleasure took on an edge, as it always did. An urgent, demanding one that in the past would have sent them in the direction of the nearest bed. Or wall. Or floor. Location hadn't always been high on their list of priorities. Only the release from this pressure cooker of heat.

But that couldn't happen now.

And Eden seemed to remember that at the same time he did because she pulled back from him. Her breath was gusting out now, and he could see she was fighting hard to rein herself in. She got some reinforcement on that when she glanced down into the crib. Tyler was still asleep, but it was best if he didn't wake up and see his parents having sex. Added to that, Rory wasn't even sure Eden was physically ready for sex. She needed rest.

And some pain meds.

Rory forced himself to move away from her, but not before he gave her a somewhat chaste kiss on the cheek. As chaste a kiss as it could be, considering their history. To avoid the temptation of pulling her right back into his arms, he went to the en suite bathroom and saw the ibuprofen that Grace or Dutton had already set out for them.

That wasn't the only thing his brother and sister-in-law had done, though. There were overnight bags for both Eden and him, things that had obviously been gathered from their houses, along with some bottles of water, bags of snacks and even a jar of bath salts on the side of the tub.

Making a mental note to thank Dutton and Grace in the morning, Rory took two of the tablets, got two more from the bottle, along with one of the waters, and brought them to Eden.

"Thanks," she whispered, and while she was downing them, Rory went to the closet and took out a pillow and a blanket.

"I'll sleep in the chair tonight," he said, tipping his head to a recliner in the sitting area. Across from it was a sofa that he knew pulled out into a bed. "You can take that or use one of the guestrooms." There were three of them, not counting the one Leslie was using, and two were on this floor.

"I'm sleeping in here," she insisted.

Rory had no intention of arguing with her about that. Yes, the guest bed would be a lot more comfortable, but she likely wouldn't get much sleep unless she could be close to Tyler.

Eden glanced at the bathroom. "But I would like a shower first."

"Take a long one," he suggested. "I'll do the same once you're finished."

She nodded, gave him a lingering look and headed toward the bathroom.

Rory silently cursed. The kiss had fueled that blasted need inside him. A need that made him forget all about his sore muscles and his banged-up body. And it took a whole lot of willpower not to follow Eden into the bathroom and finish what they'd started.

Instead, he forced himself to get a bed ready for her. Rory pulled out the sofa, took another pillow and blanket from the closet and put them on the mattress. He did the same to the recliner that was already positioned so he'd be able to see both Eden and the crib throughout the night.

The door, too.

And while he doubted the killer would come bursting in, he locked the door, anyway, and checked outside the window. Rory saw the men still guarding the house and the truck with the other hands driving around the ranch, checking for any signs of trouble while also monitoring the external security.

Satisfied that they were as secure as they could be, Rory put his phone on vibrate so the ringer wouldn't wake Tyler, and he went back to the recliner. He heard the water running in the bathroom, and he hoped Eden did as he suggested and took that long shower. While he waited for her, he used his phone to access his inbox to see if there were any updated reports.

There were.

Loads of them.

And the updates would no doubt continue throughout the night. There were many moving parts to this investigation, with two crime scenes, way too many suspects and three dead. Mellie, Brenda and Lou.

Rory didn't want anyone else added to that tally.

The first update was from Bennie, who, among other things, had been tasked with trying to locate Frank. So far, Bennie was having no luck whatsoever with that. Frank hadn't responded to multiple calls, and he hadn't answered his door when a reserve duty officer had gone to his residence. It was possible the man was simply avoiding them, but Rory could think of other reasons.

Bad ones.

If Frank was the killer, then he could be lying low after setting those IEDs and spike strips on the road. And Rory had to tamp down the anger that bubbled inside him when he thought of Frank, or anyone else, doing that. Getting revenge against Ike had already caused so much damage.

Out of all their suspects, Frank was the one who had the means to do something like that. Since he was from Renegade Canyon, he knew that road, knew the best place to set up a deadly attack. And now that he had seemingly dropped off the map, he couldn't supply them with an alibi.

Rory glanced through the background check on Frank, and while he couldn't see any experience with explosives, the man had served seven years in the Air Force, and it was possible he'd tapped into some skill he'd learned there. Of course, it was equally possible that Frank had hired someone. The man wasn't rich like Ike, Helen or Diedre, but he had more than enough assets to pay someone.

Rory moved to the next update—this one from the bomb squad—and again, it wasn't good news. There was no obvious signature on the IEDs. No trace, DNA or prints, either, that could help identify who'd made them. So that was a dead end.

The next report was on the photos that they'd gotten from Carter. According to the lab, the images hadn't been doctored. So Frank had indeed been at Diedre's when the woman had sped away in her Jeep.

The time stamp on the photos didn't clear either Frank or Carter as far as giving them an alibi since Brenda was almost certainly alive at the time the photos had been taken. That meant either man could have had time to leave Diedre's, get to Brenda, stab her and leave her to die in the barn.

So, yeah, not stellar news there.

The next report did offer a glimmer of something more positive. Carter had indeed gone into both Renegade Canyon PD and SAPD to give his statements, and he'd told SAPD Detective Vernon about the photos, which were now also at their crime lab. Vernon had used the info to obtain a search warrant for Diedre's car, home and office. The warrant would be executed in the morning and a team of CSIs would be looking for anything that could point to her being the killer.

Rory wished the detective could get a warrant for Helen's place, too, but he had no evidence against her that would help in that area. Still, he couldn't shut out the images of his aunt orchestrating all of this to get back at Ike.

And, yes, that included killing Eden and him.

Ike might have plenty of ill will toward Dutton, Eden and him, but it would still be a deep cut if someone murdered his family to get back at him. Plus, Helen might not find it any great loss to kill off her sister's children since she blamed them for not doing enough to save their mother.

Killing Eden and him would accomplish something else, too. It could throw the investigation into a tailspin.

The next report he pulled up was from the medical examiner, stating that the blade that'd killed Brenda could indeed have come from a Swiss Army knife. Rory sighed.

Because that put Ike right back in the center of suspicion. According to Dutton, Helen had threatened Ike with such a knife, and Ike had taken it from her. Ike would need to be questioned about that.

Rory looked up from the report and sighed when he heard Eden coming back into the room. Clearly, she hadn't opted for the long shower, and there was still a lot of tension in her eyes. But at least she was dressed for bed in loose joggers and a T-shirt.

He considered pulling her back into his arms but knew that was a bad idea. Instead, he tipped his head to the sofa. "Get some rest. I won't be long in the shower."

And he wasn't. He didn't want to leave Eden and Tyler alone, so he hurried, ignoring his protesting muscles. Rory didn't go with sleepwear, though. He put on some clean jeans and a black T-shirt just so he'd be ready if anything went wrong during the night.

When he went back into the nursery, Eden was already on the sofa bed and was in the process of putting her phone on vibrate. Once she'd done that, she lay down and gave him a long look before lifting the portion of the blanket that was on the empty side of the bed.

"I know it's a lot to ask, but I want you next to me," she muttered. "It's the only way I'll get any sleep."

"It's not a lot to ask at all." Rory put his holster on the end table.

He wanted to do this for her. Needed it. Yes, it would be torture having her so close but not kissing her. Or making love to her. But she didn't need kisses or sex. She just needed him.

So that's what he gave her.

Rory slid in next to her and eased Eden into his arms.

Chapter Eleven

Eden woke, slowly, parts of her seemingly protesting the mere opening of her eyes. But other parts alerted her to the warm, solid man pressed against her.

Rory.

She knew his scent and the feel of him. And those certain parts of her suddenly wanted more. Eden looked at him, to see if he was awake. He was, and her gaze collided with his intense brown eyes. They didn't move toward each other, but Eden was certainly thinking about doing that when she heard two sounds.

"Mama, Dada," Tyler babbled. He had pulled himself to a standing position in the crib and was smiling at them.

Eden automatically smiled back, and then she realized there was another sound. Rory's phone was vibrating and was practically dancing across the end table. She glanced at the time. Barely 7:00 a.m., which meant this almost certainly wasn't good news.

"It's Bennie," Rory revealed, groaning. "I'll take the call if you want to see to Tyler."

She definitely wanted to go to their son, and Eden understood why Rory didn't put the call on speaker. There was no telling what gruesome details of the investigation Bennie might mention.

Tyler gave her a sloppy kiss, and he tightened his arms around her neck when she picked him up. Just that slight pressure caused some discomfort, but no way would she loosen his grip. She needed this contact. This moment with him.

Eden held Tyler, and he babbled his way to the changing table, where there were plenty of supplies. Not just diapers and wipes, but extra clothes for their son, too.

While she changed him, she looked back at Rory. One glimpse at his expression, and she got confirmation that something bad had happened.

Please, not another murder.

But with the killer unidentified and therefore at large, it was possible he'd struck again.

She finished changing Tyler just as Rory ended the call. "Let's take Tyler to Leslie," he said, giving the baby a kiss, "and then we can talk."

Eden didn't press him for info. She stepped into the hall and practically ran right into Leslie.

"Me," Tyler squealed, which was as close as he'd come to saying the nanny's name. When he reached for her, Leslie took him into her arms. She also studied Eden's face for a moment.

"Rory just got a work call," Eden explained.

Leslie nodded, and even though she must have noticed Eden's dour expression, she managed to smile at Tyler. "Let's go downstairs and get some oatmeal," she offered.

"Me, me, me," Tyler gushed, using a slightly different inflection from what he'd called Leslie.

Eden sneaked in another quick kiss to Tyler's cheek, and then she went back into the nursery. Rory had already put on his boots and was in the process of strapping on his shoulder holster.

"About an hour ago, Dispatch received an anonymous call saying there was a body by the welcome sign for town. Judson and Garrison responded," he said, referring to their fellow deputies, Judson Docherty and Garrison Zimmer, who was a rookie. "And they did indeed find a body." He paused. "It's Carter."

Eden had to do a mental double take, and she shook her head. "Carter?" she repeated. "Does Ike even know him?"

"We'll soon find out because when Judson and Garrison got to the scene, Ike was there," Rory explained.

Oh, mercy. "Did Ike kill him?"

Rory groaned and scrubbed his hand over his face. "To be determined. I'm going out there now, but if you'd rather stay here—"

"I'll get dressed and go with you." Yes, part of her did want to stay with Tyler, but this was their investigation, and she also wanted a chance to talk to Ike.

Especially since Ike might be on the verge of being arrested.

Eden tried not to speculate as to what had happened. Instead, she hurried to the bathroom to get dressed while Rory made his way downstairs. When she joined him less than five minutes later, she found him in the kitchen with Dutton, Grace, Nash, Leslie and Tyler. Tyler was in a high chair and was making a mess with his oatmeal.

"Rory told us," Grace said, and even though she had her baby cuddled in her arms, it was obvious she was champing at the bit to be involved with the case. Thankfully, she didn't insist, though. "Bennie dropped off a cruiser about a half hour ago," she added a moment later.

Rory nodded his thanks and took the keys that Grace motioned to on the table. "We'll let you know the details as soon as we have them," Rory assured her, and then he shifted his attention to Dutton. They didn't say anything to each other, but a look passed between them.

A look of dread, mixed with relief.

Because if Ike was indeed the killer, they could arrest him so he couldn't harm anyone else. But it wouldn't be easy for them to grasp that their father had tried to kill his own son.

Dutton handed them to-go cups of coffee and two wrapped breakfast sandwiches. Eden took them, knowing she'd need the coffee but no way would she risk eating with her stomach churning the way it was.

However, Rory did start eating one as soon as they were in the cruiser. Maybe because he knew this was going to turn into a hellishly long day and that he'd need the fuel.

They drove away from the ranch and toward the sign that was only a couple of miles away. Unfortunately, it wasn't near any houses or businesses, so there probably wouldn't be any eyewitnesses. Still, they might be able to get some sort of confession from Ike or info from someone who'd driven past and saw something suspicious going on.

They were still about a half mile from the sign when Rory got a text, and the message from Detective Vernon appeared on the dash.

Search warrant executed. CSIs are going through Diedre Bennington's home, office and vehicle. She's not at her residence, but a housekeeper let us in.

Where is she? Rory texted back.

Apparently, at the gym. She's on her way to the house now. Will let you know if anything turns up.

Rory sent him back a thanks and glanced at her. "I'll fill him in, too, on Carter's death once we know what's going on."

Yes, because SAPD would need to get involved in that as well since Carter lived in San Antonio.

The moment the sign came into view, Eden saw that the deputies had already blocked off both lanes and put up a detour sign, which would basically mean any through traffic would have to do a U-turn and find another route. She also saw their cruiser parked behind Ike's truck, which was on the narrow shoulder of the road. Ike was sitting on the tailgate, and he was staring at the body.

It was Carter, all right.

The man had been propped up against one of the posts that held the sign, and his head had lolled to one side. Even before she got out of the cruiser and went closer, Eden could see the blood all over his shirt.

Rory parked the cruiser, and they fired glances around them as they made their way to Garrison, who was already walking toward them. Judson was next to Ike, and it was obvious the deputy was guarding him even though Ike's hands hadn't been restrained. Restraints were the protocol if a suspect was aggressive or likely to attempt escape, but apparently, Judson and Garrison hadn't felt the need for such measures.

"I didn't touch him, and the ME and CSIs are on the way, but I'm certain he was stabbed and bled out," Garrison told them right off.

Like Mellie and Brenda. And they had also been left in a sitting position at the barn. Since the barn no longer existed, the killer must have chosen this spot for the dump.

But, no...

Eden quickly amended that thought when she went

closer and saw the blood. Carter hadn't been dumped here. He'd been killed here.

"I'm pretty sure those are stun-gun marks on his neck," Garrison went on while all three of them studied the body.

Eden didn't go closer because she didn't want to destroy any potential evidence, but she leaned in enough to spot the marks on his neck. Yes, a stun gun.

"Has he confessed to killing Carter?" Rory asked, tipping his head to Ike, who wasn't being his usual boisterous, obnoxious self. In fact, he seemed to be in shock.

Garrison shook his head. "Nope. Just the opposite. He said someone called him to come here if he wanted to save a person from dying." His tone let them know that he wasn't buying it.

But Eden was.

Sort of.

"I don't see any blood on Ike," Eden muttered. "Was there anything in his truck? Bloody clothes? Or cleaning supplies?"

"None that I found," Garrison admitted. "I checked the truck, and there was a handgun in the glove compartment. I took that into custody, and it's locked up in the back of the cruiser. I got his phone, too, since I figured we'd need to check to see if he did get a call."

He held up the plastic evidence bag he was holding with the cell inside it, and he passed it to Eden when she motioned for it.

"Ike gave me the password to unlock the phone," Garrison went on, "and there was a call from an unknown number about thirty minutes ago."

So Ike could have been telling the truth about that. Or else this was a situation like Brenda's, with the burner sending the replies being found in her home.

"And did you find a knife on Ike or in the truck?" Eden persisted.

"No," the deputy answered. "There was a tire iron, but nothing I can see that would have been used to make those stab wounds. There are a lot of them," he murmured. "This was overkill."

Yes, it was. It was hard to tell with all the blood now soaking the dead man's clothes, but Eden could see at least five cut marks in his shirt. Then, there were the two on his neck. Those would have likely been fatal if one of the others hadn't killed him.

Eden continued to look at the body. "Rigor hasn't completely set in Carter, so he probably hasn't been dead more than a couple of hours. Added to that, if he'd been out here for long, someone would have likely spotted him."

Yes, it was early, but this was ranching country, where some started their day before sunrise.

The killer sure had.

Because if Carter had been at his home in San Antonio, the killer would have had to somehow snatch him, bring him here and murder him. After that, the body would have been posed.

All without someone seeing what was going on.

"There appears to be arterial spray," Rory commented, motioning toward the spatter on the signpost and the grass around the body. "Blood would have gotten on the killer."

Garrison lifted his shoulder. "I guess Ike couldn't have gone home and changed, or he could have been wearing some kind of protective gear. Or another possibility is that he stashed the clothes, and they're around here somewhere." But he stopped, and his forehead bunched up.

Obviously, the deputy had seen the problem with those theories. Why would Ike have murdered Carter, then left the scene, changed his clothes and returned? And if he'd had on protective gear to prevent being spattered with blood, where was it? Yes, he could have hidden it nearby, but why not just leave once he'd killed Carter?

However, Eden did think of one possible scenario that would fit what she was seeing here. "It's possible Ike came back to retrieve some kind of evidence," she muttered. "Maybe something he dropped. But that would be a huge risk."

Rory made a sound of agreement. "And if he had left something behind and found it, he could have said someone had put it there to set him up." He glanced at Garrison. "Any chance of tracing the anonymous call that reported the location of the body?"

"None," Garrison grumbled. "I checked that on the way over here, and it was a burner."

Of course, it was, but it would be interesting to hear what Ike had to say about who'd called him to the scene.

"We'll talk to him," Rory said as if reading Eden's thoughts, "but we'll move into the cruiser for that. Be careful," he added to Garrison. "If someone is setting up Ike, that someone could still be around. And there could be explosives, so go ahead and get the bomb squad out here to do a sweep before anyone starts checking the scene. Oh, and have the bomb squad check the body, too."

Garrison's eyes widened, and he muttered a single word of profanity. "You think there could be explosives underneath the body?"

"It's possible they could be anywhere out here," Rory explained.

The deputy made some glances around them, and his nerves were definitely showing. There were thick woods here, like more of the area outside of town, but there were a few trees surrounded by tall grass.

It was the perfect place to plant an IED.

Of course, if the killer still wanted Rory and her dead, this would be a good opportunity to use a sniper to gun them down. That was obviously a pressing concern for Rory because he didn't take any more time with Garrison, and they went straight to Ike and Judson.

"Garrison will fill you in on potential problems," Rory told Judson, and he hiked his thumb in the direction of the cruiser. "You're coming with us," he added to Ike.

Eden expected Ike to balk. He didn't. For once, Ike didn't lash out with any of his usual venomous remarks. With his gaze seemingly frozen on the dead man, he just got off the tailgate and followed them to the cruiser. Ike was placed in the back seat, and they took the front.

This wasn't an ideal place for questioning a murder suspect, but as acting sheriff, Rory should stay on the scene until at least some of the other responders arrived. After that, they could take Ike to the police station, where he'd need to be formally interviewed by someone other than Rory or her.

"I know Livvy read you your rights yesterday," Rory began, "but let me repeat it." And that's what he did.

Again, Ike didn't lash out. Didn't demand a lawyer. But he did ask a question the moment Rory had finished with the Miranda warning.

"Who is he?" Ike still had that frozen look of shock in his eyes.

"You don't know?" Rory countered.

That seemed to snap Ike out of his trance, and his gaze fired to Rory. "I wouldn't have asked if I already knew. Who the hell is he?"

Rory stared at his father a long time as if trying to suss out if this was an act. "Carter Rooney."

Eden carefully watched Ike's face for signs of recognition, but she didn't see any. Just the opposite. If Ike was faking all of this, then he was doing a stellar job of it.

Ike repeated the dead man's name a couple of times as if trying to jog his memory, and then he shook his head. "I don't know him," he concluded.

She and Rory exchanged a glance before he continued. "So how did you end up here at the crime scene of someone you didn't even know?"

"I got a call," Ike said after a long pause. "I don't know who from. It said 'unknown caller' on the screen, but I answered it, anyway. Sometimes, it's a horse seller who isn't in my contacts. Anyway, the person was whispering, like they were trying to disguise their voice, and he said if I wanted to stop Tyler from dying that I'd get here to the sign fast and save him."

Every muscle in Eden's body tightened. "Tyler," she blurted.

The panic came, roaring through her, and then she felt Rory take hold of her hand and give it a gentle squeeze. "Tyler's safe," he reminded her. "Grace and Dutton won't let anyone get near him."

She mentally replayed every word of that until it finally sank in. Their baby was all right. Using Tyler's name had merely been a threat. Still, it was going to take a while for her nerves to settle.

"Of course, I had to come," Ike went on several moments later. "I mean, he's my grandson no matter what's gone on between the three of us."

That wasn't exactly an outpouring of grandfatherly love, but Eden believed his concern for Tyler was the real deal.

And Ike had come here even though he must have known there was a possibility he'd be facing down a killer. That didn't erase the ugliness that'd gone on between them, but Eden would always be thankful for his response.

Well, if Ike was telling the full truth, that was.

"Why didn't you call the police station? Or us when you got a call like that?" Rory asked.

"Because the caller said if I did, then I'd never see Tyler alive again." He stopped and cursed. The words were vicious and filled with rage. "That SOB was going to hurt a baby because of me. I couldn't let that happen," he muttered. "I had to hurry here and try to save him."

"What did you see when you got here?" Rory continued after a long pause. Hearing that about Tyler had likely shaken him, too.

"Not Tyler, that's for sure. Or the two of you." Ike paused. "I thought maybe…well, I thought the killer had taken both of you, too."

So he'd expected to find all of them being held hostage. Or already dead. Again, that was the case if he was telling the truth, and Eden hadn't heard anything from him yet that felt like a flat-out lie.

"I drove up to the sign and stopped when I saw the body," Ike added to his explanation.

"Did you touch the body or anything around it?" Rory asked quickly.

"No, hell, no. I could see he was dead. Blood everywhere. And his eyes." He didn't shudder, but it was a similar reaction. "There was no life in those eyes."

Again, Eden had to agree. Even from the distance of Ike's truck to the body, she would have realized Carter was dead. No movement. All that blood, and his eyes had been wide open.

"I looked around," Ike added, "but I didn't see anyone. And then the two deputies came barreling up. That's when I knew I'd been framed." He looked at Rory. "I don't expect you to believe that, but it's the truth, and that means you don't have a killer here in this cruiser. He or she is out there, ready to strike again until I'm locked up for murder."

"Who would do that?" Rory asked.

"Helen or Diedre," Ike said without any hesitation. "Hell, they could be working together."

That was indeed possible since the women had been together at Diedre's house.

"And, no, I don't have any proof that one or both is behind this," Ike went on. "But Helen sure as hell could have gotten access to my house to plant those bugs."

True, but Diedre could have as well, if she'd hired someone to break in. Normally, the ranch wasn't as secure as it was now, and the gate was often left open for deliveries and such.

Eden looked up when she heard the sound of an approaching engine, and she silently cursed the flashback that she got of the collision and explosion the day before. It was going to be a while, if ever, before those images left her, but she shoved them aside and saw both CSI and ME vans pull to a stop behind the other cruiser.

"I'll be right back," Rory said, and stepped out. But then he leaned down and gave Ike a warning glance through the metal grating before he started toward the responders.

Since the back doors couldn't open from the inside, Eden wasn't worried about Ike trying to escape. The man wasn't stupid, and he would know something like that would lead to an immediate takedown and arrest.

"I wouldn't try to kill either of you." Ike's grumble

was barely audible. "What happens now?" he asked, loud enough for her to hear.

Eden tried to keep her cop's voice in place despite feeling so darn shaky. "We go back to the station, where you'll be processed. We'll need your clothes for testing, and Livvy will have some questions for you."

"Right." And the sarcasm and snark had returned. "No more questions until my lawyers are there. I'm not saying another damn word that could get me in even hotter water than I already am."

So some of the old Ike had returned, but she couldn't blame him for lawyering up again. If there was any physical evidence linking him to this murder, then he would almost certainly be arrested.

Since Ike had clammed up, Eden used her phone to text Detective Vernon to ask him to check on the alibis for Helen and Diedre. Even if they had them, the women would need to be brought in for another round of interviews.

Eden tried not to be frustrated that the investigation seemed to be going in circles. Three murders, and they still hadn't managed to positively ID or arrest the killer. With her and Rory's names on that hit list, the pressure was skyrocketing for them to put a stop to this, especially since the killer knew about Tyler.

Rory returned to the cruiser, and he slid in behind the wheel, automatically studying her face. No doubt to see if Ike had said anything in his absence.

"Ike wants his lawyers," Eden informed him.

Rory huffed but didn't seem surprised. Nor did he discuss the murder. Probably because Ike would have been able to hear every word. He just started the cruiser, then drove past the other responders and straight into town. It took them less than two minutes to reach the police station, a reminder of just how bold the killer had been to leave Carter's body practically right on their doorstep.

They led Ike inside, where Livvy was already waiting for them. "His phone's been taken into evidence," Rory informed her. "So he'll need to use the landline to contact his lawyers."

Livvy nodded and volleyed glances at the three of them. She was probably trying to figure out what the heck was going on. Sadly, Eden and Rory were doing the same thing.

"I can let him use the phone on my desk," Livvy said. "And then I can take him to interview room one. Do you also want me to get the contact info for the victim's next of kin so they can be notified?"

"Yes, do that. And thanks," Rory told her.

Livvy tipped her head toward Grace's office. "You two have a visitor, and he's insisting on talking to you."

Eden looked in that direction and saw Frank Mott. So, apparently, he had surfaced after all. Since the man hadn't returned their calls and no one had seen or heard from him, Eden had thought he might have met the same fate as Carter.

Frank came to the doorway of Grace's office, doling out a scowl to Ike. And Ike scowled right back.

"Are you the one setting me up?" Ike snarled.

Frank lifted his shoulder as if the question had been about something mundane rather than about murder.

"Frank," Rory greeted as they went into the office. "We've been trying to contact you."

The man nodded. "Yes, I was out at my fishing cabin on the lake. No cell service. I didn't get your messages until I got home late last night. I figured rather than call you so late, I'd just come and see you face-to-face." He paused. "Did Ike kill that man?"

"How did you know someone was dead?" Rory countered.

Frank shrugged. "Hard not to hear something like that. The two deputies were hurrying to the scene when I got here. Why did you want to talk to me?" he quickly added, and Eden didn't think it was her imagination that he was trying to curtail any more discussion as to how he'd learned about Carter's death.

Rory gave him a long, hard look before he went to a laptop on the desk and he pulled up the photos that Carter had given them. The lab had already enhanced them so that the images were much clearer now. Rory pulled up the shot of Frank and turned the laptop so the man could see the screen.

"What? Where was that taken…?" But Frank's voice trailed off when he must have recognized the surroundings. "Who took that photo?" he demanded.

Rory didn't give him the answer. "Want to explain to me why you were there and what you were doing?"

A flash of panic went through his eyes. "Am I under arrest? Do you think I killed that man?" He didn't wait for Rory to respond. "Because I didn't. I thought you were trying to get in touch with me about something else…" Again, his words slowed to a crawl, and he squeezed his eyes shut a moment.

"What's the *something else* you thought I'd want to know?" Rory demanded, and he was all cop now. Then, he held up his hand. "Let me go ahead and read you your Miranda rights."

Frank shook his head as if not believing this was happening, but he didn't speak when Rory read him his rights. Nor did he lawyer up at the end of it.

"I didn't kill anyone," Frank blurted the moment Rory

had finished. He motioned toward the photo still on the screen. "And I was there because, uh, I've been seeing Diedre."

"Seeing?" Rory queried.

Frank swallowed hard. "I'm in a relationship with her. Or at least I was, but she broke it off a couple of days ago."

Interesting. "Before or after Brenda's murder?" Eden asked.

"Before," Frank muttered. "I didn't want things to end between us so I drove to her place to talk to her, but I parked and watched the house for a little while so I could see if she was alone. Helen is there sometimes."

Eden was sure she had a puzzled look in her eyes. Rory had one as well. "Explain that," Rory insisted.

Frank certainly didn't jump right on that. He took a couple of moments and groaned under his breath, as if this wasn't something he wanted to spill. "Diedre wanted to keep our relationship a secret."

Again, Eden was puzzled. "Why?" she persisted. "You're both single, aren't you?"

"We are, but then there's Helen." Frank's groan turned to a loud huff. "Helen and I saw each other for a while—"

"Wait," Eden interrupted. "You told us you hadn't been romantically involved with Helen."

"I told you we hadn't been when I was a teenager," Frank snapped out. "Back then, I was seeing Mellie. And, no, I didn't bring that up when she was killed because it was a hell of a long time ago."

Eden folded her arms over her chest. "You didn't think it was pertinent to tell us that you had a romantic history with a woman who was murdered in the very barn where you two used to work?"

"No." He stopped, scowled. "It wasn't relevant," he insisted. "Mellie and I dated for a couple of months, and we broke up. It was just teenage stuff, definitely nothing serious. I got involved with Miranda shortly thereafter, and Mellie inherited the place she eventually turned into the foster ranch. Mellie and I moved on with our lives."

"And then became enemies," Eden reminded him.

He shot her a stony look. "Yeah, we did, but that was on Mellie. You were raised in that foster home, and you know what some of those kids were always doing to my property. Knocking down fences, letting the livestock out. Hell, even taking some of my horses for joyrides."

All of that had indeed happened, and while Eden didn't believe any serious damage had been done, she could understand why Mellie and Frank had butted heads over the years. Mellie had been trying to raise kids, and Frank had been trying to run his ranch. However, she had to wonder if their past had played into the ferocity of some of the conflicts. Eden recalled plenty of loud arguments between the two and heated threats from Frank.

Frank was obviously experiencing some of that anger now, but he didn't make any threats. He just stood there a few moments as if steadying himself. Eden did the same, and she shifted the conversation back to the original topic.

"Helen," she stated. "When did you get romantically involved with her?"

"Romance," he muttered, as if that wasn't anywhere close to the truth. "We hooked up for the first time right before she left for college. That's continued over the years. Not while I was married. I never cheated on my wife," he insisted. "But a couple of years after she passed away, Helen and I ran into each other, and we…reconnected. We still have what I guess you'd call an open-ended arrangement."

Eden wondered if that was his way of saying friends with benefits.

"Look," Frank went on, shifting his attention to Rory, "Helen has had it in for Diedre since your mom died. And, yes, I understand that, what with Diedre having an affair with her sister's husband, but Helen seems to have finally put that behind her. She's not trying to make Diedre's life miserable."

"Had Helen been doing that?" Eden prompted when the man fell silent.

"Definitely. Helen and Ike were essentially doing the same thing. Dissing Diedre to potential clients, taking every opportunity to badmouth her. It put Diedre under a lot of stress, and I don't want her to have to go back to that kind of relationship with Helen." He stopped and seemed to have a debate about what he was going to say. It took him a couple of moments to continue. "At times, Helen can be very scary."

"Scary?" Rory repeated, and it was very much a question.

"Yes." Another pause. "Last month she asked me about explosives."

That grabbed Eden and Rory's attention. "What specifically did she ask?" Rory asked.

"She wanted to know if I had any experience with them when I was in the military. I didn't. I was a cargo pilot," he explained. "When I pressed her as to why she wanted to know, she said she was considering donating to a foundation that helped veterans injured by IEDs."

Rory kept his intense gaze on Frank. "Did you believe her?"

Frank shrugged, hardly a wholehearted confirmation that he thought she'd told him the truth. "Like I said, Helen can be scary, and that's why I don't want you to mention that I've been seeing Diedre. Don't say anything about it to Ike, either."

Once again, Eden was surprised. "Why not? Why would he care if Diedre had been with you?"

Another shrug from Frank. "I think some of the bad-mouthing that Ike does is because he still has feelings for Diedre. I have no proof of that," Frank said quickly, "but Diedre is a very desirable woman, and she dumped Ike. He'll say it was the other way around, but it wasn't. She dumped him, and he wasn't ready for things to end."

Eden wasn't sure it mattered who'd been the one to break things off. And she didn't believe Ike's venom for the woman was seeded in him still having feelings for her. Of course, it was possible. She just couldn't see that as a motive for the murders.

"You also didn't mention that you knew Brenda," Rory mused.

Frank seemed to freeze for a moment. "I didn't know her. Not really."

"Not really?" Eden repeated and waited to see if he was going to mention Brenda calling him about going to the I-hate-Ike luncheon she'd arranged.

"Not really," he snapped. "The woman was a pest, wanting me to team up with her to take Ike down. I declined. I told her to let karma deal with Ike."

Frank didn't seem like a karma-believing sort of guy. But Eden could see Brenda pressing him to join the group she was assembling. Could see Frank declining, too, especially if he didn't want to be in the same room with Helen and Diedre.

"Did you ever go to Brenda's house?" Rory asked.

"No," Frank responded. "But she dropped by mine once.

I didn't even let her in. So, no, her DNA won't be at my place, and mine won't be at hers. You're barking up the wrong tree, deputies. I have absolutely no motive to kill Mellie or Brenda."

That wasn't true in Mellie's case. Bad blood was often a motive for murder. But Eden couldn't see that bad blood extending to Brenda. Yes, she'd seemingly pressured Frank into joining her anti-Ike group, but turning her down wasn't a reason to kill her.

"I need to go," Frank insisted, checking the time. "I'm meeting someone for breakfast."

"Sorry, but I'm going to need you to make a formal statement about that photo," Rory explained. "Go down the hall to interview room two and wait. I'll be there in a couple of minutes."

Frank glared at both of them for a long time, and for a moment Eden thought the man was going to refuse. He didn't. He stormed off, taking out his phone, maybe to call a lawyer.

Rory didn't add anything else until Frank was out of hearing range. "I can't tell if he just threw Helen under the bus so we'd think she's the killer, or if he's truly worried she could be behind the murders."

"Same," Eden agreed. But either way, Frank was now solidly a suspect.

Rory turned to her. "I can take his statement solo if you want to find out what's going on at the latest crime scene."

She nodded, already coming up with a mental list of things she needed to do. Touching base with the bomb squad was a high priority. But she also wanted to check Frank's military service records to see if he did indeed have the explosives experience that he had denied.

However, Eden had barely made it a step toward her

desk when Rory's phone rang, and she stopped when she heard him say, "It's Detective Vernon."

She turned back into the office, and he answered the call. He didn't put it on speaker, but after just a handful of seconds, Eden knew something was wrong. She prayed there hadn't been yet another murder.

"All right, do that," Rory said to Vernon after a couple of snail-crawling moments—moments that Eden spent on edge. "And have the lab contact me as soon as they know."

He ended the call and looked at her. "The CSIs searching Diedre's house found a Swiss Army knife."

Eden immediately thought of the incident that Dutton had witnessed. The one where Helen had threatened Ike, and he'd snatched the knife from her. That one had been a Swiss Army knife.

"Is it the murder weapon?" she asked, wondering how it'd gotten from Ike to Diedre's.

"Maybe. The lab will have to determine that. There are no prints on it, the handle has been wiped clean, but the CSIs thought they spotted something at the base of the blade, so they did a preliminary test on scene." Rory stopped and gathered his breath. "It tested positive for human blood."

Chapter Twelve

Rory stared at his phone and filled Eden in on the rest of the conversation that he'd just had with the detective. "Vernon volunteered to have one of the uniformed officers who was already on the scene at her house escort Diedre here to Renegade Canyon. I took him up on that. She'll be here soon."

"Good," Eden muttered.

Rory could practically hear Eden making a mental tally of what was on their slate today. Diedre was yet one more thing on their to-do list on what would undoubtedly turn out to be a hellishly long day. A day that had barely gotten started.

But he didn't have an option when it came to talking to Diedre. He had to get her in for an official interrogation not only about the knife, but also because of what Frank had said about them being in a relationship. Along with that, he needed to confirm if Frank had been telling the truth. Because if he'd lied, then that put the guilty spotlight right on the man since he could have planted the knife in Diedre's house.

However, if Diedre was the killer, if she was the one responsible for those three deaths and for Eden and him nearly being killed, then Rory wanted to know so he could lock her up. That could prevent others from being killed.

Including Eden.

She was holding it together, but he could see the strain in her eyes. And the fear. Not for herself but because Tyler was potentially in danger as well. That was the worst kind of pressure for a parent.

Even though the timing sucked, he closed the office door and pulled her to him. He didn't kiss her. Nope. Not nearly enough time for that, but the hug was enough to steady him some. When he eased back from her, he thought it'd done the same for her. They would definitely need steadying because of what they had to do next.

"Did Vernon say if Diedre admitted that the knife was hers?" she asked.

He shook his head. "She insisted someone planted it, that maybe we even did it when we visited her."

Eden sighed. "She's reaching. We weren't out of her sight the whole time we were there at her place." She paused. "But Helen was."

"Yep." His aunt had come into the room while Eden and he had been talking to Diedre, so she would have had free rein of the rest of the house before her entrance. "And we'll need to talk to her today, too."

To get that ball rolling, Rory located his aunt's number in his contacts and called her. Because it was still fairly early, he figured the call might go to voice mail, but she answered right away.

"Are Eden and you all right?" Helen asked, but there was no real concern, or even interest, in her voice. It seemed more like something she should say rather than something she especially wanted to know. "I heard there was another murder."

Rory didn't bother to huff. Yeah, bad news was definitely traveling fast. "We weren't hurt," he simply said, since they were far from all right. "But I need to talk to you."

"About what?" she asked after a long pause.

"Some questions have come up, and I want to discuss a couple of things with you." Rory made sure he used his cop's tone so she'd know this was all business. "How soon can you come to the police station?"

He heard Helen take in a long breath. "I can be there in about ten minutes. I'm in Renegade Canyon," she added. Judging from the background, he thought she was in her car.

Now, it was his turn to pause. "Were you visiting your friend in the hospital, the one who had an appendectomy?" Rory asked. "What was her name again?" he added.

"Sheila Mendoza," Helen informed him without hesitation. "But, no, I wasn't visiting her. I'm on the way to the cemetery to put flowers on my sister's grave. She's been on my mind a lot lately, and I brought her some roses."

Rory knew that Helen had done that in the past, but he didn't like the timing of this visit. Then again, with Ike being front and center in the investigation, his mother had been on Rory's mind, too. So maybe Helen was telling the truth.

Maybe.

"I'll be at the police station soon," Helen assured him and ended the call.

Rory didn't put his phone away, though. He accessed the database that had contact info for most people in town, and he located the number he was looking for.

"You're calling Sheila Mendoza," Eden murmured after

glancing at what he was doing. She moved closer, so she'd be able to hear.

"Yep. I want to hear what she has to say…" He had to stop when Sheila answered on the first ring.

Since he didn't know the woman that well, Rory made the greeting more formal. "Mrs. Mendoza, this is Deputy Rory McClennan."

"Rory," she said, sounding a whole lot friendlier than Helen had been. "I didn't expect to hear from someone in the police station. Is everything all right?"

Maybe there was someone who hadn't heard about the murder after all. "I just want to verify something. Are you still in the hospital?"

"Oh, no. I'm home. I just had that one night's stay. Nothing serious. Why?" she asked.

Rory evaded the question and jumped straight to the reason for the call. "Did my Aunt Helen visit you while you were still in the hospital?"

"Yes, she did," Sheila confirmed. "That was so sweet of her."

So Helen was telling the truth. That nixed his theory that Helen had murdered Brenda and then shown up at the hospital only to give herself a possible alibi if someone had indeed spotted her near or in town.

"A sweet surprise," Sheila went on.

"A surprise, how?" Rory persisted.

"Well, I mean because I didn't know she was coming. And we're not exactly friends. Don't get me wrong," she continued, "she's always been friendly enough to me, but I hadn't actually talked to her since your mom's funeral, and that was just to say hello and how sorry I was. It was so kind of her to think of visiting me on a trip to town."

"She didn't mention if visiting you was the main reason for her trip?" Rory queried.

"Golly, I don't think so. She just showed up, and we chatted for a while before she left."

Rory had to put a mental question mark by his earlier conclusion of Helen telling the truth. The visit could have still been to cover up her presence in town.

"Was there, uh, anything unusual about Helen during that visit?" Rory went on. "I mean, did she seem upset or nervous? How did she look?"

He wasn't surprised when the woman didn't answer right away. She was no doubt wondering what this was all about. "I guess she seemed fine. She looked all right, too. What happened? What's wrong? Did something happen to Helen?"

"Helen is okay," he assured her. "I'm just trying to pinpoint a lot of different people's movements that night, and you've helped with that. Thank you."

He wrapped up the call with Sheila and then immediately groaned. "I should have found an excuse to have Helen's clothes and hands tested for blood when we saw her in the hospital."

Eden rolled her eyes. "There would have been no legal excuse for that. Helen wasn't even a suspect at the time."

"No, but she should have been. I should have had her on the suspect list right from the start, because of her extreme hatred for Ike. My mother's death could have been the trigger that set all of these murders in motion."

"Maybe, but why not just go after Ike?" Eden asked, clearly playing devil's advocate.

"Having him rot in jail would be a lot more punishment," Rory replied.

Of course, that didn't explain why Helen hadn't just gone

after Diedre first since Diedre had caused Rory's mom so much pain by having an affair with Ike.

Unless…

"Maybe Helen is planning on setting up Diedre for the murders, too," he muttered. "That way, she could maybe get both Diedre and Ike behind bars."

Eden didn't disagree this time, and he could see her processing that theory. It had plenty of merit, but obviously there were some pieces that didn't fit, and Eden voiced one of them.

"Why kill Carter?" she asked.

Rory had to shrug. "The man liked to take pictures, so maybe Helen thought he'd taken an incriminating one of her. Or one that would inadvertently give Diedre an alibi that Helen wouldn't want her to have."

Again, Eden didn't disagree, but she also didn't have a chance to dole out any more potential questions because they heard the voices in the squad room and turned in that direction. It was Ike's legal team, and Stephen Arnette was making a beeline toward them. Judging from his irate expression and body language, Rory figured he knew what the lawyer was about to say.

"I demand that my client be immediately released," Arnette snarled.

Yep, that's exactly what Rory figured Arnette would demand. "It's not happening. Your client was found at the scene with someone who'd been murdered. At minimum, he needs to be questioned and give a statement."

Arnette's eyes narrowed. "Is he under arrest?"

"Not at the moment, but it's a possibility," Rory admitted. He didn't add more because he saw Helen come in. "Your client is in interview room one," he said, and he stepped around the team to head toward Helen.

Helen's eyes weren't narrowed, not yet, anyway, but her hard expression made it clear she wasn't happy to be here.

"This way," Rory said, leading her toward Grace's office. Thankfully, the lawyers were already on their way to interview so Rory didn't have to deal with them.

Once he had Helen inside the office, he closed the door and motioned for her to take a seat next to the desk. Eden took the one next to her, causing Helen to flick her a glance that seemed to be tinged with annoyance. He wasn't positive what Helen's beef was with Eden, but he suspected it was because Eden was the mother of his child. Any association with him would spur Helen's disapproval, since his aunt blamed him for not doing more to save his mother's life.

"Do you need me to go over your Miranda rights again?" Rory asked, leaning his hip against the edge of the desk.

"No. I haven't suddenly developed amnesia," she said. "Just ask your questions, and if I decide I want my lawyer here, I'll call him. But please be quick. Your mother's flowers are still in my car, and I don't want them to wilt."

He didn't bother to point out that they'd soon wilt in this heat. Or remind her that his mom hadn't actually been a flower lover because of her allergies. No need to dive into the petty stuff since he had bigger fish to fry.

"What's this about?" Helen demanded.

"The knife. Your knife," he amended. "The one you pulled on Ike during the middle of an argument."

She huffed. "I already explained that I didn't *pull* it on him. That makes it sound as if I planned on attacking him. I didn't. I simply wanted to scare him. It didn't work. He ripped the knife from my hand and took it." Helen leaned forward in the chair, pinning her gaze on Rory. "And once again, I have to know if Ike is using that knife to set me up. Did he use it to kill Brenda and that dead man you found earlier?"

Rory went with a similar response to the one he'd given her at Diedre's. "No proof of that. But I do have proof that Ike had the knife returned to you."

That was close to the truth, anyway. The photo Ike's assistant had taken showed something in an envelope being left on Helen's doorstep.

Helen stared at him and shook her head. "He didn't, and if Ike said he did, he's lying."

"Proof," Rory repeated. "The knife was left at your house."

Helen shook her head again. "No, it wasn't. Or if it was, I never received it." Her denial seemed genuine.

Seemed.

"If the knife was left at my house, then it was stolen," Helen went on. "Or else Ike faked sending it. I'll say it again—Ike will use that knife to try to set me up. Or murder me with it. Why haven't you arrested him?"

"Because I need proof for that," Rory said, honestly. "And so far, it looks more as if someone is setting up Ike, not you."

If looks could kill, Helen would have ended him right then, right there. "Are you accusing me of murder?"

"Not accusing. Asking," he clarified. "Did you kill Mellie and Brenda?" He didn't add Carter's name since the man's family hadn't been notified yet.

"No, I did not," she snapped, and she stood. "And if that's all you want—"

"It's not," Rory said, stepping in front of her to block her from leaving. "Have you had any recent conversations with anyone about explosives?"

For just a second, Helen got that deer-caught-in-the-headlights look, but she quickly reined in her shock. "Why do you ask?"

"Just answer the question," he insisted.

She took her time doing that. "Frank Mott. He told you I was asking about that." Helen waved a dismissive hand. "I certainly didn't want to know so I could blow something up." She paused again. "I was trying to make a connection with him, all right?"

Rory was sure he looked confused, because he was. "Excuse me?"

Not shock this time from Helen, but what he thought was embarrassment. "A connection. I wanted to talk about something that I thought would interest him since he has all these guns and military magazines around his house. Frank and I have been seeing each other, but he seemed to be losing interest so I wanted to…connect," she explained.

Rory wasn't sure he bought that, but he would now need to ask Frank about those magazines. They might turn out to be nothing, but since the killer had used IEDs twice now, that was definitely an angle that needed to be investigated.

"Would you agree to having your home searched?" Rory asked her.

Muscles stirred and tightened in Helen's jaw. "And what exactly would you hope to find in such a search?" But she didn't wait for an answer. She began to snap out the possibilities. "A knife that I've already told you I don't have? Clothes with Brenda's and Mellie's blood on them? A printed-out confession of crimes I didn't do? Or maybe you'll actually find something that Ike planted to try to get back at me. How about all of the above?"

Rory ignored her sarcasm, but if she was innocent she shouldn't have anything to hide. Well, unless she was truly worried that something had been planted. If so, they needed to find whatever that was and try to sort everything out.

"If you don't agree to a search, I could request a warrant," Rory told her.

Helen didn't react. She just seemed to hold her ground, though he figured there was a firestorm of anger boiling inside her.

"Get the warrant," she growled. "And I truly hope your mother isn't watching you right now from her grave because she'd be sick at what her son is trying to do to her only sister."

Rory had a comeback for that. "She'd be even sicker if her sister didn't cooperate with a murder investigation that could save lives. Maybe even Eden's and mine."

Helen opened her mouth to say something, but with her jaw clenched, she was going to have trouble speaking. Maybe that's why she didn't add anything else for several long moments.

"Is there something else you want to badger me with, or am I free to leave this witch hunt?" Helen demanded.

Rory glanced at Eden to see if she had any other questions, and when she shook her head, he gave Helen a nod. She didn't waste a second throwing open the door and heading out.

And nearly ran into Diedre.

The two women seemed to startle each other, and then they both stood there for a couple of seconds as if waiting for the other to speak.

"Your turn in the box," Helen finally muttered before she walked away.

Part of Rory wanted to go after his aunt because, after all, she was his mother's sister. But he had no idea what to say to her. He certainly couldn't assure her that everything would be all right because there was a killer still at large.

And that killer could be Helen.

However, if it turned out not to be her, then he was going to owe her an apology when this was all over. But for now, he had to do his job, and part of that job was turning over every stone to stop a killer from striking again.

"You didn't say anything to Helen about Frank and me, did you?" Diedre whispered, casting an uneasy glance at Helen from over her shoulder.

Rory was about to answer and let her know that he hadn't, but he saw Livvy making her way to him, so he and Eden stepped out of the office to see what Livvy wanted.

"Wait in the office," Rory told Diedre. "We won't be long."

Livvy waited until Diedre was out of earshot before she spoke. "The ME just called," Livvy whispered, "and he used facial recognition to confirm that the body is Carter Rooney."

Not a surprise since both he and Eden had recognized him, but the official confirmation from the ME was a necessary step in this process.

"Did the ME find anything else?" Rory asked.

Livvy shook her head. "Not yet. He hasn't actually examined the body yet. The bomb squad just arrived, and they're checking the area first. Once it's clear, he'll go in and do his initial assessment before the body is taken to the morgue for a postmortem."

Good. Rory didn't want any of the responders at risk because of other IEDs. Which made him think of something Helen had said.

"See if Bennie has the time to do some more digging into Frank's background," Rory said. "Helen told us that he was into explosives, and I'd like to know if that's true. And if so, just how into it is he. I need to know if Frank has the expertise to have made those explosive devices."

Again, Livvy nodded. "You also want me to try to get a search warrant for Frank's house?"

Rory thought of the workload that was already on Livvy since she'd be the one who had to deal with Ike. "Have Bennie do that, too. And we need to try to get a search warrant for Helen's house."

Livvy sighed. Not because she was shocked by the news. She was aware Helen was a suspect. But the sigh was no doubt because the woman was his aunt, and that meant two of his family members were suspects in a triple murder.

"I'll let Bennie know," Livvy assured him, and then she showed him the sticky note she was holding. It had the names and contact number for Reva and Harry Rooney. "They're Carter's parents, but they live in Tucson."

Part of Rory was relieved that he wouldn't have to be doing a death notification, but it also meant losing out on the opportunity to ask the couple questions about their son. Still, he figured the Tucson cops would be doing that and passing along any info they got from the parents.

Rory took the sticky note. "When we're done talking to Diedre, I'll call Tucson PD and ask that someone there go out to speak with the Rooneys. Maybe by then, we'll have a bit more from the ME that I can pass along."

"All right. Let me touch base with Bennie on getting those warrants and doing the research on Frank," Livvy said, checking the time, "and then I'll go in and see if Ike is ready to give a statement. Anything specific you want me to press him on?"

Rory considered that a moment and shook his head. "His lawyers will keep him on a tight leash so he doesn't say anything incriminating. Or rather, more incriminating since he was found at the scene with a dead body."

Livvy made a sound of agreement. "I'll press about that phone call he got," she replied. "He might remember something that can help her ID whoever it was that called him."

"Good luck," Rory told her. "As soon as we're done interviewing Diedre, we'll try to observe the rest of the interview with Ike."

Livvy glanced in the direction of Grace's office. "Will you be arresting Diedre?" she asked.

"It's possible. The knife was found in her house, but we have no confirmation yet that it was actually the murder weapon."

But there was the human blood that'd been found on it. That and the fact the knife was technically in her possession were enough to make an arrest. Rory wanted more, though. Hell, he wanted a confession so he could put an end to this nightmare.

Since Rory wanted to do this by the book, he stepped back into the office and motioned for Diedre to follow him. "We'll talk in interview room three," he insisted. "This way."

Diedre did follow Eden and him, but she also glanced back over her shoulder. "Is Helen gone?"

Rory frowned and found it strange that Diedre seemed to be more concerned about Helen than she was an interview with the cops about a murder investigation. Still, Rory didn't question her about that. He led Diedre into interview, and he started the recording. After he'd recited the time, date and the names of those present, he repeated the Miranda warning to Diedre.

"Did you tell Helen about me seeing Frank?" Diedre asked the moment Rory had finished.

Again, he was puzzled by both the woman's reaction and why she would be asking that particular question. But since she'd brought up the subject, he decided to go with it for now.

"You're in a relationship with Frank Mott?" Rory asked.

She huffed. "You know I am. Frank told you, and he called me when the officer was driving me here."

"What exactly did Frank say?" Because Rory needed to know if Frank had coached Diedre about the info she was telling them.

Annoyance, and concern, put some steel in the muscles of her jaw, and she was also nibbling on her bottom lip. "I don't remember his exact words, but he said he'd confessed to seeing me. We don't want Helen to know."

"And why is that?" Eden asked.

The annoyance went up a notch. "Because Helen can be a spiteful woman, and she'd try to get back at Frank and me. You know she would," Diedre insisted. "And I don't want to get on her bad side again."

Yes, Rory did indeed know that Helen could be spiteful, but he figured Diedre would always be on his aunt's bad side. Helen was playing nice with Diedre now for the sake of getting back at Ike, but that didn't mean Helen was finished with hating the woman who was her dead sister's rival.

"You have to promise you won't tell Helen about Frank and me," Diedre added a moment later.

Rory looked her straight in the eyes. "This is a murder investigation," he said coldly. "And I can't promise what info will or won't be divulged."

Alarm shot through Diedre's eyes. "But Helen might kill me if she finds out."

"Kill you for sleeping with a man she had a casual relationship with?" Rory said, lacing his question with some obvious skepticism.

Diedre looked ready to blurt something out, but then she seemed to rethink her response. Rory didn't give her much time before he fired off another question.

"Did Helen kill Mellie, Brenda and Carter? Is that why you're afraid she'll murder you, too?"

Diedre didn't jump to answer, but that alarm was still there. Rory had no idea if it was fake or real. And if it was warranted. Diedre could be reacting this way simply to make them more suspicious of Helen.

"Have you ever seen Helen be violent toward anyone or anything?" Eden said.

"Well, no," Diedre admitted after a long pause. "But she did pull that knife on Ike, and because of my affair with Ike, she already has a reason to hate me. I just don't want her coming after Frank and me."

Rory took a moment to process that. "Does anyone else know about your relationship with Frank?"

Diedre did more chewing on her lip. "I told Mellie. And then a few months later, I told Brenda," she finally admitted.

Well, hell. That was either a seriously bad coincidence or a motive for murder, since both women were now dead. But an affair between two consenting adults couldn't spur a murdering spree.

Could it?

If so, how did Carter fit into it?

When Carter had been in Diedre's neighborhood, she had said she didn't know him. And maybe she didn't. It was possible Carter had photographed something that he shouldn't have. Like Frank and Diedre together. But Rory still couldn't wrap his head around that being the motive for these murders.

To test those waters, though, Rory took out his phone and pulled up a photo of Carter to show Diedre. "Tell me about this man."

Her forehead creased as she studied the picture. "It's that guy who was near my house. Who is he?" The question might or might not have been genuine.

Rory didn't give her the name since the next of kin likely hadn't been notified yet. "He was murdered this morning."

Diedre's eyes widened. "That's the dead man Frank mentioned." She made a gasping sound. "You think Ike killed him?"

"Someone did," Rory answered, and it put a knot in his gut to realize he could be seated across from the actual killer.

He let Diedre stew in the silence for a couple of moments while he kept his hard stare on her. She showed no signs of breaking. Then again, she had to be a tough woman to have ever gotten involved with Ike.

Rory decided to shift the conversation in a different direction. "Tell me about the knife that the CSIs found in your house."

This time, Diedre didn't hesitate. "It's not mine, and I have no idea how it got there. Someone must have tried to frame me with it."

Nothing about that response surprised him, but Rory kept pushing. "I know that Helen has been to your house. What about Frank or Brenda?"

Diedre nodded. "Yes, both have been there…" Her voice trailed off, and she started shaking her head. "You can't think Frank would have left the knife there. He wouldn't," she insisted. "He just wouldn't."

"Maybe," Rory muttered. "What about Brenda? Could she have left it?"

She shook her head, but there was a lot less resolve in her expression this time. "Why would she? And if it's the murder weapon, then it would have been used on her, right? She couldn't have been the one to leave it."

Rory went with another *maybe*, but it was silent this time. They had no idea if Mellie and Brenda had been killed with the same weapon. But he had a problem believing Brenda would have murdered Mellie, tried to frame Diedre and then had been murdered herself. If so, that meant there were two killers.

Brenda. And the one who'd ended her life.

Rory was still considering that possibility when his phone rang, and when he saw Garrison's name on the screen, he knew he had to take the call from the deputy.

"Interview paused," Rory said for the recording. "Deputies McClennan and Gallagher exiting the room." He and Eden stepped out into the hall before he answered and put the call on speaker.

"Rory," Garrison said the moment he was on the line. "The bomb squad cleared the immediate area around the body, and the ME was able to start his exam. There's a message of sorts on the dead guy."

"What kind of message?" Rory asked.

"We're not sure. It's numbers. The ME found it beneath the bloody shirt. And it's not a note," Garrison said, the strain obvious in his voice. "It was, uh, cut into his body. I think you and Eden need to see it."

Chapter Thirteen

Eden kept watch around their surroundings as Rory and she drove away from the police station and back to the crime scene. Rory was darting glances around, too. Because both of them were aware that a trip to, well, to pretty much anywhere could result in another attempt to kill them. Still, this "message" was something they wanted to see.

Numbers that'd been carved into Carter's body.

After hearing that bit of detail from Garrison, they'd quickly postponed the interview with Frank and wrapped up the one with Diedre. While there was some circumstantial evidence against her, it hadn't been enough for them to hold her. Eden suspected the same would be true for Ike, though if any of the four—Diedre, Helen, Frank or Ike— would be arrested today, Ike would likely be the one.

But an arrest was nowhere close to getting a conviction.

There were huge holes in the case against Ike. So either Ike had put those holes in place to assure a nonguilty verdict or he wasn't the killer.

Eden was going with the second option on this. As much as she and Ike despised each other, she just couldn't see him going about getting revenge this way. Too risky. Too cat-and-mouse. She figured if Ike turned killer, then the bodies would have never been discovered, much less placed where they'd be found.

Once they reached the crime scene, Rory pulled to a stop behind the line of vehicles. The other deputies' cruiser, Ike's truck, and the three vans from the ME, CSIs and the bomb squad. The road was still blocked off in both directions and would likely remain that way for most of the day.

Eden spotted two members of the bomb squad using a small robotic device to scan an area about ten yards behind the welcome sign. While they worked, the CSIs were searching the immediate area around the body.

Along with Dewey Galway, the ME, their two fellow deputies were next to Carter. A photographer was snapping pictures.

All the responders looked up, acknowledging Rory and her with nods and muttered greetings as they got out of the cruiser and made their way to the murdered man. The body was still sitting up, propped against the sign, but his shirt had been pulled up to expose his torso. At first, Eden didn't see a message, only the blood and the stab wounds. But as she got closer, she spotted something.

The three numbers, 653.

"Mean anything to you?" the ME asked, looking up at them from his semistooped position over the body.

Eden repeated the numbers several times, but then shook her head. Rory did the same.

"I did a search of them on my phone," Judson explained. "I think it could be part of an address. Or rather it used to be the first three numbers of the address for the Devil's Hideout when it was still called a farm road."

Eden groaned. The site of the first two murders. But with the barn now reduced to rubble by the IED, maybe the killer wanted to use some of the address numbers to connect the trio of dead bodies.

"But it could also be the number of a case file," Judson went on. "I'm talking way back before any of our time on the force. Forty-three years ago," he said, reading notes from his phone. "Mellie and Frank Mott, who were both sixteen at the time, filed a report of someone firing a shot into the barn when they were inside it."

Eden was sure she gave him a blank look because this was the first she was hearing of such an incident. "A shooting at the Devil's Hideout barn?"

Judson nodded. "Of course, it wasn't called that back then, and apparently, Frank was working there as a part-time hand after school."

"So was Mellie, according to Frank," Eden remarked. "I'm guessing she was there for work?"

"It doesn't say, and the deputy who wrote the report, Cliff Marquez, died more than a decade ago," Judson explained. "But from the impression I get, I think Mellie and Frank must have been dating or just been friends, and she met him there after school. Someone fired a shot into the barn, but they never found out who, and in his notes Cliff didn't speculate as to who might have done it."

Eden looked at Rory to see if this was ringing any bells. Obviously, it wasn't. "I'll call Aileen later," he said, referring to his former boss, retired Sheriff Aileen Granger, who was Grace's mother.

Even though the incident had happened decades ago, Aileen was still as sharp as a tack and would almost certainly recall a shooting. She might even be able to speculate as to whether or not it was playing into the current murders.

They would also need to talk to Frank. And Eden was already dreading it. The man was uncooperative, and this wasn't going to improve things. However, Eden did find it interesting that they'd talked to Frank about when he'd worked with Mellie, and he hadn't mentioned a shooting. The odds were he simply hadn't forgotten something as serious as that.

Rory shifted his attention back to the ME and the body. "Can you give us an idea of time of death?"

"Within the past four hours," he answered. "No signs of a struggle. No defense wounds, but you saw the stungun marks?"

Eden and Rory nodded.

"There were four total," the ME added. "Those two on his neck and another set on his back." He eased the body forward a little, lifting the shirt to show them the two lesions.

So maybe the killer had sneaked up on him. But then why stun him twice? Unless the killer had wanted to immobilize Carter a second time after they'd arrived at the current location. That was the likely scenario since the first hit from the stun gun wouldn't have lasted that long.

"He was stabbed seven times, mainly in the chest and stomach," the ME continued after he'd maneuvered the body back against the sign post. "Not sure if one or more of the wounds hit anything vital, but I'll be able to determine that in the postmortem. My guess is the numbers were carved after he was dead." He looked up at his assistant, who'd been taking the photos. "Let's go ahead and get the body back to the morgue so I can get started on—"

The ME stopped, interrupted by a strange hissing sound.

"What the hell?" Judson muttered, and like Eden, Rory and Garrison, he was glancing all around them, looking for the source.

And they soon saw it.

About five yards away in the ditch, a fire ignited. It had been barely noticeable at first. But it didn't stay that way. It soon soared up into a high flame. A flame that didn't stay contained to that one spot. It burst out in all directions.

Mercy.

It was coming right at them like a giant fireball.

They all started running, but Eden glanced over her shoulder to make sure they weren't about to be gunned down. She couldn't see anything, including the bomb squad, because of the thick black smoke billowing out from the flames.

What the heck was this?

Maybe some kind of incendiary IED? If so, no one had stepped on it. And no one had been near it since they'd arrived on scene. So it could have been on some kind of timer.

And if there was one, there could be more.

Eden quickly got confirmation of that theory when two more fires ignited. One of the other side of the road and one in the ditch right next to the responder vehicles. Smoke was coming at them from multiple sides now, and she could even feel the heat from the flames licking through the air.

"I called the fire department," Judson shouted. "They're on the way. I told them to approach with caution."

Good. Eden hadn't seen any IEDs on the road itself, but that didn't mean there weren't any.

A fourth fire burst to life in the ditch practically right next to Rory and her. That gave her another jolt of adrenaline and sent her already accelerated heartbeat racing even more. She couldn't breathe. Couldn't see.

But she could hear.

And she heard something she definitely didn't want to hear.

Gunshots.

Rory took hold of her arm and pulled her down on the road, trying to keep her out of the line of fire. She prayed the others were doing the same thing.

On her belly now, Eden drew her gun and lifted her head just enough so she could continue to look around. Beside her, Rory was doing the same, and like her, he was obviously trying to pick through the smoke to see their attacker so they could return fire and stop this.

But nothing.

More shots came. All at once. Dozens of them.

And they seemed to be coming from multiple directions. Sweet heaven. How many shooters were there? Had the killer sent a small army after them? If so, she wasn't sure how they were going to escape. Every one of them could be killed right here.

The image of Tyler flashed through her mind, and she added more prayers. That her precious little boy was safe, that this wasn't some two-pronged attack, where gunmen were at the ranch to go after him.

Eden dug out her phone from her pocket, and since she wasn't even sure she'd be able to hear Grace, she sent her a text. Under attack here at the latest murder scene. Is everything okay there?

Everything's fine here, Grace quickly texted back. Update me about the attack as soon as you can.

Eden would do just that. If they made it out of this alive.

"Do you see the shooters?" Garrison called out. It was hard to hear him with the barrage of shots slamming through the air and all around them.

Garrison was somewhere to her left, which meant he was closer to the ditch. Maybe another of those fire devices wouldn't be going off there.

A bullet smacked into the road just a couple of inches

from her, sending up some small pieces of asphalt. The projectiles flew through the air, one of them slicing across the sleeve of her shirt.

It'd come close.

Too close.

But she couldn't say the same for most of the other shots. They seemed to be landing everywhere. So either the shooters had lousy aim, or...

Eden didn't get to finish that train of thought because Rory finished it for her.

"I don't think it's gunmen," Rory said, shouting to be heard about the deafening racket. "I think bullets have been planted in the fires."

Yes, Eden realized that was exactly what was happening. The term was "cooking off" when ammunition was heated up enough in a fire to cause them to discharge. It didn't make the situation less deadly, but it could mean there wasn't actually a shooter nearby.

Could.

It was possible there was indeed a sniper, waiting to finish the job if the heated bullets didn't kill them.

"Everyone stay down," Rory shouted, and Eden saw him glancing in the direction of the cruiser.

He was no doubt wondering if they could make it there. Maybe. But if they stood, it would make them an easier target for those random shots.

In the distance, she heard the sound of a fire engine and hoped none of the responders would get hurt when they approached. Rory must have been concerned about the same thing because he took out his phone and called Dispatch to have their situation relayed to the fire chief.

Another fire shot up on the side of the road just ahead, and it didn't take long before bullets started going off there, too. It seemed to go on for an eternity, but she knew it was probably less than two minutes before the fire engine roared to a stop not far from the other vehicles.

The crew didn't immediately get out, and when they did, they were wearing helmets and vests that she was pretty sure were bullet-resistant. More minutes crawled by, the hail of bullets continuing, while the firefighters hooked up the hose. The moment they'd done that, they started dousing the flames.

Since the fires weren't huge, they weren't that difficult to put out, but there were four of them, so it took a while. Second by second, though, the sound of the gunfire began to trail off.

Rory and she stayed put, waiting. Hoping. Praying.

"Is anyone hurt?" Rory shouted.

"Okay, here," the ME said. And one by one, the others reported in. All except Garrison.

"I took a bullet to the leg," the deputy finally said, prompting Rory and her to start scrambling in his direction. Depending on the location of the injury, he could bleed out.

"Ambulance is on the way," Judson told them, and he hurried over.

One look at the young deputy, and Eden knew it was bad.

Chapter Fourteen

Rory paced across the guestroom while he listened to the latest update on Garrison. The deputy was alive, barely, but, according to Bennie, Garrison had been medevacked to a medical center in San Antonio, where he was in critical condition.

At least he was alive. And Rory was clinging to the hope he'd recover.

What he didn't have a lot of hope about at the moment was that they'd be able to stop the killer from launching another attack. But he was working on it. Eden, too, but they'd opted to do that at Dutton's rather than return to the police station. This way, they could be near Tyler.

Right now, they needed that.

After they'd dealt with the mop-up of yet another crime scene, they'd come back to the ranch and set up a makeshift office in one of the guestrooms. Tyler was just across the hall in the nursery with Leslie, and Eden and he had been popping over there all afternoon. They'd continue to do that even though Tyler was down for the night in his crib. But for now, they had the monitor on, and it was on the end table of a sitting area where they both could see it.

He finished his call with Bennie, knowing if there was

a change in Garrison's condition, that Bennie or someone else would let them know. Rory put away his phone and looked at Eden. She was sitting on the floor, her back against the small sofa, and she was volleying glances between him, her laptop screen and the baby monitor.

"Garrison's in ICU," he disclosed. Rory had already shut the guestroom door so their calls and conversations wouldn't disturb anyone, meaning there was no reason for him to whisper. "And he's still critical."

She sighed and closed her eyes a moment. "He's barely twenty-two years old," she muttered.

Yeah, by far the youngest currently on the police force. That ate away at Rory. But then, a lot of things were eating away at him right now.

He tipped his head to her phone, which was on the floor next to her. "Any luck getting in touch with Aileen?" They needed to ask her about that shooting incident at the barn. They'd opted out of bringing it up to Frank until they had Aileen's take on it.

Eden shook her head. "I left her a voice mail. Grace said her mom was in San Antonio visiting friends, and she often turns off her phone while she's there."

That eased some of his tension. When Aileen hadn't answered their initial call, he'd been concerned that something might have happened to her, but if this was her norm, then maybe she was all right. He wouldn't breathe easier about that, though, until he heard from her.

"A report came in a couple of minutes ago from the bomb squad," Eden informed him.

Rory went to her, and since she was on the floor, that's where he sat, too, and he soon saw that the report was three pages, and she was on the last one. Eden had obviously been reading it while he was getting the update on Garrison.

She moved the laptop closer to him and started the recap. "Each of the fires were ignited with small incendiary devices triggered by a remote. Maybe even a cell phone. The devices had been placed in holes in the ground from when there used to be underground mineral springs in that area."

Rory knew about those holes. Knew, too, that some of them could be quite wide and deep. On the surface, most of them looked like gopher holes or just shallow depressions in the ground, but sometimes when people stepped in them, they'd end up with a broken foot or leg. Obviously, the killer had known about the holes, too.

And had made use of them.

"The IEDs were positioned over a mix of plastic bottles filled with gasoline and boxes of bullets," Eden went on. "Dried leaves and grass had likely been used to cover the holes so they wouldn't be easily visible."

Rory considered that. The items themselves wouldn't be that hard to get, but it would have taken time to plant all of that. And the rigging wouldn't have necessarily happened this morning. No. The killer could have set all of that up earlier before he or she had brought Carter there.

"It was all a huge risk," Rory muttered.

"Yes," she agreed. "But it wouldn't have taken much strength," Eden added. "Which means it doesn't rule out Diedre or Helen."

No, it did not, and Rory could see how this might have played out. "All three of the victims could have been lured to the places where they were killed. No lifting or dragging required for the killer. Just get them there and murder them. In Mellie's and Brenda's cases, the killer could have even been reasonably sure they wouldn't be interrupted by someone just passing by."

"Not the case with Carter, though," Eden murmured.

"True, but since it was dark, the killer might have parked off the road and dropped down into the ditch if they saw headlights. That was still a risk, but if someone had stopped, then that person might have been killed, too."

It twisted at his gut to think of that possibility, but this killer hadn't had an issue with collateral damage. One CSI was already dead, and a deputy was clinging to life. So, yes, killing any potential witnesses could have happened.

Eden stayed quiet a moment. "Any of our suspects could have done this," she said on a groan.

Again, she was right. Because none of them, including Ike, had an actual alibi for the time of Carter's death.

When Eden groaned again, he turned to her, and Rory automatically pulled her into his arms. Just touching her helped with this tangle of nerves and spent adrenaline, and she dropped her head on his shoulder.

Her breath was slow and rhythmic, hitting against his neck. Almost like a kiss. His body thought so, anyway, but his body didn't get a chance to fuel that fantasy, or actually kiss her, because Eden's phone buzzed with a call.

"It's Aileen," she said, glancing at the screen, answering the call. "You're on speaker and Rory is here with me," she told Aileen.

"I figured he would be. I just spoke with Grace, and she filled me on what's been going on. I hope I'm not calling too late."

"No," Eden assured her, though it was past nine, not a common time for a phone call in a town where people often went to bed early and got up early, but then there wasn't anything common about this situation. "Did Grace tell you we wanted to ask you about the shooting incident at the barn back when Mellie and Frank were teenagers?"

"She did," Aileen confirmed. "And even though it wasn't my case, I remember that Mellie was the one who reported it. She called it into the station, and she was upset and crying. Cliff Marquez responded and came back a couple of hours later, and he went over the details. Mellie and Frank were basically making out in one of the stalls, and someone fired a shot into the barn."

"Did they see who?" Rory asked.

"No, but Mellie thought it was Helen," Aileen said.

Everything inside Rory went still. "That wasn't in the report."

"It wasn't." Aileen huffed. "Because as you're aware, Helen's family had money and influence. Her father claimed she wasn't anywhere near the barn, and since there was no evidence to prove otherwise, Cliff had to let her go. And while I don't know this for sure, I believe Cliff caved to pressure from Helen's folks to keep her name out of it."

"But you believe Helen might have done it," Eden concluded.

"Believed it but couldn't prove it," Aileen said quickly. "Mellie said she'd seen Helen about a half hour earlier, and she was glaring at Frank and her as they were making their way to the barn. I suspect there was some kind of jealousy or love triangle going on, and Helen was a hothead back then. Still is," she added.

Rory had to agree with that. Both Ike and Helen were cut from the same cloth when it came to temperament. And holding grudges.

"Did Frank believe Helen had fired the shot?" Rory queried.

"If he did, he didn't voice it to Cliff or anyone else that

I know of. Back then, though, Frank wasn't what I would call a wave maker. He was a star wrestler. A jock. Very popular in high school, and he loved the girls. Not for long, though, since he seemed to leave a trail of broken hearts. Until he met his wife, that is."

"Was Helen one of his broken-heart relationships?" Eden asked.

"I think so," Aileen said after a short hesitation. "Helen moved away when Frank got married, and she rarely came back to town. Then, after Miranda died, Helen started showing up again. I'm not sure she was actually in love with Frank. More like he was that guy Helen just couldn't get out of her system."

Rory made the mistake of glancing at Eden just as she was glancing at him. And he saw it in her eyes. They hadn't been able to get each other out of their systems, either, so he knew how Helen felt.

Man, he knew.

The heat was always there. Always. If it'd been just the attraction, he might have been able to put that on the back burner. But there were these deep feelings he'd had for her since, well, for as long as he'd known her. Some might say she was his soul mate, but Rory knew that Eden would always be the love of his life.

"Both Helen and Frank have had relationships over the years," Aileen went on, snapping Rory's attention back to her, "but they always seemed to find their way back to each other." She stopped again. "And that has to have you wondering if Helen's obsession with Frank is playing into the murders."

It was indeed. "Mellie had been involved with Frank, and she's dead," Rory explained. "But I can't find any indications that Frank and Mellie had resumed their teenage romance."

"It doesn't have to have been a real relationship for Helen to believe it was," Aileen pointed out. "Frank was spending a lot of time going to Mellie to complain about the foster kids. Helen might have seen that as Frank's attempts to spend time with Mellie and maybe win her back."

Yes, that was possible. Then, Helen might have killed Mellie in a jealous rage. But how did the other two murders play into this? The only thing Rory could think of was that Helen had maybe decided to keep going and try to pin the murders on Ike. Then again, all three murders could have been designed for that right from the start, and jealousy might not have anything to do with this.

"I know this shooting happened a long time ago," Rory said to Aileen, "but I want to use it and the other circumstantial evidence that we have to get a search warrant for Helen's house."

Aileen made a sound of agreement. "I can help with that if you want."

"I do. Thanks." Rory wasn't going to turn down an offer like that. Aileen still had a lot of support in town, and even though the former sheriff would never bend the law, she would be able to cut through the red tape much faster than he could.

"All right. I'll get right on that," Aileen assured him. "Are you going to talk to Frank and ask him about the shooting?"

"I am. Thanks again, Aileen." Rory ended the call and immediately pressed Frank's number. It took four rings before the man finally answered.

"It's late, Deputy McClennan," Frank snapped. He'd obviously seen Rory's name on the screen.

Rory didn't bother with an apology, and he got right to the point. "Think back to that shooting in the barn when you were a teenager. Do you believe Helen could have been the one to fire that shot?"

Frank was silent for so long that Rory wasn't sure the man was going to answer, but he finally said, "Yes."

"Any reason you didn't tell the cops that?" Rory asked.

"It would have only made matters worse. And the shot wouldn't have hit Mellie or me since it was fired into the hayloft. We weren't in any kind of real danger."

"Maybe, but someone shot at you," Rory reminded him. "I'd think you would want to say who did that."

"I didn't have any proof," Frank insisted. "It would have been my word against Helen's. Her family had power and money. Mine didn't. I would have likely ended up losing my job, and my name would have been mud in Renegade Canyon."

Rory wished that wasn't true. But it was.

"If you truly thought Helen had fired the shot, why did you continue to see her over the years?" Rory asked.

Frank sighed. "Helen was there for me after my wife died. I was an emotional mess, and if I hadn't had Helen, I wouldn't have gotten through it. I owe her. She also helped me get my ranch. She used her family's influence to get me the best deal possible on the place and even lent me part of the down payment."

Rory thought of what Aileen had said about Helen not being able to let go of Frank, but it seemed to Rory that the same could be said of Frank. He didn't press the man on his feelings for Helen. Instead, he went in a different direction.

"Will you voluntarily agree to a search of your house?" Rory asked. "I could get a warrant," he added.

Frank muttered some profanity. "Do the search. I consent to it," he said, surprising Rory. "Just not tonight because I'm about to head to bed. But you can send someone out first thing in the morning."

"Thank you," Rory said, but he was talking to the air because Frank had already ended the call.

"That was easier than expected," Eden muttered. She stayed quiet a moment. "You're mentally comparing Helen and Frank to you and me."

He nodded. Then shook his head. "I don't think you'd shoot at me if I was with another woman."

She surprised him by smiling. "Well, I might have when we'd been teenagers. Especially if you'd been with Tracy Muldoon."

He smiled, too, because Tracy had been the head cheerleader, and she'd made no secret that she wanted to replace Eden as his girlfriend. Tracy had done that via the mean-girl route of making Eden's life miserable in high school.

Her expression turned serious, and the levity of the moment was gone. "No, even then I wouldn't have shot at you."

She hadn't needed to spell that out. "We were both cops in the making even back then."

"Yes," she muttered, and she didn't take her gaze off him.

The energy and the heat between them went up a notch, and that's why Rory didn't kiss her. Didn't touch her. If he did, there'd be no turning back.

But then, Eden leaned in and kissed him.

Not a sweet peck on the mouth, either. She really kissed him, instantly making it long and deep. Instantly cranking up that heat and energy even more.

Rory was about to issue a warning that his resolve wasn't that strong right now, but Eden didn't give him a chance. Hard to talk when they were French kissing. And when things were escalating to beyond just this kiss.

Turning, Eden moved her leg over him and shifted her position until she was on his lap. That didn't just amp up the heat. It caused it to skyrocket, and it snapped every bit of his restraint. It suddenly didn't matter that sex could turn out to be a mistake.

Nope.

Because it was going to happen.

That was the problem, and the huge advantage, of being with someone whose body and mind he knew so well. Rory could feel this wasn't just a kiss to soothe. This wasn't about soothing at all. It was about feeling. It was about needing.

It was about them.

He slid his arm around her, snapping Eden closer to him, until her breasts were pressed against his chest. And he did some escalating of his own. The kiss went from hot to scalding. The need went from urgent to an absolute necessity.

Rory had to have her now.

Thankfully, Eden seemed to feel the same way.

She took those scalding kisses to his neck, doling out some torture and pleasure with the flick of her tongue over his skin. She knew all his hot spots. Hell, she'd been the one to discover them since they'd been each other's firsts. They had a long history of torture and pleasure.

Needing to do some kissing of his own, Rory turned the tables on her and went after her breasts. Eden's hot spots. He pushed up her top, shoved down the bra and used his mouth and tongue on her nipples.

Eden moaned, that sound of pleasure he knew all too well. A sound that shot through every part of his body. Especially one part that was urging him to move faster. To take everything she was offering.

Rory did just that, and he pulled off her top. Rid her of the bra, too. And the battle began. Because the clothes were obviously the enemy now, and they wanted each other naked.

Even then, the kissing and touching didn't stop, and somehow they managed not to injure themselves when the battle of the clothing escalated. Eden yanked off his shirt, sliding some tongue kisses on his chest while she fumbled with his jeans.

Rory ended up helping her with that, which led to some rolling around on the floor while holsters, boots and jeans all came off. The frantic pace continued when they were naked—their mouths met again, and the kiss roared past the hungry stage. The pleasure and need consumed him, and he was ready to take her here and now, but Eden said something that got through his lust-hazed mind.

"Condom," she muttered through her gusting breath.

Hell. He'd nearly forgotten again, and the last time, he'd gotten her pregnant. Since he doubted she wanted that to happen again, he forced himself to move away from her and locate his jeans. Then, his wallet. Then, the condom he kept there.

Eden made her way toward him, and the second he had the condom on, she straddled him, taking her inside him. The pleasure wasn't just a roar now. It was an avalanche of all the sensations that confirmed to him that this wasn't a mistake.

Eden was the right woman.

And despite the investigation, it was the right time.

Eden started the maddening strokes, taking him deep inside her, and he could see the pleasure on her face. Could feel it in her body as he slid his hands down her breasts and stomach. She rode him, drawing out every bit of that pleasure. Building it. Making them both climb.

And desperate.

Because that's what happened with great sex. The need became overwhelming, impossible to stave off. But Rory held on, savoring it. Savoring her. And when Eden's body finally found the release, Rory let himself take the plunge with her.

Yeah, this was right.

Chapter Fifteen

Eden stood in the shower and let the pulsing jets go to work on her tight muscles. She was sore and bruised and had some scrapes from both the barn explosion and having to dive onto the road after the firebombs.

The romp on the floor with Rory had maybe added a few new bruises, but the sex had made that all worth it. In fact, the sex had made a lot of things worth it.

Including the doubts and regrets.

Being with Rory had definitely muddied the waters of their already complicated relationship, but there was no chance of regretting it. She'd needed him, and he'd given her exactly what Rory was capable of giving.

Which was pretty much everything.

Rory cared for her. He loved their son. And he was a good man. Soon, she was going to have to decide if being with him was worth the daily battles that Ike would dole out. Then again, if Ike was in jail, then he couldn't make trouble for them.

But she still couldn't see Ike committing these murders.

No, and that meant eventually the evidence would clear his name. Eventually, the real killer would be caught and put in jail. And then life would get back to…

"Normal," she muttered.

That should have made her feel better, but there were some question marks on catching the killer. It was possible that once the killer had run through the list of Ike's enemies, the murders would stop. There might never be justice for Mellie, Brenda or Carter.

And as for going back to normal?

That might not happen. Not after these emotional barriers had come down between Rory and her. They might never go back to the way things had been just a few days ago. Now, she needed to decide how she felt about that.

With that thought weaving its way through her mind, she stepped out of the shower to a variety of sounds. She could hear Rory and Tyler on the baby monitor that she'd brought into the bathroom with her after they'd all had breakfast with Dutton, Grace, Leslie and Nash. Tyler and Rory were now back in the nursery, and her son was babbling while Rory was reading to him.

But there was another sound—her buzzing phone.

And on the monitor she could hear Rory's buzzing as well.

Despite her son's happy sounds, the dread raced through her, and she steeled herself to hear more bad news. She prayed there hadn't been another murder.

It wasn't that early, already a little past ten, and Livvy and Bennie had been sending them text updates, but this was the first call of the morning.

She looked at her phone screen and saw not only Livvy's name, but also that it was a group call to Bennie, Rory and her. On the monitor, she heard Rory answer, muttering to Livvy that he was going to leave Tyler with Leslie in the nursery and step out in the hall so they could talk.

Eden answered as well, putting it on speaker so she could dry off and get dressed in the clothes that Dutton had had brought over from her place. She needed to be ready since it was possible she and Rory would be leaving soon to put out another fire.

Maybe a literal one.

"I'm here," Eden said to the group. "Did something happen?"

"No one else is dead," Livvy answered, clearly picking up on Eden's concern. "But I thought you should know about the latest on Garrison. And the searches that are going on as we speak at Frank's and Helen's."

Yes, she definitely wanted to hear about Garrison. Eden had known about Aileen coming through on the search warrant. They'd gotten that info in a text while they were eating breakfast. Aileen had also let them know that SAPD would be the ones executing the warrant and sending in their own CSIs, so none of the deputies would have to go into San Antonio to do it. But Eden hadn't been aware that the actual searches would take place so soon.

"Garrison's still in ICU," Livvy began, "but his condition is improving. The doctors are a lot more optimistic about his condition now than they were last night. They believe he's going to make it."

Good. Eden hoped that he made a full recovery, and once he was out of ICU, she would try to go see him.

"I haven't heard anything back yet on Helen's search," Livvy went on, "but Bennie wants to give us an update about what he found at Frank's."

"Or rather what I didn't find," Bennie interjected. She heard the man huff. "I know in one of the reports that Helen said Frank had lots of magazines about guns and explosives, but we didn't find anything like that anywhere in his house. In fact, no magazines, just a handful of nonfiction books about histories of various wars."

"Maybe Frank hid or destroyed them?" Eden suggested.

"Yeah, I considered that so I checked the attic and any possible hidey-hole I could think of. Nothing there, and there were no fresh ashes in the fireplace or the barbecue grill," Bennie informed them. "The man's not a pack rat, that's for sure. There was practically nothing in the attic. That minimalism applied to the house, too. No clutter, everything in its place and I didn't see a spot where a bunch of magazines had once been. Of course, that doesn't mean he didn't get rid of them before I showed up."

"True," Rory agreed, "but it also could mean Helen was lying. And there's only one reason I can think of for her doing that. She wants Frank to look guilty."

"I think I'm going with that option," Bennie muttered. "While I was looking around, Frank and I chatted, and I got the feeling the man was scared of Helen. Maybe not actually scared for himself but for anyone who crossed her."

"Diedre," Rory and Eden said in unison. It was Eden who continued. "Both Frank and Diedre want to keep their relationship a secret, but if Helen found out, she might have wanted to get back at Frank by making him look guilty." She stopped, groaned. "Has anyone checked in with Diedre this morning?"

There were more groans. "I'll do that now," Livvy said. "Just stay on the phone with Bennie, and I'll use a landline."

"Bennie, did Frank happen to mention Diedre?" Eden asked after Livvy had left the group chat.

"He didn't bring her up, but she's something else I

worked into the conversation while I was searching. I asked him the last time he saw her, and get this—he said it was night before last."

"The night of Brenda's murder," Eden muttered. It was also when Carter had taken those photos of Diedre returning home in different clothes.

"Yep. That puts Diedre in Renegade Canyon at the time of the attack," Bennie said. "Well, it does if Frank is telling the truth."

And that was the problem with this investigation. Someone was lying, since Diedre had said she wasn't in town that night. Unfortunately, Eden didn't think they were going to get the truth from the killer.

But what exactly was the truth?

"Diedre's not answering her phone," Livvy said, coming back on the line. "Should I have SAPD check on her?"

"Yes," Rory said immediately, and Eden knew why.

If Diedre wasn't the killer, then she could be the next target. Then again, the same could be said about Rory and her.

"Did anything else turn up in the search of Frank's house?" Rory asked, obviously directing that question at Bennie.

"Not a thing." But then the deputy paused. "It seemed too clean. Maybe that's just Frank's thing, and I could way off base here, but to me it looked as if everything might have been…staged," he said. She heard him gather his breath. "I'm about to check in with SAPD on the search at Helen's. If anything turns up, I'll let you know."

Rory thanked Livvy and him, and he ended the call. Seconds later, just as Eden was putting on the rest of her clothes, there was a knock at the bathroom door.

"It's me," Rory said.

She opened it, and despite the serious conversation they'd just had, Eden had to deal with the stomach flutters she got whenever she was around Rory. The flutters must have shown on her face because the corners of Rory's mouth lifted.

"You do the same to me," he muttered, and then he leaned in and melted her with a kiss.

She was toast.

No way could she not sink into that kiss and make it last a whole lot longer and turn a whole lot hotter than it should be. Apparently, she was going to continue to muddy these relationship waters with him.

He eased back, that slight smile still in place on his clever mouth, and he smoothed his hand over her cheek. Again, she must not have had a poker face because he seemed to know exactly what she was thinking.

"Let's not overthink this," he muttered.

"Good. Because I don't believe I can cram anything else into my head right now." Eden didn't get a chance to add more because their phones buzzed again, and this time it was Bennie who'd initiated the call.

"The CSIs going through Helen's house found something," Bennie blurted the moment they answered. "And it's not good."

Eden and Rory both groaned, and Eden could think of many incriminating things they could find in the house of a possible killer. "What?" Rory asked.

"They found some traces of the supplies that were used to make those IEDs," Bennie explained. "They were in a plastic bag at the bottom of her trash can."

Rory's gaze met hers, and she saw the relief. And the sickening dread. They might finally have their killer, but it was horrific to think of his blood kin committing these horrible crimes.

"There are also some deleted computer searches on how to make explosives," Bennie added. "Her laptop will be sent to the lab to see what else they can find on it."

"They're certain it's the same supplies as those in the IEDs?" Rory asked.

"They seem plenty certain to me. Of course, everything will be tested, but they had the components of the IEDs from the bomb-squad guys and matched them to what they found in that plastic bag."

Rory stayed quiet a moment, obviously processing that revelation. "What did Helen have to say about that bag and the computer searches?"

Bennie huffed. "She's not here. According to the CSIs, she left shortly after the search began. And they say she's not answering her phone."

"Hell," Rory grumbled. "Put out an APB on Helen. I wanted her found *now.*"

Rory TRIED NOT to curse when he read the latest text from Detective Vernon. Tried and failed. Because it wasn't good news.

Still no sign of Helen.

It'd been hours since his aunt had walked out of her house during a CSI search. Hours since the CSIs had found the components that had been used to make those deadly IEDs. And after she'd walked out, Helen had seemingly vanished.

Was she out setting up another murder?

Or had Helen been set up by someone who'd planted

that plastic bag in her trash bin? Her outdoor trash bin that was on the side of her garage where anyone could have gotten to it.

Either of those were possible, but Rory couldn't ask her about them because she couldn't be found.

He looked over at Eden and showed her the text from the detective. She seemed to be on the verge of cursing, too.

"I'm not having any better luck," she told him.

She was seated at Grace's desk at the police station, with not one but two laptops in front of her. One was for the reports and updates that seemed to be coming in nonstop—Rory was dealing with those and fielding the calls. Eden was using the other laptop to review the traffic camera feed around Helen's neighborhood to see if she could spot anyone coming or going from Helen's house.

"The problem is there isn't a traffic cam right at her subdivision," Eden explained. "The closest one is a quarter of a mile away so even if I don't see, say, Diedre or Frank, it doesn't mean they weren't there. They could have just used an alternate route."

Yeah, and if one of them was the killer, they might have scoped out where the cameras were and made sure to avoid them.

Rory heard the dinging sound on the second laptop, an indication that a new report had arrived, so he dropped down in the chair he'd pulled next to Eden's and saw the latest from Livvy.

Again, he had to clamp down the urge to curse.

"No unusual withdrawals from Helen's bank account," he advised Eden. "Ditto for Ike, Diedre and Frank."

Eden stopped the traffic camera feed and looked at him. "These weren't expensive attacks. Well, unless one of them hired someone to make the IEDs. But any of them could have made smaller withdrawals for that months in advance so it wouldn't send up any red flags."

"True. And Helen, Ike, Frank and Diedre all should have known they'd be persons of interest or suspects for these killings."

"Ike," Eden repeated under her breath. "Where is he? He's not missing, too, is he?"

"He's not. He's at his lawyers' firm. He'll be coming back in soon to finish up his interview with Livvy." Though Rory wasn't holding out much hope they'd get anything useful from him.

Rory checked the time and saw they'd been at this for going on six hours now. It was midafternoon, and Eden looked more than ready for a break. He was about to suggest calling in an order from the diner up the street, but his phone rang.

"Diedre," he told Eden, and he took the call on speaker. "Where are you?" Rory demanded.

The woman huffed loud enough for him to hear it. Rory could also hear a car engine, which meant she was likely driving. "Look, I'm tired of you calling and leaving me messages. Can't you just leave me in peace?"

"No," he snarled, "and I wouldn't have to keep calling you if you'd just answer your phone. FYI, you're on speaker, and Deputy Gallagher is with me."

"Of course, she is," Diedre groaned. "She left me a voice mail, too."

Eden had indeed done that, but that had been hours ago. "Where are you?" Rory repeated.

Another loud huff. "I'm driving back from a business meeting. And, no, you don't need to verify if I had one or not because I mixed up the dates. The meeting isn't until next week. When I realized that, I turned around, and now,

I'm heading back home. Why are you calling me?" she snorted.

Rory had a couple of things he needed to ask her, but he went with the most important one. "Where is Helen?"

"How should I know…?" But she stopped at what had sounded as if it might be a rant. "Is something wrong?"

"That's what I'm trying to find out. She's not answering her phone. Has she been in touch with you?"

"No." And now, Diedre sounded concerned. Of course, that might be a pretense. "I can try to call her."

"Do that once you answer a few more questions." And Rory went with the second thing on his list. "Were you at Frank's two nights ago?"

"No," she blurted, but again, she stopped. "Sorry, that's a knee-jerk reaction. It's become second nature to deny I've been with Frank. But, yes, I was there. Briefly," she added. "I was out for a drive and dropped by to see if he was busy. He was. He said he had a Zoom meeting with a cattle broker."

"So you were in Renegade Canyon when Brenda was attacked?" Rory made sure he used his cop's tone on that one.

"Good grief, you just don't give up, do you?" She didn't wait for him to respond to that. "Yes, I was there. Again, it was very brief. I went to Frank's, talked to him for a couple of minutes and then I left. That's it. I didn't stop off on the way home to murder a woman I hardly knew."

"But you did know her," Rory argued. "You had lunch with her. The two of you discussed your mutual hatred for Ike."

"So what?" Diedre growled at him. "I discussed that with Helen, too. And Frank. I haven't murdered either of them."

The sarcasm dripped from her voice, but Rory felt the icy chill go through him, and he resisted muttering "not yet."

"Are you done accusing me of things I didn't do?" Diedre snapped.

"No," he snapped right back, and Rory moved on to the final thing on his list. "Think back to a couple of months ago to a fight that took place between Frank and Ike at the cemetery."

"That," she choked out, and the sarcasm was gone. In its place was a hefty amount of anger. "That's when Ike acted like his usual SOB self and upset Frank."

"Were you there?" Rory asked.

"No, but Frank told me all about it," Diedre insisted, and he didn't have to prompt the woman to continue. She just started spewing out the venom. "Ike's a vile monster. First, he cheated on his wife with a lot of women. Yes, that included me, but I wasn't married at the time. But he also cheated with Frank's wife. And then he rubbed the cheating in Frank's face."

"You know this for sure?" Rory asked.

"I know Ike, and he doesn't care who he hurts. And he hurt Frank that day at the cemetery." The woman's voice cracked on those last words.

Rory jumped right on that. "How did he hurt him?"

Diedre didn't say anything for a long time. "Ike was there visiting your mom's grave, and Frank was clear on the other side of the cemetery visiting Miranda's. Ike made a point of walking over to him and blowing a kiss at Miranda's tombstone. Ike did that," she snorted. Not a shout. But the anger was there. So much anger.

If Ike had truly done that, and Rory didn't doubt that he had, then it was an SOB thing to do. Then again, Ike made a habit of doing whatever he could to hurt people. Nearly everyone in town had been on the receiving end of Ike's wrath at one time or another.

"What's wrong with him?" Diedre asked. "Is it just plain meanness?" Again, she didn't wait for an answer, and she ended the call.

Rory and Eden sat in silence for a while, going over everything Diedre had just said. "That could be motive for the murders," Eden muttered.

Yeah, it could be, but it was motive for both Diedre and Frank. As for Helen, she had a motive of a different kind. To get rid of any competition she might have for Frank. That's why it was so critical for them to find her.

He took out his phone to try again to call her, but it rang before he could do that. "It's Ike's lawyer," he told Eden, and he figured Arnette was calling to reschedule his client's interview.

But Rory was wrong.

"Where's your father?" Arnette demanded the moment Rory answered. There was a frantic urge to the lawyer's normally cocky tone.

"He should be on his way here," Rory said. "Why?" And because he suddenly had a bad feeling about this, he put the call on speaker so Eden could hear as well.

"Because we had a meeting scheduled for well over an hour ago, and when Ike didn't show up or answer his phone, I started driving to the ranch. I figured he was maybe out riding or perhaps he'd lost track of time. But then I saw his truck," Arnette added, the strain in his voice going up a significant notch. "It was parked on a trail close to where that barn blew up."

An icy chill raced through Rory. Yeah, that bad feeling was warranted. "I take it he wasn't in the truck?" he asked, already standing. And Eden stood, too.

"No. He wasn't in it." Arnette's voice was shaking now. "But there was blood. So much blood." He made a loud groan. "Rory, I think somebody killed your father."

Chapter Sixteen

Eden was ready to take hold of Rory's arm to stop him from bolting out of the station and hurrying to get to Ike's truck.

But he thankfully didn't do that.

In fact, he muted the call with the lawyer and voiced the first thought that had occurred to her when she'd heard Arnette say "so much blood."

"This could be a trap," Rory muttered, and he fixed his gaze on her.

"Yes," she agreed. "One that the killer set, hoping we'd rush to the scene where we could be killed."

He nodded and unmuted his phone. "Arnette, move away from the truck and get back in your vehicle to wait for us. Walk backward, retracing your steps, because there could be IEDs."

That was highly likely since it had been the killer's preferred method in the previous attack. But Eden didn't doubt Ike had been taken.

Or hurt.

However, he was likely alive, for now, anyway, if the killer planned to use him as a lure. The killer could have taken Ike and then set up the explosives for anyone responding to the scene.

"An IED?" the lawyer repeated, and now there was some serious panic in his voice to go along with the worry. Eden hoped that panic didn't send Arnette running because it could get him blown to bits.

"Get in your vehicle," Rory repeated. "But don't drive away."

Good advice, because if Arnette had pulled off the side of the road, he could hit an IED when he tried to leave.

"Stay put," Rory added. "Help will be there soon."

He ended the call, continuing to keep his gaze fixed on her, and then cursed. She knew the reason for his profanity, too, so Eden went ahead and spelled out what needed to happen.

"I'll go with you in a cruiser," she stated. "You can't leave me holed up here since the killer could just find another way to get to us. Let's try to end this now."

Oh, he didn't care for that, but Rory knew it was the right thing to do. Like him, it was her job to go after a killer.

He nodded, gave her one last look that was laced with worry and they went back into the squad room. Livvy, Judson and Bennie were all working at their desks, and they must have realized something was wrong because they got to their feet.

"Arnette found Ike's truck near the rubble of the old Sanderson barn," Rory explained. "There was blood. Eden and I will respond in one cruiser. Judson and Bennie, you'll go in a second one. Livvy, I need you here at the station. Call the bomb squad and get them out to the scene. Hell, the fire department, too, in case there are any more of those gasoline bombs. And let Grace and Dutton know what's going on."

"What about a roadblock?" Livvy asked.

"We'll do that after we arrive on scene, but get out the word that the road will be closed indefinitely."

Livvy nodded, already taking out her phone. "Where's Ike?"

"No idea," Rory said, and then motioned for Judson and Bennie to follow them, and they all headed outside.

Rory reached for the door handle of the cruiser and then stopped. "Check underneath for any explosives," he called out to Judson and Bennie.

That gave Eden a jolt because it was something that she hadn't even considered. But she sure as heck should have. With the cruisers just sitting there in the parking lot, the killer could have planted IEDs on the vehicles.

All four of them lowered to the ground, and they did a search of the undercarriage. Eden didn't see anything suspicious, but she didn't know if the killer had tucked it away, somewhere out of sight. Still, it would have been awfully bold to try to do something like that with the police station only a few yards away.

"Nothing," Judson said several moments later, and Rory echoed the same.

They got in their respective cruisers, and Eden suspected all of them were doing some praying when they started the engines. But thankfully, the cruisers didn't explode, so with sirens and lights on, they started toward the scene.

It was bold, too, for the killer to do anything in this area, since it had already been the scene of three murders. Then again, the CSIs were long gone, so maybe the killer figured that cops and responders wouldn't be around anytime soon. Still, it was gutsy.

"This isn't on the route from the ranch to town," Eden pointed out. "So what was Ike doing out here?"

"Maybe he was forced to come," Rory said without hesitation, letting her know he'd thought of the question, too. "The killer could have been waiting for him in his truck." He paused. "Or done something to lure him here. Hell, or even taken him from the house."

All of those possibilities could have happened. There was plenty of extra security at the ranch, but that was mainly around Dutton's house, and that was for protecting Tyler. Since the main house couldn't be seen from Dutton's, it was possible that someone had sneaked onto the grounds, waited and attacked Ike.

"Remember, too, that Ike came to Carter's scene because of that message he could save someone," Rory went on. "I doubt Ike would fall for that again, but it could have been a different tactic."

"Like what?" she asked.

He looked at her, and she saw the worry in his eyes. "The killer could have called for a showdown, a way for Ike to put an end to this. Ike might not have turned that down."

True. After all, Rory and she hadn't, and this could have all been put in place to get them killed. But something about that bothered her.

"If the killer's intentions are to flat-out murder us," she said, "then why not just shoot us when we were at the barn or when we were with Carter's body?"

Rory lifted his shoulder. "It could be that shooting isn't part of his or her skill set. We know Frank had firearms training in the military, but I don't have any idea how sharp his skills are. And I don't recall anything in Helen's or Diedre's background to indicate they're markswomen." He paused. "Then again, there's nothing to link Diedre to having the know-how to make explosives."

No, but there was that link to Helen. And perhaps one to Frank, if Helen had been telling the truth about the magazines she saw. But even then, owning magazines like that didn't mean someone knew how to construct an IED.

Just in case the killer did decide to launch a sniper attack, Eden kept watch around them as they drove to the scene. It didn't take long, and they only passed one other vehicle during the five-minute drive.

She soon spotted Arnette's sleek silver Jaguar on the side of the road, and just as the man had said, Ike's truck was on one of the trails. Definitely not out of sight, though. In fact, it was barely on the trail itself, which meant the killer had likely wanted it to be found.

Rory pulled to a stop, not on the side of the road but right smack in the middle of it. He turned off the sirens but kept the lights on. Behind him, Judson did the same, and when Bennie and he got out, they all looked around on the road and the shoulder.

Nothing.

Well, nothing visible, anyway.

Eden took out two sets of latex gloves from the supply kit under her seat. She shoved one pair into her pocket, and Rory did the same to the pair she handed him.

"Get the roadblocks up," Rory told Judson and Bennie.

The two deputies went straight to the trunk and brought out the bright yellow plastic barricades. Livvy would send out a road crew to set up signs farther up, but this would do for now. At least there weren't any steep curves, so anyone traveling here would be able to see the barriers and the whirling blue cruiser lights in time to stop.

No repeats of what had happened to Rory and her with those strips of spikes.

Arnette didn't get out of his car as she and Rory approached, but he did lower his window a fraction. The lawyer was clearly rattled. He was sweating, and his hands were shaking.

"Is there a bomb?" Arnette blurted.

"Haven't had time to look yet, but I don't want you driving off. Go ahead and move to one of the cruisers. They're bullet-resistant."

That didn't ease the panicked look in Arnette's eyes, but with a shaky nod, he got out of the Jag and scurried toward a cruiser. There were no keys in the ignition, so the man wouldn't just be able to drive off. At least this way, though, he'd be semiprotected if all hell broke loose.

Again.

"Watch where you step," Rory muttered to her as they started toward Ike's truck. "And look for any footprints."

She did and so did Rory, along with firing lots of glances around them. As for spotting footprints, she soon realized that would be next to impossible. The entire surface here was fine gravel. It was perhaps why the killer had chosen it, since some of the other trails were dirt.

Rory went to the driver's side, and she went to the passenger's. Both doors were closed, but she had no trouble seeing what had alarmed Arnette.

The blood.

It was spattered on the windshield, the dash, the seat and the coffee mug that was in the cupholder. The total amount probably wasn't enough to indicate a fatal blood loss, but she could understand why Arnette had been so alarmed. The spatter likely meant Ike had received a blow to the head.

Or someone else had.

Because, after all, they had no idea if the blood was Ike's. He could have been involved in some kind of altercation and maybe had been the one who'd delivered such a blow. But if that was the case, where was he?

She slipped on one of the gloves and was about to open the door for a closer look, but Rory's warning of "no" came through loud and clear.

"The doors could be rigged with explosives," he reminded her.

Eden mentally cursed. Of course. That's something this killer could do to ensure their death.

After taking off the glove and shoving it back in her pocket, Eden settled for doing a visual of the interior and outside of the truck. There were way too many places where an explosive could have been set, and out of sight. Best to leave this for the bomb squad ,and eventually, the CSIs.

"More blood," Rory said. "It's on the ground."

She carefully went around the back of the truck so she could join him, and she followed his gaze to the drops on the gravel. Again, not a huge amount, but it looked as if the blood hadn't been there that long.

"And more," Rory added, pointing just ahead on the trail.

Eden saw, too, and went with him to the spot. It didn't take long before they saw more just ahead.

"This feels a little like following breadcrumbs," he muttered.

Yes, it did. Breadcrumbs that would lead them straight into an attack. That's why they both drew their guns and kept moving, slowly, checking for anything that could help them make sense of this scene.

If the killer had been leading Ike along this trail, then where was the killer's vehicle? It lent credence to the theory that the killer had been in Ike's truck and forced him here. Maybe that meant the killer had left some DNA or trace evidence inside the truck.

As they moved, she spotted one of those holes left over from the dried-up mineral springs. Unlike the ones the killer had used around Carter, this one was huge, a caved-in section of the ground the size of a bathtub. If the killer had planted IEDs in this one, she couldn't see them because it was too deep.

They kept moving, kept following the blood drops, but they both stopped when there was a sound.

A low, hoarse moan.

Maybe.

Since this was in the sticks by anyone's standards, it was possible an animal had made the sound. But Eden didn't believe that. No. The sound had been human. A human in pain.

Rory must have thought so, too, because he quickened the pace just a little, but he also continued to keep watch. Eden did the same.

And she heard it again.

That moan.

And thankfully, this time she could better pinpoint the location. It'd come from just ahead and to her right, where there was a cluster of thick cedars.

Because of the underbrush, they couldn't just step off the trail, where there might be explosives, so they continued ahead. When they reached the cedars, though, she didn't see Ike.

Not at first, anyway.

But then she spotted him.

And her heart dropped to her knees.

Because the blood was streaming down the side of Ike's head, and he appeared to be barely conscious. He was sitting, but he'd been tied to a tree. Not just his hands and feet. The rope had been coiled around his torso, anchoring him in place.

That wasn't all, though.

No.

Around him, mere inches away from where Ike sat, there was a perfect semicircle of something Eden hadn't wanted to see.

Four IEDs.

RORY SUCKED IN a hard breath and immediately glanced all around the area. Because even though the IEDs had gotten their attention, that didn't mean the killer wasn't going to try to capitalize on the distraction and kill them.

He took hold of Eden's arm, moving her next to one of the larger trees. As cover went, it sucked, but at least it was better than them standing out in the open.

"Ike?" Eden called out to his father while Rory texted Livvy to send an ambulance.

Of course, the EMTs wouldn't be able to get to Ike, not until the bomb squad had cleared the IEDs, but Rory wanted medical help on hand. Not just for Ike, but for anyone else who ended up hurt in this ordeal.

But what was the ordeal?

If the killer had used Ike to lure them to their deaths, then why put the IEDs in plain sight? Was it because the explosive devices were meant to be a distraction? If so, they were working. Hard to completely focus when the whole area might blow up.

"Ike?" Eden repeated.

This time, Ike struggled to get one of his eyes open. He was clearly dazed but alive. Not for long, though, if they didn't do something fast.

ETA on the bomb squad? he texted Livvy.

Fifteen minutes, she replied.

That time would no doubt crawl by, while Ike sat there, bleeding.

"Ike, who did this to you?" Eden asked.

His father turned to look at Eden, but Rory wasn't sure he was actually seeing her. There was blood in his left eye, and his face was a mask of pain with the one good eye barely open to a slit.

"Who did this?" she repeated.

Ike shook his head. "Someone hit me over the head when I got in my truck." Like his face, his voice was a tangle of pain as well. "I didn't see who." Blinking hard, he glanced around. "Where am I? How did I get here?"

Rory cursed. So Ike wasn't going to be able to tell them much, but the area around him offered a few clues. There were no drag marks, which meant the killer had carried Ike—which would eliminate Diedre because of her size. And while Helen was strong, he doubted even she could carry Ike.

That left Frank.

He could do the carrying, but that didn't mean he was the killer. Ike could have been bludgeoned and then drugged just enough to make him incapable of fighting back, but still able to walk. If so, the killer could have led him straight to this spot, tied him up and maybe given him another hit on the head or some drugs.

Which meant he couldn't rule out any of their suspects.

Heck, he couldn't even rule out Ike, who could have perhaps staged all of this. But that didn't feel right. There were easier ways for Ike to get to Eden and him.

Unless they weren't the targets.

Maybe he and Eden were the lures for someone else. For someone whom Ike wanted dead.

"Helen," Ike muttered.

And that sure as hell got Rory's attention. "What about her?" Rory demanded.

"Uh, she was here. Wasn't she?" Ike looked at him as if he might know the answer. Rory didn't.

"Where did you see her?" Eden asked.

Ike ran his tongue over his bottom lip and grimaced. "Here," he said but then shook his head. "Just up the trail."

Rory glanced in that direction, but he didn't see anyone. No surprise there. The narrow trail was jammed on both sides by trees and thick underbrush. Added to that, it curved around just about ten yards ahead. It was impossible to see who or what could be on the other side.

"Did Helen do this to you?" Eden asked.

Again, Ike shook his head. "Maybe. I don't know. I'm hurt. I need to get to the hospital."

"The ambulance will be here soon," Eden said. "How badly are you hurt? Is it just your head or do you have other injuries?"

Ike seemed to consider that a moment. "I'm not sure. Can't think straight, and everything's a blur."

So if he wasn't lying or faking, Ike either had a serious concussion or he'd indeed been drugged. It could be both, and he could even have brain damage. Again, that was true if this wasn't all some ploy.

But Rory was positive that the blood was the real deal.

And it was continuing to seep down the side of Ike's head.

Rory whirled around at the sound of footsteps, and the adrenaline shot through him. Unnecessarily, though, because it was Bennie.

"Judson's keeping an eye on the road and Arnette…"

Bennie said, but his words trailed off when he got a glimpse of Ike and those IEDs. "Hell," he muttered.

That summed up Rory's feelings, too, and he debated their next step. If Helen was indeed somewhere on the trail, and she was the killer, Rory needed to neutralize her before the bomb squad arrived.

Especially if she had a detonator for those IEDs.

"Wait here for the bomb squad," Rory told Bennie, and he looked at Ike. "Don't move. Don't try to get out of those ropes. Don't even kick out your feet."

Because if he did, Ike would almost certainly set off one of the IEDs.

Ike muttered something that sounded like agreement. Whether it was or not, Rory needed to get moving.

"Eden, with me," he said, motioning for her to follow him up the trail. "I don't want to go too far," he added to her in a whisper. "I don't want to risk the killer going after Bennie."

"Yes," she answered so quickly that he understood that possibility had already occurred to her.

They didn't say anything else. They just took slow, cautious steps up the trail toward that blind curve while they tried to keep watch around them. He didn't know what game the killer was playing, but he sure as hell didn't like any part of this.

He paused for a moment when he heard something. A rustling sound in the bushes to his left. But moments later, a rabbit darted out and disappeared into the woods. Normally, that wouldn't have put a hard knot in his gut, but even a creature as small as a rabbit could set off one of those IEDs.

And there might be more than just the ones surrounding Ike.

Unlike the spot where Ike's truck had been left, this part of the trail wasn't nearly as visible from the road. The killer could have taken his time here. But when had she or he brought in the IEDs? Maybe that had been done during the night, and then they could have been positioned once Ike was here.

Rory drew in a long breath when he reached the curve, and even though he knew Eden wouldn't like it, he stepped in front of her, trying to shield her in case they were about to face down a killer.

Eden didn't balk, though. Instead, she turned to the side, watching their backs while they kept moving. Good. He didn't want them ambushed, and like that rabbit, the killer could be hiding in the underbrush, ready to spring.

But no one did.

And no one was on the other side of the curve, either.

Of course, that didn't mean Helen hadn't been here, but she could be long gone by now. Rory didn't think so, though. He was pretty sure they were being watched, but he couldn't see or hear anyone.

Not at first, anyway.

There was more of that rustling sound. Not on the trail, but to the left side of it. Bringing up his gun, he whipped in that direction, and spotted Helen.

She was there, standing by a tree.

And she had a gun.

Chapter Seventeen

Eden jolted when she saw Helen with that gun pointed at them, and she was already dropping to the ground, catching hold of Rory to pull him down with her. She wanted both of them out of the line of fire.

Mercy, her heart had jumped to her throat, and it wasn't budging. It was stuck there like a rock. Of course, she'd known the killer could be Helen, but it still had been a shock to see her and that weapon.

Rory immediately rolled to the side and came up, taking aim at his aunt. "Put down your gun," he shouted.

But Helen didn't respond. Didn't move.

The woman stayed seemingly frozen there against the tree. No. Not frozen, Eden realized. But Helen was unable to move.

"I think she's been taped to the tree," Eden muttered.

The clear, wide kind of tape used for securing packages. It was hard to tell from this distance, but Eden thought she could see the light on the shiny surface. If that was it, then her neck had perhaps been taped as well, since her head was upright. The gun could be taped in place, too, since it was aimed outward, but Helen wasn't adjusting it so that it would be aimed at them.

"The killer could have put her here," Rory added.

Yes, that could have happened, but like Ike, this could be a ruse. A deadly one.

"Helen?" Rory shouted.

There was still no response, and the woman still wasn't trying to shift that gun around and shoot them. Was she waiting for them to get closer so she could get a better shot? Heck, was she even alive? Unlike Ike, there was no blood, but there were no obvious signs of life, either.

"I'm moving closer," Rory said.

Since he didn't order her to stay put, Eden didn't. When he started to belly-crawl closer to Helen, so did she. If this took a turn for the worst, she wanted to be by his side to help him.

Rory kept his attention pinned to his aunt, and Eden continued to keep watch behind and around them. She also kept an eye out for IEDs, and that was a little easier to do with her face only inches from the ground.

She cringed when she saw another of those deep holes off to the side. Any minute now, there could be an explosion. Any minute, Rory and she could die.

Of course, living with that threat of possible death was part of the job, but they had so many reasons to live, and she hoped she got a chance to tell Rory how she felt about it. She promised herself then and there if they made it out of this alive, she wouldn't put up another barrier between them.

And she would tell him that she loved him.

For now, she had to push that thought away and keep moving.

They finally got close enough to Helen for them to see there was indeed tape around her torso and her neck. Her hand, too, the one holding the gun in place.

Had the killer done that so that they would see the weapon and then shoot first, killing her? Or was this all Helen's doing? Maybe a way to try to make herself look innocent of the other murders since she was now seemingly a victim, too.

She was alive because Eden could see her chest moving. But her eyes were closed, and the woman definitely wasn't responding when they called out to her.

"I don't see any IEDs around her," Rory whispered.

"Neither do I."

Eden wasn't sure what to make of that. Again, if this was the killer's doing, then he or she hadn't staged the scene like Ike's.

There were differences in Mellie's and Brenda's stagings as well, with Brenda left at the back of the barn and Mellie's body toward the front. And Carter's murder was nothing like the other victims except for the cause of death. That's the only thing that all of them had in common.

They'd been stabbed and left to die.

As far as she knew, Ike hadn't been stabbed. Judging by the lack of blood, neither had Helen. So as far as Eden was concerned, both of them stayed on the list of potential suspects.

Eden thought back to the way Ike had been tied up against that tree, and that was something he could have done himself. Ditto for the head wound. It would have taken a lot of guts to hit himself on the head, but it might be a small price to pay to make himself look innocent.

And it was the same for Helen.

They had no idea if that tape went all the way around the tree so Helen could have posed herself this way and be lying in wait. A clever way to get them closer and kill them. Still, that didn't feel right. If the plan was to pin all of this on Ike, then why hit him and tie him up? Helen could have probably figured out a way to get him on scene, so he could be blamed for the latest attack.

Eden didn't voice that thought, and she continued to move with Rory, inch by excruciating inch. They were still a good ten feet away from Helen when Eden saw another of those holes in the ground.

Right in front of Helen.

If they'd charged toward her, they would have fallen in. Maybe landing right on an IED that would have then exploded.

"Frank!" someone shouted.

Eden groaned because she instantly recognized the voice. What the heck was she doing there?

Diedre.

"Frank," the woman shouted again.

Eden looked behind them to see Diedre running up the trail toward them. Bennie was right behind her, and he practically tackled the woman before she could get to Rory and her.

Diedre shrieked, and there was probably some pain that went along with the tackle. But Eden was glad Bennie had done that because they had no idea what the woman's intentions were.

"Where's Frank?" Diedre called out, her voice breaking into a sob. "Did Helen kill him?"

"Sorry," Bennie said. He was huffing and fighting to hang on to Diedre, who was trying to wriggle out of his grip. "I didn't see her until she started running right past me. She didn't drive up in a vehicle, and she must have cut her way through the woods, so Judson didn't spot her."

So Diedre had sneaked onto the scene, and Eden couldn't think of a single good reason for her to do that.

"Did Helen kill him?" Diedre repeated, and she was flat-out crying now.

Maybe it was an act, but if so, she was certainly putting a lot into it. Then again, she might need that effort to try to convince them she wasn't there to kill them.

"Why are you here?" Rory snapped.

"For Frank," Diedre said quickly. "I know he's here… somewhere."

"And how would you know that?" he asked.

"Because I put a tracker app on his phone," Diedre blurted, but then stopped and gasped as if she hadn't meant to say that aloud. "I, uh, I thought he was seeing Helen or someone else."

So…jealousy. Or a way to track him so she could kill him. But if so, then it was stupid of her to admit that she was tracking him.

"I went to his house, and when he wasn't there," the woman continued, "I used the tracker, and it led me here. To her," she spluttered, her gaze landing on Helen. There was rage in Diedre's eyes now. "Did you kill him?" she shouted to Helen.

"What makes you think Frank is dead?" Eden asked.

"There was blood on his porch. So he's been hurt. She hurt him and brought him here to kill him the way she did Brenda and Mellie," Diedre said.

Rory was quick to respond to that. "You're certain Helen killed them? You have proof?"

"No, but she did it," Diedre snarled. "She must have so she could set up Ike."

Diedre's gaze met Eden's, and suddenly the woman didn't seem so certain of that. Again, it could all be an act, but there seemed to be some doubt now.

"Oh, God," Diedre muttered, her gaze slashing to her

left, where there were more of those clustered cedar trees. "Frank?" The sobbing came to a quick halt, and there was shock coating both her voice and her face.

Eden was still on her belly, but she automatically turned in that direction, too, bringing up her gun. Beside her, Rory did the same. And they both took aim at Frank, who stepped out from behind one of the trees.

He didn't have a gun, but there was something else in his hand. Something that Eden knew could kill them all.

Frank was holding an IED.

Rory bolted to his feet, getting in a firing stance.

But he didn't have a safe shot.

Not with Frank's fingers on what Rory was pretty sure was the detonator of that IED he was holding.

"This ends here," Frank said, glancing at all of them. "It'll end for Ike, too, since he'll be blown to bits in ten minutes or so. Those IEDs are all on timers. And there won't be enough time for the bomb squad to get in here and defuse them."

Rory silently cursed. So Frank was cleaning house. Or rather, that was his plan, anyway, but Rory didn't intend to let that plan come to fruition. Somehow, he had to stop this.

But how?

And why had Frank gone off the deep end like this?

Diedre had started sobbing again, and she was muttering stuff that Rory couldn't make out. But she wasn't the only one making sounds. So was Helen. She was moaning, regaining consciousness.

"Rory?" Judson shouted. "What the devil is going on?" He was running toward them, but pulled up when he saw the answer to his own question.

All hell was about to break loose.

"What will it take to get you to put down that IED and surrender?" Rory asked Frank.

Frank laughed, but there was no humor in it. In fact, just the opposite. He groaned, the sound of a man in emotional agony. Rory didn't have a shred of sympathy for him, though, since he was looking at the face of a killer.

"No surrender," Frank muttered. "This ends now." And he shifted the IED as if ready to set it off.

Think. Think fast. Rory had to do something.

"At least tell us why we're dying," Rory insisted. "You can do that much for us. We deserve answers."

Frank seemed to consider that, and Rory could feel the seconds ticking by. He had no idea how much firepower was in those IEDs around Ike, but it was possible they'd blow up the entire area. If that was the case, though, then Frank likely wouldn't be holding yet another IED. Unless that was insurance that they all die.

Frank included.

But maybe that had been his plan all along.

"I didn't mean for Mellie to die," Frank finally said. "That was an accident. She'd seen Ike and me fighting at my wife's grave, and she came to my ranch to check on me. I didn't hear her when she drove up, and she walked right in to my workshop. She saw me making one of these." He lowered his gaze to the IED. "She knew what it was, and she turned to run. I caught her, and, I, uh, had a knife in my hand that I was using to strip some wires…" His voice trailed off.

"And you murdered her," Eden said, finishing his sentence. "You murdered her!"

Rory could only imagine the firestorm of emotions that she was feeling right now. Frank had killed her foster mother, and it didn't matter that he'd just called it an accident. Mellie was dead. So were Lou Garcia, Brenda and Carter. Garrison had nearly been killed, too.

And Frank had clearly tried to cover his tracks.

Clearly taken steps to prevent him from being ID'ed as the killer. The CSIs had found no IED-making equipment during their search, so that meant Frank had cleaned up that area and had obviously moved his IED factory elsewhere.

"No," Diedre sobbed. "No, please say this isn't true."

Everyone, including Frank, ignored her, and from the corner of his eye, he could see Judson easing back a few steps. Rory doubted the deputy was trying to distance himself from the blast, though. No. He was likely trying to get to Ike to see what he could do about saving him.

"Did Brenda walk in on you, too?" Eden snapped. "Did you kill her by accident as well?"

Frank didn't react to the anger. "No," he said with an eerie calmness, "but Mellie had apparently called her to tell her what had happened at the cemetery with Ike, and she told Brenda that she was coming to see me."

So there was the motive for two murders. Heck, for framing Ike as well, since it was obvious now that the altercation at the cemetery had been what set Frank off. That had caused him to snap, and this was the result.

But there was something about this that didn't make sense.

"There was five months between Mellie's and Brenda's murders," Eden pointed out. "That's a long time to wait to tie up any loose ends."

Frank nodded. "Brenda kept asking me about Mellie, kept bringing up the visit that Mellie told her she was going to make to see me. I think Brenda was looking for evidence to prove that I'd been the one to kill her. Playing detective," he grumbled under his breath.

"Brenda never said anything to the cops about Mellie's plans to visit you," Rory informed Frank.

"Because I told her that Mellie hadn't come," Frank admitted, "and I turned the tables on her by saying that Mellie had told me that she was going to see her, to see Brenda. So it was sort of an impasse. I wouldn't tell on Brenda, and she wouldn't tell on me. But I couldn't risk Brenda staying quiet forever. So I asked her if I could meet her at her house to discuss it. She agreed."

Frank stopped again. Rory didn't know how much of those ten minutes were gone now, but each second counted.

"I drugged Brenda, planted those burner phones, took her to the barn. And I killed her," Frank admitted. "At least I thought I had. When I left her, I believed she was dead."

"But you set an IED just in case," Eden snapped. "An IED that killed a CSI."

"I'm sorry about that. He wasn't meant to die. But I wanted to bring down the whole damn barn because I thought it was over. I thought Ike would be blamed for Brenda's death, and that he'd end up rotting in jail. But you didn't arrest him," he practically shouted. "He was a free man, walking around, continuing to spread his hatred. Not paying for the misery he brought to my life."

Rory didn't voice the reason for that misery. It wasn't just the incident in the cemetery, but the fact that Ike had had an affair with Frank's wife. A wife he had obviously loved.

"It was supposed to be over," Frank continued, his voice lower now. And he was too composed, considering what he had done. Considering what he was about to do. "But

Carter had taken some pictures of me going into Brenda's house that night, and he tried to blackmail me with them."

"And you killed him, too," Rory concluded. "Three. That's makes you a serial killer."

Frank didn't have time to react to that because Diedre spoke before he could say anything.

"But I saw blood on your porch," the woman said, like some kind of plea to help her make sense of this. "I saw it and thought you'd been hurt or killed."

Frank shook his head and tipped his head to his arm. "I cut myself when I was moving some of the IEDs."

So no one had harmed him. Not physically, anyway.

"You son of a bitch," Helen yelled. She was conscious now, and she had her narrowed eyes pinned on Frank. "I trusted you. I was in love with you. And this is how you repay me? You asked me to meet you so you could give me proof that Diedre had murdered Mellie and Brenda."

"What?" Diedre howled.

A surge of anger must have gone through Diedre because she tried to get up. No doubt to charge at Frank so she could try to have a go at him. Bennie, thankfully, shut that down by wrapping his arms around the woman and holding on tight.

"I wasn't going to pin the murders on you," Frank insisted, sparing Diedre a dismissive glance. "In fact, you weren't even supposed to be here. You were supposed to… live," he muttered.

"But I was supposed to die?" Helen snapped. She was struggling to get out of the tape restraints, and she was succeeding. Rory only hoped the gun wasn't loaded, because if she tried to shoot Frank, he'd set off the IED. "Why did you lump me with Mellie, Brenda and Carter? I wasn't blackmailing you. I didn't know you were a killer."

"You're insurance," Frank said. "Ike's fingerprints are on the tape and gun. After this is over, the CSIs would have found that. They would have found his prints on some of the IEDs, too. And the equipment to make the IEDs is in the cargo bed of his truck. There's a note back at my house, saying that I learned that Ike was going to kill you and that I came here to try to stop him."

Rory cursed. "But Ike would have been dead."

He nodded. "Dead, but always remembered as a cold-blooded killer. That's the legacy I want for him. The legacy he deserves."

"And what legacy do you deserve?" Rory snapped to get his attention. "You're killing innocent people."

Much to Rory's surprise, Frank seemed to consider that, and he looked at Diedre. "There's a big hole from the old mineral springs right in front of Helen. Get in it now. You, too," he added, spearing Eden with his intense gaze. "And Bennie. It might protect the three of you from the blast."

Rory didn't even have to think about this. "Go," he ordered Diedre, Bennie and Eden.

Bennie and Diedre quickly moved toward the hole. So did Helen, who had managed to get out of the tape. Eden didn't. Damn it. She stayed put.

"I'm not leaving you to die," she said, and then she added something that perhaps stunned them both. "I'm in love with you."

Despite everything, Rory managed a brief smile. Those were words he'd waited a long time to hear. And to say.

"I'm in love with you, too," he told her. Now, he had to play dirty. He had to say or do whatever it took to save her. "I need you to stay alive for Tyler. He can't lose both of his parents. Our son needs you."

She shook her head. "He needs you, too. I need you," Eden added.

"This ends now," Frank repeated in a mutter.

Rory knew the man meant it, and moving as fast as he could, he hooked his arm around Eden, diving toward that hole with her in tow.

Behind them, the blast ripped through the air.

Chapter Eighteen

Eden wasn't sure if Rory or the blast had propelled them into the hole. Maybe a combination of both. But they landed on top of Bennie, Diedre and Helen.

It wasn't exactly a cushioned fall, since bodies slamming against bodies was rough, and Eden saw stars when her elbow rammed against the rock wall. And she couldn't breathe. The air was gone, and her lungs were clamped into a vise.

She wasn't the only one, either. All of them were gasping, and Eden thought that maybe the IED had created some kind of vacuum. Still, the fact that she could feel the pain meant she was alive.

She turned—well, as much as she could turn in the small space—and saw Rory. He was right behind her. Alive, too, thank goodness. They had survived. But were they out of danger?

Dragging in some much needed air, Eden looked at the others, and in a blink, she knew there was no threat here. Diedre was trying to scream, and she was clinging to Bennie. Helen was groaning, the sound of raw pain, and Eden realized the gun still taped to her hand had apparently gouged into her left arm. The barrel had been rammed into her skin.

Eden unraveled the rest of the tape, checking to see if the gun was loaded. It wasn't. Then she checked the wound. It was bleeding. Not a fatal injury, but she'd need medical attention. Heck, they all would.

"Ike," Rory blurted on a gasp of breath.

That put her heart right back in her throat, and the images flashed like neon signs in her head. Ike with all those IEDs around him. And Judson had gone back to try to help him.

Rory caught on to the top of the hole, and he levered himself out, his gaze sweeping around. He'd managed to hold on to his gun. Unlike Eden. She had to pick hers up from the bottom of the hole.

"I'll go check on Judson and Ike," Rory insisted.

She'd had no doubts that was his plan, but Eden crawled out with him, and she glanced around at the disaster Frank had created. There was rubble everywhere, along with his body. Or rather, what was left of it. He was dead, and she was glad of it. Mellie's killer had finally gotten the justice he deserved.

Too bad he'd hurt and killed so many other people in the process.

Eden whirled back toward Rory, who had started to move toward Ike. She moved, too, ready to help.

But she didn't get the chance.

There was another blast, even louder than the other one, and it shook the very ground beneath them. She saw the sickening dread go over Rory's face. Felt the same emotion in every part of her body.

And they took off running.

They could have an officer down. Judson could be seriously injured. Or worse. They had to get to him and Ike.

The adrenaline gave them a boost of speed, and they

sprinted toward the spot where they'd left Ike. There wasn't much left of it. The cedars had all been ripped apart like giant toothpicks, and there was a huge hole in the ground.

But no bodies.

"Here," someone called out.

Judson. She whirled around and saw the deputy near one of the cruisers. And he wasn't alone. He had Ike with him. He'd saved Rory's father.

Rory didn't take off running. Instead, he looked down at the ground, no doubt checking for more IEDs. That slowed them down considerably, but they eventually made it to Judson and Ike. Like Rory and her, they were both gasping for breath, while Arnette looked on in horror from the cruiser.

"Frank's dead," Rory informed them. "He confessed to everything."

Later, there'd be a ton of reports to do. Witness accounts needed to be taken, and the whole scene would have to be examined, but for now, they all just stood there a moment, trying to come to terms with the nightmare they'd just escaped.

"How'd you get Ike to safety?" Rory asked Judson.

"I circled behind him. No IEDs there. So I got him loose, and we got the hell out of there as fast as we could."

"Barely escaped," Ike muttered, using his forearm to wipe away the blood on his head.

"You and Helen need an ambulance," Eden finally said.

"It's on the way," Judson assured her, and there were indeed the sounds of sirens in the distance. He opened his mouth, probably to ask about Bennie, but he stopped, motioning toward Bennie, Helen and Diedre, who were all making their way toward them.

Neither of the women was saying anything, which meant

the shock had likely set in. After the shock, well, there'd be a lot of emotional turmoil. But they were alive, and Eden figured that reminder would be setting in soon as well. They'd all gotten lucky and were here despite Frank's sick plan of revenge.

The irony of that plan was Ike was alive, too, and he wouldn't be rotting in jail as Frank had wanted.

Arnette finally got out of the cruiser, went straight to Ike and taking him by the arm, he looked at Rory. "I'd like to get my client out of here and take him to the ER. Any objections?"

Rory looked at his dad. "You could go in an ambulance." He tipped his head as it came into sight.

"I'd rather go with Arnette." But he didn't budge. Ike just stood there a couple of moment. "Thanks for saving my life," he muttered, glancing at Judson, Rory and, yes, even at Eden.

The three of them muttered some variations of "you're welcome." And they meant it. Despite Ike being a despicable human being, he hadn't deserved to die, though Eden hoped he'd learned a lesson about taunting a man over his wife's grave.

"You're going to owe my client an apology," Arnette snapped, clearly stepping back into his lawyer role.

"Shut the hell up, Arnette," Ike told him, and he headed toward the Jag with the lawyer trailing right along behind him.

Eden was finally ready to take a breath to try to tamp down some of this adrenaline, but then Rory spoke.

"Put Helen in the ambulance," Rory instructed Judson. "There might be other IEDs."

Sweet heaven. Eden hoped that wasn't true, but as enraged as Frank had been, there could be more.

"Go in the ambulance with her to the hospital," Rory added to Judson. "And take a statement from her if you can."

After Judson gave him a nod, Rory shifted to Diedre, who looked on the verge of starting that shrieking again. "Where are you parked?"

She motioned toward a trail up the road.

"Don't go there," Rory ordered her. "Get in the cruiser with Bennie. He'll take you to the station, and after the bomb squad has cleared the area, someone will bring you your car. Oh, and FYI, it's against the law to put a tracker on someone's phone. You're lucky it didn't lead you to getting killed."

Diedre didn't shriek, but she started to sob as Bennie led her to the cruiser. Eden doubted they'd actually file charges against Diedre, especially since they had so many other loose ends to wrap up. For starters, checking for IEDs and recovering the explosive-making equipment that Frank said he'd put in Ike's truck. The bomb squad would see to that, and then the CSIs and ME would have to come in. It could take days to clean up this crime scene.

"I want to see Tyler," Eden said simply.

He nodded, and he motioned for her to move into the cruiser with him. "So do I. We can leave as soon as the bomb squad gets here."

Good. Because holding their son might start untangling this mass of nerve.

She slid into the passenger's seat and did something else to start that untangling. Eden reached over and pulled Rory to her.

Yes, instant relief.

Along with so many other feelings. Not the nerves. No, this was something much stronger.

"I'm not taking it back," she told him while they clung to each other.

"Taking what back?" he asked.

"That *I love you*. I meant it, and I'm not going to claim it was part of the fear or adrenaline surge."

Rory eased back from her, a slow smile forming on his mouth. A mouth he promptly used to kiss her. An incredible kiss that worked wonders. The nightmare of the attack didn't exactly vanish, but the kiss put a serious dent in it.

When he eased back, Rory was still smiling. "I'm not taking it back, either. I'm in love with you, Eden, and no, that wasn't the adrenaline talking. That was all me."

"Ike is never going to approve of us being together," she reminded him. And she returned the favor by giving him one of those scalding kisses.

Rory didn't even attempt to end the kiss so he could respond. He just kissed and kissed and kissed, until he stirred up a ton of heat inside her.

"Ike has no say in…us," he said. "This love is between you and me. And Tyler," he added.

Now, she smiled. Because, yes, Tyler was in on this, too.

The weight just lifted off her heart. Weight that felt as if it'd been there for a very long time. Eden suddenly felt as if everything was going to be fine.

Better than fine, she amended.

Everything was finally going to be *right*.

* * * * *

MEMORY OF MURDER

DEBRA WEBB

Chapter One

Chicago
Monday, July 7
Colby Agency, 9:30 a.m.

Jamie Colby waited in her grandmother's office, the package sitting in her lap. Her fingers tapped out a tune on the box that had gotten slightly battered in transit. The package and its contents had been in Jamie's possession for a mere three days, but already she was convinced of what needed to be done. Quickly, she reminded herself. This had to happen as soon as possible.

Somehow she would make the indomitable Victoria Colby-Camp see that her plan was a good one. A necessary one that had to be carried out, even if pro bono. The agency did pro bono work all the time. Did it really matter that the actual client was deceased?

Not in Jamie's opinion. The woman deserved to have her reputation restored. Some things transcended death.

The door opened, and Victoria breezed into the office and settled behind her desk. "Good morning." She smiled brightly as she always did whenever she saw Jamie for the first time each day.

Jamie adored her grandmother. Her entire life Jamie had always known she wanted to be just like her.

No matter that she and Jamie had been working together now for nearly seven months, each day was like the first with her grandmother. Calling Victoria *Grandmother* almost always put off anyone who met them for the first time. Primarily because Victoria looked far younger than her seventy-two years. The silver threaded through her black hair spoke of sophistication and wisdom rather than age. But it was her keen eyes that warned she was no little old lady.

Jamie smiled. "Good morning, Grandmother."

Victoria eyed the package in Jamie's lap. "I understand you have a special case under consideration."

So, Ian had spoken to her already. Jamie wasn't surprised. It wasn't as if she had told him not to tell Victoria. Perhaps he'd hoped to grease the wheels, so to speak. Ian Michaels was one of her grandmother's closest friends and colleagues. His recommendation would go a long way— assuming he leaned in Jamie's favor, and she suspected he would.

"Yes." Jamie stood. She placed the box on the edge of her grandmother's desk and removed the contents piece by piece. First the handwritten journal. Then the photos, the newspaper clippings, a locket, Polaroid-type photos and the baby blanket—the sort of receiving blanket given at birth, usually by a hospital. A detailed letter from the accused killer had accompanied the box.

As Victoria shuffled through the photos, Jamie explained, "Mary Morton was charged with first-degree murder thirty years ago. She was sentenced to life in prison. At the time she was pregnant, and the baby—a girl—was later born and subsequently taken from her. Since Mary had no other family or close friends able or willing to take the child, she was introduced into the foster system."

Victoria moved on to the newspaper clippings. "Has the child—woman," she amended, "been contacted about her mother's death?"

Jamie nodded. "I spoke with the warden. He gives his best, by the way." Her grandmother knew everyone who was anyone in key positions in the state and no small number of VIPs across the country. "A notification was sent to her last known address. I checked out the address, and she does live there. There's every reason to believe she's aware of the situation."

Victoria reached for the journal. "Tell me why we should be interested in this convicted murderer's history."

Jamie resumed her seat. "At the time of the murder, Mary Morton was twenty-four years old. She had just completed her master's in teaching, and she was already employed at an elementary school in Crystal Lake. On a personal level, she was engaged to a law student set to graduate the upcoming year. His name was Neil Reed. Both Mary and Neil grew up in Crystal Lake. Her parents were deceased, but his still lived in the area."

"Reed was the victim in the murder case." Victoria placed the journal with the other items.

Obviously her grandmother had already looked into the details. Possibly a good sign.

"Yes. Mary insisted throughout the trial that she was innocent, but the preponderance of evidence was overwhelming. Her prints were on the murder weapon. She had blood on her clothes. Her court-appointed attorney—a man swamped with cases—didn't stand a chance against the newly elected hotshot district attorney determined to make a name for himself. My impression is that the case was decided even before a jury was selected."

Victoria picked up a newspaper clipping, considered it a moment. "Why are we talking about this case, Jamie? The poor woman, guilty or innocent, is dead. I really don't see how we can help her."

"We can," Jamie countered. "Mary's greatest regret was that she couldn't clear her name to prove to her only child that she was not the daughter of a murderer. According to her letter, Mary didn't care if she was ever released. She only wanted to clear her name for her daughter's sake. Her attorney promised to appeal her conviction, but his meager efforts proved futile. Still Mary never gave up. No matter how earnest her efforts, it was as if whatever legal maneuvers she attempted were doomed from the outset. Every single time she was met with defeat. No reporter ever showed interest in her story. Fate simply turned a blind eye to her. I feel strongly that the justice system let her down."

Victoria studied Jamie. "Or she was simply guilty and no one wanted to help change a righteous verdict."

"That's possible, yes. However, everyone—even the guilty—has the right to petition for an appeal. But guilt is not the sense I'm getting from what we have here." Jamie gestured to the contents of the box spread over her grandmother's desk. "Just before she died, Mary had lost all hope. She saw an article about you, Grandmother, and the story gave her hope that there were still good people in the world who might be able to help her. She put together this package and asked that it be mailed to our office. An indifferent guard never bothered to see that it was done. But after her death, there was some question about why all her personal items were missing, and another guard discovered the box in an office. She checked the contents and then hand delivered it here."

Victoria continued to study her, waiting, apparently, for her to go on.

"After a thorough examination of all you see, and a review of the available public information on the case, I feel compelled to open a case and assign an investigator."

"Who do you have in mind?" Victoria leaned forward and placed the items back in the box.

"Jack Brenner. He has extensive experience with cold cases. I believe if there is something to be found, he can find it."

Victoria sat back once more and resumed her analysis of Jamie. "Jack is an excellent choice."

Anticipation flared. "Is that a yes?"

"On one condition," Victoria pointed out.

Hesitation slowed Jamie's mental victory celebration. "What condition?"

"The daughter will be notified and asked to participate in the investigation. We're not going to do this without giving her an opportunity for input. In fact, I would prefer she be actively involved."

Jamie nodded. "Fair enough."

"Brief Jackson," Victoria went on. "When he's ready have him reach out to the daughter and make an appointment to discuss the possibility."

Jamie stood. "Very well." She placed the items back into the box and picked it up. "Thank you. You won't regret your decision."

"I'm sure I won't."

VICTORIA SMILED AS the door closed behind Jamie. For a while Victoria had worried about her. Jamie was so young.

The commitment here at the agency was different from her previous work with the government. It was far more personal. Often, the inexperienced in the field of private investigations poured their hearts and souls into the work on a level that was impossible to maintain for any length of time. Victoria knew that her granddaughter would do this. The best investigators always gave their all but paced themselves for the long haul. That skill came with time. Surprisingly, Jamie had found a good balance very quickly.

Having Jamie here had fulfilled Victoria's longtime dream that her grandchildren would one day take over. Both Jamie and her brother Luke had seemed intent on different career paths. To have Jamie make this leap had been an incredible joy. Particularly since Jim, Victoria's son and Jamie and Luke's father, was still helping their mother, Tasha, recover from her horrendous illness, and quite frankly, he had no desire to take the position as head of the agency. He had made himself clear on that point some time ago and had not changed his mind. The need for Jamie to come onboard had never been more apparent, but Victoria had not wanted to push the idea on the girl— young woman.

Jamie was here now and seemed immensely happy with her work. The fact that she had taken the initiative on a somewhat delicate situation warmed Victoria's heart. Jamie was going to make an amazing leader for this agency one day.

Victoria could not wait to share this news with Lucas. Her husband had insisted all along that Jamie was happy at the agency, but Victoria had allowed a few doubts to seep in. Lucas remained convinced that having Kenny— Kendrick Poe—on board at the agency with Jamie had helped to ensure her continued happiness. Kenny, too, was a great asset. Victoria often wondered how long it would be before Jamie and Kenny took their relationship to the next level. Victoria's heart thumped faster at the idea of a Colby wedding.

There were times when her seventh decade of life seemed to fly by so very fast that she couldn't help but wonder about all she would miss when she was gone. But then she reminded herself that it was far more important to stay focused on not missing anything today than to worry about what she might miss tomorrow.

She pushed back her chair and walked to the window overlooking the street below. The Chicago weather was particularly warm, even in July.

She smiled. The future looked exactly as she had hoped it would.

Chapter Two

Aurora, Illinois
Tuesday, July 8
Griffin Residence
Borkshire Lane, 1:30 p.m.

Anne Griffin smiled as she ended the call. The job was hers!

Her smile stretched into a happy, relieved, grateful grin. "I got the job!"

She tossed her cell phone onto her desk, set her hands on her hips and walked to the window that overlooked her small, enclosed backyard. A celebratory cocktail and a few minutes of relaxing was in order, she decided. The weather was perfect, and that new chaise lounge on her little flagstone patio was calling her name.

With a deep breath, she padded to the kitchen and prepared her favorite drink. Three fresh strawberries went into the glass, along with a generous serving of lemonade and then a splash of vodka. Just a little. It was early for a cocktail, but it was nice to celebrate now and then. After all, this was her first really big contract since going out on her own at the beginning of the year.

These last few months had been a bit of an uphill climb, professionally speaking. Thankfully she'd been prepared for a period of little or no income. But recently, knowing her savings would soon be gone had her a little nervous. Luckily, she had also braced herself for the doubts that would arise.

How many times had she second-guessed her decision? Far too many. It was the curse of a worrier.

She lifted her glass in a silent toast. But all those uncertainties were behind her now. Griffin Interior Concepts was officially off the ground and running. Her scant client list was expanding. So far most of the work had been smaller scale—a kitchen or bath remodel, the occasional principal bedroom and one over-the-top screened-in porch. But this contract was big. Really big, as in a whole-house renovation. The owners had narrowed their choices to three designers, and Anne had been one of them. Two weeks ago, all three designers had submitted fully developed plans and cost estimates. To be honest, she'd been incredibly thankful to even be in the running.

And now the job was hers.

She did a happy dance and then sipped her drink. A little sun was in order. Far too much time was spent behind her desk lately so she wandered out to her patio. Her home was an end-unit town house, with a patio slightly larger than most. She had a square of flagstone for entertaining and a little patch of grass. Shrubbery and flowers formed a pleasing border against the fence. It was really quite lovely. She couldn't complain. Frankly, any more than this would take up too much of her time in maintenance. Building a business, she needed every available minute to keep the momentum going. One day, when she had more employees to do the leg work, she wouldn't mind having a larger home and garden.

"One day," she repeated aloud.

With a sigh, she settled onto the chaise lounge and enjoyed her fruity drink. After she figured out a late lunch she would take a drive to the exclusive neighborhood where her first whole-house reno would be taking place. A few more shots of the home wouldn't hurt. Maybe a walk around the block.

Another grin tugged at her lips. Taking on the project would be like buying a major ad campaign. This couple was very involved in the community. The wife was a social media influencer, so she would certainly use the renovation as fodder for her numerous posts and reels. The couple socialized in real life a lot as well. Their big parties were widely known—and promoted on her media pages. Anne couldn't be more delighted at the idea of how much publicity this one job would provide. To top it off, she was being paid particularly well for the work. A truly win-win situation.

For the next few moments, she considered the steps she needed to take moving forward. She would make a call to each of her go-to contractors and see how this job would fit into their schedules. There was at least one floor tile she would need to get ordered as soon as possible. Thankfully the scheduling of contractors wouldn't be much of a problem. The clients were busy people who traveled a good deal of the time, particularly in the summer. So getting the work done wouldn't be nearly as difficult as it was when clients were home, trying to live and/or work around construction. That part was always tricky.

The doorbell drew Anne's attention back to the present. It was a miracle she'd heard it. As she got to her feet she noted that she'd left the French doors ajar, which was likely the only reason she had. Knowing her new client, it could very well be a congratulatory flower delivery.

She walked inside, finished off her drink and put the glass in the sink before making her way to the front door. One of the things she loved about this town home was that the entire downstairs was one large open space. There was a short hallway that led to a powder room and drop zone for coats and shoes, but all else was wide open. The floating staircase to the left of the front door led up to an exposed second-floor hallway and the bedrooms—one of which she had turned into an office.

It was everything she needed while staying in budget.

Budgets were particularly important when deciding to go into business for oneself.

Before opening the door, she checked through the security viewfinder to get a look at the visitor.

Male. Tall. Dark hair. Broad shoulders. Navy trousers with a matching lightweight business jacket, pale blue button-down shirt, open at the throat. No flowers anywhere to be seen.

Salesman, maybe.

Then she spotted the box in his right hand. Perhaps a deliveryman? If so, he was a bit overdressed for the occasion. It wasn't her birthday, so it wouldn't be a surprise gift from one of her colleagues.

"May I help you?" she asked through the door.

"Afternoon, Ms. Griffin." He smiled.

Deep voice. Pleasant smile. Handsome. A little flutter in her belly reminded her that while pinching pennies for this independent business launch, she'd also neglected all forms of social life.

"I'm Jackson Brenner. I work with the Colby Agency."

He removed his wallet from a hip pocket and held his credentials up to the viewfinder. She stared at the photo that was indeed him. "I'd like to speak with you, if you have a few minutes."

The Colby Agency. A frown furrowed her brow. She had no idea what sort of business he represented. "I'm afraid you have me at a disadvantage, Mr. Brenner. I don't know what your agency is or does."

Certainly, she had no clue why someone from said agency would be at her door. Unless he was selling insurance or something else she did not need.

"The Colby Agency is a private investigations firm, ma'am. I'm here about your mother, Mary Morton."

Anne drew back as if the words had been stones flung at her. A barrage of confusing emotions twisted inside her. Mary Morton was dead. Why would anyone be contacting Anne now? Surely there was some mistake.

"I was informed that she passed away." Anne eased closer to the viewfinder once more.

"Yes, ma'am. That's why I'm here. Your mother left some personal items intended for you."

Anne's gaze shifted to the box once more. She bit her lip. From time to time since she was a teenager she had been approached by reporters, even a private detective once. All had wanted to question her about her mother and the murder. None had wanted to help Mary Morton in any way. It was all for documentaries or books that served only the person pursuing the research. The best stories were always about cold-hearted monsters, and the hope had been that Anne would reiterate that idea about her biological mother.

In reality, Anne knew nothing about the murder or her biological mother. She had never met Mary Morton. Obviously when she was born in that prison infirmary she had been with her mother for a brief time. Not for even a moment since then. They had never met and they had never spoken. Anne had nothing to add to the woman's painfully sad story.

"I'm afraid I'm not clear on what it is you're delivering." She still wasn't ready to open the door and deal with whatever this unexpected visit actually involved.

"I understand your hesitancy, ma'am." His voice was soft, his face kind. "But I assure you this is something you will want to see and hear." He shrugged. "Otherwise I wouldn't be knocking on your door. The agency doesn't do this sort of thing unless there is a very good reason."

Anne drew back once more. What could it hurt? She would hear what he had to say, accept the box and then send him on his way. Ten minutes at most. She still had to call her assistant, Lisa, and tell her the good news about the contract. There was much she had to do. A stroll into a past she didn't recall or understand was not part of her agenda for the day.

Determined not to allow this strange development to dampen her spirits, Anne opened the door. *Just get it over with and move on.* Once he was on his way, she could go back to celebrating.

"Come in." She opened the door wider.

He entered, glanced around, then set his gaze on hers. "Thank you."

Anne closed the door and walked to the center of the room where the sofa and two chairs surrounded a coffee table and fronted a fireplace.

"Have a seat." She settled into her favorite chair and mentally braced for whatever he had to say.

He placed the box on the coffee table and lowered onto the sofa.

"What's in the box?" No need to wait for him to begin. The sooner the conversation was started the sooner it would be done.

"Your mother's personal items."

Her gaze shifted from him to the box. It was a relatively small box. Apparently her biological mother's life had been reduced to this. She swallowed, annoyed at the tightness in her throat. "I received a letter from Logan Correctional Center informing me of her death. Why didn't they send this box at that time?" Wasn't that the typical way it was done? Personal effects were mailed to the next of kin.

"Your mother—"

"Wait." She held up a hand. "It's true that Mary Morton was my biological mother." Anne took a moment, drew in a steadying breath. "But that's all she was to me. We never met. Never spoke. She never wrote to me. Twenty-nine years ago, all she left me was alone. I went from the prison infirmary to a hospital and then to a foster family. From there I bounced from one family to the next. No one wanted to adopt the child of a murderer. So, honestly, I genuinely have no desire to receive anything from her now."

Now that she thought about it, why had she even opened the door? All those emotions from her earliest childhood memories flooded her: Disappointment. Sadness. Fear. Hatred. More fear.

He nodded. "I understand how you might feel that way. But my dilemma is that the Colby Agency received a request from Ms. Morton, and we have an obligation to honor it."

Somehow Anne couldn't see her mother's name in the same sentence with the word *honor*, but there it was.

"In that case," she relented, "just get it over with. What's in the box, and why did you feel compelled to hand deliver it?"

The man—Jackson Brenner—reached out and opened the flaps of the box. "Inside you'll find a detailed journal, newspaper clippings and a few items I imagine were precious to your—to Ms. Morton."

Anne stood, crossed the four feet to the table and picked up the box. She took it back to her chair and sat it in her lap. Inside, the item on top was the journal. She picked it up and flipped through the pages. She wanted to remain unaffected, but the handwriting—her mother's handwriting—shifted something deep inside her even when she wanted desperately not to feel anything at all.

She was not your mother. The words echoed through her soul. Somehow holding that journal… She couldn't chase away the idea so easily.

"Five months before you were born," Jackson explained, "your mother was charged with the murder of Neil Reed. All who knew the two, who were engaged at the time, considered them the perfect couple. There hadn't been any trouble between Neil and Mary, and both had good reputations at their places of employment and in the community."

"Until the murder," Anne spoke up, setting the journal aside. Her skin seemed to tingle from touching it. A glutton for punishment, she reached for the next item in the box—newspaper clippings.

"Yes," Jackson agreed. "In her letter to my employer, Ms. Morton urged us to find the truth. She insisted that no one had even tried in all these years. At the time she wrote the letter she was aware that her time was limited. She'd just learned she had cancer. Her request was a final attempt to prod someone into finding the truth. Though it wouldn't help her, she hoped it would be of some comfort to you to learn that your mother was not a murderer."

The impact of his words hit her hard. Anne rode out the unsettling emotions, then grabbed back her protective shield. "Well, I'm afraid she will be very disappointed. You see, when I was nineteen I suddenly felt I needed to know the whole story. So I did a little digging myself. I have to say that I found nothing to indicate she was innocent. In fact, everything I discovered suggested the opposite. I can't imagine that you will find anything different."

"Perhaps I won't." He shrugged. "But I will look. I won't stop until I have irrefutable evidence one way or the other. She deserves that confirmation."

Deserves. Anne considered the idea for a moment. How was it that this stranger could believe a woman he didn't know deserved anything?

"What does this have to do with me?" Anne didn't want to sound uncaring, but frankly, she was. She had no reason to feel anything for this woman. In fact, she remembered well the moment when she had stopped feeling anything. It had been her twelfth birthday. All those years—at every birthday—she had told herself that would be the day her mother would come for her. She would be released from prison, and she would finally come to reclaim the child taken from her.

Except that never happened.

She never even sent a letter offering happy birthday to her only child.

And on her twelfth birthday, after running away from her newest foster home, Anne had understood that her mother was never coming. The fairy tale she had told herself as a child was nothing more than a self-comforting technique designed to keep the overwhelming sadness at bay.

No one was coming—least of all her mother.

"I won't pursue your mother's last request if you ask me not to." Jackson startled her from the painful thoughts. "If you tell me to let it go, I will. Those are my instructions from the top. This investigation won't move forward without your approval. I do, however, believe that if that is your decision, you will one day come to regret it."

Oh, she saw the endgame now. "Am I supposed to pay for this endeavor?" She almost laughed. Please. Absolutely no way. Was this Colby Agency nothing more than some shameful version of ambulance chasers?

"No," he assured her. "There is no fee involved with this investigation. But I do need your approval to move forward. Victoria made that point very clear."

"Victoria?" His boss, she presumed.

"The head of the Colby Agency."

Anne's first inclination was to say no. She did not agree with this ridiculous idea. She did not want the stuff in the box. She surely did not feel an obligation to the woman who gave birth to her.

But then she saw the photo. An old Polaroid-style photograph of a woman holding a tiny baby.

Her, she realized.

This was probably the only photo of her and her mother together that existed. Something pink grabbed her attention then. She touched it. A baby blanket.

The rip in her chest was abrupt, painful. Anne willed the sharp sensation away. The ache…the lost hope and childish desperation refused to go.

"Really," she insisted even as her throat tightened further. "I don't care. Do what she asked. It makes no difference to me." She tossed the photo back into the box and struggled to tamp down the emotions shearing through her.

This woman—this murderer—would not cause her more pain. Not now. Not ever again.

He nodded. "There's just one catch, you see. In order to proceed we need your cooperation."

Her gaze narrowed on the man who had intruded on her day. "What does that mean? My cooperation?"

"Victoria feels strongly that I shouldn't move forward with my investigation unless you agree to be a part of the investigation."

No way. Anne would not go digging around in a past she knew nothing about for a woman who was a stranger to her.

Absolutely no way.

Chapter Three

Anne watched from the front window as Jackson Brenner drove away.

Despite her misgivings, she had assured him that she would have an answer in the morning.

On some level she wanted to simply say no. Mary Morton didn't deserve the time of day from Anne, much less a day or more of her life. The very idea was ludicrous. But in her current emotional state, Anne didn't trust herself to make the right decision. As he so cleverly pointed out, she didn't want to have future regrets.

As soon as the man from the Colby Agency had walked out the door she had called the one person she trusted— her friend and personal assistant, Lisa Gilbert. Lisa was on her way over.

Anne crossed to the chair she had vacated and picked up the box.

The box.

It sounded so ominous…as if her mother's ashes or some dark secret were ensconced inside.

Her mother. Anne moved her head side to side. She

had no mother. This woman—the biological mother—had never been a mother to her. None of the foster moms had been anything more than a supervisor. Anne felt confident there were good foster parents out there. Probably plenty of them. Sadly she had never been placed with a good one. She closed her eyes and pushed away the memories that tried to surface. Maybe her long run of bad luck had been in part due to the attitude she developed by age three, but mostly, she was certain, it was about her being the child of a murderer—born in prison.

No one had wanted her.

Anne forced her eyes open and kicked aside all those painful feelings. She had survived. And eventually she had thrived. All on her own, damn it.

Lips tight with frustration, she picked up the box and carried it to the dining area. Unlike many who kept some sort of decor on the table, Anne left hers clean for the purpose of spreading out her work. The one she'd chosen was larger than her sofa, its size necessary since she used it as a multipurpose piece. Although her office was upstairs, she often worked here with the French doors open so she could enjoy the fresh air. Not this time of year, obviously, because it was too hot. Open doors or not, she regularly used this as a conference table for meetings with clients. With Lisa on her way to *confer*, Anne removed the items from the box and spread them out over the tabletop as if they were samples related to a potential customer.

Flooring, paint, cabinetry… All sorts of sample pieces ended up on her table during a brainstorming session with Lisa or a meeting with clients. Generally, there were photographs of the space in need of a redo. Sometimes there were blueprints. Always there were options, photos from previous projects or magazines or Pinterest, for consideration.

For this unexpected session there were only the things from the box. The journal. A fist formed in Anne's chest. The photographs she'd never seen. Knots tightened in her belly. A dozen or more newspaper clippings. A key. Curiosity joined the mix of emotions. She picked up the key and turned it over. No markings, but there was a number stamped into the metal: 168. Could be an apartment key. Maybe a lockbox key. Anne had no idea.

Then there was the necklace. Delicate silver chain with a locket. There were two tiny photos inside. One was of a woman she believed to be Mary Morton with a young man. The other was even harder to distinguish other than the fact that there appeared to be three women huddled together.

Maybe there was something in the journal about the locket.

The pink blanket… Anne pulled it from the box and smoothed her hand over it. Was this the blanket she'd been wrapped in after she was born? Tiny white flowers dotted the soft pink fabric. She set it aside.

These items represented the life of Mary Morton. A murderer who had died in prison at the age of fifty-two after nearly twenty-nine years served.

The doorbell sounded, and Anne jumped. She pressed her hand to her chest and forced a breath. This whole thing had her far too jumpy. Of all the surprises she had hoped might come into her life, this was not one of them.

She hurried to the door, checked the viewfinder. *Lisa.* When Anne had called her, she'd told her friend first about the business news. Like her, Lisa had been ecstatic. She wanted to celebrate. Then Anne had spilled about the unexpected visitor. Lisa couldn't believe it. On some level, Anne still didn't.

She unlocked the door and wrenched it open. Anne had

gotten so caught up in the contents of the box she hadn't realized enough time had passed for Lisa to be here already. "Thanks for coming. This is…" She took a breath. "This is something I just can't do alone."

There were few things Anne had ever felt she wasn't prepared to face alone—God knew she'd had no real choice in the matter—but this… This was different. She really needed an objective voice here.

Rather than immediately respond, Lisa grabbed her in a hug and squeezed. "I'm so sorry this is happening."

For a few seconds Anne sagged into her dear friend's embrace. Then she drew back. "It's okay. I just need to be sure that I make a decision that won't come back to haunt me in the future."

As much as she hated to admit it, Mr. Brenner had been right about that. Mary Morton was dead. Anne wanted to put her and the nightmare legacy behind her. But first, she needed to do this…maybe. The final decision was still up in the air.

Lisa closed the door and locked it. "Of course you do. This is a big deal. It's like if you don't do it, you'll always be wondering. And if you do…" She shrugged. "It's an enormous decision."

Her friend was right, even if Anne didn't want to acknowledge it. If she simply said no without further consideration, she might truly regret the decision in the future. Why not just do this and move on once and for all? Sounded simple enough. Well, maybe not simple, but straightforward.

Doubt nudged her. Or not. One way or the other she had only a few hours to make a decision with which she could live.

"Would you like something to drink?" Anne led the

way to the dining table. "I've already had a cocktail, but I could go for another."

Lisa dropped her shoulder bag onto a chair and set her attention on Anne. "Have you had lunch?"

Her friend knew her too well. "I was just about to when that guy arrived." She stared at the items spread across her table. "I forgot all about food after that."

"I'm ordering pizza. Now."

Anne didn't argue. She needed to eat, and she sure didn't need another cocktail. At least not until after she'd eaten. If there ever was one, *this* was definitely a two-or three-cocktail afternoon.

She was supposed to be celebrating this new big deal. Instead she was fretting over the past.

"Okay." Finished with the pizza order, Lisa tossed her phone onto the table, pulled out a chair and settled into it. "Let's see what we have here."

While her friend studied the items from the box, Anne went up to her office and grabbed the portfolio for her new clients. In spite of all else, she smiled. Not just clients, she amended, but her big-deal clients who were going to make this little firm a household name. At least in the greater Chicago area.

Hopefully.

At the bottom of the stairs, she contemplated her friend. With this new contract, it was time to make the offer she'd been secretly putting together. If her friend accepted, she and Lisa would become partners.

Smiling to herself, Anne made her way back to the dining table. Lisa was studying the newspaper clippings, her face lined in concentration. She was such a great assistant. Always going above and beyond. Anne knew without a doubt that she would make an amazing partner as well.

"She was young," Lisa said without looking up.

"Yeah." Anne sat down at the table. "She'd just finished her master's in education. She was starting her third year of teaching at an elementary school when the murder happened."

Lisa glanced at her. "You look a lot like her." Anne nodded. "I mean, *a lot* like her."

"I know. It used to bother me," she admitted. "But I blocked it from my mind. In fact, I haven't thought about her—really thought about her—in years. It seems surreal that this is happening." She dropped into a chair across the table from Lisa. "I'm still reeling at the shock. I feel torn in a dozen directions. Afraid. Seriously, I feel like a kid who doesn't want to look under the bed."

"Understandable." Lisa placed the newspaper clipping back on the table. "Give me the gist of what happened based on what you actually know."

Anne moistened her lips, took a breath and launched into the story. "Mary Morton met Neil Reed in high school. They'd known each other forever, and they were sweethearts all through senior year and through college—though long distance. Mary went to Wheaton with a major in education, and Neil was a student at Northwestern's Pritzker School of Law. They were only an hour or so apart, but still, it made living together difficult. Neil shared an apartment with three other students while Mary got a small studio apartment without roommates, which allowed them to spend their weekends and holidays together."

Lisa frowned. "How do you know those specifics?"

"When I was nineteen I watched a documentary about them." Anne turned her hands up. "I went through something. Maybe because I was in college and the reality of adulthood had hit me hard. I felt like I needed to know all

I could." She surveyed the items on the table. "But to tell you the truth, the only thing I learned was what the police discovered and released to the public. There was quite a bit about the trial but basically nothing after that. No really deep details from before or after, you know. There wasn't a lot of attention on the case—ever. That one low-level documentary was the only thing I ever found, and I can't be sure everything in it was accurate."

Lisa nodded. "I get it." She gestured to the journal. "Anything in there?"

"I don't know. I haven't looked beyond the first page. It's almost like I don't want to look." She smirked. "That maybe I'll find something that changes everything—as if the possibility that nothing I thought I knew was right. I'm not sure I'm adequately prepared for that journey. Pathetic, huh?"

"Not pathetic at all." Lisa studied her for a moment. "Did you ever try to visit her?"

Anne looked away. The answer to that question was maybe the most painful of all. Finally, she turned to her friend. "Yes. During that same time, when I was a sophomore in college. After the documentary. I realized I had so many questions. I wanted to talk to her. To know the truth or at least her side of it. So I went to the prison. But she wouldn't see me." She laughed dryly. "No matter how many times I went, she wouldn't see me. Eventually I stopped going, and that was when I decided I was never looking back. I told myself Mary Morton was nothing to me and I was nothing to her. End of story."

"That's really awful. My first thought is what mother would deny her only child a few minutes of her time when time was all she had." Lisa shook her head. "But the truth is what I'm getting from you is that you've never heard her side of what happened."

The words shook Anne just a little. "Well, no, I suppose not. I mean, I read all these back then." She indicated the clippings with a sweep of her arm. "And everything else that was available ten years ago online. Like I said, I watched the documentary. But that's it. There was nothing else. She wouldn't talk to me, so what was I supposed to do?"

"You did what you could. The situation is not your fault." Lisa surveyed the items on the table once more. "All right, then. As your best friend, this is my advice, for what it's worth. Read the journal. Get her side of things or whatever she wants you to know from those pages. Then decide if you want to do this thing—for you, not for her. None of this is about her anymore. She's gone. This, Anne, is about you."

The suggestion made almost too much sense.

"That's a good idea." Anne's gaze fixed on the journal. "I can read it tonight and then give him my answer in the morning as promised."

The doorbell rang.

Anne jumped, almost laughed. She rarely had unscheduled visitors. Most of the time appearances at her door were either a client or Lisa. Today she felt like she was living at Grand Central Station.

Lisa stood. "That will be the pizza."

Of course. Right. Anne had entirely forgotten the pizza order.

While Lisa went to the door, Anne gathered the clippings and placed them back in the box. She'd read all those articles on the internet. No need to read them again. The locket and key she decided she might need. She held that one photo of the two of them for a moment, stared at the image of herself as a newborn. Then she studied the vague smile on Mary Morton's face. Anne traced the image with the pad of her thumb. The woman in the photo, nearly five years younger at the time than Anne was now, looked happy and at the same time terrified. Why wouldn't she be the latter? She was facing life in prison, and she'd just given birth to a child.

Mary's parents were dead. She'd been accused of murder, and certainly her friends had turned their backs on her. She'd been alone…

Anne knew that feeling all too well.

"Here we go." Lisa placed the pizza box in the center of the table. The scent of freshly baked dough and cheese and meats wafted from it.

Anne tucked the photograph into the journal, then put both, as well as the locket and key, into the box. "I'll get paper plates."

"And cocktails," Lisa reminded her.

Anne smiled in spite of herself. "Coming up!"

She arranged paper plates on the table. Made sure a roll of paper towels was handy. Then she prepared two more of those lovely strawberry-lemonade cocktails—adding extra vodka this time. For a little while they gorged on pizza and sipped their drinks.

"If I decide to do this," Anne said, a new worry niggling at her, "I can't say for sure if I'll be losing a day or a week, and this is really not a good time to be doing that."

Lisa smiled. "If it's our new big client you're worried about—don't. I can handle things for a few days while you do what you have to do."

Admittedly, the idea was troubling. They had just landed this amazing opportunity, and the thought of suddenly being unavailable was terrifying. Anne couldn't help wondering if her distant past was really worth the risk.

That part was still up in the air.

"I know one hundred percent that I can trust you to go above and beyond. That's not a question. But, just to make sure we're on the same page, let's go over everything." Anne reached for the portfolio she'd brought down from her office. "Of course, you can call me any time no matter where I am."

Did that mean she had made up her mind already?

The idea had her pulse quickening.

"Going over the details is a good idea," Lisa agreed, drawing her back to the here and now. "We're only human." She grinned. "We can't be perfect all the time."

Anne grinned. "Just most of it."

They grabbed more slices of pizza and continued eating as they discussed the details.

"I'll call the contractors and suppliers," Anne said. "Make sure we're good there and send you an email with the dates they give me."

"I can lay out a schedule and pass it along to all parties," Lisa suggested before biting into the thick-crusted slice of pie.

"Add reminders to our calendar." Anne then took a bit of her own slice.

"Will do." Lisa held up her half empty glass. "To the future."

Anne tapped her glass against it. "The future."

She just hoped it wasn't about to turn into a nightmare.

7:30 p.m.

ANNE HAD TOUCHED base with all the necessary contractors and suppliers, then passed along the results of her conversations to Lisa by phone and via email. There appeared to be no glitches to worry about with scheduling. During the calls to the suppliers, she had ordered the items—like the special floor tile—that required additional lead time.

Now, a fourth cocktail in hand—she never had four cocktails in a single day, but somehow this day called for it—she settled onto the sofa to begin reading the journal.

Deep breath. This is the right decision. She opened the slightly worn cover and stared at her mother's handwriting. Then she sipped her cocktail to wash down the lump that had risen in her throat.

Reading this journal was a necessary journey into whatever had been happening when her mother committed murder—or not. Like the documentary, it would be one-sided. That said, in order to have both sides of the issue she had no choice but to do this.

It was often said that the truth would set you free. Anne had no idea if that was true. Mostly the only thing this particular truth had done for her in the past was to make her a pariah. Kids at school had tortured her. Even foster parents had treated her differently. Some had been afraid of her, while others had decided she was something with which to be toyed, and not in a good way. After all she was the daughter of a monster. Why not treat her like a little monster? She'd been mistreated and abused…but mostly she had been neglected and unloved.

No child should grow up believing he or she was alone and unloved.

But it happened all too often.

Maybe that was why she had never managed a long-term relationship. She hadn't been able to trust anyone to care for her or to love her properly as a child. How could she possibly trust anyone as an adult? The answer was she could not.

She'd had the occasional date. Even an official boyfriend once or twice, but nothing lasted more than a month or two. The first one had only been interested in sex, as were most teenage boys. The other was obsessed with true crime and, as it turned out, only dated her in hopes of learning the dirty details.

Nothing ever lasted.

"Get over it," she muttered. This was her life.

To her credit she had made the most of it, and damn it, she was proud of her accomplishments. Once this unexpected bump in the road was behind her, she wasn't looking back ever again. Forward would be her only direction.

Satisfied that she had made the right decision, she began to read, starting with the *Present Day* note that had been added to page one by taping pink pieces of notepaper on top.

Chapter Four

Sorry—this part is the present, but I had already begun by writing *Thirty Years Ago* when I realized I needed to explain, and it's ink so… Oh well. I didn't have a diary or a journal back then—when I was young and in love and pregnant with you. I was far too busy planning my wedding and working to worry about writing anything down. Besides, who worries about the worst-possible situation actually happening at the most unlikely time? Not me apparently. This I now deeply regret. It's the second biggest regret of my life. It would have been so much easier if I'd kept a log of the details. Oh well, hindsight is twenty-twenty, as they say.

Although it has been three decades since these events occurred, I realized just recently that it was necessary for me to put certain parts in writing. I skip around a little, ensuring that I get the most relevant dates and information down. With my recent cancer diagnosis, my time and energy are limited, and in truth, I can't say that I won't go to sleep tonight and not wake up. If I am able to finish, I hope this journal makes it to you. I know I don't deserve your time or your attention, but this isn't for me. This is for *you*. I want you to know the truth so that whatever bad feelings about who you are and where you came from will be alleviated to some degree.

Also, no matter what you believe, I have always loved you. I loved you before you were born, and I love you now. Your father loved you as well. What happened was the sort of nightmare you might see in a movie or read in a book. It was not something I ever dreamed would happen to us. To this day I wonder how it could have happened without at least some sort of warning.

Anyway, I hope you won't be put off or ignore this journal simply because you hate me. Or perhaps you feel nothing for or about me. Please know that I understand. If I were you I would hate me too. But please keep reading. I beg you to keep reading. Find the truth…for *you*.

I'm sure you're likely wondering why now. Why did I wait all this time to contact you in any way? After all, you came to the prison several times, and I refused to see you. That is my first and biggest regret in this life. Once it was clear an appeal was not going to happen, I thought I was doing the right thing by staying out of your life and never allowing you to be part of mine. It was the most difficult decision of my existence. I wanted you to be free of me and the regret and pain I carried. And the stigma, of course. I noticed you changed your name, and I'm glad. You deserve to be free of any connection to the horror that was my final year of freedom.

I'm sure you're laughing as you read. Why wouldn't the murder be my biggest regret? The answer is painfully simple. I did not murder anyone. I swear this to you. I am innocent. I don't expect you to believe me, which is why

I have started this journal. When it's done I'm sending all that I have left along with the journal to the Colby Agency. Another inmate told me that the Colby Agency are the best private investigators. Not that she ever used them, but she knows people who know people. I did a little research on the internet, and it seems to be true. In the end, I'm counting on someone at the Colby Agency to find the truth. You see, I don't know who killed the love of my life. Neil's murder, I am confident, was committed by someone close to us. I can tell you the people I believe did this, but I cannot prove anything. My hope is that the Colby Agency can do what I and the police could not. Actually, I'm praying they will. Again, not for me, but for *you*.

Anyway, here goes. Please, please keep reading.

May 5
Thirty Years Ago

I HAD JUST found out I was pregnant. I was so thrilled. I can't even find the words to describe how amazing it felt. I couldn't wait to tell Neil. He was going to be over the moon. Although we had intended to wait until we were a little more settled—at least until after the wedding—to start a family, it didn't matter. This was amazing. And maybe under the circumstances we could forego the bigger wedding his mother had planned and just elope. That would have actually been pretty perfect.

We had been looking at houses with our best friends, Eve Redford and Kevin Langston. Eve and I had known each other since we were children. She met Kevin at a sorority party sophomore year, and they have been a couple since. It was nice that Kevin and Neil hit it off. Eve and I couldn't have been happy unless our future husbands were friends. That's the way best friends were supposed to be, you know. We wanted to do things together...to be friends forever. We had lost the third member of our bestie trio—Carin Carter. She was one of us until she wasn't. I don't know what happened, but one day she just decided we couldn't be friends anymore. She had not spoken to me or to Eve in weeks. We later learned she moved to Chicago and never looked back. Which is all the more reason Eve and I understood we had to stick together. We would never allow anything to come between us. Best friends forever.

Except something did...something unthinkable...something straight out of a horror movie. Something I never saw coming.

SIDE NOTE: YOU SHOULD know that what I felt that long ago May all changed by August of that same year. Eve Redford was not my friend after all. I later wondered if who she really was is the reason Carin left. I can't be sure about that. But what I can say with absolute certainty is that Eve Redford was not who she appeared to be. I imagine she is still that same deceitful person. Did she murder my sweet Neil? I don't know, but I believe she knows who did. Whatever you do, be careful around her. Do not trust her under any circumstances. I have no proof...no evidence whatsoever. But what I can say is that I know in my heart with utter certainty that someone close to me murdered my future husband—your father. I just don't know which of the three—Eve or Kevin or, maybe, Carin.

If I could have figured out the motive maybe I could have uncovered the truth. I can only assume that the evil person who killed him did not want me to continue being happy. There simply is no other explanation. Neil was the kindest, most honorable man I have ever known. No one, and I mean no one, could have found a single thing bad in him that warranted harm, much less murder.

Obviously, the killer didn't want the man I loved because he or she killed him. She didn't want the child I carried. Otherwise he or she would have taken you in under the guise of friendship. I just don't know. The one thing I know with absolute certainty is that you cannot trust those three or anyone close to them. Bottom line: Do not trust anyone who was close to me. And please, please be careful.

Chapter Five

Anne sat in her car for a while. She'd been sitting here ten minutes already. When she called Jackson Brenner she told him she would arrive at his hotel at nine. And she was here, but somehow she wasn't ready to get out and do this thing. It was a foolish reaction, but there it was.

He had offered to come to her house, but she'd preferred to do this in neutral territory. For now, she wanted—no, needed—this to be separate from her real life. She was Anne Griffin, a survivor. A college graduate against all odds who had started her own business. A girl who had built something out of nothing.

This…*this* thing from before she was born had no place in her real life, and she intended to keep it that way until she knew more. She had worked far too hard to become her own person—not the child of a murderer—to risk that reputation. Despite those feelings and her determination, on some level she understood that if she didn't do this the mystery and shame of that past would forever follow her like a lost and unwanted shadow. She needed it behind her permanently and irrevocably.

Deep breath.

With effort, she opened the car door and got out. Squaring her shoulders, she elbowed the door closed and tapped the handle to secure it. A soft beep confirmed the vehicle was locked.

Anne strode to the entrance of the hotel and hesitated long enough to draw in another deep, solidifying breath before entering the lobby. She followed a corridor to the elevator and then rode up to the second floor. Heart pounding, she walked along the upstairs corridor until she reached the room number he'd given her. Then she knocked on the door.

This was it. The point of no return.

The slab of stained and polished wood opened instantly as if he'd been standing on the other side waiting for her arrival.

He smiled. "Ms. Griffin, come in."

He stepped away, giving her space. She entered the room and closed the door. She was really doing this. He'd offered to meet her in the lobby or the parking lot, but she had wanted to do this in private. Besides, if she couldn't trust this man in his hotel room she certainly couldn't trust him as a near constant companion for the next day…or few days.

Go big or go home.

She had used that motto throughout her post-college struggle to create her own company. No doubting herself. She could do this. She had to do this. Moving on required this one big step.

"Would you like to sit?" He gestured to the table and

chairs that fronted the lone, large window. "Coffee? Anything?"

A carafe and cups, along with two bottles of water, sat on the table.

She walked to the table and sat. "No coffee for me." She did, however, accept a bottle of water. Her throat was bone dry.

"I presume you read the journal?" He eased into a chair at the table, took the other bottle of water.

"I did." She twisted off the cap and had a sip to moisten her throat.

"What's your decision, then?"

"To be honest…" She looked him square in the eyes. He had nice eyes. "I'm still torn. Part of me feels the whole thing is preposterous. But I decided to give your agency the benefit of the doubt. The Colby Agency has a stellar reputation." She had done some deep digging on the agency last night and been duly impressed. "Since you decided to take the case, I'm confident you see something I cannot."

He nodded. "We do."

She held the bottle tighter, considered another swallow. "Please, tell me—what is it that you see?"

His blue eyes searched hers for a moment before he answered. He really did have nice eyes. "Holes. We see holes."

"In the investigation, or in Mary Morton's story?"

He shrugged. "Both, to some degree, but primarily in the investigation. We're of the opinion that your mother was railroaded into the conviction. That said, we can't assure you that she was innocent and wrongly convicted, but we feel there are serious enough questions to doubt her guilt."

Anne's chest tightened. "So you believe this can be proven one way or the other even now…three decades later."

"Yes."

He seemed so certain. How could he be based on the journal that a convicted murderer had written in her final days of life? "I don't see how. I mean, yes, her story does suggest the possibility of other suspects, and certainly she insists on her innocence. But how could the police have gotten it so wrong?"

For a long moment he studied her as if attempting to determine how best to answer her question. After a bit he said, "The police are only human. They make mistakes. Once in a while a member of that upstanding group decides to do something bad. Maybe because he's just not a good guy or maybe for the money. Either way, no unit or agency is exempt from the occasional bad apple or mistake. Then again, the detective who investigated the case was fairly young. The issue may have been nothing more than inexperience."

"He was thirty-two," Anne argued. She wasn't even thirty yet. Thirty-two didn't seem so young to her.

"But he'd only been a detective for two years—that's the issue, in my opinion. He was inexperienced in this sort of investigation."

The idea took her aback. "Are you saying he had never investigated a murder before?"

"He had—twice, in fact. But both were cut-and-dry cases where the evidence was clear and the suspects more than apparent—one even came with a confession. The Reed case was complicated with no clear-cut evidence. There should have been a seasoned detective assigned to the case."

Anne couldn't sit any longer. She stood. Paced the length of the room. "Then why did her attorney have trouble trying for an appeal? I mean, if the lack of a thorough investigation was so evident, it seems to me an appeal should have been almost automatic."

"The attorney is another bone of contention, in our opinion," Brenner explained. "He was a public defender. Not to say there aren't plenty of great attorneys in a public defender's office, but this one was also really young, with few cases under his belt. Worse, he was overworked—as most are. The circumstances were ripe for failure."

He turned his hands up. "As for appeals, they're granted when there is proof of ineffective counsel, prosecutorial or jury misconduct, or maybe some sort of evidence that was left out or newly discovered evidence—something that suggests the defendant deserves a second chance at proving her innocence. All the attorney or the judge had to do in order to deny an appeal was to say there was no legal standing for appeal—which he did because there was nothing brought to his attention that would suggest otherwise. The attorney should have been helping her find what she needed to persuade the judge."

Anne paused in her pacing and allowed a deeper breath. "What you're saying is that whatever happened, Mary Morton had lost before the investigation and the trial even began?"

"That's what I'm saying."

The notion sat like a load of rocks on her shoulders. "What are the chances you can actually find the truth?" She held up a hand before he could answer. "I'm not asking if you can overturn the verdict. What good would that do at this point? I'm asking if you realistically believe you can uncover what really happened."

He stood, pushed in his chair, then pressed her with his gaze. "If you allow me, I will find the truth. Do not doubt it. The Colby Agency hired me because I have a knack for solving cold cases." He shrugged. "You don't know me, and this is a sensitive situation, so I get why you feel hesitant. But know this—if you allow me to look into the case, I will find the answers. If the truth is what you're looking for, whatever that truth is, I will give it to you when I'm finished."

If she'd had any doubts when she walked into this room, he had satisfied those uncertainties. Whatever else Jackson Brenner was, the man was convincing. "Then let's get this done."

Jack had worried when he left Anne Griffin's home yesterday that she wouldn't want to move forward with the investigation. Then, when she'd showed up this morning he had still felt on some level that she wasn't fully convinced it was the right thing to do. Whether he had persuaded her or she'd talked herself into it, he was glad the answer was yes.

This was the kind of case he liked best—one where there was an opportunity to see justice done in an unjust situation.

"Thank you," he said, relieved. "For trusting me."

She gave a vague nod. "What do we do next?"

"I would suggest we take your car back to your place and go to Crystal Lake together. We can discuss the case during the drive."

A frown marred her brow. "I would feel better taking my car."

He got it. Frankly, he would have been surprised if she'd agreed to ride with him, a total stranger. "No problem. We'll drive to Crystal Lake. I've reserved two connecting rooms at the Water's Edge Hotel. Once we're settled in, we'll begin by taking a tour of the area—where Mary

Morton and Neil Reed lived. Where their friends lived then and now. Where they worked, past and present."

"We'll get the lay of the land, so to speak," she suggested.

"Yes. After that we'll go over what the agency has found related to the friends your mother—Mary mentioned in the journal."

"We can't do that part now?" Her expression had taken on a decidedly interested appearance. "I'd really like to know what you've found."

He indicated the table and the chairs they had abandoned. "Why not? Since we're driving separately, it'll give you something to think about en route."

The drive was just over an hour. If she had details to consider hopefully she wouldn't have time to doubt her decision to dive in.

She eased into the chair she'd deserted, and he did the same.

"Coffee?" He'd had two cups already, so he was set.

Anne held up a hand. "I don't think my nerves can handle more caffeine. I had two cups before driving over here."

He smiled. "I'm regretting that second cup I downed as well."

Her face told him she was ready to listen to something beyond small talk. She was even more attractive in person than in the photos he had seen. Her brown hair was long. It swept from a side part and hung around her shoulders. But her eyes were the most flattering asset in his opinion. Deep chocolate brown. Wide and expressive.

"So…" She dragged out the one syllable.

Jack snapped to attention, kicking himself for getting caught up in analyzing her. "So, Mary Morton's best friend, Eve Redford, married the year after the trial. She married

Kevin Langston—her boyfriend at the time of Neil Reed's murder. Kevin went on to do the bigger things he touted as his plan back in law school at the University of Chicago—according to interviews I watched from ten years ago. He worked as head legal counsel for one of the top research companies, BioTech, for the first nine years after law school, then he ran for the state senate. He served there for two terms and then ran for the US Senate, which is where he has served since. His wife, Eve, has made a career as a socialite, though she started out as a social worker." He chuckled. "A bit of a turnaround for her. I would say by her many efforts to show up in the papers and on social media that she loves every minute of it."

"What about Carin Carter?" Anne asked. "According to the journal, she parted ways with Mary and Eve before the murder. There was some sort of falling out, I presume."

"She did. The reasons for the parting of ways remains unknown, but Carin left Crystal Lake and married an investor in Chicago. She worked as a secretary in various state government offices, eventually becoming a personal assistant to the Illinois governor at the time. By then her husband had passed away and she'd inherited a small fortune. This is where things start to twist backward a bit. When Kevin Langston got elected to the US Senate, Carin joined him there as a personal assistant. The two have worked together since. If you peruse photos of the Langstons online, you'll find Carin somewhere in the background in most of them. Though none ever show Carin and Eve looking all chummy the way they once did when they were younger."

"I tried searching for Carin online." Anne visibly relaxed as they talked. "I didn't find much of anything."

"That's because she goes by her married name—Wallace. She never used her maiden name for anything relevant to her work in politics, so considering the timing, most everything about her that hit and stuck on the internet as it evolved has always been under the name Wallace. Her life as a Carter was during the internet's infancy, so it's not unusual that you didn't find anything."

"Then those three are back together."

"For the past decade or so, yes."

Anne took a minute to evaluate the information he'd passed along. "What are your thoughts about the three, based on what you know at this point?"

He smiled. "You know the old saying—you don't get far in politics without a few skeletons in your closet. Does that mean that Kevin Langston or his personal assistant, Carin Carter Wallace, is guilty of murder or an accessory to murder? Who knows. It tells me that they're fearless on some level. Not afraid to face negativity or tough battles. They're determined and maybe a little on the ruthless side. As for the wife, Eve, I would say the same. None have had so much as a traffic ticket. Can we be sure they've never done anything illegal because of the lack of negative hits? Not at all. But as for what this indicates relative to our investigation, we're looking at people who are high profile, have some level of loyalty in their community and who have everything to lose."

"We're facing an uphill battle," Anne surmised.

"We are. But all any of this ultimately suggests is that we have no specific thing to look at. No particular time frame beyond that of the murder. Which dictates that we must go back to the beginning and trace these people and what they did, who they did it with and what resulted from their actions until we find what we're looking for. It takes a little longer, but the result is the same."

Anne's slim shoulders sagged. "This may take a while."

He couldn't pretend otherwise. "It's possible that it will take some time, yes. But in my experience, whenever an investigation begins word gets around pretty quickly. Once that happens anyone who has something to hide will get nervous. When people get nervous they make mistakes."

She nodded slowly as understanding sank in. "They do things they might not otherwise do in an effort to protect themselves."

He grinned. "They do. The more nervous they get, the more risks they take, which allows for more noticeable mistakes. That's when we'll start to see whatever one or all are hiding. That," he emphasized, "is when the real story will start to emerge."

A blink, followed by another and then another warned that her emotions were getting the better of her. "I…" She took a moment, then pressed her fingertips to her eyes. "I didn't want to do this." She met his gaze, her dark brown eyes liquid with the mounting emotion. "But after I read the journal, I felt like I had to know in order to get on with my life without this…this nightmarish history hanging around my neck."

He wanted to reach out and squeeze her hand, give her a pat on the shoulder…something to comfort her, but that wouldn't be a good move. He imagined that trust wasn't easily gained with this woman. "I—all of us at the Colby Agency—recognize how difficult this must be for you. In truth, I wrestled with the idea of including you in the investigation. My boss, Victoria, insisted, but I wasn't so sure it was the right thing to do."

Anne searched his face, hers uncertain. "What changed your mind?"

"The more I looked at the case as a whole, I realized

something important. As much as Mary Morton wanted the truth to come out—as insistent as she was that she was innocent—this really was never about her. She had accepted her fate. Which is why she stopped fighting the appeals process. It's why she refused to see you when you became of age. She didn't want you to live the rest of your life with this thing hovering in the background like a dark cloud ready to rain on you at the worst possible time."

Anne visibly held her breath...waited for him to go on.

He shook his head, dead certain in his assessment. "As time went on she recognized that there was only one way to make this right. Then she learned of the cancer and that her time was short and she grew desperate, which is why she contacted the agency. But this was not about her. She confirmed as much in her journal. This is, and always has been, about *you*."

The mixture of emotions on Anne's face spoke loudly and clearly of her understanding. She got it, and she appeared prepared to do this for herself and maybe even for her mother.

Chapter Six

The rooms were on the second floor and had balconies that overlooked the water. Not such a bad way to spend the next few days. The community of Johnsburg was one of many smaller ones that surrounded Crystal Lake.

Anne wandered from the closed sliding door that led onto the balcony back to the queen-size bed that stood in the center of the room. She opened the small suitcase she had tossed there. She had packed for a stay through the weekend. Being home by Monday was, in her mind, a hard deadline.

Not that she couldn't nudge it deeper into next week if necessary, but she preferred to be home by then. Since going out on her own she had never spent more than a day or two from work. Lisa would handle things. No need, really, to worry about the business, but somehow she couldn't help herself.

Jackson Brenner had been right, she realized. He'd given her a lot to think about on the drive here. It hadn't taken that long. Just over an hour. She'd spent that time wondering why none of her mother's supposed closest friends had checked on Anne after she was moved into foster care. She imagined it was possible one or the other had attempted to take her in and had been turned down. Anne couldn't see any reason that would have happened. The more likely scenario was that no one had tried. None testified on Mary's behalf. Given their testimony, why in the world would any have wanted to welcome her child into their lives? Eve Redford (now Langston) and Kevin Langston had been called as defense witnesses, but their testimony had been damaging rather than helpful. Carin Carter, now Wallace, had been out of the picture by then.

Was the lack of support from close friends because Mary had been guilty?

Apparently so—in their minds anyway.

Anne pushed the thoughts away for the moment and removed the clothes from her bag. She hung up the tees and jeans along with the two more businesslike blouses she had added at the last moment. One pair of dress pants and two pairs of jeans. She'd worn her favorite sneakers and packed a pair of leather loafers to go with the dressier attire.

Her cosmetics bag she stored in the bathroom. Not that she wore that much makeup. Mascara and a very basic foundation. Occasionally she added a little blush, so she'd brought that too. Makeup and nail polish weren't her things. She preferred simple and easy to maintain. A hairbrush and deodorant along with a toothbrush and paste were necessary.

The skin lotion she used at night was her only fragrance. And it was so subtle no one ever noticed it.

But that was Anne. Simple. Basic. Rarely noticed beyond her design skills.

She thought of the man in the next room. He was tall, broad shouldered. Very nice eyes. They were kind, expressive. He had a nice smile too. Most important, he seemed really good at his work. She supposed the next few days would tell the tale on that one. She had no reason to expect otherwise given that the Colby Agency had such a prestigious reputation. She'd actually been surprised at what a big deal the agency was. The fact that they had taken up her mother's case was almost shocking. Anne felt confident it wasn't for any sort of accolades—and certainly not for money.

Maybe it was because they liked championing the underdog.

A soft knock on the door drew her in that direction. She checked the viewfinder. Her partner for this endeavor. *Time to get this show started.* She took a deep breath and opened the door. "Let me grab my purse and I'm ready."

"Lunch first, or straight into the tour?"

Brenner waited in the door while she grabbed her shoulder bag from the desk. Her stomach said eat, but her brain wanted to get on with what they'd come to do. Her brain generally won out in these sorts of debates, which was why Lisa was constantly after her about forgetting to eat.

"If it's okay," she said as she approached the door once more, "we can start the tour and eat a little later."

"Absolutely." He held up a hand, two protein bars fisted there. "I thought you might say that."

She accepted one of the bars. "Thank you." She opened the wrapper as they walked to the stairs. Her stomach had decided to remind her that she actually was hungry.

By the time they reached the lobby she had scarfed down the bar. Brenner grabbed a couple of bottles of water from the machine in the niche near the exit and tossed one to her. Funny how quickly she was beginning to really like this guy.

In the lot he opened the passenger-side door of his car and waited for her to climb in. Once he'd closed the door and settled behind the steering wheel she asked, "What should I call you? Do you prefer Mr. Brenner or Jackson?"

Seemed like she would have asked or he would have said before now. But it had been a strange twenty odd hours. Maybe he had and she'd simply forgotten.

"Most people call me Jack," he said as he backed out of the parking slot.

"Jack it is, then." She watched as he navigated from the lot and onto the road. "Everyone calls me Anne. My name is actually Marianne but I've never gone by that."

"So, Anne." He glanced at her, smiled. "What made you decide to keep your first name when you changed your last name?"

She considered the question and the passing landscape as he drove. "It was the last name and all the baggage it carried that I wanted to get away from. The other didn't seem relevant at the time."

"You could have used your father's last name."

A valid point. "The newspapers and online articles all quoted Mary's friends as saying that Neil Reed was her longtime boyfriend and future husband and, of course, my father, but he wasn't named on the birth certificate. I don't know if it was an error due to the circumstances." She shrugged. "I mean, being born in a prison isn't exactly an ideal situation. But, in the end, I opted for something completely different. I read a book once with a character named Anne Griffin and..." She shrugged. "I guess it stuck with me and it certainly took me out of the situation altogether."

"I get that." He flashed her a smile as he turned onto

Big Hollow Road. "I'm sure, as you say, the birth certificate was an error. Mary never deviated in her certainty that Neil Reed was your father."

"No one else questioned it either, to my knowledge. I've always assumed that made it true." She turned her attention to the landscape then. They were nearly *there*...to the place where her parents had lived before disaster struck.

Mostly trees and houses dotted both sides of the road until they reached the little town of Round Lake. Johnsburg, Round Lake—they were all bedroom communities near Crystal Lake. All within a few minutes driving distance of each other.

He made the turn onto Washington Street and then onto Fairlawn Drive before he started to slow. "This is the place."

If they had turned in the opposite direction on Washington Street, Fairlawn would have taken them to the waterfront homes on Lake Shore Drive.

But this was no waterfront home, and it was nothing like Lake Shore Drive.

This was a little house built eighty or more years ago. It looked like a rehab special that no one had decided to tear down but obviously should have. The narrow lot was overgrown. It was easy to see why anyone would just pass it by and never consider a rehab or rebuild.

This was where the woman who had given birth to her had lived when her life went to hell in the proverbial handbasket.

"Wow. Looks as if no one has lived here in decades." A real dump. The photo from the newspaper back then hadn't shown it this way. It had been a neat little cottage surrounded by blooming flowers and mature trees. The tiny lawn had been well kept. The paint hadn't been peeling.

"I spoke to a clerk in the property office," Jack told her, "and she says the place was and still is owned by Neil Reed's father. They've sent warnings about the condition of the property, but he never does anything. Just last week they labeled it condemned."

"Why haven't they razed it? Don't cities do that in extreme cases where owners refuse to take the proper action?" In her line of work, she had heard about those sorts of situations, especially in neighborhoods being gentrified. Or under consideration for gentrification. Failure to pay taxes and/or to properly maintain a property often resulted in the city taking action—sometimes extreme action.

"Apparently," Jack explained, "Preston Reed, Neil's father—your grandfather—has an in with someone on the city's hierarchy and action is never taken. This isn't the first time it's been listed as condemned and then later removed from that status. I suppose Mr. Reed has his reasons for wanting to leave it as is."

Grandfather. At some point Anne had read that her purported biological father had a living father. But she had assumed since he hadn't taken her in as an infant that he wanted nothing to do with her either.

She stared at the house where Mary had lived the last two years of her freedom. There was no reason to believe that because Mr. Reed had kept his son's home for all those years that he cared one iota for his grandchild. Hanging on to the house might've only been related to it being the last place where his son lived. As for why he would ignore Anne, maybe he had reason to believe Mary had cheated on Neil. If she murdered him, she was certainly capable of other atrocities.

Anne dismissed the thoughts. Really, she had no idea

what sort of people her biological mother and father and grandparents were.

Jack pulled into the drive—a strip of lesser overgrowth rendering the driveway very nearly hidden.

"Are we going in?" She instinctively leaned forward. The possibility suddenly had her heart beating faster. Her palms itched with anticipation.

"Might not be safe to go inside, but we can look through the windows and make that determination. The clerk said whatever we do, they are not responsible for any injuries we might sustain since it is listed as condemned. Not to mention, there's always the trespassing and breaking-and-entering charges if we're caught."

Anne felt giddy suddenly. "I'm willing to take the risk if you are. I would really like to go inside if possible." Especially if no one else had lived in the house in all these years. On some level she recognized this was a bit on the foolish side. What difference did where they lived make? Why take such a risk?

What was she even doing here, really?

Just stop. She ordered the dissenting voice away. She had to do this. Had to know as much as possible…to understand before she could put the past fully behind her. After reading that journal Mary had written, there was no way for Anne to pretend she no longer cared. The disinterest she had feigned all these years had been a lie she told herself so she wouldn't look back. No more lying to herself.

Jack shut off the engine. "We'll have a look and go from there." He gave her a nod and got out.

"Works for me."

Moving quickly, she did the same before he could hustle around to open her door. She joined him at the front of the car. A long survey of the small yard had her thankful she'd worn her sneakers and jeans. Gardening boots would have been better, but at least she wasn't wearing sandals or high heels.

He walked ahead of her, threading his way through the massive shrubs to follow the barely visible brick walk that led to the porch steps. The scrape of branches had her wishing she'd chosen a long-sleeved blouse too, no matter that the temperature was well into the eighties. She frowned at the condition of the porch and steps. Both looked less than reliable.

With a careful step onto the first tread and then the next, Jack tested the steps. When he reached the porch, he gave her a nod. "So far, so good."

She followed the path he'd taken. The porch itself was missing a board or two, but the section that led to the front door felt sound enough. No creaking or bouncing. At the door he gave the knob a twist, but it was locked. Anne's hopes deflated.

"Wait." She thought of the key in the box of personal items. "What was the house number?"

He met her gaze, grinned as if the same thought had just occurred to him as well. "168. I'll get that key."

She'd brought the box along, not wanting to leave it in the hotel room. As foolish as it might've sounded considering there really was nothing of true value inside, she hadn't wanted to risk it disappearing.

Maybe it was a little paranoid to be afraid to leave it, but now she was glad she'd made the decision. She was also very grateful that Jack Brenner was such a gentleman.

Jack returned with the key, the steps creaking this time. "Here goes nothing." He inserted it into the lock. The door opened.

Anne gave a nod. "We didn't have to do any breaking and entering after all."

"Feels like an arguable point if we're caught."

She liked this man more all the time.

Inside was dark considering that trees and bushes surrounded the place as if preparing to swallow it up. Any sunlight that might have been afforded by the windows was effectively blocked. Anne tried a switch, but no light came on.

"And—" there was a clicking sound followed by a beam of light "—I grabbed the flashlight from the glove box."

"I'm glad one of us came prepared." Anne hadn't even considered the possibilities of what they would find, much less what they would need at this house. Based on how many houses requiring rehab she'd been inside, she, of all people, should have thought of a flashlight if nothing else. The flashlight apps on phones were great in a pinch but not quite as good as the original thing.

The front door entered directly into the living room. An old sofa still remained in the middle of the room, along with an end table and coffee table. There was an old-fashioned cabinet-style television. No rug or other pieces.

Anne stared at the floor in the center of the room, her heart pounding once more. That spot was where Neil Reed had fallen...had died. The rug she'd seen in the one photo of the place was, she supposed, why there was no blood soaked into the wood. The rug had been amid the photos of the crime scene in one or more articles she'd read. Now the only thing on the wood floor was decades of dust. She blinked and turned away.

The smell of grime and that closed-up odor assaulted her senses as if she'd just awakened from a deep sleep and found herself in this unknown place.

Wood floors…white walls adorned with cobwebs in every corner. No crown molding. Dark-stained wood baseboards, door and window trim. A number of framed photographs hung on the wall. The one that drew Anne was an eight-by-ten of Mary Morton and Neil Reed. Their smiling faces and the way they embraced each other while staring at the camera made Anne's breath catch. They looked so young. And very much in love. Anne wondered when the photograph had been taken. Compared to the ones she had seen of the two in the newspaper clippings and online, this was likely taken months or perhaps a year before the murder.

But none of those details were responsible for her pulse suddenly racing faster with each breath. It was the realization of how very much she looked like Mary. They had the same color hair and eyes. But the online and newspaper images had not shown so shockingly clear how closely Anne's facial features resembled Mary's. They were like twins.

Anne drew in a steadying breath and moved on.

To the left of the front door was a short hallway with three doors lining it. To the right was the living room and the kitchen. No separate dining room. She decided on the hallway to the left and that first door, which led into a bedroom. She tried the switch. Same as in the living room—no light. The power had likely long ago been disconnected.

There was a bed, covers straightened, pillows arranged at the headboard as if someone had just made the bed and hurried away to work. Except the covers were laden with dust and what appeared to be rat feces. She stood in the middle of the room, took out her phone and turned on the flashlight app so she wasn't tethered to Jack. She could follow her instincts rather than just tagging along after him. Dust and swags of cobwebs layered the once-white walls and bare-wood floors just as in the living room. Wherever she stepped, a shoeprint was left behind in the thick dust. The bed was a double, small by today's standards for a couple.

There was a dresser with a mirror, both covered with dust as well. Anne wandered in that direction. An empty bottle of perfume stood amid the grime, its label worn by time and use. Anne picked it up and sniffed the pump-sprayer head. Had Mary worn this perfume daily or just on special occasions? The idea that she had touched this perfume bottle shivered through Anne. She set the bottle aside and checked the drawers. All but one was empty save for more dust and a mud-dauber nest. The one drawer contained men's socks and underwear.

The only thing hanging on the wall besides cobwebs was a floral painting above the bed. The closet was empty of female belongings, but there was a suit and a few men's shirts hanging on one end. Neil Reed's, Anne imagined. She slid her fingers along the sleeve. A pair of men's loafers sat on the floor. Like everywhere else, years of disuse and neglect covered the items like a layer of fine, brownish snow.

Why had these things been left here and others taken away? It was almost like a shrine to the murder victim. Then she understood. This was the last place the owner's—supposedly her grandfather's—son had lived, and Mr. Reed couldn't bring himself to change or do away with his belongings. Of course, that was assuming he was a nice and sentimental person.

Anne had her doubts considering he never bothered to check on her.

Jack caught up with her, and they moved on to the next door in the narrow little hall. It was a second, even smaller bedroom that held a desk and bookcases. Ungraded school papers lay on top of the desk. Jack went through the three drawers in the desk while Anne checked the tiny closet. The door had been turned into a makeshift bulletin board complete with corkboard. A couple of school notices were posted there, the pages yellowed and the corners curled. A business card from a local law firm had been pinned near the top. If Anne recalled correctly it was the firm where Neil had interned during his final year of law school.

Jack reached down and closed the final drawer of the desk. "Nothing beyond more school papers and supplies in here. I didn't see anything that belonged to Neil."

Anne scanned the books on the shelves. "Apparently Mary was fond of romance novels." One entire shelf was lined with the paperbacks. Another held books on education and teachers' manuals.

Jack joined her. "My mother is a huge fan of romance novels." He sent her a sideways glance. "How about you?"

"Sadly, there is never enough time in the day for me to indulge in reading."

"You should make time for yourself."

With that profound statement, he moved on to the next room. Anne followed, pondering the idea that maybe he was right.

The one bathroom was miniscule. Typical three-piece, sink, tub and toilet, and seriously dusty. Shampoo and soap as well as a razor and aftershave remained.

The kitchen was another small space, shoehorned between the side of the house that was bedrooms and the larger room up front that was the living room. Jack looked through the cabinets and in the fridge and oven. The man was thorough for sure.

Anne lingered at the fridge and studied the small photos peppering the surface. Most were held against the appliance with magnets of various shapes and colors. One magnet was a back-to-school shout-out. Another was an apple with a pencil next to it. But it was the photos that tugged at her senses.

Another smaller version of the eight-by-ten on the wall in the living room. Other candid shots of Mary with her friends. Anne recognized Eve and Carin in two of the photos. Their faces and hairstyles were the same as the photo in the locket. Anne decided those were going with her. One by one she removed the photos from beneath the magnets. She tucked them into her shoulder bag. When they interviewed Mr. Reed, she would offer them to the man. If he didn't seem to care about them, Anne would keep them. Surely he cared since the house remained standing. But if he didn't take action eventually, the house would likely be torn down. Maybe that was his intention after all this time.

Putting thoughts of him out of her mind, she considered all that she had seen. Overall, she imagined that thirty or more years ago the little house would have been considered a nice starter home. Good bones and all the necessary options. But now, like the rest of Mary Morton's existence, it was disintegrating. The thought made Anne sad on some level beyond her control. No matter that she hadn't known the woman... Mary had been her mother.

From there they locked the front door and went out the back. The stoop and its two steps were far ricketier than the front porch and steps. There wasn't a lot to see out back beyond the thick greenery and knee-deep grass. Jack cut through the heavy overgrowth and went inside the detached shed-style garage. It wasn't large enough for today's SUVs or trucks. Absolutely tiny by today's standards.

He came out swiping at a spiderweb he'd walked through.

"Anything?" Anne already knew the answer.

He shook his head.

She turned and stared at the house once more. This was where the couple had, from all accounts, been happy. No one had seen the trouble coming—according to the documentary she had watched. Had Mary hurried home to this place each day after school to prepare dinner for her soon-to-be husband? Had they made love on that double bed and conceived a child in that same room? It would seem so.

But then, if this was home to the fairy tale, what went wrong?

Why shoot and kill the man she loved? The father of her child?

Unfortunately, it was very possible that Anne would never know the answers to those questions. But she intended to give it this one shot. Her gaze lit on Jack. He had insisted he could find the answers.

Would those answers be the ones she wanted to hear?

Anne shook her head. Funny, the end result suddenly mattered in a way she hadn't anticipated.

Chapter Seven

Judith's Cocktail Lounge was quite an upscale place, with soft music playing from hidden speakers and tables tucked in cozy niches as well as a bar that offered more seating. The elegant menu offered "small plates" of international appetizers and entrees that smelled as wonderful as they looked. The accompanying menu photos showed the entrees artistically arranged on pure white plates. As a designer, Anne appreciated the pleasing visuals.

She had not realized she was starving until the charcuterie board for two was placed on the table. Once she started eating, any talk had to wait. By the time the wooden board was bare, Anne was utterly stuffed. She sipped her lemon water and finally allowed her mind to replay the tour through the cottage on Fairlawn Drive.

She reached into her bag and pulled out the photos she'd taken from the fridge door. After pushing the board aside, she spread the photos in front of her like a deck of tarot cards. Somehow the images in the photos were every bit as ominous. She tapped the one photo that showed all three of the female friends. "This is the same photo that's in the locket."

Jack nodded. Then he flashed Anne a wide grin. "Look around. That was taken here." He pointed to the elegant bar. "Right there."

She looked from the bar to the photo and nodded. "You're right. Is that why you suggested this place?" She studied the photo again and then surveyed the intimate cocktail bar with new interest.

Jack followed her gaze, taking in the details as well. "It is. The place had a different name then." He shifted his attention to Anne. "She mentioned—in the journal—coming here once a week after school for a girls' night out."

Anne hadn't made the connection considering the new name. "With the headline change," she pointed out, "it's likely under new ownership."

Before he could comment, the waitress paused at their table. "Would you care for a cocktail or coffee?"

Anne smiled. "I'm good—thank you."

"This place has a new name," Jack said when the waitress's attention swung to him, then he gifted her with a charming smile that clearly dazzled her. "Has the management or owner changed as well?"

The waitress, Cherry, returned the smile with a dreamy one of her own. "It used to be JJ's," she confirmed. "For Jerry and Judith Trenton, but the owners got divorced. The wife ended up with the bar in the settlement, and she changed the name to Judith's."

"Is Judith here by any chance?" Anne mentally crossed her fingers.

Cherry, who couldn't have been more than twenty-two or-three, nodded eagerly. "She is. Wednesdays are ladies' poker night, and she's setting up the club room."

"We'd love to say hello," Anne said hopefully. "My mother used to come here. She told me all about the place."

Cherry nodded. "I'll let her know you're here." She looked to Jack once more. "Would you like anything else?"

"No, thanks."

When the waitress had hurried away, Jack gave Anne a thumbs-up. "Good move."

"It's mostly true." She sipped her water. "Like you said, the journal mentioned this place."

"When we leave, we'll drive by the address where the Langstons lived then and now. You won't believe the change—talk about moving up. The apartment building where Carin Carter Wallace lived is gone. There's a huge supermarket there now. Like the Langstons, based on her current address, she's moved way up as well."

"Rumor is," Anne pointed out, "there's money to be made in the world of politics."

Jack chuckled. "There is that."

A gasp drew their attention to the woman suddenly standing next to their table. She looked to be in her late sixties or early seventies. Her white hair was arranged in a youthful bob around an unexpectedly smooth complexion. Her pantsuit was silk and a spectacular blue that emphasized the color of her eyes.

Judith, no doubt. Anticipation and no small dash of anxiety swelled inside Anne.

"Oh my God," the older woman murmured. "You are the spitting image of your mother."

Anne flinched, couldn't help herself. She recovered quickly and held out her hand. "Anne. The long-lost daughter."

Judith shook her hand but then placed her own against her chest. "It's utterly uncanny."

"And you're Judith," Anne suggested.

"I am indeed."

Jack scooted over, making room on his side of the booth. "Please, join us."

The older lady settled into the seat next to him. She smiled at him, her shiny pink lips parting to show off straight, white teeth. "Thank you. And you are…"

"Jack." He offered his hand then. "Jack Brenner from the Colby Agency. I'm helping Anne find the answers she needs."

Her hand fell away from Jack's, and another gasp hissed across her lips. She put her fingers there as if needing to hold back whatever might have popped out next. When her hand dropped to the table, she looked from Jack to Anne. "You're here because we're closing in on the thirtieth anniversary, and you want the whole story."

Anne nodded, going along with the narrative Jack had opened. "I felt it was time."

"Oh, and Mary just passed." Judith made a sad face and shook her head. "Such a tragic story."

"Mary left me her journal and other evidence." Anne stretched the facts just a little. "We're going through everything piece by piece."

Judith's jaw fell open for a moment before she snapped it closed once more. "Things are going to hit the fan, aren't they?"

The twinkle in her eyes told Anne she wasn't sad or angry about the notion.

"Possibly. The truth deserves to be told. In fact—" she turned to Jack "—we were just talking about paying a visit to the Langstons and to Carin Carter Wallace."

That twinkle brightened, and the older woman's grin

widened. "This is going to be epic." She nodded sagely. "Finding the whole truth should have happened ages ago."

Anne couldn't help but laugh. Her heart rate had finally started to slow, and she was feeling a little elated. "Any help you can provide with our efforts will be greatly appreciated."

"Well—" Judith nodded "—I'm more than happy to do so." She glanced at Jack. "I'm not a big fan of our illustrious senator and his wife—or his assistant. That said, I was going through a divorce at the time of the murder, so I wasn't with it and available as much as I might have otherwise been."

She turned fully to Anne then. "Mary was here every week with her friends. They had dinner and cocktails. Oh, and they laughed." She sighed, her expression melancholy. "I just don't understand what happened. Mary loved Neil so much. They came by nearly every weekend and had a cocktail, usually on Saturday evenings before going out to dinner. They always made it a point to say hello if I was here. I just can't believe…" She shook her head and fell silent.

Anne's heart was racing again.

Jack leaned in close to Judith. "Don't worry—we're going to find the truth."

Judith smiled at him again. "I cannot wait to watch the fireworks."

A HALF HOUR LATER, they left the bar. Anne drew in a lungful of air as they walked side by side to his car. Her heart rate had only just fallen back down to normal. Not for a moment had she expected to be so moved…so absorbed in this journey.

"You were amazing back there." Jack sent her a sideways look. "Talk about getting the grapevine stirred up. I'm certain, as Judith said, fireworks will follow."

Anne waited while he opened her door. "I don't know what got into me. I felt like Miss Marple. I just couldn't slow the momentum."

She settled into the passenger seat and realized she could not wait to tell Lisa all about the day. As much doubt and uncertainty as she had suffered at the idea of doing this... she was so very glad she'd agreed. There was something here...something that had been rotting away for thirty years...decaying bit by bit. Anne intended to find it before it disappeared completely.

Jack slid behind the steering wheel. "You should watch out. The Colby Agency will be trying to recruit you."

Anne laughed, and for the first time in too long to remember, it felt deep and real and relaxed.

Maybe this had been a really good idea.

Truly, how was she supposed to move on with her life without settling the past once and for all?

This effort really was essential to her future.

FROM THE OUTER limits of Crystal Lake where they did a drive-by of the vintage, aka rundown, apartment building where twenty-and thirtysomethings Eve and Kevin had lived, they drove the twenty minutes to Barrington. Senator Kevin Langton and his wife, Eve, currently lived in a fifteen-thousand-square-foot mansion on Plum Tree Road, recently valued at nearly six million dollars. The place looked more like a castle than a home. Although the property was not on the market, there was a listing on Zillow that showed that the estate included a vast thirty-seven acres. There were walking trails and a barn for horses. The lavish details went on and on.

"This is—" Anne stared at the towering gate that fronted the drive leading to the property "—crazy luxurious."

"Ready to see where the assistant lives?"

Anne had a feeling Carin Carter Wallace's rise from an administrative assistant in a small-town mayor's office to where she was now would be equally astonishing. "I can't wait."

"Like I said, the apartment building was replaced with a big super store," he reminded her. "For perspective, the images of the building before demolition were very much like the one where the senator and his wife once lived."

"I'm amazed at the amount of research you did." His work put hers to shame.

He glanced at her. "Just doing my job."

And Anne was pleased that he'd been so very thorough. It hit her then that they really did have a shot at finding the truth.

The drive was only a couple of minutes from Plum Tree Road and onto Rolling Hills Drive in the same high-end community.

Carin Carter Wallace, the senator's assistant, lived in a far more modern residence consisting of a mere six thousand square feet ensconced on an intimate five acres, valued at just over four million, according to Zillow.

Soaring windows sat in a cutting-edge contemporary design. This home, too, was fronted by a towering gate. Anne wondered if their secrets made them yearn for extra security. But that was petty of her. She didn't know these people.

"Not too shabby," Jack commented.

"One of my foster mothers used to say, 'Pretty is as pretty does.' Maybe we'll find out if all this is representative of what's in their hearts."

Anne had never been one to judge a book by its cover, but something about these people felt very wrong even if she didn't know them. Maybe it was the journal and all that it insinuated. But those words could be nothing more than Mary's bitterness. Time would tell, Anne supposed.

The drive back to the hotel gave Anne time to do a good deal of thinking. The journal suggested that someone close to Mary and Neil was responsible for the murder. At the moment, the big question in Anne's mind was, Did the astonishing transformation in the lives of those close to Mary and Neil have anything to do with the murder?

Frankly she couldn't see how at this point. But what she could see was the possibility of people who were ambitious, ruthless…maybe capable of anything and who perhaps knew more than they'd told the police. But did that make one or all a murderer? No…but it certainly merited further consideration.

On the other hand, it was very possible these suspicions were popping into her head because those were the things she wanted to see. Was she superimposing their extravagant personal gains onto a scenario of evil that was actually only a theory?

This was personal for Anne—more personal than she would ever have believed. As hard as she might try, remaining completely objective was likely impossible. Though she'd had no relationship with her parents, there was the potential for wanting some tiny aspect of their story to not be a heinous murder story.

All the more reason to be grateful for the Colby Agency's involvement. Jack would keep her grounded and on the right track. He would be objective as it became more and more clear that she might not be able to.

Anne was exhausted when they reached the hotel. At

her door she turned to Jack. "Thank you. I'll be honest—
I had major reservations about doing this…all the way up
until this morning actually. But now, just talking to someone like Judith and seeing where Mary and Neil lived, I
can truthfully say that I'm glad I came."

He smiled. "I'm glad too." His gaze was direct when
he started to speak once more. "But fair warning—don't
thank me until we're done. The part that comes next may
not be nearly as much fun."

Anne wasn't put off by his warning. Not yet anyway.

Chapter Eight

Barrington
Thursday, July 10
Langston Residence
Plum Tree Road, 9:30 a.m.

Jack parked down the block from the turn onto the Langston property. He checked his cell since there had been a couple of vibrations during the drive over. The two waiting text messages made him smile. One was from his contact at the Mayo Clinic, the other from Jamie Colby. Each wanted to ensure he'd received the latest information sent to his email.

Having the power of the Colby Agency as backup was the best. He glanced at the woman in the passenger seat. He wondered if she understood yet how lucky she was that her mother had chosen the Colby Agency.

"Did you have a chance to look over the information I sent you?" He turned his attention to Anne.

They'd had breakfast in their respective rooms, so they hadn't really talked this morning. On the drive here she'd been focused on a call from her assistant about an in-progress project.

But now, before knocking on this door and kicking off the day with a serious bang, they needed to talk.

"I did." She stared toward the property that was their destination. "The Langstons made an investment in the research company, BioTech, where the senator worked the first decade of his law career. As he left the company to start his political career, the stocks soared, making them multimillionaires when they sold out. It would seem they have a legitimate explanation for their super lifestyle change."

He was surprised she hadn't made the connection that came with the rest of the information he'd sent her via email. "Maybe you didn't notice that Carin Carter Wallace's husband was an angel investor in BioTech well before she met him…well before the Langstons invested."

She frowned. "So Carin's husband was one of the original investors."

"He was." Jack grinned. "Just one year after his investment in a fledgling company, she shows up in his life and they end up married."

Anne bobbed her head slowly. "Okay, but what's the connection to my parents?"

Surprised didn't begin to cover his reaction to her use of the term *parents*. This was the first time he'd heard her refer to Mary Morton and Neil Reed as parents…out loud anyway. He suspected it was her first time period. He hoped what they found during this investigation didn't make her regret that development.

"I can't confirm anything with any degree of certainty," he said honestly. "But Carin disappeared from the Crystal Lake area and appeared in Wallace's orbit just a couple of months before Neil's murder."

Anne nodded slowly, as if trying to make the connection

he meant, then surprise flared in her expression. "Kevin, Eve and Carin were all trying to get involved with this Bio-Tech. With that in mind, maybe Carin didn't just get mad and leave. She may have left with an agenda—to weave her way into Wallace's life."

"Right. And FYI, BioTech got its start right here in Chicago by a young med student, Michael Smith, at North-western's Feinberg School of Medicine."

Her eyes widened. "Neil was at Northwestern."

Jack held up his cell. "One of my sources who attended Northwestern just confirmed that the two were friends. But the really interesting part is that Michael Smith and Neil Reed were two of four who shared an apartment for a while."

"Are you serious?"

He nodded. "I am." Even Jack had found this news particularly exciting.

"Wow." She took a breath. "I can see how this company—BioTech—is a definite connection of some sort." She bit her lip, confusion replacing the other emotions that had danced across her face. "But how did that lead to murder?"

"That's what we intend to find out. I can't say for sure this is the connection—*the thread*—that led to murder. But it's one that wasn't explored in the investigation." He shifted back into Drive. "And money matters have long been motives for murder."

"True. But Neil was a law student. The only money matters he had at the time was the mounting debt."

"Still—" Jack braked for the turn into the imposing driveway "—it's a starting place for our search."

"It is a starting place. The fact that all the players except

Mary and Neil wound up a part of BioTech does seem a little suspicious."

"Definitely a little suspicious considering that Mary mentioned a new start-up business that wanted Neil on board."

Anne's eyes widened. "You're right. If it was BioTech, then that's a thread that binds them all."

He nodded. "Exactly."

Jack braked again at the gate and powered down his window. Now, if they were lucky, Mrs. Langston was home. He pressed the button on the intercom.

"Good morning," a female voice said. "Please state your name and business."

"Jackson Brenner with the Colby Agency and my colleague, Anne Griffin." He glanced at her. "We're here to see Eve Redford Langston."

He used the woman's maiden name as well to suggest some knowledge of her prior to becoming the senator's wife.

Anne's eyebrows lifted in question. Likely the same question he had. Would the lady of the house allow them into her domain? Would she dare satisfy her curiosity as to why the daughter of Mary Morton was at her gate? He had no doubt the Langstons had already heard the news. Judith Hudson, owner of Judith's, had photos with her lifelong friend, Eve Langston, all over her social media pages. Jack had spent some time perusing those pages last night. The woman no doubt called Langston the instant they left her establishment.

"One moment please."

The seconds ticked off, but neither spoke while they waited. The pulse at the base of Anne's throat fluttered rapidly. She was nervous…anxious. Who wouldn't be?

This was her life—well, her history anyway. Like anyone else, she wanted to understand…to clear up the mystery. He couldn't imagine growing up and finding his way through this world without the strong foundation of his personal history…without the love of his parents and siblings.

So much of Anne's was unknown. Hung in the balance of multiple unanswered questions. And that didn't even take into account the murder.

The gate suddenly started a slow swing inward.

He and Anne exchanged a look. Evidently they were in. The smile that stretched across her face no doubt mirrored his own.

"Drive forward," the seemingly disembodied voice directed. "Park near the fountain and approach the front door."

"Will do." He powered the window up and rolled forward. "We're in."

Anne exhaled a big breath. "She didn't say Eve wasn't in."

"She did not. I'm guessing Eve intends to see us, otherwise why allow the visit to her home?"

"I'm sure the Colby Agency name was persuasive."

"Possibly."

The name often got him through doors he might not have been able to enter. But he suspected Eve Redford Langston knew exactly who Anne Griffin was and why she was here. If Anne hadn't decided Judith had given them up, he'd let her have that one for a bit longer. Judith had pretended to be such a good friend of Mary's. He had a feeling Anne preferred giving people the benefit of the doubt. Surprising in light of the childhood she'd lived.

She was a nice person, he decided. Maybe too nice.

Jack parked on the cobblestone drive that circled a massive fountain which looked exactly like something one might come across in Italy. He exited the car and moved toward Anne's door.

She emerged, staring at the fountain, then the monstrosity of a house with its grand turret. "This is just too much," she said for his ears only.

He agreed. This, he surmised, was not a home. It was bragging rights.

A short set of broad steps led to a grand porch—if you could call the architectural detail fronting a castle-like structure a porch.

The double doors opened as they approached. A woman, middle aged, well dressed, waited just inside.

"This way please." She gestured to the grand foyer.

Once they were across the threshold, the woman closed the doors, then led the way across the marble-floored foyer. The ceiling towered at least three stories, rising to the very top of the turret that fronted the mansion. They crossed under the upstairs landing that was flanked on either side by a stone staircase.

Jack had expected they would be ushered to a parlor of some sort, but instead the next set of double doors the woman opened revealed a library as large as the one in his hometown. The walls were lined with book-filled shelves. The flow was interrupted only by a large arched window on the opposite side from the doors, ensuring an inspiring view of the rear gardens. Near the window was a seating area, with a sofa and a couple of chairs surrounding a table.

A woman, her back turned, waited at the window that looked out over the meticulously and lushly cultivated landscape.

When the double doors closed, leaving Jack and Anne standing in the center of the room, the woman at the window turned to them. Eve Redford Langston took a couple of steps toward the seating area. Her attention first rested on Jack. It wasn't until she paused at the sofa that she shifted her attention to Anne. Her eyes widened. Jack was almost positive he heard a sharp intake of breath.

Eve gestured to the two upholstered chairs. "Sit. Please."

She lowered onto the sofa, her gaze tracking their movements toward the chairs.

When they were seated, she turned to Anne. "It's amazing how much you look like your mother."

IN THE PAST Anne would have stiffened if anyone had made such a remark to her, but somehow in the past few hours she had come to terms with many things. Her resemblance to her mother was one of them. It almost felt like a compliment.

"Thank you." She gazed steadily at the former best friend of Mary's. "And thank you for seeing us. Jack and I have a great deal of research to do."

The older woman's lips twitched in what might've been construed as a smile, but the effort was vague and lackluster.

"I assume the two of you are looking into your mother's history—at least, that's what I've heard. If that's the case, I'm happy to help any way I can."

Well, well. It seemed the kindly Judith had put the word out. Good. Anne had hoped she would. At the same time, Anne was a little disappointed. The woman had claimed to be a friend of her mother's. Apparently that loyalty only went as far as the senator's address. Anne wondered if Jack had assumed or hoped for the same.

"We'd like to hear about the days and weeks leading up to the murder." Jack launched into the questions. "I've read the statements from the investigation, and they seem a tad incomplete."

"Incomplete?" Eve eyed him speculatively. "How so?"

"According to what we know, you, Mary Morton and Carin Carter Wallace spent a good deal of time together. You had been friends for many years at the time of the murder."

Eve made a single nod. "That's correct. You should have read as much in my statement."

"We did." Anne waded in. "My question is given the fact that you and Mary were so close, didn't you suspect or sense something was wrong—wrong enough to result in murder?"

The silence that followed echoed in the room like the nothingness that trailed a sonic blast.

Eve smiled then, something more than a mere twitch. She appeared to find the question amusing. "The detective asked me this as well."

"Your answer," Jack inserted, "was not documented in the file. There was some vague mention of you being out of town."

This time she actually laughed. The sound was dry, half-hearted. "Detective Jones was young. Only a few years older than we were at the time. I'm not sure he had a clue what he was doing."

"Jack said the same thing," Anne pointed out. "It's insane that not a single appeal was granted considering the incompetent investigation and the subpar legal counsel Mary received."

Eve lifted her chin ever so slightly. "If that's how you feel, have you looked into what avenues you have to rectify those shortfalls? I can't imagine the city would want to enter into any sort of civil litigation. A settlement would likely be far more appealing."

Was the woman subtlety offering a payoff to shut Anne down? She didn't have to say the words outright. Anne saw it in her eyes—the anticipation. The offer was loud and clear. "So you agree there was negligence involved. Mary's conviction may have been a miscarriage of justice."

"Sadly, I don't agree." Eve sighed, crossed her hands on her lap. "As difficult as it was to believe in the beginning, I long ago faced the reality that Mary must have killed Neil. It was the only logical answer. Was the murder investigated as it should have been? Unquestionably not. Did she receive proper legal representation? Probably not. But that doesn't mean she wasn't guilty. If you're looking to clear her name, I must warn you that you will be gravely disappointed. You're far more likely to prove she wasn't properly represented by counsel."

Startled by the woman's certainty, Anne held up a hand. "I'm not looking to do anything but find the truth. That's why I need your help. You were her best friend, after all."

A standoff of sorts passed between them. Eve broke first.

"As your friend pointed out—" she gestured to Jack "—I was not here in the days that led up to the murder. Mary was busy with wedding plans and with her pregnancy. We didn't spend a lot of time together those final weeks."

"Where were you that final week before the murder?" Jack asked. "You stated that you were visiting your grandmother in Rockford, but I didn't find any statement from your grandmother confirming your alibi."

A hint of pink flushed her cheeks, and Anne barely resisted the urge to grin.

"It should be there," Eve argued. "Perhaps it was lost."

"Can anyone confirm you were at your grandmother's?" he asked.

"Well, since my grandmother is deceased, as are my parents," she admitted, "I suppose you'll have to take my word for it. She was ill at the time and needed me. My parents were on a month-long cruise."

"The prosecution suggested that Neil Reed was having an affair." Anne moved in a hopefully more constructive direction. "Were you aware of this? Did Mary give any indication of being worried about something like this?"

"She did mention having concerns about him." Eve's full attention turned to Anne. "Your mother was very intuitive. If Neil lied to her, she would have seen right through his efforts."

"If he was aware of this," Anne countered, "why would he bother lying? Then again, Mary had no history of violence. She didn't own a gun. There was never an explanation of where the gun came from."

"I'm afraid I have no idea. I can only say that she had concerns about her future husband. Perhaps it was merely cold feet." Eve lifted her hand toward Anne. "Or perhaps it was because she'd learned she was pregnant and any second thoughts were a little late. Whatever the case, she is the only person who could possibly have had a motive to kill Neil. There was no one else." She stood, obviously ready to dismiss them.

"One final question," Jack said as he, too, stood.

Anne followed suit. Hoped his question was one that would leave the woman with something to think about.

Eve looked to him in expectation.

"Was Neil the one who introduced the senator to Michael Smith? It seems his work and investments in BioTech were very good moves." He glanced around the room. "Obviously it changed your life."

She blinked once, twice. "I'm afraid I have no idea. My husband served as lead counsel to Michael Smith and his company for a decade. I don't recall how they met. You would have to ask my husband, and he is very busy. He has to return to DC next week for the new session. I doubt he'll have time to meet with you before then."

"No problem," Jack insisted. "There are public records I can look through. I'm sure the senator disclosed his employment with and investment ties to BioTech when he took office."

"I'm sure." The senator's wife led the way back to the front door. She waited there and watched as they exited.

When she would have closed the door Anne decided to take one last shot at unsettling her. If the endgame was to rouse a reaction, they needed a good, strong final move.

"I've always wondered," she said to the woman standing in the doorway to her own private castle, "why no one—and you were her best friend—visited Mary in prison or helped with me after I was born. It was a shame I had to be thrust into foster care."

Eve stared at Anne for a long moment. "I can't speak for anyone else, but I can tell you that I was young and uncertain about my future. Kevin hadn't proposed, and frankly, I had no idea where my future was going. I simply couldn't take on the added responsibility." She looked away for a few seconds before meeting Anne's gaze once more. "It's a shame, though, what happened to you. I hope you won't allow the past to define your future."

When Anne and Jack were in his car driving away, she couldn't decide if she wanted to scream or to cry.

She had worked very hard not to allow her past to define her present or her future.

But this…this thing they were doing was different.

Wasn't it?

Suddenly she felt uncertain again. Why even go down this path? What did it matter, really?

"She wanted to make you feel unsure of yourself." Jack apparently read her mind.

"She did that rightly enough." Anne collapsed deeper into the seat and stared out the window. All those hurtful feelings related to her mother and the loneliness crushed in on her.

"I'm guessing," he said with a quick glance at her, "that we completely unhinged the lady. I'll bet she's on the phone right now calling her husband and demanding he take some sort of action."

A smile tugged at Anne's lips. "And next she'll call her friend Carin and warn her that the you-know-what is hitting the fan."

Jack laughed. "Exactly."

Anne drew in a really big breath and let it out slowly. "I swear it felt exactly like she was trying to tell me there was money to be had if I was willing to let this whole thing go."

"The conversation did take a bit of a turn in that direction. If that was her intent, she was definitely sly about it."

"Sly like a fox," Anne noted. "I'm getting this feeling that something is wrong where this BioTech business is concerned. Kevin Langston served as lead counsel for the start-up, but it sounded in the journal as if that was the position Neil was being considered for."

"I'll get someone looking into the possibility. Particularly now that we can make the connection between the friends."

"Thanks." Anne stared forward. "All right, so what's next?"

"I checked with the senior living community, and we've been added to Mr. Reed's visitor's list."

"How did you manage that?" The fact that her pulse rate suddenly shot into rapid-fire had her feeling uncertain again. The man was her grandfather…and yet he had abandoned her just like everyone else.

"I can't give away all my secrets."

Anne laughed, the sound a little strangled. As long as his secret skills got the job done, she could live without knowing.

Reed Residence
The Sparkling Springs
Crystal Lake, 1:00 p.m.

THIS WAS DEFINITELY not your typical senior living community.

Anne surveyed the beautiful property as they walked from the parking area to the main office. The place was gated and, quite frankly, gorgeous. Nestled in a treed landscape, rows and rows of tiny cottages flanked the perimeter while taller apartment-style buildings filled the inner space. But everything between and around was like a park. Walking paths and ponds were bordered by lush shrubs and blooming plants. It was peaceful and elegant. It was amazing.

Not at all what Anne had expected.

They hadn't been able to come directly here after the meeting with Eve. Although Jack had called and provided all the necessary details required, Mr. Reed wasn't available for a visit until one. To kill time, they'd had lunch and discussed the senator's wife. They both agreed that she was nervous. Anne found Jack easy to talk to, and she continued to be surprised at how comfortable she felt with him and this deep dive into the past. She still had her moments of anxiety and trepidation, but not enough to make her hesitate.

"Does he have health issues?" she asked as they approached the grand entrance.

"Not that I've been able to determine. He has a huge real estate portfolio. The home where he lived with his family thirty years ago is sitting vacant now—much like the one Mary and Neil lived in—only well cared for. Last year, he suddenly moved here. If there was a health reason, he's kept it quiet."

Maybe all the memories had become too much for him.

Once in the main office lobby, they were met by a representative who signed them in, provided name badges and escorted them to Mr. Reed's door. He lived in one of the small cottages.

"Enjoy your visit," the representative said before scurrying away.

"Wow," Anne said quietly as they watched her go. "This place is amazing. It must cost a small fortune."

Jack nodded. "Including all the fees, you're talking in the neighborhood of a hundred K per year."

Anne felt her eyes nearly pop out. Oh well, why not enjoy your later years being waited on hand and foot if you had the means?

Jack knocked on the door. "Hopefully the serene environment keeps him happy and cooperative."

Anne would appreciate cooperative.

The door opened, and an elderly man stared out at them. Despite his age, eighty, he stood tall and appeared strong and clear eyed. His hair was completely gray, and his attire looked as if he had an afternoon on the golf course planned—pressed khakis and a polo shirt.

He stared at Anne for a long moment before he spoke. "So you're the daughter."

In that instant it hit Anne fully, deeply that this man was her grandfather. An actual relative. She had no others. A man, she realized, who opted not to come for her after she was born in that prison infirmary. A man who allowed her to be thrust into foster care. A man who had abandoned her.

"And you're the grandfather," she said with perhaps more sarcasm than necessary.

He stared a moment more, then glanced at Jack. "Come in. Let's get this over with."

Now she was flat-out angry, but she did all in her power to keep the emotion to herself. Deep breaths and slow releases. She had Jack at her side. She could do this.

Once inside his cottage, she focused on the details around her rather than the man. The cottage was even lovelier inside than out. Nicely decorated and efficiently designed. Furnished for comfort but with an eye toward charm and sophistication.

"Join me." Preston Reed settled on the sofa.

He made no offer of refreshments, and that was just as well. Anne felt sick to her stomach. The shaking prompted by that blast of anger had started deep inside her and now spread through her limbs.

When they'd all taken seats, Jack said, "We appreciate your time, Mr. Reed."

Reed looked to Anne. "Why are you here?"

The man really knew how to get on her last nerve. "I—we—" she glanced at Jack "—are attempting to find answers about what really happened the day Neil was murdered."

Reed's expression remained passive, and he said nothing.

"The Colby Agency has looked into the way the investigation was conducted," Jack jumped in, drawing Reed's attention. "We don't believe the work was thorough. We'd like to remedy that."

The older man set his gaze on Anne once more. "The detective was young, probably not the best choice for the job. But I don't have any doubts as to the conclusion he reached. Mary killed my son. I'm certain of that."

"Why?" Anne held his gaze, her chin raised in defiance of his unwavering claim. "What makes you so certain?"

"Because my son said she would."

The words stunned Anne—hit her in the face like a blow from a closed fist.

"When did he say this?" Jack prodded. "Under what circumstances?"

"He'd decided to take a risk. He wanted to borrow against his trust fund and invest in some start-up company. She was against him taking a job with an up-and-coming company, so he thought an investment would be wise instead. He had come to see Mary's concerns about the risk considering she was unexpectedly pregnant."

Anne's breath caught softly before she could stop the reaction.

Reed scrutinized her for a moment before going on. "They wanted you. No need to worry about that. But you did show up before they'd planned to start a family."

She relaxed a little. "Why are you so convinced she would kill the father of her child?"

"Why do mothers kill their children?" He flung his arms upward. "Or fathers abandon their families? Who the hell knows? She wasn't crazy—I can tell you that. She was smart. Maybe a little too clever. All I know is she told Neil she would kill him, and that's what I told the police."

"When did she make this statement?" Anne pushed. He still hadn't explained that shocker to any real degree. And it sounded as if the statement was hearsay.

"He told me she said she would kill him if he dared take the risk of that position with a company just getting started." He stared at the floor a moment. "I don't think he really thought she would do it."

Anne glared at him, in part astonished but mostly just angry. "People say things like that all the time. It's just a way of getting the point across. It doesn't mean they really intend to kill the person to whom they made the statement."

"I felt that way too, until my son was dead."

Dear God. Anne barely resisted the need to roll her eyes. She already knew the answer to what she was about to ask, but it would be helpful to have it substantiated by someone who was there at the time. "What was the name of this company?"

He shook his head. "I don't recall. It's not relevant."

Anne wanted to shake him. He was purposely evading the question.

"We believe," Jack interjected, "Mary was innocent. We believe she was set up by someone close to her and Neil."

The silence that followed had Anne's heart starting to pound. If there was even a remote possibility the police had the wrong person, why had this man done nothing? If he'd felt the investigation wasn't thorough, why not hire a private detective? Why just sit back and let whatever would happen just happen? His son was dead! Murdered! Just because he believed his future daughter-in-law committed the crime did not make it true. For God's sake, he lost his son!

The mounting fury had her glaring at the man who was

her grandfather. "Mary loved him. More than anything. She would not have killed him."

The journal... Anne fought to catch her breath. Even after all those years, Mary's love for Neil had been clear in her words.

Preston Reed looked away. "It doesn't matter. They're both dead now."

Fury slammed into her chest. "But I'm not and you're not. Why allow this travesty to stand?"

His gaze narrowed on her. "If it's money you want, you'll just have to wait for that. I've set up a trust fund that distributes to you when you reach age thirty. In, if memory serves, four months from now."

Anne drew back. "I didn't come here for your money." She launched to her feet. "I don't want your money. I want the truth."

Jack was at her side, a hand on her elbow. "We can go if you'd like," he offered.

Reed peered up at her, his face void of emotion. "Don't waste your time digging around in the past."

Anne couldn't speak. There were no words that accurately articulated what she wanted to say to him. Instead, she left. Couldn't get out of there fast enough.

Once they were in the car driving away, she said out loud, mostly to herself, "How could he ignore me all these years and then throw money at me?"

"It takes courage to step forward and do the right thing in times of loss. He was grieving the loss of his son—his only child. He may have seen you as an extension of Mary, and the idea of having you in his life was unbearable under the circumstances. But on some level, even now, he recognizes his obligation to his son's child."

She pressed her hands to her face, fought the urge to cry.

Damn it. She would not cry. "When I agreed to do this, I didn't expect…this…*him*."

"There will be more." He glanced at her. "And some of it will be painful, maybe more than what just happened. But it's the only way to find what you're looking for."

Defeat crushed at her chest. He was right. But she had to be strong. She'd endured far more painful times growing up. On the scale of her childhood misery, this was nothing.

Chapter Nine

They stood outside the door of Beatrice Farrell's house. This was a cold call, so Jack wasn't sure how it would go.

Farrell was one of the teachers at Crystal Lake Elementary who had worked with Morton. She had been interviewed by the detective investigating the case, but she'd had no helpful information to share, according to his report.

She had retired at the end of this school year, so hopefully she was home and not traveling to celebrate her newfound freedom.

Anne pressed the doorbell a second time, and they continued to wait.

Jack had been a little worried about her after the visit with Preston Reed. She'd been more upset by the man than Jack had anticipated. He suspected all these years of ignoring the situation had not prevented Anne from forming feelings for the family she had never known except through newspaper clippings and online articles.

What little girl abandoned by a parent, whatever the

circumstances, didn't dream of the fairy tale that could have been?

He hoped Farrell would be helpful. Of the three teachers who had been fairly close to Morton back then, Farrell was the only one still alive.

Finding someone who had relevant memories of Mary Morton and who was willing to share them would be good about now. Not only for the investigation but for Anne. She needed to see progress.

The door opened, and the woman who matched the photos from the school's website stood before them. Beatrice was petite, with hair that was more blond than gray and kept in a long braid. She had pale eyes, almost a blue, but they were actually a very light shade of silver. The knee-length shorts and cotton t-shirt she wore said she went for comfort over fashion. Judging by her weathered skin and the sheer number of blooming plants in her landscape, she liked spending her free time outside.

She looked to Jack. "I'm sure you noticed the no-soliciting sign next to the sidewalk."

"Mrs. Farrell," Anne said, drawing her attention, "my name is Anne Griffin."

Farrell shifted her attention toward Anne. Her hand went to her mouth. "Oh my word, you're Mary's daughter."

Jack watched Anne's reaction. This just kept happening. If she'd had any doubts about how much she looked like her mother, she shouldn't have any now. He'd noticed the remarkable resemblance the first time he googled her.

Anne produced a realistic smile. "I am."

Maybe she was getting attached—or at least accustomed—to the idea.

The older woman pressed her hand to her chest now. "I was so sorry to hear that she passed." She smiled sadly. "I wrote to her every month all these years." She shrugged. "Even though she never wrote me back, I felt it was the least I could do considering everyone else had turned on her."

The relief on Anne's face was palpable. "Would you have a few minutes for us to ask some questions about Mary and the time surrounding...what happened?"

"Of course." Farrell drew the door open wider. "Come in."

Jack followed Anne, then closed the door since Farrell was busy explaining how her husband had passed away last year and now it was just her.

He followed the two to the kitchen, where Farrell insisted on putting on a pot of tea. The house was a typical ranch style. A good-sized yard surrounded it, all enclosed with an aged picket fence. A gray cat appeared, rubbed against its master's legs and then eyed Jack suspiciously before disappearing.

"Sit at the table with me." Farrell ushered them to the dining table.

The kitchen-dining combo was just off the living room. You could actually see both the front and back doors from the table.

"I have lots of questions for you," Farrell said to Anne, "but you go first. I'm sure yours are far more important than mine."

"Thank you." Anne accepted a cup of tea from their host.

"Would you like cream or sugar?" Farrell asked.

"No, thank you." Anne cradled the fragile cup in both hands as if she needed the warmth.

Farrell looked to Jack. "The same for me."

When the lady had poured a cup for Jack and then one for herself, she turned back to Anne. "Please, ask away."

"First," she began, "you said you wrote to Mary. But she never once wrote you back?"

Farrell shook her head. "No, she didn't, but I understood. The lack of a response never put me off. I continued to write to her. Usually only a page, but something to let her know I was thinking of her."

"That was very kind of you. Before the murder, were you aware of any issues between Mary and Neil?"

Farrell shook her head. "Absolutely not. Those two were madly in love. The only time I ever heard her mention being upset with Neil was when he wanted to accept that position with some start-up company." She frowned, set her cup aside as if holding it splintered her concentration. "They'd just found out about you." She smiled at Anne. "Mary was worried that some start-up company wouldn't provide the stability they would need going forward with a baby on the way."

"Do you remember the name of the company?" Jack asked. There was mention of Neil's offer from a start-up company, but the journal never mentioned the name.

Farrell appeared to ponder the question for a time. "I can't… Wait. Bio something, I think. Some sort of medical something." She shook her head. "Sorry. I swear the memory is the first thing to go once you pass sixty."

"I feel that way," Anne said, "and I'm not even thirty."

"Life is busy," Farrell said. "Too much on our minds these days."

"Some have suggested," Anne went on, "that Neil was cheating on Mary."

Another firm shake of her head. "Absolutely not. I would have known." She laughed softly. "I wasn't Mary's closest friend, but we teachers spend so much time together discussing students and the headaches and heartaches of being an educator that we're bound to share personal difficulties. She would have told me. I'm certain. She adored Neil and never spoke negatively of him. Never."

"Do you," Jack said, "remember anything at all that gave you pause during the days that led up to the murder?"

Farrell took a moment before she answered. "The only thing I recall is that Mary was furious with her friend Eve—you know, the senator's wife." She cringed an unpleasant expression. "It was the first time I'd heard Mary sound so put out by her. I think they were friends since childhood."

"Did she mention any specific trouble?"

Farrell hesitated for five or so seconds but then looked at Anne. "I swore to Mary that I would never tell this." She sighed. "I suppose it doesn't matter now that she's gone." Farrell tilted her head and frowned. "Not that I would tell a soul except you."

She inhaled a big breath as if what she had to say was quite the burden. "Mary was looking into how to do a reliable paternity test without Neil knowing anything about it. She couldn't let him find out."

Anne drew back as if the woman had slugged her. "What?"

"I'm so sorry. If Mary didn't tell you this, then I'm guessing she found a way and determined that all was as it should be." She stared into her cup a moment. "I probably shouldn't have told you." Her gaze lifted to Anne's once more. "But Mary was beside herself about it for reasons she never explained. Of course, it was easy enough to assume the reason. I suppose Eve didn't agree with some aspect of the situation. Whatever the case, the two were out of sorts."

Jack watched Anne carefully to ensure she was going to

hold it together after that revelation. There certainly hadn't been anything in the diary about another love interest.

Anne moistened her lips. "You're right. I didn't know, but now it's important that I know everything possible if I'm going to find the truth."

"Do you know if she spoke to Eve or to her other friend, Carin about this?" Jack chimed in, hoping to usher things forward. He felt bad at the sorrow clouding Anne's eyes.

"I don't know." Farrell picked up her tea once more. "I actually found out by accident. It was Mary's planning period, and her class was in the gym. It was mine as well. My class was in art, but I went to the gym for a personal reason. The PE instructor at the time was my husband's first cousin. We were planning a cookout that weekend, so I popped into the gym to run the date and time by him."

"Was Mary in the gym?" Anne asked.

"No. No. She was in her classroom." A frown furrowed across the older woman's brow. "As I walked into the gym one of Mary's third graders stopped playing and started crying. She said she didn't feel well and wanted to go home." Her gaze grew distant as if the memory was playing like a movie reel in her mind. "Suddenly the little girl fell to the floor and had a seizure. While Winston, our cousin, saw to her, I ran to the nurse's office. I sent her to the gym, then I rushed to Mary and told her what had happened. She hurried out of the room, and I collapsed into her chair to catch my breath."

"Was the little girl okay?"

Farrell nodded at Anne. "Oh, yes. A fever caused the seizure. She had a thorough checkup and spent a few days at home, and then she was fine."

Farrell hesitated a moment. "When I stood to go from Mary's room I noticed a brochure open on her desk. I didn't mean to be nosy, but it was right there. Later, I asked her if everything was all right, and she broke down into tears and said she had to be sure about who the father was before she and Neil could move ahead with their wedding plans."

Her face pale, Anne tackled the next realistic question. "Was she planning an abortion if things didn't turn out the way she hoped?"

The hollow sound of her voice tore at Jack.

"Oh, no," Farrell insisted. "She'd already picked out names and nursery furniture. She said she just had to know so she could tell Neil. She was adamant that he should know the truth."

When Anne said nothing more, Jack asked, "Mrs. Farrell, did Mary mention who the father might be if not Neil Reed?"

Another fervent shake of her head. "No. She wouldn't talk about it. When I asked she grew very upset…angry, even." She looked Jack directly in the eyes. "But I can tell you one thing for certain—Mary Morton was a good woman. Kind and loyal to a fault. Whatever happened, she didn't mean for it to happen. As good a person as she was, she was only human." Beatrice shook her head again. "Still, I cannot imagine how the situation came about. The next thing I knew, Neil was dead and Mary had been charged with his murder. I tried to see her, but they wouldn't let me. They said she didn't want to see me, but I didn't believe them."

"Did you tell the police about the paternity test?"

Farrell looked away. When she turned back to Anne, tears sat on her lashes. "No, I didn't. Because I believed with all my heart that Mary would never have hurt Neil or anyone else. I wasn't about to give them any more ammunition to use against her."

"I'm sure she appreciated that," Anne said softly. "Do you recall the name of the lab?"

"Well, you would think so. I stared at the brochure for several seconds. I guess I was a bit stunned. But I don't recall the name. It's been a long time."

Anne nodded.

When the silence lingered, Jack pulled a business card from his pocket and passed it to the former teacher. "I hope you'll call if you think of anything at all that might help us."

She stared at the card a moment and nodded, then she placed it on the table. Her hand went to Anne's. "I am so sorry if this news hurt you, but please don't hold it against your mother. However the question of paternity came about, she suffered enough when Neil was murdered."

"I guess I don't understand. If Mary was such a good person, why did no one stand up for her at trial?" Anne held up a hand. "I recognize that you did by not telling the police about the paternity test, but why no one else? No other teacher? None of her other friends? No one?"

The pain in her voice and on her face twisted a knot in Jack's gut. He had known this would be hard. But that didn't make watching it happen any easier.

"Perhaps you don't realize how powerful Preston Reed was at the time," Beatrice said quietly. "Throughout his life he has stayed behind the scenes. Never put himself out there for political office. But make no mistake—he ran things. Three days after his son was murdered, his wife had a heart attack and died. He was devastated. The rumor was that he blamed Mary for his wife's death as well as his son's. No one would have dared to step on Preston's toes. Your mother was doomed from the moment she was charged."

Anne thanked Mrs. Farrell, but she didn't say another word until they were in the car driving away.

"Is there a way to find out what lab she used?" She turned to face Jack.

"We can try." He slowed for the upcoming turn. "The one she used may have gone out of business or been gobbled up by another one, so I wouldn't count on finding the exact place."

Anne sat back in her seat and chewed on her lips. "She mentioned in the journal about an issue, but she also said that it turned out okay." She shook her head. "That was also the point when she mentioned her friends had basically abandoned her. It has to mean something. The trouble—the new job—all of it was somehow connected."

"I agree, and my money is on Langston. After all, he was one of the best friends. The chances of an encounter occurring were far more likely and would certainly have created the rift between Mary and Eve."

"Could have been another teacher," Anne argued. "Or the principal."

Jack shrugged. "Could have been. But schools aren't exactly the best place for secrets. I would bet money that someone—Mrs. Farrell, for sure—would have known if something was going on there." He sent Anne a sideways look. "I don't know about you, but I got the impression Mrs. Farrell felt the incident would not have been something Mary agreed to."

Anne stared out her window. "Maybe she just doesn't want to think badly of Mary."

Jack wasn't going any further down that road. Although, next to money, an affair was a major motive discovered in murder investigations. The biggest sticking point in Jack's opinion was the fact that her closest friends, meaning the

Langstons and Carin Carter Wallace, hadn't appeared to know. Based on the statements the three gave in court, if they had known anything else negative, it would have come out of their mouths.

Unless…it involved the future senator.

Jack's attention shifted to the rearview mirror. A black sedan had been following them since leaving Farrell's neighborhood.

Coincidence? Maybe.

Only one way to find out.

"Brace yourself." Jack made a sudden right.

The tires squealed. Anne grabbed the armrest, then shot him a look. "What the heck, Jack?"

The sedan didn't make the turn.

Jack relaxed the narrowest margin. "Almost missed my turn." He didn't want to worry her until he had no choice.

"Maybe next time you could give me a little more warning."

"You got it." But then, at the next intersection, he swore under his breath.

The black sedan had taken a right at the next block. It was back.

The driver was male. Sunglasses on.

"Brace yourself again." Jack punched the accelerator and made a hard left.

He continued to turn here and there until he was confident the sedan wasn't reappearing.

When he felt it was safe to slow down, he glanced at his passenger. "You up for an early dinner?"

She sent him a pointed look, her grip on the dash loosening. "If it means you'll stop driving like a crazy person."

He laughed. The sedan by now would be waiting for them at their hotel since he wasn't able to keep up. "Sorry about that, but we had a tail, and I wanted to give him a hard time."

She groaned. "They're already watching us?"

"They are. Actually, I'm surprised it took this long." He flashed her a smile. "But this is good."

Anne made a face. "If you say so."

"It means they're worried," he explained. "If they had nothing to hide they wouldn't be worried."

She turned to him, and a smile spread across her pretty face. "You're right. This is good."

Chapter Ten

I realized by then that I had no true friends. There were my colleagues at work who were nice and whom I adored working with, but we were not friends in the true sense of the word. I was getting a little paranoid actually. At least the other worry had passed. The lab results were what I had hoped for. But I won't talk about that since it worked out for the best. Thank God. I don't think I could have lived with myself if it had turned out differently.

Still, Neil was considering a new venture for after he graduated next year. It was a start-up company that he felt would explode with opportunity in the near future. He was offered a part-time position starting late July. The trouble was that the company was untried. He would be brand new out of law school and serving as the company's head legal counsel. It was quite the prestigious offer for him, except for all the reasons I just named.

By then you would have been born and maybe even trying to crawl. But I didn't want to go back to work that first year. I really wanted to spend some time being your mom. The health insurance was the issue. At the time, my insurance was with my work. Who knew what this new company just starting out would offer. If I took a year off, there might not have been any health insurance. That would not have worked. I told myself that Neil would make the right decision.

Carin had not come back, and by this point Eve and I were not speaking. It was awful the way we had fallen apart. All for such stupid reasons…all because of one person.

By that point I realized I should have told Neil the truth when it happened, and this would have been behind us. But I didn't, and by mid-July I was living with that nightmare hanging over my head. I had no idea what the right thing to do was. I was so young. Neil's life was so busy with his last year of law school and the decisions about our future. He had no time for distraction.

The best I could do was hope all would work out and we could move forward with our lives and never look back. Even then I had begun to believe we had outgrown our friends anyway. It was time to make new friends. I didn't want to raise a child with friends like our old ones.

With that in mind, I told myself we would get through it and maybe in a couple of years we would try for another child. It would have been so wonderful to have a boy and a girl. I remember thinking these things. Although I hadn't had a scan yet, I was convinced you would be a girl. If that turned out to be the case, I planned to name you Marianne. The *Mari* part after me, of course, and the *Anne* after Neil's mom. She was such a good mom and wife. Far better than her husband deserved. I hoped I could be half as good as she was. Just so you know, it wasn't because my mother was a bad one. She just wasn't the kind of mom I wanted to be. I loved her, but I wanted to be better.

I often sat in our little cottage and wondered if one day we would have a bigger house. I even pondered the idea that I should be thankful Neil was considering that start-up company. If it went the way he believed it would, we could end up very comfortable. Possibly even rich.

Maybe some things were worth the risk.

I had decided to talk to him about it again. Just because we were having a baby we shouldn't have been afraid to go for a better life.

I was happy with the decision, and I couldn't wait to tell Neil.

But I had no idea what was coming.

Chapter Eleven

Crystal Lake
Friday, July 11
Latham & Hirsh Law Firm
Virginia Street, 10:00 a.m.

Anne was on edge this morning. She had been since she awakened at five o'clock. Walking the floors of her room for an hour hadn't helped. Then finally around six or so she'd gone outside and stared at the water in hopes the serenity of its stillness would help her find her center.

Hadn't happened.

By seven she'd gone back inside and made a cup of coffee. She couldn't stop thinking about the house where Mary and Neil had lived or the details Beatrice Farrell had shared with her. Specifically, the idea that Neil might not be the father of the child Mary had been carrying.

Her father, Anne amended. She was trying—she really was—to get right with consistently acknowledging the people who had brought her into this world. Not so easy after all these years of resentment and of pretending they didn't exist or were irrelevant. Growing up, she had learned to turn off those feelings. It was the only way to protect herself.

She pushed aside the thought. That little girl no longer needed protecting. She was a grown woman, and she owed it to herself—and maybe to her parents—to do this. The journal had mentioned some sort of situation Mary had worried about and that it had been straightened out. Anne had no idea what the problem—or situation—was until yesterday. Obviously it was the concern about paternity.

When Jack knocked on the door to her room this morning and let her know it was time to go, she'd been startled. She had been far too deep in the swarm of new discoveries to notice the passage of time. After the murder, her mother had basically gone through the horrors of her situation alone. Her own parents were long dead. Her friends had abandoned her. She really was completely alone.

For the first time in her entire life, Anne felt sympathy for the woman who had given birth to her. Perhaps those feelings were misguided. After all, being here and talking to the people who had known Mary and Neil made all of it so real. Quite honestly the whole story—what little she had known about it—had seemed like a work of fiction to Anne. Not part of her actual life. Nothing she had actually experienced.

As a child she'd experienced only resentment and disappointment related to her biological parents. But this had changed everything far faster than she could have imagined possible. Had Victoria, the head of the Colby Agency, known this would happen? Was that why she insisted Anne participate in the investigation?

Anne would hold off until this was done before thanking her…or not.

Too many confusing emotions roiled inside her just now to visualize how this would all settle down.

Since today was forecast to be another scorcher, she

had selected her lightest-weight blouse and the blue dress pants. It was important to represent herself well at this meeting, given that she was also representing her parents, so to speak.

It really was the oddest, somewhat unsettling urge.

"You ready?"

Jack's voice dragged her attention back to the present for the second time this morning. They were here—at the office where Neil had worked part-time during his final year of law school and the final months and weeks of his life. Anne blinked. She hadn't realized they had arrived or that the car had stopped. She gave herself a mental shake. Keeping her focus on the now was far too important to be allowing herself to get caught up in the what-ifs and oh-my-gods of thirty years ago.

Jack looked from her to the office building in front of them. He had taken the last parking slot on the same side of the street. Mr. Hirsh would see them at 10:15. He was the only remaining partner who had been with the firm for more than thirty years—making him the only one who had known Neil Reed. Without hesitation, he had agreed to the meeting. No questions. But that had been late yesterday. Maybe sleeping on the idea will have changed his mind. He might share nothing at all or have questions of his own. Anne wouldn't be surprised either way.

"Anne?"

She jerked to attention once more. "Yes. Sorry. I'm ready." Anne reached for the door.

Jack did the same. They met on the sidewalk at the front of the car. He'd finally learned not to bother rushing to her side of the vehicle to open the door. It was so not necessary, and she felt foolish waiting for him to do so. Still, the notion that he would if she opted to go that route was refreshing in an old-fashioned sort of way. There was something to be said for chivalry. She was pretty much convinced that he was a very nice man.

Despite her determination there was no stopping him from opening the door to the law firm for her. She thanked him with a smile and walked in. At the reception desk, she deferred to Jack. He had made the call for the meeting.

"Good morning," Sandra, according to the nameplate, announced.

"Good morning. Jack Brenner and Anne Griffin to see Mr. Hirsh."

After checking the calendar, Sandra nodded. "He's ready for you now." She stood. "This way, please."

They followed her along a carpeted corridor. Paintings of the partners, retired or deceased ones first, lined the walls. At the end of the corridor was a table topped with a large, lush flower arrangement. Reminded Anne a little of a funeral home.

Sandra rapped on the door to the left, then opened it. "Mr. Hirsh, your ten fifteen is here." She swept her right hand in a gesture for Anne and Jack to enter the office.

The gray-haired gentleman behind the gleaming, wide wooden desk stood. "Thank you, Sandra."

She left the room, closing the door behind her.

"Mr. Brenner, I presume," Hirsh said to Jack before turning to Anne. "Ms. Griffin. Take a seat, and let's dive in. I worked you in between appointments, so my time is limited."

"Thank you for that," Jack said as he waited for Anne to settle. Then he claimed the chair next to her.

Always the gentleman, she mused.

"As I told your assistant, I'm from the Colby Agency—a private investigations firm in Chicago," Jack explained, cutting straight to the chase. "We have questions about Neil Reed."

Mr. Hirsh clasped his hands on his desk. "Well, that goes back a bit. Neil interned here for a few months as I'm sure you're aware. We had high hopes for him. He was a brilliant student of the law. The goal was when he graduated and passed the bar to work with Oscar Nelson. Oscar was nearing retirement age, and we wanted to get someone good on board to absorb as much of his wisdom as possible before that happened. We felt Neil was a promising young man with a natural gift for the work we do here."

"When was the decision made that he would join your firm?" Jack inquired. "We've found some indication that he had other plans."

"BioTech." Hirsh nodded. "I believe that was his first choice, but there was a glitch, as I recall, and he opted to take the offer we made."

"Glitch?" Anne echoed, speaking for the first time.

The attorney's attention shifted to her. "I can't say for certain, of course, since those details were never made public or shared with anyone at this firm. The rumor was that Mike Smith, the BioTech CEO, withdrew the offer and hired someone else."

They knew part of this already. Jack's research department at the Colby Agency determined that Langston had taken the position instead of her father. But no one appeared to know how that change came about. And as Hirsh said, any fallout was kept under wraps. The whole ordeal took place so quietly and so far behind the scenes it was as if it never happened…except it had, and Anne's instincts warned it had served as an impetus for the storm that descended on Mary Morton's and Neil Reed's lives.

Frankly, to Anne's way of thinking, anything kept so secretive couldn't have been good for all parties involved.

"We've learned that Neil and his fiancée," Anne said, "were concerned about BioTech being new without the potential security and benefits of a more established firm like yours. Perhaps that was the only glitch."

"I'd like to think," Hirsh said, "that our package was the better offer, and that was the reason we were able to lock him in well in advance of his being able to join us as an attorney. But there was talk to the contrary."

Anne was surprised he opted to share what was clearly hearsay.

"Did you or any of the partners," Jack probed, "at the time have any concerns or hesitations before making the offer? He was months from graduating, and then there was the bar exam after that. How could you be certain he'd pull it all off?"

"One only needed to review his transcript to know that—barring a grave illness or death—there was no question Neil Reed would do those things and do them particularly well. The fact is if you expect to get the best coming out of law school, you have to make the preliminary offers early. We learned that lesson the hard way. It's a situation that continues to be a concern with maintaining a larger firm, which is why we've downsized somewhat in recent years."

"In the days before his murder," Anne ventured, "were you aware of any issues going on in his private life? Did he seem worried or upset here at the office?"

"We've read the statement you made to the investigating detective," Jack pointed out. "What we're in search of is anything that, looking back, may have been more important than you realized at the time."

A very good point, in Anne's opinion, since Hirsh's statement told them basically nothing other than Neil was brilliant, dependable and charming.

"In particular," Anne tossed in while Hirsch pondered Jack's question, "any issues between Neil and Kevin Langston? Perhaps there was bad blood after the way things turned out with the BioTech offer." The fact that Hirsh hadn't mentioned Langston in connection to the so-called glitch was certainly no indication that he didn't know. She would wager that he was well aware.

The hesitation dragged on a bit. Jack pulled out his phone and checked it as if to show his impatience. Anne, on the other hand, kept her attention fixed on the attorney. She wanted that answer. There had to be an issue between the two men. Everything pointed in that direction.

"It was my opinion," Hirsh said finally, "that there was a rift between the two men afterward, yes."

"Can you elaborate on that?" Jack tucked his phone away.

"Not really. Whatever issues arose from the quandary, I'm sure the two worked those out. But, of course, I have no way of knowing those private details. Frankly it takes little or no imagination to recognize it was an issue. Neil never spoke of it or of his friend which, in my opinion, was telling in itself."

"That would suggest the two didn't work out the issues at all," Anne tossed in. "Neil was murdered soon after. If there was some underhanded step that caused Langston to steal the position Neil had already accepted, that's the sort of story that makes life complicated for a politician."

Anne understood before she made the statement that Hirsh would have no comment, but she wanted him to realize she wasn't blind. What Langston did was motive whether he killed Neil or not. The bigger question was why the police didn't investigate that avenue.

Hirsh's expression closed instantly. "I'm afraid I am unaware of any such step. Senator Langston has a long-standing reputation of exceptional accomplishments in this city and in representing this state. I would be remiss if I didn't warn you that such unfounded rumors can be constituted as libelous. Which is why I shall refrain from further comment."

"This is exactly the sort of brick wall," Jack remarked, "as I'm sure you're aware, that prevents those searching from finding the truth."

"Well." Hirsh stood. "I hope I've been of some assistance to you. I do have another appointment waiting. Good luck with your endeavor."

Anne and Jack had almost made it to the door when he hesitated and turned back to the attorney. "Just one other thing. Did your firm handle the nondisclosure agreement for the senator when a former intern came forward accusing him of sexual assault?"

Anne stared at Jack for a moment, shock radiating through her. This was certainly news to her. She quickly banished the reaction and turned to Hirsh to hear the answer. Inside, she couldn't stop wondering why Jack hadn't mentioned a sexual-assault accusation in Langton's history. She certainly hadn't found anything even remotely negative related to the man in her searches. His history—according to the World Wide Web—was as clean as a whistle.

Hirsh's face blanched. "As I'm sure *you* are aware, I can't discuss the work we do at this firm unless, of course, you are in need of one or more of those services."

Jack smiled. "Never mind. I have the answer now."

They exited the office. Anne barely kept her mouth shut

until they were outside and in the car. "You didn't mention anything about a sexual-assault accusation."

"I just found out—that text I received a few minutes ago."

"You have someone still digging?" The frustration drained away, and she had to admit she was impressed.

He shifted in his seat, faced her. "To be clear, our people will be working on finding whatever there is to find until this is done."

"Okay." Talk about the full treatment. She couldn't ask for more than that. She also couldn't stop looking into his eyes. He really did have nice eyes, but it was the certainty, the reassurance there that had her lingering.

He turned back to the steering wheel, reversed out of the slot and headed for Williams Street. They were having an early lunch at Judith's. Jack wanted to rattle her cage again. Anne was fully on board with the plan.

As he drove in that direction, she chewed at her lip. "I'm thinking that if your discovery is illustrative of the sort of man Langston is or was, he could very well have forced an encounter with Mary. That may be why she wanted the paternity test. It makes the most sense—don't you think?"

Something definitely happened between the longtime friends. Maybe it was money, aka the BioTech position, *and* sex. Maybe one or the other, but it had happened. All they had to do was prove it.

"I think it's a strong possibility."

Or maybe Anne only wanted it to be Langston after the things she had learned he'd done. Stealing the job Neil had hoped for. Abusing an intern. On the other hand, in both instances, they were hearing just one side of the story. Maybe more so than ever, she recognized that there were two sides to every story.

She wished it hadn't taken her so long to realize this. Perhaps she should have tried visiting her mother again. Maybe if she hadn't stopped Mary would have eventually given in before it was too late. Anne would never know about that. All she could do was keep digging until someone told the truth.

What they needed was to talk to the senator. Anne considered herself pretty good at spotting untruths and insincerities. She'd certainly felt seriously bad vibes from Eve Langston. They also very much needed to get an interview with Carin Carter Wallace. She was closer to the Langstons than anyone else. Anne imagined the woman was privy to all their secrets.

Jack pulled out his cell phone and accepted a call.

While he spoke quietly with the caller, Anne pondered the well-prepared answers they had gotten from Hirsh. The man had wanted to appear cooperative with his little well-couched innuendos. She had a feeling the only thing he had done was give answers that would lead absolutely nowhere. And if his firm had represented Langston before…perhaps they still did. In which case, his agreement to meet with them was in all likelihood just an opportunity to get information for the senator.

If Jack had the name of the woman who'd claimed the assault—

"We have to go back to the hotel," Jack announced before she'd finished the thought.

"Why? Did you forget something?"

His hands tightened on the steering wheel. "There was a fire in your room. Several rooms along that corridor suffered smoke damage." He glanced at her. "We'll need to find a new place to stay."

He'd lost her at *a fire in your room*. "How in the world

did that happen?" The possibilities swirled in her head. She had not used an iron or a hair dryer or any other product that required electricity except the coffeemaker which stayed plugged in. She hadn't touched it other than to brew a cup of coffee. Whatever happened, she didn't think it was related to her use of the room.

"At the moment they don't know the cause. Only that it started in your room."

In her opinion that said it all. Anne sank into the seat. Did someone want them to stop their investigation that badly? Desperately enough to do this?

Thank God she had the box and all its contents with her.

What about the photos? She grabbed her purse and dug through it. A deep breath was impossible until her fingers found those irreplaceable photos. They were there. Thank God.

If she'd left them in the room...

She shook off the thought. She hadn't.

The secrets and the lies and now a fire? It had been almost thirty years since Neil Reed was murdered and Mary Morton went to prison. What could anyone be trying to hide at this point?

Fear slid cold and oily through her chest.

There was only one answer—the truth about who murdered Neil Reed.

Just like Mary Morton said.

Water's Edge Hotel
Chapel Hill Road, Johnsburg, Noon

JACK STARED AT the blackened walls, the burned bed and curtains, the partially melted and charred desk and chair that had been a part of Anne's room. He was damned glad they had already left before this thing started. But then, whoever did this had known they weren't in their rooms. The goal was to destroy any evidence Anne might have left in the room and to scare her.

If Jack had doubted the conclusion, the fire marshal confirmed it by admitting that arson was suspected.

"Did anything survive?" Anne asked when he walked to where she waited near the stairwell at the end of the corridor.

"I wouldn't think so. Either way, they aren't going to give us access to the room or its contents anytime soon."

"We'll need new rooms." She sighed. "And clothes."

"Agreed." He glanced around. "We can do that now if you're ready."

She looked up at him. "I say we go to Judith's as planned. While we wait for the food, I'll look for a new hotel online, and you check in with the senator's people again. I want to see that man today."

Jack couldn't help but grin. She'd been so hesitant about going along with this investigation, and now she was leading the charge. He loved it.

She frowned. "Why are you smiling?"

"Just thinking how lucky I am to have you as a partner on this. What a good plan." He hitched his head toward the parking lot. "You ready? If the manager here needs anything else he has my number."

As they walked away she grumbled something about *partner* and shot him a look, but the smile her expression melted into told him she kind of liked the idea. He did too. Maybe too much.

When they reached the car, Jack held up a hand. "Hang on." With the fire in the rooms, he wasn't taking any risks that whoever had started it might not decide on some other route to deter them.

He checked the car doors—still locked. No way anyone was opening the hood or the trunk without getting into the car. Then he got down onto his hands and knees on the pavement, lowered onto his back and had a look at the undercarriage. He checked all the way around the vehicle and in the wheel wells.

No tracking devices. No other unexpected additions. He got to his feet and dusted himself off.

"You think they would try to tamper with the car?" Fear made its way into her eyes.

"At this point, we can't pretend it isn't a possibility."

She dusted off the back of his shirt, stopping at his waist. "The idea is a little unsettling, but I suppose I shouldn't be surprised."

"It is unsettling." He rested his gaze on hers then. "Being extra careful is the guide now. We don't do anything without being abundantly cautious."

"Got it." She made a face. "You see this kind of thing in the movies. On the news. You just don't expect to have it happen in your real life."

"I can talk to Victoria." Worry nudged him. "Maybe I should finish this on my own."

"No way." She shook her head firmly from side to side. "I'm all in—especially now. I'm not going anywhere until this is done. I'm your partner, you said," she reminded him.

"All right, then. But if you change your mind at any point, say the word."

He had a feeling that would never happen. This lady was tougher than she looked.

Just another thing he liked about her. Truth was he liked everything about her.

Chapter Twelve

Barrington
Langston Residence
Plum Tree Road, 3:00 p.m.

Anne could barely remain seated. They had arrived and were shown to the senator's home office. The room was exactly what she had expected. Lots of dark wood, a massive desk and a wall filled with shelves in the same dark walnut. Each shelf was lined with law books. If he arrived wearing a tweed jacket and smoking a pipe her visual image would be complete.

Though the design was quite traditional, it felt heavy and outdated. The space needed a serious update, in Anne's opinion.

Jack glanced at her. She managed a smile. He would be wondering if she was anxious. The answer was yes. She was nervous for sure. But learning all possible from and about this man was essential. She would do whatever was necessary to make that happen.

Except she really didn't want to die trying to find answers.

The memory of how the aftermath in her hotel room had looked and smelled haunted her. If she sniffed her blouse the odor still lingered. The fire marshal had mentioned that the fire had moved fast. They would be testing for an accelerant, which he suspected would be found. Whoever set that fire hadn't been playing around. Sadly, the hotel had no security cameras, and no one they had questioned so far had seen a single thing out of the ordinary.

Deep inside, she shivered at the thought of how someone could have been injured or killed because she had kicked a hornet's nest. It was impossible to ignore the fact that someone or several someones did not want the truth dug up and were willing to do anything to stop it.

Was finding a thirty-year-old truth really worth the risk to her safety and that of others?

Then again, if she didn't finish this, it could happen again. If the senator was the one who murdered Neil, then he could still be hurting people. Case in point, the sexual-assault allegation. She could only imagine what he might be capable of in the future. He certainly had no place in a position of such significant power.

If he was the one, he had to be stopped.

The door opened and the man himself walked in. She and Jack stood. Part of her had wanted to stay seated. He wasn't royalty, just another possibly crooked politician. Maybe a killer...certainly an abuser. She suddenly felt foolish for showing him any regard whatsoever.

"I apologize for keeping you waiting." He paused and thrust out his hand, first to Anne.

She brushed her palm against his, barely touching his hand. "Anne Griffin."

Jack took his hand next, gave it a firm pump. "Jack Brenner."

The senator was a tall man. Even nearing sixty, the only gray in his hair was at his temples. He carried himself with an air of importance—as if anyone he encountered should recognize his worth. There were many things Anne instantly recognized about the man—arrogant, self-serving, to name a few. But then, she'd drawn that conclusion before he set foot in the room.

He skirted his desk and settled into the leather chair behind it. "I understand you're conducting some sort of investigation into Neil Reed's murder." His attention moved between the two of them coming to rest on Jack. "I'm familiar with the Colby Agency's stellar reputation. I'm sure you'll be thorough."

"We appreciate your time, Senator. Our primary goal at this time is to determine what was happening in Mary Morton's and Neil Reed's personal lives just before the murder. We've reviewed the official case file and, frankly, found it lacking. Perhaps it was inexperience on the detective's part. Given the many holes in the work, we're basically going over all the steps."

Langston leaned back in his chair, his forearms and hands resting on the chair arms. "My wife mentioned that you spoke with her already." He glanced at Anne for the first time since they brushed palms. "Eve was right. You do look so much like your mother."

Anne forced a smile. "You and your wife were very close to my parents. Were you aware of any trouble between them or with any of their friends just before the murder?" Like *you*, she wanted to say but did not. Who could doubt the possibility considering what this man had taken from Neil Reed? Even if he wasn't guilty of murder, he knew things—things that could make a difference.

He paused for consideration of the question before responding. "I was unaware of any personal trouble between Mary and Neil. As for issues with friends, I can't say that the relationship he and I once had was the same. Obviously not, since I was chosen over him for a position he really wanted. But like politics, the field of law is competitive. Fiercely so. There are no in-betweens. You're either winning or you're losing. In that case, I was the winner."

Anne bit her lips together to hold back the retort that sprang to the tip of her tongue.

"What about your relationship with Mary?" Jack said. "Was their trouble between you and Reed where she was concerned?"

Like the attorney they had met with this morning, Langston's face cleared of emotion. He turned his hands up as if to say he didn't understand the question. But then he spoke. "Mary and Eve were very good friends. Best friends, I would say," he insisted. "I, of course, was friends with her as well but only through Eve. There was never anything beyond that between Mary and me. She was busy with her teaching, and I was even busier with building my career. We hardly had time for anything else. I can't imagine where you stumbled upon such an idea."

Stumbled? Anne bit her teeth together hard to prevent a retort.

Jack looked from Anne to Langston, she suspected to build the anticipation of his next question. "Was there anyone else," he pressed, "close to the four of you who may have taken an unsolicited interest in Mary?"

"Are you implying Mary had an affair?" Langston's tone was imbued with surprise or something on that order. Probably faked. He appeared every bit the type to act his way out of a troubling situation.

"We know there was—let's just say," Jack explained, "an event with another man. We're currently running down a paternity test that should answer the question."

The senator's expression closed completely then.

"We have reason to believe the encounter was not a welcome one," Anne added without saying *the word*.

Despite his restraint, the man's face turned deathly pale. His eyes widened like saucers. She and Jack seemed to have that effect during interviews, even with someone as practiced at disguise as this man clearly was. Anne had to clutch the armrests of her chair to remain seated. She wanted to jump up and demand that he admit what he had done.

This man was somehow involved in what happened. Anne was sure of it.

"I've been reading her journal," she said, only at that moment deciding to share this information. He apparently had lost his ability to speak, at least momentarily. "I believe we're getting very close to uncovering evidence of the details she shared. Once we have what we need, I'm confident the murder case will be reopened. But this time, there will be a different defendant. My only regret is that I couldn't make that happen before she died in prison for a crime she did not commit."

The emotion that poured out of her with the revelations left her weak and on the verge of shaking. She should not have ignored her mother all those years. No matter that her mother had turned away her only attempts for a connection after high school, Anne should have kept trying. She should have fought for the truth. Regret and pain welled inside her so fast she could hardly breathe.

"I can understand your need to somehow make this right." Langston seemed to have gathered his wits once more. "But Mary is dead. What good can come of turning your own life upside down to find answers that likely will not change a thing?"

"She was innocent." Anne surprised herself by saying the words with strength and determination. "Her name should be cleared. She deserves—I deserve—the truth."

The senator inclined his head and studied her. "At what expense to you? In your line of work, reputation is everything. You need clients to trust you on all levels. It would be a shame to neglect your career for this futile endeavor."

Anne shook visibly with the impact of his words. Had he just threatened to damage her reputation? Clearly a US senator had the power to do such a thing. Also very clear was the idea that he had looked into her life.

"Particularly," Jack cut in, "if those rumors are false. I'm sure you felt the same way when Adrina Wilson made her allegations. Thankfully you were able to keep those out of the media for the most part—which is a major feat in itself these days."

The blood drained from Langston's face once more. "That," he said, his voice tight, "was a woman out to get something for nothing. I never touched her. She smelled money, and she wanted it." He snapped his mouth shut as if he'd only just realized that he wasn't supposed to speak of the matter.

So much for the nondisclosure agreement.

"But it was the other—the physical relationship," Anne suggested, "Adrina didn't want. Was that the true issue? Mary's journal reflects much the same. She didn't want what happened, and yet fear kept her from going to the proper authorities." She was really reaching here, but somehow she couldn't stop herself.

"This conversation is over." Langston stood. "I'm certain you can see yourselves out."

Anne and Jack rose from their chairs.

"Again," Jack said, "we appreciate your time. Would you

let your assistant, Carin Wallace, know that we're trying to get in touch? I'm confident she has some of the answers we're looking for."

Langston remained silent. Fury burned red on his face, glowing in his eyes.

No one, not even the woman who had greeted them when they arrived, waited outside the office to escort them from the house. This surprised Anne. They walked along the marble-floored hall and into the grand foyer. No sign of Eve or an assistant or a member of the household staff.

Apparently the senator had wanted to ensure today's conversation was kept absolutely quiet.

Again, Jack checked the vehicle before they got in to leave. At the end of the driveway, they waited for the gates to open and rolled forward.

They had a new place to stay. Anne had taken care of that matter while they waited for their lunch at Judith's. If the woman had been in today, she hadn't come out to say hello. Maybe she couldn't bear to face Anne after what she'd done—filling Eve in on their conversation. But then perhaps Judith didn't realize she'd done exactly what they'd wanted her to do—spread the word they were here and looking for information.

"Our tail is back." Jack nodded toward the rearview mirror.

"Are we still going to shop?" She watched the black sedan in the side mirror.

"Why not. He can follow us there, and we'll lose him after that. Just be prepared in case he makes some sort of aggressive move."

Vividly recalling yesterday's driving adventures, Anne leaned deeper into the seat, braced one hand on the door's armrest and the other on the console between them. "Got it."

The drive via US-14 from Barrington to Crystal Lake took all of five minutes. Another five or so minutes later and they arrived in the parking lot of the superstore they'd agreed upon.

Jack watched as the black sedan drove on past where they had parked. It wound through the lines of parked cars, finally sliding into a slot three rows away.

"I guess they want to know the location of our new hotel," Anne surmised. Motel actually. The one she'd chosen wasn't one those watching them would likely consider.

"We'll just have to make sure that doesn't happen."

They emerged from the car. Jack reached into the back seat and got the box. "Just in case." He looked at Anne over the top of the car.

"Good idea."

They walked together to the entrance. Anne had never shopped for clothes with a man. This would be a unique experience for sure. She grabbed a cart. Jack deposited the box in the cart, and she placed her shoulder bag on top of it.

"Ladies first," Jack suggested.

"Works for me." Anne headed for the women's department.

While she perused the racks of tops, Jack stepped a short distance away and made a call. She glanced at him from time to time, hoping there wasn't bad news. Or maybe this was a good call and she would have something better to think about instead of being frustrated over the meeting with Langston. What a jerk the man was.

The sound of her own cell phone vibrating tugged her attention to her purse. She poked around inside until she found it.

Lisa.

Worry sent a flare of adrenaline in her chest. "Hey, what's going on?"

"Hey, Anne. I hope I'm not catching you at a bad time."

"No." She rifled through the tops on the rack in front of her. "It's fine. Everything okay?"

"I'm not sure."

Her assistant did not sound okay. "What's going on?"

"The tile supplier just called about our new job. He said he'd forgotten about a customer on the list ahead of us who apparently wants the exact same tile we ordered for the principal bathroom."

Anne's stomach dipped. Not good. "What kind of delay are we looking at?"

"Two to three weeks from today. He claims the tile we ordered that will arrive next week will have to go to the other customer."

That kind of delay absolutely would not work.

"Hold on," Lisa said before Anne could respond. "Got another call."

Anne forced herself to focus on the task at hand despite the news from Lisa. She grabbed a mustard-colored tee without a logo or image plastered across the front. She tossed it into the cart and carried on sorting through the offerings on the rack. When the seconds continued to tick off, she glanced at the screen to ensure the call was still connected. It was and she was still on hold.

She hoped this was not more trouble. The idea that the timing was worrisome wasn't lost on her. Could Langston really work that fast? They'd only left the meeting a few minutes ago. Then again, he could have started this as soon as he heard she was in town.

A black tee caught her attention. Plain. Good. She plucked it from the rack and tossed it into the cart as well.

Maybe one more, and that would be enough. She settled on a pale rose-colored one, and it joined the others in the cart. She glanced at Jack, who lingered close and still appeared to be in deep conversation on his own phone.

She grabbed two pairs of jeans and headed for the lingerie department, which was next to this one. She glanced back to ensure Jack followed. He did, but thankfully he kept his distance while she grabbed the necessary bras and undies as well as a nightshirt.

All she needed now was a few toiletries like deodorant and a disposable razor. Maybe some mascara.

"Sorry!" Lisa said into her ear, making her jump. "You are really not going to believe this. It was the same guy— the tile supplier. Now he says the kitchen-floor tile is on back order. But I know it's not because I spoke to one of the guys who works there this morning to go over the suggested coordinating trim. It was not on back order, Anne. Something is going on with this guy. I mean, I can call around and see what I find out from other wholesalers, but this is very strange."

Anne's fingers tightened around the cart handle. Nothing she could do from here…except stay calm. "Just do what you can to ensure we have what we need to start in fourteen days."

"Don't worry," Lisa assured her. "I will. I just wanted you to know that something weird is happening here."

"I'm sorry for the trouble, Lisa. I promise there will be a big bonus in this one."

Lisa laughed. "I got you. Don't worry. Bonus or not, this is going to get done."

Anne thanked her and ended the call. She tossed her phone back into her bag. Outrage rushed through her veins, and she wanted to scream. How the hell had he done this so fast? Even if he'd started yesterday…this was incredibly quick. His statements in the meeting suggested he had already done a background search on her. But the details of her latest client's contract? That was over the top.

Well, of course he had gotten in-depth information. He was rich and powerful…and a scumbag.

How much money did it take, she mused, to turn long-time suppliers against her?

"Everything okay?"

Jack must have noticed the look on her face because he was suddenly beside her.

"I don't know. It seems we have a problem with our tile supplier." She looked directly at Jack, hoping he would read the innuendo in her eyes. "This morning all was well with our orders, and now suddenly there are delays. I want to believe this has nothing to do with what's going on here…" She moved her head side to side. "But after that veiled threat he made about my life, I'm not so sure."

Her phone sounded the warning that she had a new text message. She grabbed it from her bag and stared at the screen.

You will not believe this!

Her heart dropping, she opened the text box.

There may be a snag with our permit for the job!!!

Anne typed a quick message letting Lisa know to call if she couldn't get it straightened out.

"And now——" she looked at Jack "——there's a holdup on our permit."

"Now, that one," he said, his own frustration showing, "I

would put money on being prompted by a call from someone on the senator's personal staff."

Anne was angrier than she had been in…she couldn't remember when. She forced the worries aside. "We heading to the men's department now?"

"Yeah. Let's get this done and get out of here."

They started that way, and then she realized she hadn't asked him about his call.

"Everything okay on your end?"

"My call was all good." He flashed her a grin.

She liked his smiles, and she was immensely thankful he hadn't laid another issue at her feet. "We'll need to stop at health and beauty aids too."

"Deodorant," he noted with a nod.

"For sure."

Unlike her, he was quick with his shopping. They even swung through the aisle where camping supplies were sold and grabbed another flashlight and batteries. Then after a quick stroll through Health and Beauty, they were off to the checkout lanes. Once they were checked out and ready to go, rather than walk out the main exit, he ushered her in a different direction.

"Where are we going?"

He flashed her another of those adorable grins. "To the garden department."

The garden department was on the opposite end of the enormous superstore from where they had parked. She wasn't sure how that would help, but obviously the man had a plan. To her surprise, she trusted him completely.

As they reached the area stocked with all manner of grilling and pool supplies as well as loads of plants, he checked his cell and continued toward the exit.

Outside a car waited at the pedestrian crosswalk. Jack

opened the rear passenger door for her. She climbed in, her bag of goods in hand, and he slid in next to her, the box and his own bag in tow.

"All set?" the driver asked.

"We are. If you don't mind, go out on this end of the lot."

"Will do."

Jack turned to her. "Uber," he whispered. "He's taking us to the car-rental center. We'll pick up our new car and head to our hotel."

Anne twisted around in the seat and looked for the black sedan that had parked just beyond the grocery entrance—all the way at the other end of the massive building.

Then she grinned at Jack. "That was good." Worry tugged her lips into a frown. "What about your car?"

"Someone from the agency will pick it up."

Anne relaxed and settled back into the seat. She was grateful to be in such good hands. She just hoped he was good enough to keep this search for the truth from turning into a bigger nightmare.

Though she hated admitting as much, she hadn't expected her business and certainly not her life to be in danger while pursuing this quest.

But then, she hadn't fully embraced the idea that Mary—her mother—had been telling the truth.

And that someone would be willing to do anything to prevent that truth from coming out.

Chapter Thirteen

Moody Motel
Carpenter Street, 6:00 p.m.

The place wasn't as bad as Anne had feared. Not that Jack had given her any particular specifications regarding where to book a room. Still, she sort of wanted him to be pleased, if not impressed, with her choice. The place was far from impressive, but that wasn't the primary requirement this go-around.

There had been two rooms with a connecting door available. The motel was not an upscale place by any stretch of the imagination. The upside was that the rooms were clean. A little shabby, but in a charming sort of way. The outside had been painted recently in one of those popular dark bluish-black colors. The inside was freshly painted in a very pale shade of gray. No carpet. Hardwood and tile. The tiny bathroom was, to be kind, vintage—including a clawfoot tub.

Anne liked it. She wasn't sure how Jack felt. He was probably accustomed to staying in the higher-end hotels. Her goal had been to find a decent place where no one would look—at least not at first.

This was, she figured, exactly that sort of place.

It was funny, she considered as she hung up her new clothes in the very tiny closet, how easily appeased she was with accommodations. She went to great lengths to provide beautiful, elegant and trending designs to her clients. Personally, if she didn't work from home, she would live in a little cottage by the water somewhere. Vintage was her favorite style. But clients expected certain things when they met with a designer. So she lived in an upscale neighborhood in a trendy town house that would hopefully whet their appetites and earn their trust.

Her hands fell to her sides. At university one of her professors had warned that she shouldn't be afraid to color outside the lines. He'd done this because she never took risks with her designs. She was very good, he had insisted, but she needed to extend outside her boundaries. Over time her work had grown and taken on more of a cutting edge. But her personal life—the person she was—stayed in that *safe* zone.

Which probably explained how she'd almost reached thirty with few romantic relationships.

It wasn't that she didn't try. She did. She just didn't try very hard…or often.

Her gaze swung to the connecting door. Jack kind of made her want to jump outside that safe zone she'd built around her personal life. It was easy to imagine coloring outside the lines with him.

She shook her head. He was here to do a job, not become a romantic interest for a lonely designer about to hit the big 3-0.

A knock on the connecting door made her jump.

She pressed a hand to her chest and sucked in the breath that had deserted her. Squaring her shoulders, she walked to the door and opened it. Better to keep her head out of those dreamy places.

He smiled. He really had the nicest smile. Nice lips too. Great eyes. Anne almost sighed out loud. She chased away the thoughts.

"What's up?" She was tired...mentally and physically. Not herself. It wasn't like her to fantasize about random men. Not that there was really anything at all random about this one. *Enough, Anne!*

"I thought I'd order dinner in. Have it delivered since there's no restaurant on the property."

She frowned. "I know this place is kind of low end. I hope it's okay. I figured it wouldn't be somewhere they would consider—at least not the first place on their list anyway." She laughed at herself. "I may have read too many mystery novels."

He chuckled. "It was a good choice. Really."

"Thanks." She relaxed a little. "So...food. What did you have in mind?"

"Chinese? Mexican? Mediterranean? Regular old American? There's quite a list who deliver."

"Chinese. Pick a variety of things, and we'll share." Immediately the image of her using chopsticks to feed him came to mind. She banished it. She so had to get her head on straight. Maybe it was the stress. Had to be.

"Another good choice." He tapped the screen of his cell phone and started the process.

She left him in the doorway between their rooms and went back to unbagging her purchases. It was either that or stare at his perfect profile while he ordered their dinner. *Strange behavior, Anne.* Apparently digging into her mother's sad love story was getting to her...making her desperate.

That had to be it. Otherwise, what in the world had her suddenly daydreaming about an encounter with the man assigned to investigate her case? She decided it was that age-old problem of needing to take her mind off her troubles. Hadn't she learned that in Psych 101 back during her freshman year of college?

Either that or the other age-old suggestion that barreling toward thirty had her biological clock acting up. At this point she hadn't even considered children.

No. Stop it.

She'd been dateless for ages now. Hadn't been kissed or hugged by a man in months—maybe a year. She groaned. Pretty pathetic. But no reason to go all desperate and sex crazed. She wandered to the bathroom to stash her necessities. With no room on the tiny sink, she lined them up on the toilet tank lid.

She considered the tub. She loved its curves and the deeper depth. Maybe she'd have a soak later. She needed to relax, and a leisurely bath might just do the trick. Get her mind off the ancient history of an abandoned baby and the present dilemma of a lonely woman.

Her eyes rolled. Pathetic.

Back in her room, Jack waited at the shared door, one broad shoulder braced against the doorframe. Could he not look so...sexy? Another groan welled inside her, but she tamped it down.

"Thirty-to-forty minutes," he announced.

"Thanks."

She stood there a moment, uncertain what to do. Maybe he'd say something, get a conversation going about the investigation. Otherwise, her mounting tension would continue. She was obviously going through something, and it was ridiculous. She was no teenager, and this was no game.

"You handling today okay? I know some of it wasn't exactly comfortable."

She lifted one shoulder and let it fall, fixed her attention on the events of the day. "I had this idea of how things would go." She dropped onto the foot of the bed—thankfully the mattress seemed fairly comfortable. "But I was way off in my assumptions."

"You thought—" he stepped into her space, pulled the chair from the small desk and took a seat "—you'd find the same thing the detective did. You'd feel you had done your due diligence, and then you could go home and put this all behind you."

Wow. He was a mind reader too.

"Something like that."

"Assuming the most complicated situation or ending isn't the route our minds usually take." He braced his forearms on his thighs. "But sometimes that's just where life takes us."

She tried to ignore how their knees almost touched. The room was so small the end of the bed was only about three or four feet from the desk and the connecting door. But she wasn't complaining. His nearness was comforting. It made her feel warm and safe. Gave her the courage to keep her chin up and her shoulders square in this situation so alien to her. Her only experience with this sort of thing was the occasional true crime documentary.

"I thought I knew what happened. The woman who gave birth to me killed the man who fathered me. For reasons I would likely never know or understand." She shook her head. "She'd never written to me. Wouldn't see me when I tried to visit her. I assumed she never wanted me—the same story some of my foster mothers told me while they were pointing out how happy I should be to have what they provided. Which wasn't always what a child needed."

"I get that your childhood wasn't what it should have been." His eyes searched hers. "But you rose above it. You've done really well for yourself. You have every reason to be proud of your accomplishments. If your mother knew anything about your life, I'm sure she was proud as well."

"Thank you. I hope so. I haven't really worried about what she thought since I was a kid, but I would be lying if I didn't say my feelings have changed. This whole endeavor has certainly been eye opening." She glanced at the journal that lay on her bed. She'd taken it out of the box with the intention of reviewing certain entries. "When I read the journal, I wasn't convinced of anything beyond what I already felt. Not really. I mean anyone can write words on a page. Everyone has their story. I had little confidence that her story would prove accurate to any real degree. Maybe it was what she believed to be the truth…but that's not always the same as the real truth."

But she had begun to see the full picture now. Her gaze settled on the man watching her. About many things—like her own story. The way she ignored her personal needs. How she pretended work was everything and that there was no time for anything else.

Slow down, girl.

"I, as well as the team at the agency, fully believe that Mary was innocent. I personally am confident that what we've heard so far confirms as much."

Anne crossed her legs in an effort to get more comfortable. Her foot nudged his shin, and she uncrossed and then recrossed in the other direction. "Sorry."

"No problem—I'm the one who's crowding you." He shifted a little.

"It's fine. Really." *Focus on the case!* Deep breath. "Do you think there's any chance Adrina Wilson would talk to me?" If the senator had taken advantage of his assistant, that would make believing he'd done the same to Mary far easier to accept for anyone hearing the story.

"It's doubtful. She signed an NDA. She would be setting herself up for serious legal repercussions if she did."

Anne had thought as much, but it never hurt to get a second opinion. "The fact that he paid her to sign this agreement suggests he was guilty, right?"

"Most people see it that way. There's always the possibility that even if he was innocent of the charge he didn't want to deal with being trashed in the media. Like you, I see the agreement as hush money for his crossing the line. How far over that line he went" he shrugged "—who knows. I will say that this business with Wilson was ten years ago—just as he was assuming his current office, so keeping negative reports out of the media was more important than ever."

She supposed that was a valid point.

"Thirty years ago," he went on, "Langston was younger and had far less to lose. I'm guessing he wasn't worried about Mary coming forward. She had to protect her reputation as a teacher of young children, and she was engaged to be married. She had everything to lose at the time, and he had basically nothing to worry about. It was her word against his. No matter who their friends and colleagues believed, the damage would be done to Mary's reputation."

A very smart analysis. Not a fair conclusion, but the most likely one that would have been reached at the time. Jack was really good at his job. Handsome, charming, kind and smart. Why was it that she never ran into a guy like him in her everyday life? Would she have even noticed?

Not fair, she decided. She no doubt ran into really nice men often, but she ignored them. Her attention was more often than not on work. The truth was if she didn't put herself out there, she didn't have to worry about being hurt. Relationships and marriage led to other things like children and...

It was difficult to see going down that road after the childhood she'd had.

As much as she hated blaming so much on her childhood, her inability to take the usual relationship risks was a direct result of those early years. On some level she understood that this moment—this time with Jack—was temporary and less risky maybe. In the end they would go their own ways. No real jeopardy involved when the relationship was temporary, right?

She had lost her mind. With a deep breath, she dismissed the thoughts and concentrated on what they were here to do. "I feel like the things we've learned from Mrs. Farrell and then about the position at BioTech lends credibility to Mary's claims. I don't know if finding that lab she used will tell us anything about who, besides Neil, might have been my father, but the idea that she was worried is a potential motive for the other person involved. It's proof of the involvement of a third party. Someone who could have committed the murder to shut her up and/or to protect himself."

"You're right about that. Even if it's best not to attempt a meeting with Wilson, we still have Carin Carter Wallace to locate. She has stayed under the radar a lot. There has to be a reason for that."

Anne had pondered the idea as well. "When you look at the time frame that she went to work for Langston, it was not long before he took higher office and only a few months after her husband died. Do you think she had decided to come back and demand some sort of compensation for the secret she'd kept all those years? At that point, she didn't have to worry about her husband learning whatever secrets she had. He was dead."

"You might not be far off in your assessment. Carin married a wealthy investor after leaving her life here behind. He was a good deal older than her, and he'd been married before. When he died her inheritance was a pittance compared to what his grown children received. There was likely a prenup, so she couldn't exactly contest it with any hope of winning. I'm guessing she was ready to move on to the next option for living the good life."

Anne contemplated the idea. "We still don't know the reason Carin left in the first place. She may have seen or heard something that put her in a position to be concerned for her safety. Getting out of here may have felt like the safest thing to do at the time. But after the murder, she realized she had a sort of insurance policy that would protect her, but she didn't come back because she'd already met her rich widower."

Jack smiled. "Exactly. You're a natural at this. You sure you don't want to change careers?"

She laughed. "Whether I'm good at this or not—which remains to be seen—I love what I do."

"You're very good at what you do." He made a *what can I say* face. "I checked out your website. Perused your gallery." He flashed that smile again. "Tell me about your plans for the future. Beyond all this, I mean."

"My plan is to keep building my business—which is why this big client with the tile issues…and now the permit glitch—is so important." She thought about all the things she envisioned for the future. "I have this five-year plan I hope takes us—my assistant, Lisa, and me—to the next level. I'll get an office in downtown Aurora, and I'd like to buy one of the amazing historic homes and make it mine." She rolled her eyes. "I'm sure you're wishing you hadn't asked."

The way he was watching her she felt certain she'd over answered the question. Good grief, she'd never had such trouble in a man's presence. One of her best business assets was her ability to keep her cool in the most stressful situation. Then again, this wasn't business.

"You're not going to believe this." Jack reached into his pocket for his cell phone. "I'm renovating this nineteenth-century Victorian on Augusta Street in Oak Park."

Stunned, Anne accepted his phone and swiped through the photos. The house was perfect. The wood floors looked very salvageable. The walls appeared to be in good shape. It was exactly the sort of home she hoped to have one day.

"It's great. I'd love to hear your plans. Are you remodeling or restoring?"

His fingers brushed hers as he took the phone from her hand. Heat shot up her arm. She tried to stifle the gasp but didn't quite accomplish her mission.

"I want to restore as much as possible." He ignored or was hopefully oblivious to her reaction. "I'll save the remodeling for areas like the kitchen, where a more modern update is most convenient."

"Good plan." She managed a smile, no matter that the way he studied her now was deeply unsettling…in a good way. She leaned forward slightly, unable to drag her gaze from his.

He stared at her lips. "The food should be here…"

Her breath foolishly caught again. He had to know she was attracted to him. God, she was so embarrassed.

"I'm sorry." She drew away slightly. "I guess I was so

caught up in our conversation I…" She shook her head. "Sorry."

He sat his phone on the desk without taking his eyes off her, then he reached out, gently traced the outline of her cheek with the tips of his fingers. Desire ignited inside her, and her heart started to pound.

He dropped his hand away. "I should be the one to apologize. I couldn't stop staring at you, and I shouldn't have let myself get carried away."

"Please," she urged, her voice barely a whisper, "get carried away some more."

He leaned closer, brushed his lips across hers. "I can do that," he murmured against the lips he had set on fire. Then he kissed her again, softly, slowly.

She put her arms around his neck and leaned into the kiss. Oh, how she wanted to feel this…this fire and anticipation.

A pounding on his door tore them apart.

"The food," he said hoarsely. He turned back to her, licked his lips hungrily. "To be continued."

He walked out of the room.

Anne braced her elbows on her knees and plunked her face into her hands. What was she thinking? This was not supposed to happen. She forced her lungs to fill with air. Not smart. Not smart.

She stood. To heck with smart! Her fingers fumbled as she quickly unfastened the buttons of her blouse—the one she'd been wearing this morning, which saved it from the fire. She tore it off and reached for the waist of her pants.

Jack came back into the room carrying bags of food. He stalled, stared at the blouse on the floor and then her.

She shrugged, her fingers still clutching her waistband.

"I thought we could eat later…after we do the to-be-continued part."

He placed the bags on the desk and moved toward her.

Her heart thumped so hard she couldn't catch her breath.

And then he kissed her, his hands roving over her bare back until he found the place where her bra fastened.

Her body melted against him. No more thinking.

Chapter Fourteen

Journal Entry
Thirty Years Ago
August 10

This was the worst that could have happened.

No, not the worst. But close. The position Neil had wanted so badly was stolen by a friend. He was devastated, and I was devastated for him.

The so-called friend who stole it was a year ahead of Neil. He had graduated in May. Not at the top of his class either as Neil was set to do. No, he was mediocre at best. So far he'd taken his bar exam multiple times without passing it.

He was no Neil, and the company had made a huge mistake choosing the other man over Neil.

I wanted to scream then, still do now whenever I think about it.

No matter that I preferred he didn't go with that company, it was unfair.

At the time Eve was still avoiding me, which was just as well. I wanted nothing to do with her or her lowlife fiancé. Carin hadn't returned. I wondered if she did come back whether she would take Eve's side in all that had happened. At that point I didn't trust anyone to be who they claimed to be. How could Neil and I have been friends with those two for so long and not have seen the duplicity they were capable of?

I knew then that I would never forgive them. Never.

I wish I could have told Neil about the other, but I feared there would be terrible repercussions. The worry there would be physical violence if he ever learned what had happened was a true concern. Although Neil and I didn't have a gun in the house, I felt as if he would get one if he learned that awful truth. I could never tell him. It was better if he didn't know. We just had to move on with our lives and not look back. The law firm in Crystal Lake had been pushing hard to have Neil come on board when he graduated. It was a reputable, long-standing firm. The offer was a generous one. There was no reason not to take it. The potential for the big leagues wasn't as great, but it would work. As long as we had each other, what else really mattered?

I was certain I would feel much better when all of that was behind us. I had a terrible feeling about it. I recognized that we couldn't trust the people we thought were our friends. And I also understood that they would never want the things I knew to be revealed. Everyone had their secrets. Some more than others, and the knowledge of those secrets made me very nervous.

I made the decision to focus on the future and pretend I didn't know what those evil so-called friends were capable of. School was about to start back, so that would occupy much of my time. I had you to get ready for the baby and the wedding. Neil had finally agreed to something far more low-key. I was glad because I just wanted to be happy and settled and not draw a lot of attention to ourselves. It sounds strange, I know, but I thought I needed to stay very small so they would ignore me and the things I knew.

I read once that the universe gives back to you what you put out to it. With that in mind, I focused on being extra kind to all. I thought good thoughts most of the time. I had hoped that attitude would get me through until we were safe again.

Apparently I was wrong to assume the threat to us would just go away.

I wish I didn't have to be so cryptic as I write this. I would very much like to spell out all that I know for sure. That would make finding the rest much easier. But I don't dare. I'm in prison, so nothing—not even my body—is private and certainly not safe.

I have to be careful…and should you ever take up this challenge to find the truth, you should be very careful too.

Chapter Fifteen

Crystal Lake
Saturday, July 12
Jones Residence
Maplewood Lane, 9:30 a.m.

Anne had expected breakfast to be awkward.

Jack had already been up and in the shower in his room when she woke up. There were no adequate words for how relieved she was that she had been alone in her own room when she woke. Not that there had been a single regret—at least on her part, but she'd felt a little embarrassed. Her neediness had been more than obvious, and he'd been so attentive…and so amazing.

Trying not to swoon with the memories, she had taken a shower—though she had wanted a long hot soak so badly—and hurriedly dried her hair. She had chosen to wear the black tee. It felt weird wearing jeans that hadn't been washed, but there was no way to change that now. Since she'd forgotten to grab a pair of sneakers at the store, she was stuck with wearing the loafers. They were fairly comfortable, but she was a sneakers girl.

Then Jack had knocked on the connecting door, and

she'd been dazed and out of sorts just seeing him. They had stopped for breakfast at a local diner. He'd carried the conversation as they'd eaten. She had managed the occasional nod or hummed agreement. Then they'd gotten back into the rental car and driven to Barrington to see if Carin Carter Wallace was home.

Whoever answered the intercom at the gate had said she wasn't, so from there they'd driven back to Crystal Lake to the home of Detective Harlan Jones.

Anne suspected he would not be happy about their visit on a Saturday morning, but she was immensely thankful for diving directly into the investigation. Even at breakfast, Jack had kept the conversation focused on what they had discovered so far and what he hoped to accomplish going forward.

The prospect of potentially discussing last night had been terrifying. It had been so long since she'd dealt with a morning after, and she felt completely off balance.

Not that it hadn't been awesome, she considered again. It was completely amazing. Jack had made her experience things she had not known were possible. She'd lost count of the times he had made her…well, feel really, really good.

The first thing she'd wanted to do this morning was to call Lisa and tell her all about it. Except she couldn't with him in the next room and the connecting door ajar. Not to mention that talking about it to another person would equate to it being real. Last night had not been real—as in some sort of declaration of a personal connection or the start of a relationship.

It was just something that happened at the end of the day between two people involved in an intense situation.

That was it. No big deal.

Except she still felt warm inside this morning. She felt…

Stop. The fact was that they were together because of his job. It wasn't about anything personal. When the investigation concluded he would go back to Chicago and she would go home…to work.

Funny how the work she loved suddenly felt lacking.

Just stop.

Jack parked in the driveway behind an SUV. Next to the SUV was a fishing boat. Nothing large or elaborate, just a flat-bottom boat with a small motor sitting atop a trailer. A man who matched the online images of Detective Jones placed a cooler in the boat and then a pair of fishing rods. His weekend plans appeared to include fishing. Hopefully that meant he was in a good mood. This was another cold call. The detective might or might not talk to them. Particularly if he figured out they were looking into one of his old cases.

Anne mentally crossed her fingers and turned to the man behind the wheel. "Looks like he's home."

"And perhaps in a good mood." Jack smiled, and her pulse reacted.

She was so overreacting to last night. "I was thinking the same thing."

They got out of the car at the same time. He glanced across the top of the rental at her and gave her a nod as if he understood she was a little nervous. She was. This interview would be a bit touchier than the others, and she needed to be on her toes. This man was a cop—the one who investigated the murder thirty years ago. He was retired now, but that didn't mean he would want to admit mistakes. Though thirty years older than the images from the newspaper clippings in Mary's box of saved things, the man had stayed fit. His dark hair was sprinkled with gray now, and the beard was new. He wore jeans and a tee and sneakers. He was ready for his weekend…and they were stepping into his path.

Harlan Jones stared at them as they approached. He braced one hand on the boat and with the other reached up and adjusted his glasses. Those were new too. "Good morning."

"Good morning, Mr. Jones," Jack responded. "I'm Jack Brenner, and this is Anne Griffin." She forced her lips into a smile.

The man with fishing on his mind narrowed his gaze, looked them each over. "If you're here to preach to me, don't waste your breath," he warned. "Or if you're here selling something, I'm a retired police detective, which means I live on a budget, so don't waste your time."

"Fair enough." Jack nodded. "Actually, I'm from the Colby Agency—a private investigations firm in Chicago."

The detective's head went up in acknowledgment. "I've heard of the Colby Agency. What brings you to my home?"

Anne was surprised he hadn't already gotten wind of their endeavor. Maybe retirement meant he'd lost touch with the local grapevine.

"We're looking into the Neil Reed murder."

Surprise flared in his eyes. "Talk about an old one. I'm surprised anyone even remembers the case."

"Mary Morton was my mother," Anne explained, finally finding her footing. "She passed away recently."

The former detective's surprise was overtaken by the guard that went up. His expression closed. All signs of what he was thinking or feeling vanished.

"She left a journal," Jack said, "and we're looking into some of the allegations she made about others involved in the events leading up to and including the murder of Reed."

The former detective's jaw tightened, but to his credit,

Mr. Jones didn't make a run for the house. "I haven't heard about the case being reopened."

"That's coming, I suspect." Jack surveyed the man's boat. "Looks as if you have your day planned out."

Jones nodded. "I fish every chance I get. It's my favorite thing to do. Thirty-five-plus years as a cop... I figure I earned all the fishing I can get in before old age takes over."

"Law enforcement takes a toll," Jack agreed. "Would you have a few minutes for a couple of questions?"

He looked from Jack to Anne, then shrugged. "I suppose so. Shoot."

Anne was still stuck on the words *That's coming.* Did Jack really believe their—his—investigation could make that happen? The official reopening of the case? Once more she felt as if her head was spinning. Not that she didn't want the case reopened. She did. She just had been skeptical and... Wow, this might really be happening. *Pay attention to the now, Anne!*

"There was never any determination about where the weapon came from." Jack went straight for one of the bigger missing elements of the investigation.

"The ballistics didn't match anything we had on file," Jones admitted. "There was no 4473—firearms transaction record—submitted for Morton or Reed, so we can only assume the weapon was purchased illegally. No one we interviewed was aware the couple owned a firearm. However they came into possession of that gun, her prints were the only ones on it."

Anne spoke up, "But she said in her statement that she picked up the gun from where it lay on the floor when she found Neil. She had no idea where it came from or who fired it. Most anyone would have done the same thing.

It's instinct to pick up and inspect something unexpected found in your home."

He nodded. "That's what she said, but I wasn't buying it." He turned his hands up. "I get that she was your mother, but she had blood on her clothes, and she was the only person seen coming in or out of the house around the time of the murder."

"There was no gun powder residue on her hands," Jack pointed out. "As for the blood, it was smeared on her clothes from trying to render emergency care to the man she loved. There was no blood splatter pattern from standing close when the weapon fired and the bullet hit him in the chest."

"We're confident she washed her hands and forearms," Jones countered. "Morton was smart. She knew what to do and what to say. Her story about picking up the gun before we even asked felt too accommodating and detailed for someone overcome with emotion. As for the blood, a splatter pattern couldn't be found after she smeared blood over it. She made sure of it. Besides, no one else had motive—not like her anyway. And she was the one to find him. It was all just a little too convenient."

"What about her friend, Eve Langston—Redford at the time?" Fury simmered inside Anne. So this was what her mother had been up against. "She was seen in the neighborhood that day, according to one of the neighbors you interviewed."

"It's possible the neighbor who saw her," Jack added, "got the time wrong."

Anne wished that neighbor was still alive. It would have been helpful to hear directly from her.

Mr. Jones laughed. "The senator's wife? I can't imagine what motive she would have had to murder her best friend's husband." He sent a pointed look at Jack. "I do know how to conduct a homicide investigation, you know."

There it was. No more Mr. Nice Guy.

"First," Anne argued, "he wasn't a senator at the time, and Eve wasn't his wife until later. So neither of those scenarios had anything to do with what happened." Her gaze narrowed on the man. "I'm guessing," she went on, trying not to let her irritation show, "you didn't consider Eve's husband, Kevin, as a person of interest either. No matter that he'd just stolen a position with BioTech that had been offered to Neil. I can't imagine that wouldn't be considered motive."

Anne wanted to toss in the possible sexual-assault allegation she'd learned about and the paternity test…but Mrs. Farrell was right. It would only make her mother look guiltier. As for the previous sexual-assault allegation involving Adrina Wilson, surely any good cop would have dug up that one.

Then again, she wasn't sure this man fit the definition of a good cop.

The former detective actually laughed this time. "She really pulled out all the stops in that journal, didn't she? The fact is Kevin Langston could not have killed Neil Reed any more than his future wife could have because they were having drinks together in town at the time of the murder. Their alibi was confirmed."

"I noticed that in the file," Jack commented. "But the location and the person who verified their alibi weren't named."

Jones held up his hands in a signal of surrender. "That one is on me. I must have failed to list those items. They were at JJ's, and the owner, Jerry Trenton, confirmed their alibi." He dropped his hands to his sides. "The truth is it was crystal clear who the shooter was. The rest was just a matter of filling in the blanks."

Anne required a moment to ride out the shock of that news. No wonder Judith had gone straight to Eve about Anne and Jack's visit. Her ex-husband had been the Langstons' alibi. Oh, how the plot thickened.

"You're saying," Anne pressed, her anger stirring once more, "that you were so certain my mother killed my father that you really didn't consider anyone else."

The detective's hands went to his hips then, and he glared at her, his face hard with his own rising anger. "I did not say that. I looked at several other persons of interest. The fact is, lady, Mary Morton killed him. End of story. As sad as that might make you, it's the truth."

Anne wasn't a cop but she found it suspicious that he could remember all these details so well thirty years later. More likely, someone had spoken to him already. Made sure he remembered all the right answers.

"You never mentioned a motive," Jack said, dragging the guy's attention to him. "What was her motive for killing the man she intended to marry…the father of her unborn child? Any way I look at it, I can't find how doing so helped her in the slightest. He had no life insurance. You and I both know that for a young woman—a pregnant one—with no history of violence to suddenly obtain a weapon illegally and then shoot and kill the man she loved takes a strong motive. If there was nothing for her to gain, why did she do it? You found no evidence he'd cheated on her. No evidence of any sort of abuse. Nothing. That's a stretch, Detective."

Jones face lined with rage, he snapped, "I guess you had to be there. You had to see the lack of emotion when she was found hovering over his body. The dull, lifeless look in her eyes while I questioned her. The methodical, almost rehearsed answers."

"Did you consider that she was pregnant and emotionally devastated?" Jack argued. "What you're describing could easily have been shock."

The detective laughed, shook his head. "We can debate this all day, but I was there. I know what I saw and heard. She was guilty, and the case was closed."

"Did you interview Michael Smith to find out why he chose Langston for the position at his company after already making a deal with Reed?" Jack demanded next.

"I didn't see the point."

"What about Carin Carter Wallace?" Anne demanded. "She took off just before the murder. She was friends with Mary and Neil as well as Eve and Kevin. She's the senator's personal assistant now. Has been for years. You found nothing suspicious about any of their activities? Never considered that close friends might know things useful to your investigation?"

His eyebrows lifted at her sarcastic tone. "Carter was not in Crystal Lake at the time of the murder. Her fiancé confirmed she was at home in Chicago. Even though she visited for a couple of days after the murder, she didn't hang around long."

"You didn't put that in the file either," Jack noted.

The man exhaled a big, put upon breath. "Looking back, I can see where I didn't do several things I would have done later on. Experience changes how you do things. I still had a lot to learn thirty years ago."

"I'm glad you mentioned that," Jack said. "Why were you put on the case, considering your lack of experience at the time?"

Another of those impatient exhales from the former detective. "It was Labor Day weekend. Everyone else was on vacation. I was low man on the seniority roster, so I got stuck on call. Once the case was mine, I wasn't giving it up. I figured a big case like that would help set my career. I may not have documented everything exactly as I should have, but I guarantee you it all got done and the killer went to jail. End of story."

"And as it turned out, considering the lack of actual evidence or motive," Anne countered, disbelief and no small amount of frustration twisting inside her, "all the judge and jury needed for the Reed murder case was your testimony in the courtroom. That's astonishing."

When he would have argued Anne's point, Jack cut him off. "The fact that no one was assigned to ensure the new kid on the block covered all the bases in the investigation kind of makes you wonder," he suggested, "if someone involved with the murder had a friend in the department."

His own frustration tightened the detective's features, but rather than argue he hitched his head toward his boat. "The morning's wasting. I'm heading to the lake. If you have a complaint or any more questions, take it up with the chief."

When they were in the car driving away, Anne had gone way past frustration and into pure anger. "Did you buy any of that?"

"Parts, to some degree," he said, surprising her. But then he braked at an intersection and shifted his attention to her. "Detective Jones did what he was told to do. Anyone who has worked with the police understands that when there's a murder—particularly in a fairly small town like this one—a detective on vacation can be called in. No one wanted this case, so they handed it off to the rookie. Any potential mistakes would be his."

Anne's frustration and anger fizzled. "He wasn't important enough to protect."

"Or," Jack said as he took a right, "someone higher up was protecting the future senator and wanted a scapegoat in place in case someone ever came along and pointed out the holes in the investigation."

"Like us." Anne hadn't thought of that one. "Kevin Langston might have had a friend in the department making sure he was never dragged into the fray."

"I would put money on it." Jack flashed her a smile.

Her heart skipped a beat. "How do we go about finding out who that is—was?"

"After the conversation we just had with Jones, I don't think we'll have to do anything except wait. Whoever decided how that investigation was to be handled will catch up with us."

In light of the fire at the hotel, the idea made Anne more than a little nervous and at the same time incredibly giddy.

She suspected the next couple of days were going to get even more interesting.

Chapter Sixteen

Barrington
Langston Residence
Plum Tree Road, 1:00 p.m.

Since the meeting with Detective Jones, Jack had driven to Carin Carter Wallace's residence on Rollings Hills Drive. Again that disembodied voice on the intercom at the gate had insisted Ms. Wallace was not home and she had no idea where she was this morning. *Personal time*, her calendar showed. He and Anne had simply shaken their heads. The woman was still avoiding them. No surprise really.

Since he felt confident the detective would make it a point to get word to the Langstons, Jack had decided that watching their home would be the right step. Anne had agreed. If Detective Jones was quick about it, one or both Langstons would likely be reacting sooner rather than later.

"If either one leaves the house—" Anne broke the extended silence "—we're going to follow, right?"

"We are." They had grabbed lunch and spent some time surveilling the Wallace house to no avail. Jack had attempted to start a conversation from time to time, but nothing stuck. More than once he had considered bringing up last night, but there hadn't been a moment that felt right.

No, that wasn't true. If he were honest with himself, he worried that he'd read far too much into the moment. He wasn't at all sure she had felt the same way he had. She'd experienced the need and the urgency—that part had been obvious. But he wasn't sure she felt the deeper attraction, the deeper connection that he had. He liked Anne. A lot. And he wanted to know her better...if she was interested.

Since she hadn't brought up the subject either, taking her lead seemed like the right move. No matter that he actually wanted to talk about it. Part of him wanted to apologize for making the first move. He should have restrained himself. But the need to kiss her had overridden his senses. He'd had no choice. After that, there had been no stopping.

Not that he regretted what they'd shared. No way. He just hoped she didn't.

Last night had been...nice. In truth, it was way better than nice. Even *great* didn't feel like an adequate description. The best way to describe it was that he wanted it to happen again...and again after that.

Still, he had crossed a line no matter that he refused to regret any aspect of it. He cared about this woman, and he wanted to spend more time with her...if she was agreeable, and last night it had felt like she was.

But he wasn't pushing the idea. She was vulnerable right now. He'd lost control last night, but if it happened again, she would have to make the first move.

"You shouldn't feel guilty about last night."

Her words yanked him back to the here and now. Surprised him. He turned to her. "Why would you think I feel guilty?"

She kept her attention focused forward. "Well, I…you haven't mentioned it, and…"

He laughed softly. "I was waiting for you to bring it up." He studied her profile, easily spotted the uncertainty and hesitation there now that he looked more closely. She was nervous. "Since you brought it up, let me assure you that guilt is not what I feel."

She met his gaze then, hers wide. "I hope you don't regret it either. It was as much my decision as yours."

He shook his head. "No regret. As long as you have no guilt or regret…"

"No regret and no guilt. I'm glad it happened. It was really…" She closed her eyes, took a breath. "It was amazing and…" She looked directly into his eyes then. "I hope when this is finished, we can do it again." She snapped her eyes shut and winced. "I mean…"

"I think I know what you mean." He took her hand in his and set his attention on the property just up the block from where they were parked. This thing between them would have to wait until his work on the case was done.

She relaxed and he did the same, then her fingers curled around his.

He was glad she trusted him and, it seemed, she liked him. He was glad about that part as well.

Putting too much stock in a relationship that developed during an intense situation was not smart. And maybe this wasn't the brightest move he'd made. But he was in for however long it lasted.

Before he could get too lost in those thoughts, the gate to the Langston home started to swing open.

"Here we go." He sat up straighter, put both hands on the steering wheel.

Beside him, Anne leaned slightly forward in anticipation of who would be leaving the Langston residence.

The sleek black Mercedes that Eve Langston drove rolled forward. She took a right out of her driveway, and Jack caught a glimpse of the woman in the driver's side window. One of their targets was on the move.

Once the Mercedes was farther down the block, Jack eased onto the street and followed.

Tension coiled inside him along with the hope that the woman would meet with someone or do something that gave them the upper hand in this investigation. What they had right now was a lot of interesting and potentially case-altering scenarios but no evidence to back it up. Not unlike what Detective Jones had when the case was originally investigated. Other than the proverbial smoking gun, he'd had nothing that proved Mary Morton had pulled the trigger. Likewise, they had nothing that proved she hadn't.

There had to be something or someone out there who could change that disappointing situation. All they had to do was find it.

"Well, what do you know," Jack announced as Langston turned onto Rolling Hills Drive.

"She's headed to Wallace's house," Anne finished the announcement for him.

"Looks that way."

Sure enough Langston pulled up to the gate in front of the Wallace residence, and the twelve or so feet of iron opened.

Jack parked across the street and far enough back from the house so as not to be easily spotted but with a line of sight to the only way in or out of the property.

"They can't talk on the phone," Anne pointed out with a satisfied smile.

"Not unless they want to risk the records being subpoenaed and the conversation being revealed."

"The best way around leaving evidence of a conversation is to have it face-to-face." Anne folded her arms over her chest. "They're getting their stories straight, I'm sure. Conferring about all the trouble we're causing."

"I agree." Jack considered another thought. "I've also been thinking about Carin's role in all this. Before Neil was murdered," he began, putting the new theory into words for the first time, "it was Eve and Kevin, Mary and Neil. Carin was a sort of fifth wheel. None of the photos you found showed her with a date or a partner. She was always the lone extra."

Anne's brow furrowed as she turned to him. "You're right. She was the extra. The tagalong."

"She was and still is," he went on, "attractive. Apparently smart. What if she was having an affair with Neil or Kevin that whole time and had no desire to have another guy in the mix? She was happy taking whatever she could get from her secret lover."

"If she'd been having an affair with Neil," Anne said, "don't you think that would have come out? It would have been a solid motive for Mary having murdered him. And if Mary had any idea about it, surely she would have mentioned it in the journal."

"Maybe." He let the theory roll around in his head for a bit. "An affair—whichever man was the offending partner—may have been the reason Carin left Crystal Lake in the first place."

"Makes sense," Anne agreed. "Her friends wanted nothing to do with her once they knew." She made a face as if recalling something. "Except Mary mentioned in her journal that she didn't understand why Carin had left. Whatever Eve knew, Mary had no idea."

"Neil could have asked her to leave considering the baby on the way. Carin," Jack offered, "may have felt guilty or abandoned and followed his suggestion."

"But why would she?" Anne countered. "If it was Neil she wanted, why not stay and confront Mary? Why give up so easily?"

Jack smiled. She really had a great mind for investigative work. "That's a very good question. We don't know enough about Carin to make an assessment. But we do know that Eve, on the other hand, was someone Carin probably didn't want to cross. Bearing in mind Kevin's big coup with Bio-Tech and his political aspirations, Eve would likely have sided with Kevin no matter what he'd done. She strikes me as the sort who follows the money. Carin would have known it was a no-win situation."

"Good point." Anne shifted to get more comfortable. "In that scenario, Carin left because Eve found out about the affair. But when the murder happened, she came back to…what? Provide emotional support? Be a cheerleader for Team Eve and Kevin? Make sure she wasn't blamed?"

The realization of what the probable answer was suddenly expanded in Jack's brain. "No, Carin came back to show she was aware of what really happened. By then she was busy sinking her claws into the mega-rich investor Irving Wallace. She was too close to a big payoff to let it go. So she dropped by to leave the message just in case she would need to take advantage of that knowledge in the future."

"And she did. Twenty years later," Anne picked the story up from there, "Irving dropped dead, and poor Carin was left only the paltry sum of five million dollars. The prenup ensured the man's grown children got everything else. So she finds herself back at square one."

"She takes her *paltry* sum and returns to Crystal Lake where her old friends have suddenly risen to fame as Senator and Mrs. Langston. She negotiates a job—one which would not cover the cost of a four-million-dollar home and a six-figure automobile. But with her recent inheritance, she buys the home and the car while the nice salary, and whatever blackmail proceeds flow in keep her afloat in the lifestyle to which she had become accustomed."

Anne smiled. "It's completely logical and fits the pattern. One of the Langstons killed Neil to get him out of the way because he planned to do something or knew something, and they used Mary as the scapegoat. The Langstons got rich from BioTech and launched their dream political career. Carin somehow knew their deep, dark secrets and has milked the couple for all she can get."

Jack held her gaze for a moment. "And your mother spent more than half her life in prison for a crime she didn't commit. She missed raising you…watching you become the amazing young woman you are." He shook his head. "They stole her life."

"They stole my childhood." Anne blinked rapidly, emotion shining in her eyes. "I want to make them pay." Her voice was thick with that emotion.

Jack placed his hand on hers. "We will see to it that happens."

The gate started to open once more. Jack watched as the Langston Mercedes rolled back out.

"I guess leaving a quick message was all she needed to do." This group of friends was definitely up to something.

Anne's breath caught. "Unless she killed her."

Jack met her gaze. Unfortunately, that was a reasonable possibility. Not the most likely one, he figured, but not improbable.

"If she's dead, we can't change that, but we do need to see where Eve goes next. Then we can come back."

"You're right." Anne fastened her seatbelt. "Let's follow her."

They tracked Eve Langston who, surprisingly, returned to her castle-like home without another stop. Then Jack drove back to the Wallace home to follow-up on Carin's status. Anne remained absorbed in her thoughts. He recognized she had a lot to take in with all this…a lot to resolve internally. Her entire adult life she'd ignored thoughts of her biological parents and their tragic history in order to go on with hers. Now she was seeing a different side. All of this had to be overwhelming.

Jack pulled the rental up to the gate and pressed the button for the intercom. He wanted desperately to find answers for her.

"Ms. Wallace is still not available." The woman recognized them from their previous visit. The gate was equipped with a camera as well as an intercom. "If you'll leave your name and number, I will be sure she knows you'd like to speak to her."

Jack leaned forward so that his face was clear for the camera that sat atop the fence. "Jack Brenner from the Colby Agency." He provided his cell number. "Tell her it's important. We know the truth about Neil Reed. She needs to contact me."

"I'll pass along the message."

Jack and Anne exchanged a glance, and then he backed out of the driveway.

"If there had been a fight or any trouble the woman who spoke to you would know it," Anne suggested.

"Which means we don't need to worry about Wallace being wounded and bleeding out on the floor."

"Okay." Anne laughed softly. "I loved your message, by the way. If that doesn't get a response, nothing will."

His cell vibrated on the console. He picked it up and greeted the caller. "Jack Brenner."

"Mr. Brenner," a female voice said, "this is Beatrice Farrell."

He glanced at Anne. "Good afternoon, Ms. Farrell."

"I hope I'm not calling at a bad time."

"Oh, no, ma'am. Your timing is perfect."

Anne was leaning toward him in hopes of hearing the conversation. He wished he had put it on speaker, but that was hard to do while driving.

"I remembered the name of that lab Mary used. It was Trust One. It was the funniest thing. I was watching television, and someone said the word *trust*, and it suddenly came to me. I hope this helps. Please give Anne my best."

Anticipation fired in Jack's veins. "Thank you, Ms. Farrell. This is very helpful."

He ended the call and placed his phone back on the console. "Trust One," he said to Anne who was waiting, staring intently at him. "That's the lab Mary used."

"What are the chances they'll give me a copy of the test?"

"Have your friend Lisa send you a copy of your birth certificate if you have one."

"I do," she said eagerly. "I also have the death certificate that came with the letter from the prison."

"Have her send that too." He drove, his fingers tightening around the steering wheel. "We might be able to get the results since you are Mary's biological daughter. Otherwise, we'll purchase some sort of genetics assessment they offer. She's in their database, so some part of the results of her testing will show up as a match to yours."

"But that takes time, and it might not give us all the information from her original request." Worry tinged Anne's voice.

"Depends on the clerk and what we offer," he suggested. "Maybe we can get everything."

Trust One Lab
Borden Street, 3:00 p.m.

THE PARKING LOT was basically empty. The couple of cars there likely belonged to employees. It was Saturday afternoon. Business had slowed with closing time nearing. Jack removed the five carefully folded one-hundred dollar bills he kept in a hidden slot in his wallet for an emergency just like this one.

"Ready?"

Anne nodded and then got out.

"If there's a chance you could get into trouble for this," she said quietly, "I can do it. I could be just a desperate woman looking for her family. Emotion drives people to do bad things."

He slipped the folded money into his front pocket. "Not necessary. I'm a PI, not a cop. Bending the rules is something I have to do sometimes. The cops don't like it, but they usually don't push it."

She squared her shoulders. "If you're sure."

"Positive." He opened the door, and they entered the waiting area. White walls, industrial-type tile and preformed plastic chairs. The typical sterile environment.

When they reached the counter, a clerk, male, mid-twenties maybe, approached them. He looked beyond ready for his day to be over. It was Saturday, so of course he did.

Having someone—a potential customer—walk in the door was not what he wanted at this hour.

"Can I help you?" he said with no enthusiasm.

"Yes." Anne smiled hopefully. "My biological mother had some prenatal paternity testing done here, and I'm hoping to get those results. I have my birth certificate. Her name was—"

"I think," he interrupted, "I'll need a legal order to give you someone else's lab results, even your mother's."

Anne's expression shifted from hopeful to desperate. "I do have my birth certificate and proof she passed away. Are you sure you need anything more?"

He shrugged. "Sorry. There are requests you can make. Or you can do a genetic test and find your matches that way."

Jack placed his hand on the counter, pushed the folded hundreds from beneath his fingers. "What testing option would you recommend for immediate results?"

The young man stared at the folded bills. He turned to Anne then. "You said you have your birth certificate and maybe a death certificate?"

She nodded. Showed him the images on her phone. "Can I email these to you?"

"Sure thing."

She hit Forward and handed the phone to him. He typed in the email address and pressed Send. Then he gave her a couple of forms.

"Fill these out, and I'll see what I can do."

He went to a desk and worked at his computer while Anne filled out the forms. Jack hoped this would work. A court order could take days or weeks.

Anne laid the pen on the counter. "All done."

"Great." The clerk walked to the printer, picked up some

documents, folded them and placed them in an envelope. When he returned to the counter, he handed Anne the envelope, then picked up her forms along with the folded bills. "You'll hear from us as soon as we have results."

He walked back to his desk. Anne glanced at Jack, and he hitched his head toward the door.

They walked out. As soon as they were back in the car he pulled out of the parking slot, and Anne rushed to rip open the envelope.

When he braked to wait for traffic to clear, she pressed her fingers to her lips and turned to him. "It's the report on the paternity test."

He searched her eyes for some sense of the contents of the report. "And?"

"Neil was my father, he's listed as Test Subject #2 and, of course there's mine, Test Subject #1. They used the noninvasive blood test to collect my sample via Mother's blood. Then there's a third set of DNA but no name, just *Test Subject #3*."

"We may not have the name, but we have the guy's DNA. This is good, Anne. Maybe an important piece of the puzzle."

He doubted that Mary Morton would have had the presence of mind to take a sample at the time of her assault. She'd likely sneaked a hair or a toothbrush from Langston's home when she realized she was pregnant and paternity became a concern. Whatever she'd done, it worked.

Before Anne said more his cell vibrated. He picked it up, checked the screen to identify the caller. *Blocked call.* He tapped accept. "Brenner."

"Mr. Brenner, this is Carin Wallace. I think we need to talk."

"I agree." His gaze caught Anne's. "When and where would you like to meet, Ms. Wallace?"

"Why not now? I'll be visiting my old friend Neil Reed at Crystal Lake Cemetery. See you there."

The sound of the call ending echoed in his ear.

"We got her attention," he told Anne as he pulled out onto the street. "She wants to meet."

"Now?" Her eyes widened. "Where?"

"She'll meet us at the cemetery where your father is buried."

The shock on Anne's face caused a literal pain in his chest.

Damn…he'd gotten way too close to this…to her.

Chapter Seventeen

Crystal Lake
Crystal Lake Cemetery
Ridgefield Road, 3:50 p.m.

Anne stared at the sleek black granite headstone. It was beautiful and at the same time cold and distant. The name *Neil Aaron Reed* was engraved in big letters. Beneath that was *Beloved son*. And of course his dates of birth and death. No mention of his wife or his child.

She hadn't expected to feel anything, but somehow she did. The man buried here was her father. He'd died at a younger age than Anne was right now. No, he hadn't just died—he had been murdered. Not because he'd been a bad man or because he'd done bad things but because someone had wanted what was his.

Fury swelled in her chest. She had never felt so wronged in her life. All those years in foster care could have been avoided. She could have grown up in a good, stable home with good, loving parents...but that opportunity had been stolen from her.

Sure there were plenty of kids in the system who got lucky and ended up with amazing families for their foster care years. But Anne had been one of the unlucky kids who'd bounced from neglectful home to abusive home to overcrowded ones where no one received the care and attention they needed. She supposed it was, in part, because she'd been somewhat difficult between the ages of five and twelve. It was hard when you reached a certain stage in childhood and understood that no one wanted you. Not a single person in the whole world loved you.

And all the stories you had heard about your mother labeled her a monster.

A barrage of those old emotions twisted inside her, had her eyes burning with the need to cry. She would never cry over those years again. Ever. Now she knew things no one had bothered to tell her as a child. According to the journal, this man—her gaze traveled over his name once more—had wanted her. He and Mary had made plans for their future—theirs and their child's. It would have helped so much if she had known this back then. Anne thought of the people closest to her parents. Eve and Kevin Langston. Carin Carter Wallace. Judith Hudson. Beatrice Farrell. Why had no one bothered to find Anne and tell her any of this? Why had they heartlessly allowed her to believe the worst?

Jack rested his hand at the small of her back as if he sensed the turmoil inside her. "You okay?"

She was shaking. She hadn't realized this until he touched her. Her fists were clenched at her sides. *Deep breath.* Reaching for calm, she steadied herself and turned her face up to his. "I will be."

"From what I've learned so far," he offered, "I don't believe your parents were responsible in any way for how this turned out. I also don't think either of them would have wanted you to suffer the hurt and unhappiness you went through as a child. This was a tragedy of someone else's making."

"I'm beginning to see that." She was. For the first time in her life she believed someone had cared and wanted her. The realization that her parents had not thrown her away was so overwhelming it was almost painful. She waffled between wanting to weep and wanting to scream.

The sound of a vehicle arriving drew their attention to the red BMW Alpina that parked behind their rental. Anne recognized the car. Carin Carter Wallace's luxury automobile—the one her dead husband's money had paid for.

Carin emerged from the driver's side, closed the door and strode toward them. The woman was a year younger than Eve. She had managed to maintain her looks considerably better than the other woman. Maybe she'd had more cosmetic surgery or simply better surgeons. Possibly better skin to begin with. Good genes often made all the difference. Additionally, unlike her friend, Carin's wardrobe appeared to be far more stylish and youthful. She could be an influencer on social media.

"Anne Griffin, I presume," Carin announced as she paused a few steps away. Her hands rested on her silk-clad hips. She wore creamy pearl-colored pants and a button-up shirt in the same elegant, flowy fabric that flared open sharply since the top three pearl buttons were unfastened. Her long blond hair and dark sunglasses were emphasized by ruby-red lips. The woman actually looked as if she'd just stepped off the set of a *Vogue* or *Vanity Fair* photo shoot.

Anne gave her a nod.

"Jack Brenner." He thrust out his hand, which prompted Carin to step closer, only the headstone separating them now.

She touched her hand to his briefly. "Carin Wallace."

"Nice of you to join us," Anne said, drawing the woman's attention from Jack.

Carin reached up, removed her designer sunglasses and hung them in the vee of her shirt, which resulted in more showing off of her cleavage. "Have you been here before? Or is this only a drive-by to settle your mother's affairs?"

Anne worked at restraining the anger building inside her. "If by *settle her affairs* you mean find the truth about who murdered my father, yes, that's why I'm here."

Carin laughed softly. "I can't imagine you'll find anything the police didn't." She eyed Jack. "Even with your world-class private investigator." She raised an eyebrow at him. "Your agency has quite the gold-standard reputation…not to mention a fascinating history."

"We do our best." Jack's tone and his expression were proof enough that he was not impressed by the lady.

Anne appreciated that more than he could know. "We've concluded a number of new scenarios since we arrived," she told the woman devouring Jack with her eyes. "You play a major role in most of them."

Her red lips parted in a laugh. "How strange when I wasn't even here during the time frame of the murder."

"You were less than an hour away," Jack countered. "An easy, quick commute."

She looked from him to Anne. "So I'm your prime suspect, am I?"

"One of them," Anne said.

"My money's still on the senator." Jack eased his hands into his pockets and studied Anne for a moment. "I know we talked at length about Carin being at the top of our list, but now that we've met in person—" he gave the older woman a once-over "—I'm not so sure she could have handled the job."

Carin laughed again, but there was no humor in the

sound. "It's nice to have someone on my side who recognizes I'm not capable of murder."

Jack was the one chuckling this time. "Oh, I'm confident you're capable. I'm just not sure you could have pulled it off without getting caught. The person who murdered Neil Reed was very careful. Meticulous, even. Unless the police were completely incompetent, the killer left no evidence whatsoever."

Anne nodded. She got where he was going now. "A mastermind." She made a *no way* face at Carin. "You're right. She's obviously not the one."

"Whatever you believe," the older woman snapped, "your mother is the *one* who murdered Neil. She was jealous and vindictive. She despised her life. I remember her fantasizing about having a life just like the one Eve had planned. I guess she thought if she got Neil out of the way—"

"She could have Kevin," Anne interrupted. "I can't deny that scenario is a possibility. Not since we found the lab she used." This idea had only just occurred to Anne. She hoped Jack would approve.

Confusion flashed on Carin's unlined face before she could restrain it. "I'm not following. What lab?"

"The one she used for a prenatal DNA test to determine whether Neil was my father or if it was…" She stared directly into the other woman's eyes. "Kevin."

The impact of the words visibly shook Carin Carter Wallace.

Anne kept going, determined not to let up now. "Her journal was very insightful. I'm just sorry she didn't allow me to see it before she died. It would have changed everything for her…for me too."

"I hate to be the one to tell you this," Carin said, the shock under control now, "but Mary Morton was a liar.

A consummate liar and a cheater. She betrayed Neil. She betrayed all of us."

"Kevin didn't seem to mind," Anne countered. She glanced at Jack then. "I think you're right. It probably was Kevin who murdered him. He stole Neil's offer from Bio-Tech, assaulted his wife and got away with it all."

"Until now," Jack pointed out.

"I would watch myself where the senator is concerned," Carin advised. "He'll react strongly to such unfounded allegations."

"What will he do?" Anne demanded, taking a step in the other woman's direction. "Kill me too? He's already started a fire at the hotel where we were staying. He has his thugs following us."

Carin's eyes narrowed to slits. "You never know what a cornered animal will do next."

Anne smiled. "Good point because he is an animal. My mother isn't the only woman he assaulted. But I'm guessing you knew that already."

"Knowledge is power in the world of politics," Jack noted.

Carin backed up a step. "I warn you—" she looked from one to the other "—do not go down this path. You will regret it."

"A lot of people are going to have regrets when we're done," Anne tossed right back at her. "But it won't be us. Believe that if you believe nothing else."

"If only you had proof," Carin bemoaned, then she laughed.

"You mean," Anne suggested, "like the DNA of the person my mother feared might be my father after he assaulted her? I have the lab report. It's all there."

Red lips pursed in fury, Carin did an about-face and marched back to her extravagant automobile.

When she'd driven away, Jack turned to Anne and clapped his hands. "Very good. I doubt she's been that rattled in decades."

"Probably around three." Anger stirred inside Anne. "I hope she rushes back to the Langstons and tells them every word we said."

"We're really going to have to watch our backs now," he cautioned.

"If we shake them up enough, one of them is bound to get fired up and make a mistake."

"That's the part that worries me," Jack confessed. "Like the woman said, when an animal gets cornered, you never know what it might do."

Anne met his gaze once more. "I'm not afraid. Not with you on my side."

He took her hand in his and gave it a squeeze. "No fear, but we will proceed with extreme caution."

Anne nodded, then looked at the headstone once more. A small flower arrangement had been tucked against it. The blooms had drooped and fallen free, and the leaves had withered and turned brown. She couldn't help wondering who had brought the flowers. Mr. Reed, perhaps?

She crouched down and looked for a card. No card. The small bundle fell over, revealing something beneath it. The bronze color almost caused her to miss the roundish object. Anne tapped it and realized it was some sort of metal. She pulled it free of the dirt. Someone had partially buried it next to the headstone. There was an inscription.

Mary Morton.

Anne's breath caught. Beneath the name was her date of birth and death as well as *Cremation Services of Crystal Lake*. It was one of those mini urns…part of her mother's ashes. But who put them here?

She pushed to her feet and showed the urn to Jack. "Someone brought her here."

Anne had been told Mary was cremated, but she never asked what became of her remains. She hadn't cared at the time.

But she cared now. Maybe her mother had one friend left in this town after all.

Jack pulled out his cell and tapped in a search. "They're still open." He looked to Anne. "We can see if they'll tell us who picked up her ashes."

"Let's do it."

Jack helped her to tuck the small urn next to the headstone and cover it properly. Anne dusted her hands off. At least her parents were together now.

Cremation Services
North Virginia Street, 5:30 p.m.

THE RATHER SMALL brick building was nothing like a funeral home. There were no rooms for services related to viewings and funerals. This was a place where cremations were performed and a lobby where the ashes were picked up for whatever the family intended. Somewhere beyond the lobby was likely the business office.

"Hello," the man behind the counter said, a faint smile on his lips. "May I help you?"

Anne worked up a smile in return. "I'm here to ask about my mother, Mary Morton. She died at Logan Correctional Center."

The man slowly nodded. "Yes, I'm familiar. I was contacted by a friend who contracted our services. We picked up Ms. Morton and fulfilled the service requested."

"Who contracted the service? I want to thank them for

taking care of her arrangements since I was unreachable. I had no idea she'd died until days later."

When the man hesitated, Jack withdrew a business card and placed it on the counter. "We want to keep this as discreet as possible. No need to involve the authorities or warrants."

The man studied the card. "Judith Hudson. She took care of everything."

"Thank you," Jack said.

Anne managed a nod of thanks before Jack ushered her outside. Why would Judith not have mentioned having taken care of the arrangements? Why be so secretive?

Frustration rolled through Anne. If she'd only been trying to help, why act as if she'd committed some crime?

Maybe the need to do this final act for Mary had been about guilt instead of friendship.

Chapter Eighteen

Judith's Cocktail Lounge
Williams Street, 7:15 p.m.

"You should eat." Jack nodded toward the plate the waiter had placed in front of Anne a good fifteen minutes ago.

She stared at the delicious-smelling orange-marinated chicken in the bed of fluffy rice. She just didn't feel the urge to eat no matter that it looked and smelled so good. "You're right." She picked up her fork and poked at the rice.

He'd started devouring the ramen he'd ordered the moment it arrived. Like her entrée, it looked great. And smelled just as good—garlicky and gingery.

But her taste buds just wouldn't rise to the occasion. She kept thinking of how her parents were finally together again after all these years. And how she had lost so much— they had lost so much—because someone decided that what they wanted was more important. It just wasn't fair.

They had asked to see Judith as soon as they arrived. She was here but busy. The waitress promised the owner would pop over to their table as soon as she could. That had been half an hour ago.

Anne poked a forkful of rice flavored with orange sauce

into her mouth and forced herself to chew. There was a lot in this life—in this world—that wasn't fair. People went to prison every day for crimes they didn't commit. Were harmed in some way when they had done nothing to deserve such treatment. She understood this, but somehow seeing an up-close look at the life her parents had lived and all the potential they had lost made her want to cry.

She squeezed her eyes shut. *Not going to cry. Not now.*

"Hey." Jack's hand rested atop hers.

She opened her eyes and met his gaze. The concern and kindness there caused hope to bloom deep inside her.

"Sometimes these things get really tough before they get better," he assured her, "but we're on the downhill side of this. We know what and who we're looking at. It's going to get better from here."

Although they were in a public place, the tables were spaced far enough apart and the music playing in the background allowed a sense of privacy. She appreciated that and his words more than she could say.

She poked at a piece of chicken. "Thanks. I really would not have gotten through this without you." When she popped it into her mouth and chewed she almost moaned. The chicken was amazing. So tender, and the spice level was the perfect balance of sweet and zesty.

He grinned. "If yours is half as good as mine..." He made a satisfied sound.

"It's great." Her appetite was at full attention now. "You were right."

"Good." He ate for a moment more. "You mentioned that you wouldn't have gotten through this without me." He shrugged. "If you recall, you wouldn't be in the middle of this if I hadn't knocked on your door."

This was true.

"You recognized something I didn't want to see," she countered. "I wanted to go on with my life without looking back." She shrugged. "Without believing that the past mattered. I was wrong, and you helped me see that. In my case anyway, I had to come back and see this through. Otherwise, sometime down the line I would have regretted not finishing this." She looked out the window for a moment. Watched the Saturday-evening traffic roll past. "Maybe when I had children of my own it would have hit me particularly hard. But the past—the story I didn't want to hear—would still have been haunting me. This was the right thing to do, and I'm so glad you helped me see that."

"I'm glad I've been able to help."

She suddenly felt a little embarrassed. "I'm sorry. I know you've only been doing your job, but it has felt like more to me." Might as well get that out there on the table. Particularly after last night.

His smile warmed her chest. "If I may be totally honest, this hasn't felt like work since I read Mary's journal. We're basically strangers, but I hope we can change that going forward."

After last night, she had been having that same thought— the same hope. It was such a relief to hear that she wasn't alone in those feelings. "I would like that very much."

"I'm so sorry to keep you waiting." Judith appeared at their table. She grabbed a nearby chair no one was using and settled in. "I'm hearing all sorts of gossip about what you two have been up to." She looked from Anne to Jack and then to their half-finished food. "I hope our amazing chef hasn't disappointed you."

"The food is great." Anne reached for her cocktail. Same one as she made at home—lemonade with strawberries and vodka. "And so is the cocktail."

"Both are excellent," Jack agreed. "But... I would be interested in the gossip you're hearing."

Judith waved off the comment. "Nothing fascinating, really." She smiled. "Other than how riled up the whole tribe is."

Anne savored the lemony vodka as she sat her glass down. "Carin and Eve aren't too happy with us. The senator either, I suspect."

"I'm sure you heard," Jack interjected, "about the Water's Edge Hotel—those were our rooms. An odd sort of coincidence, wouldn't you say?"

"Indeed," Judith agreed. "I was so glad to hear the two of you were out when that happened. Sounds exactly like one of those scare tactics they use in the movies. Hard to believe it happened right here in our little town."

"Not really," Anne argued. "It's all tied to the murder of Neil Reed. I think we both know the wrong person went to prison for that heinous crime."

The older woman's eyebrows reared up her forehead. "Some would agree with you. Others probably not."

Anne patted her lips with her linen napkin and decided to cut to the chase. "Why did you arrange for her body to be cremated?"

Judith stared back at Anne with the same firm look in her eyes. "Who else was going to do it? Would you have preferred the state did away with her? You know, they donate unclaimed bodies for research. Is that what you would have preferred?"

Anne flinched. Until a few days ago she would have preferred exactly that. To have one's body donated for medical research was a good thing. But now she wasn't sure she could say that about Mary's body. The woman had been her mother…and she had suffered more than her share of neglect and abandonment in her life.

"No," Anne admitted. "Thank you for taking care of her."

Judith blinked once, twice, three times as if having difficulty holding back the emotion shining in her eyes. "It was the least I could do."

"And thank you for seeing that some of her ashes were buried next to his headstone. I'm sure she would have appreciated that."

"It felt like the right thing to do."

"I do have one question though." Anne understood that whatever moment they'd just shared would be shattered by this single query.

Judith lifted her chin as if bracing for the unexpected. "What is that?"

"Why didn't you or any of her other friends see that I was placed in a good home? I know what you said before, but I want the truth this time."

It was a simple question, really. Mary had so-called friends. Neil had a father. And yet no one bothered to do a single thing for the child born to the two.

Anne had stopped resenting the friends and family who should have stepped in. What was done was done. But how had they lived with themselves? This was the part she would never understand.

Judith stared at the table for a moment, unable to meet Anne's eyes. "It was a difficult time for many. Neil was dead, and his father suddenly lost his wife. The man was beside himself with grief. I think he saw you—" she finally met Anne's gaze "—as an extension of your mother and, therefore, unworthy of his attention or support. It was wrong, obviously. But you can't tell a man anything when he's that wounded. I'm sure at some point he realized his mistake, but it was too late by then."

"And what about you? Carin? Eve? All of you claimed to be Mary's friends until near the end."

"I can't speak for Carin or for Eve," Judith admitted. "But I will say that something happened between those three. I have no idea what it was, but things changed. Your mother was suddenly on the outside. I tried to talk to her to find out what was going on, but she wouldn't talk to me. She avoided me and everyone else."

Anne stared at her, waiting for the rest.

The older woman closed her eyes and drew in a heavy breath. When she opened her eyes once more they were liquid with emotion. "Jerry had found someone new and younger. A woman already pregnant with his child—something I could never give him. I was in a bad place. A place I couldn't find my way back from for a very long time. By the time I realized I should have helped you, you were in the system, and no one was giving me any information. I wasn't family and my efforts were futile. I even went to Preston, your grandfather, and asked for his help, but he was still in that awful place where he hated everyone—especially you simply because you were alive and his son wasn't."

Anne wanted to resent this woman for her failure. She wanted to be angry with her for letting Mary and her down. But Judith was only human, and she'd gotten through that time period the only way she could. What happened was not her fault.

"Judith." Jack drew her attention to him. "I fully understand your reasons, as I'm sure Anne does." He looked to her, and she nodded. "But if you recall anything at all that might help us find the truth about who murdered Neil, you could help Anne now. She needs this to be settled. She deserves that, as does her mother. Help us."

Anne battled the tears stinging her eyes. She held her breath, dared to hope.

Judith placed both palms against the table as if she might push herself up out of her chair and walk away. She stared at that space where her hands rested, not meeting either of their gazes.

Finally, she looked up, this time at Jack. "There was serious trouble brewing." Her voice was low. "Neil and Kevin came to blows at dinner is the way I heard it. They were at the new house Kevin was planning to buy. They'd done one of those *trying it out for a night* deals. He and Eve were getting married in October, and they wanted to get settled before the wedding and honeymoon."

"Do you know what the fight was about?" Jack asked.

"It was…" She looked to Anne. "About the baby—you. Bear in mind that I heard all this thirdhand. Eve had told Carin and Carin told me."

"Kevin took advantage of my mother." Fury built inside Anne.

Judith nodded. "He claimed it was a one-time moment of weakness that Mary instigated, but I didn't believe it. Frankly, anyone who really knew him wouldn't have believed it. But Eve had her reasons for taking his word. She wanted to marry the man who would be a senator one day. A man who had taken a position from the *Steve Jobs* of research laboratory developers. Eve knew Kevin was moving up, and she intended to rise with him."

Anne struggled to keep her anger at bay. "Carin knew too. That's why she left."

"I can't say for sure," Judith confessed, "but she knew it was all going to hit the fan, and she wanted no part of it."

"Do you," Jack asked, "believe Kevin Langston killed Neil?"

Judith held his gaze for a long, heart pounding moment. "No."

No? Before Anne could demand an explanation, the woman went on.

"I believe Eve did it for him. Kevin would never have dared do anything that might damage his reputation. No way." She shrugged. "Although he had trouble keeping his trousers fastened, he, evidently, believed that particular sin was forgivable given the number of powerful men who've gotten away with it. But he was far too self-absorbed to consider risking it all by committing murder."

"Why," Anne demanded, "did you never tell anyone?"

Again, the older woman hesitated before answering. "I was afraid."

Anne shook her head, swung her gaze to the window to prevent the other woman from seeing the accusation there. How could a woman who operated her own successful business be afraid?

"I did try."

"How so, Judith?" Jack asked.

Anne turned back to the conversation. She certainly wanted to hear this one.

"I went to the detective—Detective Jones. Not at his office. I was too afraid. I went to his house. He and his wife had two kids, and they were living in a dump. I think he was embarrassed that I showed up there, but his financial status was irrelevant to me."

"You told him," Jack pressed, "about your suspicions."

Judith moved her head up and down with a solemness that finished the story before she said another word. "We sat on his back porch. I remember the house badly needed painting, and it was hot that evening. Just unusually miserable. But he heard me out and wrote everything down. He said he would let me know if he had any more questions."

Anne knew exactly what happened. "He never had any more questions."

"No. I, on the other hand, was suddenly in the battle of my life with my husband and with the state licensing board. It took me nearly a year to get all the local government offices related to running a business like mine off my back. I suppose I was lucky I wasn't murdered."

"You were lucky," Jack confirmed.

Anne thought of the house they had visited where Harlan Jones lived. It was certainly not the same one Judith spoke about. The high-end SUV and fishing boat weren't exactly cheap either.

"I noticed," Judith went on, "later, maybe around Christmas, that the detective had moved up in the world. He bought a really nice house, moved his family there." She laughed, a soft, bitter sound. "I suspect he quickly recognized which side his bread was buttered on."

"Did Carin or Eve or her husband ever approach you about what you told the detective?" Jack asked.

"No. Carin had moved away and was doing her own kind of fishing for a rich husband. Eve and Kevin moved to Chicago to be nearer his new job. They only returned to Crystal Lake after he was elected to the US Senate. Ten years ago, I think. They built that enormous house and have been showing off ever since."

"But they all remain friendly with you," Anne said. "I'm guessing you put the word out about us after we talked that first time."

"They pretend to be my friends," Judith clarified. "But we don't socialize unless they come here. As for passing

the word along, I apologize, but it gave me great pleasure. I simply couldn't help myself." She frowned suddenly. "Dear Lord, I hope it wasn't my fault that the hotel
was set on fire."

Jack waved off the idea. "They would have found out
from someone."

This didn't appear to assuage her guilt. "I really am
sorry if I contributed to that in any way."

"We should go." Anne finished off her cocktail. "We've
had a long day." She set her gaze on the older woman's.
"Thank you again for what you did for my mother. I should
have been the one, but I was not in the right place for that."

"I was glad I could." Judith smiled. "For the record, I
wish I had done the right thing for you as well. I've regretted that for all these years." She stood. "Tonight is on
the house." She nodded to Jack. "Thank you for bringing
her here."

"Yes, ma'am."

Anne floated between elation and anger on the drive
back to their motel. It wasn't that anything Judith had told
her helped prove who Neil's killer was—not in a strong
enough or solid enough way to have the case reopened. But
all of it made Anne feel a good deal better.

"Tomorrow," Jack said, "we'll pay another visit to the
detective. The things Judith revealed will give us some
leverage."

"I can't see Jones admitting to anything at this stage
in his life," she countered. "Not unless it involved some
deal where he got immunity. Or maybe," she added with
a laugh, "he wants rid of his wife."

"Depending on which side of the political fence the DA
in this county is on, it's possible he or she might be will-

ing to go that route—a deal, I mean—if it brought down a dirty senator."

Anne chewed her lip. "Carin probably knows all the gritty details. But I'm guessing she won't change sides for any reason."

"Not unless—" Jack glanced at Anne "—she's the one who took care of the situation. Just because she had moved away doesn't mean she didn't come back for a few hours or a day."

"I'm still leaning toward Eve. She had the most to lose—besides the senator, I mean. Judith might be right about him. He may not have had the guts to do the job." Anne stared out at the darkening sky. The sun was setting. It would be full-on dark soon. "Then again, maybe he hired someone."

"Possibly. But the more people involved in a secret, the less likely it is to stay secret. If Eve or Carin were willing, that would have been the safest route for the future."

"Unless there was something else," Anne said slowly, sharing her thoughts as they occurred, "that motivated her. I can't wrap my head around the idea that Carin would take a man's life for a friend. It just seems like something that requires a more personal motive. Unless you're nothing more than a cold-blooded killer."

"Or desperate," Jack offered.

"But again, what was her motive? What was she desperate about? Kevin Langston wasn't her husband-to-be. Why kill someone over a betrayal that had no impact on her? She was working on Irving Wallace by then. She had the most to gain by sticking with Wallace."

"Ah." Jack glanced in Anne's direction. "We can't be certain there was no impact to her. If the senator was a cheater, maybe Carin was one of his lovers. She may have believed he intended to drop Eve for her. With Wallace there was that little problem of the prenup, and she had no leverage to prevent it."

"I should have thought of that one." Anne frowned. "Perhaps Carin was friendlier with Kevin than she ever was with Eve."

"When Eve found out," Jack went on, "she was grateful Carin had taken care of one problem, just not grateful enough to share her future husband."

"Until they had no choice." Anne considered the timeline. "Once Carin's rich husband died—leaving her near penniless, in her mind—she decided to come back and call in the marker."

Jack slowed for the turn into the motel. As he shifted into Park, he pulled out his cell. He stared at the screen. "Speak of the devil." He showed a text to Anne.

It's Carin. Meet me at the house on Fairlawn. We need to talk. Can't do it on the phone.

"What if it's not really her?" Worry edged into Anne's thoughts.

"We can counter with a different meeting place."

She shook her head. "We shouldn't take the risk. If she's willing to talk, we should do this her way. She might change her mind."

"We'll take necessary precautions," he assured her as he backed out and pulled back onto the road. "We won't just walk in the door."

Anne wasn't worried. She trusted Jack completely.

Chapter Nineteen

Journal Entry
Thirty Years Ago
October 1

Neil died on the Saturday before Labor Day.

I cried nearly every waking hour for days. I didn't know how I could go on.

Somehow they had decided to fast-track the trial, and it would begin in a few weeks. I asked my court-appointed attorney to get word to Neil's father that I was innocent. But he either did not or Mr. Reed didn't believe me. I was sure he was devastated too. Especially after Mrs. Reed's heart attack. It was all completely unbelievable.

My world had fallen to pieces.

Neil was gone.

I couldn't imagine that anyone really believed I murdered him…but they did. I sat in that jail cell—without bond—because they believed it. The detective, even my own attorney, looked at me as if I was evil.

I spent most of my time with both arms wrapped around my belly and you and wondered what on earth would become of you. I realized that if the trial began as scheduled,

I would be in prison months before you were born. I was so scared for you. Neil's father wouldn't talk to me, so how could I convince him to take care of you?

The weeks passed and the trial commenced and no one believed me. They didn't even hear me. They merely looked at me and saw evil.

A social worker came to see me to discuss my signing over rights to you, but I refused. How could I willingly do that? I so hoped if I waited things would turn around. I would not lose you unless I had no other choice. You are my child—my only remaining part of Neil. You have my word that I tried everything possible to take care of you—to be your mother.

When the worst happened, I prayed that Mr. Reed would come through. I was sure he hated me. Who wouldn't under the circumstances? If he believed I killed his son—his only child—how could he feel anything else? But he shouldn't hate you. You were as much Neil's as mine.

I remember telling Neil that after you were born his father would likely be more involved in our lives, but he didn't think so. He said his father had always kept him at arm's length. I can't say that I found him particularly nice to me. I always assumed he thought I wasn't good enough for his only son. Perhaps he was simply busy with all his real estate holdings. Whatever the case, I was alone.

I had never felt so helpless in my life.

But I had to be strong. I had to somehow make them see that I would never have hurt Neil. I loved him with every part of my being.

All these years later, you, of course, know what happened. I wish I could give you the answer to why it happened the way it did and the identity of who hurt your father...but I honestly don't know. I only know that I came home and found him shot and dying. He tried to talk but no words came, and then he was gone.

I am sure he would have told me how much he loved both of us if he had been able to say the words. But those words weren't necessary. I knew without a doubt how much he loved me, just as I loved him. Still do. And we both desperately loved you. Still do.

I am sorrier than you will ever know that you came into this world with so much against you already. That is my biggest regret.

Be strong and always know that you were wanted and loved deeply.

And if somehow this journal helps you find the truth, I am glad for you. I have no regrets about the choices I have made. If I could start over, I would follow the same path to the man I loved with all my heart.

Be safe, dear daughter. I have always loved you.

Chapter Twenty

Johnsburg
Fairlawn Drive, 10:00 p.m.

The house was dark.

Jack saw no other vehicles. He eased to the side of the street opposite the house Mary and Neil had shared.

He shut off the engine, and the headlights went out.

"I don't see her snazzy red car."

"I didn't see any vehicles parked along the street." Jack reviewed the slow roll along Fairlawn they had just made. "The only two houses on the street that appear to be occupied have one vehicle each in the drives, but nothing Carin would be caught operating."

Anne released her seat belt and turned around to try and scan the street, but with only one streetlamp at the end of the block there was little to see.

"Should we go in first?" She turned back to him.

Jack had an uneasy feeling about this. He reached across the console and opened the glove box. The feel of her breath on his neck had him turning to face her. "We could always go back to our motel and insist on doing this in the daylight."

She smiled. He didn't have to see—he felt it. "There are things I would much prefer to do tonight, but maybe this will give us the rest of what we need to finish this."

"Okay." He brushed his lips across hers. Then he took the handgun and flashlight from the glove box. He didn't like carrying a handgun when digging around in a cold case. It generally wasn't necessary. But he never went on assignment without one. Tonight his instincts were on fire.

"I have the key." She dug it from her bag and held it up for him to see.

"Okay." He turned off the interior lights and reached for his door. "Stay put until I come around to your door."

The air was hot and thick with humidity as he exited the car, closing the door softly. He scanned the street. Spotted no movement, although he couldn't be certain as dark as it was. Keeping his steps as quiet as possible, he walked around to the passenger-side door and opened it. He kept watch while Anne climbed out.

They hurried across the narrow street and into the overgrown yard that fronted the abandoned house. It still struck him as odd that Mary's and Neil's things—at least some of them—remained in the house. From the looks of this part of the street there wasn't that much going on in the way of gentrification. Still, nearly thirty years was a long time for a house to sit abandoned. Why had Preston Reed kept it all this time like some sort of shrine? Actually, that was probably the answer.

As with their last visit, they made their way onto the porch, thankfully without turning on the flashlight. Anne used the light from the screen of her cell, which was far dimmer than the flashlight app, to find the door key. If anyone was watching them, Jack would prefer that they stay as invisible as possible.

The door opened before the key was even in the lock. She stared up at him, and he leaned close and whispered, "Stay behind me."

She nodded her understanding, her temple brushing against his jaw.

For several seconds he stood just beyond the doorway and listened for any sound and allowed his senses to sharpen in the darkness. When he was satisfied, he moved forward. Anne stuck close behind him. He closed the door, gritting his teeth as the click echoed in the silence.

They moved through the house, checking room after room and finding nothing beyond what had been there the first time they walked through the house.

"What was the point of this?" Anne murmured.

"Maybe she was delayed," Jack offered, keeping his voice low as well.

"Maybe." Anne walked to the back door. She held her cell up to look at the door with the light from the screen. "I don't remember the door being boarded shut."

Jack turned on the flashlight and joined her at the back door. The glass area in the upper part of the door was now covered with boards. He reached for the knob, gave it a twist, and though it turned freely the door didn't budge.

"Maybe someone saw us over here on Wednesday and Reed sent a caretaker over to secure the place."

"But they left the front door unlocked?" Anne countered. "And if there's a caretaker, why let the place grow up like this?"

Very good questions. "Let's go," he said sharply, a new kind of worry kicking him in the gut.

Before they were out of the kitchen the smell of gasoline reached his nostrils. The odor was immediately followed by a whoosh he recognized all too well.

The front door was engulfed in flames. He hurried to the nearest window. Anne rushed to yet another.

The sashes wouldn't budge. Obviously they'd been screwed or nailed shut. Or years and layers of paint had sealed them shut.

"This way," he called out.

They hurried from room to room, checked all the windows. All were secured in the closed position.

By the time they were back in the kitchen, flames were climbing up the side of the house, dancing over the windows. Smoke had started to fill the air.

Urgency fired in Jack's gut. He grabbed Anne by the hand and rushed back to the bedroom Mary had used as an office. He grabbed the chair.

"Stand back and call 911." As soon as she moved away, he crashed the window with the chair. He used the chair to shove the remaining jagged pieces of glass from the frame, then he tossed it aside and used his hands to finish busting out the wood parts. The flames were climbing that side of the house too. They only had moments before it would be too late. This old house was going up in flames like dry kindling.

"Help is on the way," she said as he pulled her toward him.

"We can't wait."

As if on cue she started to cough.

They had to get out now.

"I'm going to pick you up and set your feet on the windowsill, and then you need to jump as far forward as possible." The idea that they had no idea what was in all that overgrown grass and shrubs outside—benches, flowerpots, yard ornaments—twisted his gut. Part of him wanted to go first and check out the situation. But the smoke filling his lungs warned there was no time. He had to get Anne out of here.

She hesitated. "You'll be right behind me?"

"I'll be right behind you."

"Okay."

He put his hands on her waist and lifted her upward. She planted her feet on the windowsill and leaned forward.

"Go!" he shouted as he released her.

She jumped, landing in the dense shrubs beyond the flames.

Jack went next. He grabbed onto the sides of the window frame, the heat scorching his fingers, and lunged into the air.

He plowed into the thick brush and shrubs. His knee contacted something hard.

He clenched his jaw against the pain and scrambled to his feet. He grabbed Anne by the arm and started through the junglelike landscape. Pain roared up his leg and his knee refused to work properly, but he managed to hobble quickly forward.

He checked the rental car, then they climbed inside. His body shuddered with the effort of working through the pain.

Anne stared out the car window at the house that was now fully engulfed. Thankfully there were no inhabited properties on either side of it.

They would need to make a statement when the police arrived.

Anne turned to him. "I want to go to her house."

Jack wasn't sure that was a good idea. "We should wait for the police."

"No," she argued. "I want to see Carin Wallace's face and find out why the hell she did this if she wasn't the one to kill my father. If we wait she could be long gone."

Jack started the car and pulled onto the street. By the time they arrived at the intersection at the end of the block, firetrucks were roaring toward them, lights and sirens blaring.

Knowing that help was on-site made leaving more palatable. They drove the few miles to Barrington and the extravagant residence of Carin Carter Wallace. She likely wouldn't answer and surely wouldn't open the gate.

To Jack's surprise, the gate was open.

He rolled forward, going slowly. He scanned the landscape as best he could, following the path of the headlights as they drew closer to the house.

"Her car is here." Anne pointed to the red vehicle.

There was an SUV also. Range Rover. White. Didn't look familiar.

Jack parked. "We should approach the house with caution. We can't be sure who's in there with her and what's happened."

Anne nodded. "Got it. I'll follow your lead."

They emerged from the rental and walked toward the front door. Lights were on inside, suggesting someone was there. Only two steps separated the stone parking area from the double door entry. One of the doors was ajar.

Jack hesitated. He drew his weapon. "You should call 911 again and give them this address. Whatever has happened here, it isn't likely to be good."

Anne made the call, staying close behind him as he entered the house. He didn't have to go far before he spotted the first sign of trouble.

A suitcase on the floor by the table where a car fob lay in a glass catchall.

"In here."

The voice, male, was one Jack recognized. He moved

toward the entrance to a great room, where Preston Reed sat on the sofa. A few feet away Carin Wallace lay on the floor, blood pooled around her middle.

Anne gasped, and though Jack wanted to rush to the wounded woman's side to check her vitals, he held his position in front of Anne. He had to protect her at all costs. He surveyed the man seated on the sofa. "Do you have a gun, Mr. Reed?"

He nodded, gestured to the floor.

Jack walked closer, saw the handgun on the floor. He kicked it away, sending it under the coffee table. With the immediate threat out of the way, he checked Carin Carter Wallace for a pulse. Considering her eyes were open, pupil's fixed and dilated, and her chest wasn't moving, he didn't hold out much hope that she was still alive. Her skin was cool, no pulse at the base of her throat. He shook his head at Anne, who stood a few feet away, staring in shock.

Jack stood and approached the man on the couch. "What happened, Mr. Reed?"

"Your visit—" he looked beyond Jack to Anne "—got me to thinking. The more I thought about all that you said, the more I questioned what I thought I had always known. About seven I went to the senator's house and demanded answers. He wasn't there, of course. Or if he was he was hiding." He shook his head, his face and posture weary. "So I guess I took out my emotions on his wife. I grilled her. Even shook her. She'll probably charge me with assault, but I didn't hit her."

Anne moved closer. "What did she say?"

"She said it was Carin. That Carin was the one who killed my son. She'd been having an affair with him, and when he refused to leave Mary, she disappeared." He exhaled a big breath. "Except then she came back to try one last time. But Neil wouldn't change his mind." Preston's gaze settled on Anne's. "He loved your mother too much. He wasn't giving up her and you for anything or anyone." His jaw tightened. "He always was hardheaded, just like his mother."

Jack and Anne shared a look.

"Then you came here?" Jack suggested.

The older man nodded. "She had a gun, but I took it away from her. She was in a big rush to get out of here. We argued and I tried to force her to tell me the truth, but she just kept laughing at me. She repeated two or three times that it would all be over after tonight." He shook his head. "But I didn't understand. Then we struggled and the gun went off."

He glanced at the woman on the floor. "She killed my son."

Anne's hands went to her face.

Jack considered the man again. "Did she admit this to you, Mr. Reed?"

"She did." He nodded. "She laughed when she said it. She said it was time I knew the truth but it was too bad no one else ever would." His gaze dropped to the floor. "I had to stop her...to see that she paid for what she had done."

Sirens blaring outside drew their attention to the windows.

"The police are here now." Jack slid his arm around Anne's waist and pulled her closer to him. "You can tell them what you just told us, and they'll figure it out."

Reed pushed to his feet as if he were eager to do so. "I'm ready." He stared at Anne. "I'm sorry I didn't believe Mary."

While he continued to speak to Anne, Jack studied him closer. Something about this didn't feel right. Then he spotted the oily-looking stain on his shirt around the left shoulder area. For such a warm night he was wearing a long-sleeved shirt, and the right sleeve was torn.

"Mr. Reed—" Jack ushered Anne behind him "—I'm sure this has all been a shock. Did Carin also tell you about the fire at the Fairlawn house?"

Reed's gaze swung to Jack. "What? What fire?"

Jack was close enough to smell the odor of gasoline clinging to his clothes. And the faintest scent of smoke.

Anne suddenly stepped around Jack. "It was you. I smell the gasoline. You tried to kill us."

Reed dove for the gun.

Jack was on top of him before his fingers could wrap around the grip. Anne snatched up the gun and tossed it across the room.

"It was all her fault," he railed, his face twisted with fury as he tried to glare up at Anne. "Mary didn't want him to take the job with BioTech. It was too risky, she claimed, so he turned down the offer. I tried to change his mind. We were set to make a fortune. I'd invested heavily when he told me about Smith and his offer, and I needed him on the inside so he could feed me information. But he refused." He turned his gaze to the floor as if the rest was too awful or too humiliating to say with anyone staring at him. "He refused," he repeated, the words muffled by the rug beneath his face. "He was my son, and he refused. He chose her over me."

"What happened?"

Preston looked at Jack. "I always carried a handgun. It had belonged to my father. Being in real estate, he'd warned me to carry it when I was just a young man. And he was right. I learned the hard way how dangerous some people who didn't want to be evicted could be." He shifted into a sitting position. Exhaled a heavy breath. "All those rental properties. I was in debt over my head. I don't know what happened. Neil and I were arguing, and suddenly I had the gun in my hand. I killed him. I didn't mean to… I only wanted to make him see what my life was like. I had protected him from that ugliness." He shook his head. "It was an accident. I tried to make him listen, and it went off." He started to sob. "I killed him. I killed him."

The police poured into the house. Jack lowered his weapon to the floor and nudged it away with his foot.

Anne stood next to him and cried softly while they cuffed her grandfather.

She finally knew the truth. Her mother hadn't killed her father.

Barrington Police Department
Northwest Highway
Sunday, July 13, 5:00 a.m.

ANNE HAD NEVER been so tired in her life.

Preston Reed had officially confessed to the murder of his son as well as Carin Carter Wallace. Much of what he had told her and Jack at the Wallace home had been lies. At that point he had been trying to frame Carin for the murder. But it was him. Carin never had an affair with Neil. Preston Reed had not gone to the Langston home and confronted Eve as he claimed. He'd come up with this desperate plan to use Carin in order to lure Anne and Jack to the Fairlawn house.

None of this horrific mystery had turned out the way Anne had expected.

Senator and Eve Langston were not guilty of participating in any way in the murder of Neil Reed. The senator was only guilty of being a bad friend and trying to steal the job Neil had decided he didn't want anyway. Carin, on the other hand, had known about the senator's predilection for young interns. After her husband's death, she had returned to Crystal Lake determined to glom onto the Langstons since they were rich and powerful by that point. She had enough blackmail material based on Kevin's proclivity to cheat on his wife. It had been time, in her opinion, to cash in.

All the people who should have been there for Mary and Neil had let them down for their own selfish reasons. Eve and Kevin because they hadn't wanted to get involved and have any sort of connection to murder on the record. Judith and Carin were guilty of the same. Each had her own problems and selfishly turned their backs on Mary when she needed them most. Even Ms. Farrell had, on some level, kept her head down to avoid the fallout. No one had really tried.

No matter that Anne had never allowed herself to care about her mother, she was glad that she was able to clear her name. To do what no one else had been willing to try. The memories would be with Anne for the rest of her life—the good and the bad. She was immensely thankful to the Colby Agency—to Jack—for helping her uncover and sort out those real memories.

"We're free to go," Jack announced as he walked into the tiny office.

The chief of police had given his office to Anne for some privacy. She stood, pushed all the painful thoughts out of her mind. It was time to move on. Time to tuck away all these memories of the past and murder and look to the future. Her parents would want her to be happy. And Jack had been right—they would be proud of how far she had come despite the bumpy start she had gotten in life.

Jack smiled at her, made her feel instantly warm inside. "I'm glad this is over for you, but I'm also a little sad that you lost the only other part of your family."

He was right. Preston Reed was the last of her biological family—at least as far as she knew.

"Frankly, I'm just glad it's over. At this point, I don't have it in me to forgive him." She worked up a smile of her own. "My plan is to get on with my life and be grateful for the good memories we were able to glean from so-called friends of my parents."

"That's an excellent way to go forward." He wrapped her arm around his. "How about we find a place to have breakfast and talk about your other plans for the future."

She leaned in close. "I was thinking we could pick up something to take back to our motel and do our talking— or not—there."

He grinned. "Much better idea."

They drove away from the police station, and Anne realized she already had a great plan in mind. She would start her own family...with this man—eventually. Maybe it was a little early in the relationship, but if life had taught her anything, it was not to put off her dreams. She smiled at Jack. As long as he was willing, of course.

He flashed her a smile and reached for her hand.

She had a feeling he was more than willing.

Chapter Twenty-One

Chicago
Monday, July 14
The Colby Agency, 10:00 a.m.

Victoria spread the *Chicago Tribune* across her desk. She smiled. Mary Morton had made the headlines. After thirty years her name had been cleared. To see this and know the agency had helped make it happen warmed her heart.

The door of her office burst open, and Jamie rushed in with her own copy of the *Tribune*. "Have you seen it?"

"I have. Great work, Jamie. I am so very proud."

Her granddaughter settled in one of the chairs in front of Victoria's desk. "I had a feeling about this one."

"Always trust your instincts," Victoria agreed.

"I understand Jack has decided to take some vacation time." Jamie's eyes twinkled.

Victoria nodded. "He has. He's been such a workaholic for years. I'm so glad he finally found the time." Or the right reason, she mused.

"I'll never tire of these happy endings," Jamie enthused.

Her granddaughter was so like her. This made Victoria inordinately happy.

Jamie folded her paper and laid it aside. "Grandmother, you and Grandpa should take a vacation too. Get out of the city and enjoy yourselves. No one works harder than the two of you. We can handle things here for a few weeks."

"A few weeks?" she repeated with raised eyebrows. How could she possibly agree to such a schedule?

Jamie inclined her head. "Two or three, I mean. It would do you both good."

Victoria's gaze narrowed. "Did your grandpa put you up to this?"

"Perhaps." Jamie grinned. "Just say yes. He has a big surprise waiting for you."

Victoria loved surprises, especially from Lucas. "Well, I suppose a little time off won't hurt."

Jamie shot to her feet. "Excellent. I'll schedule a staff meeting so you can tell the others."

Before she could say a word her granddaughter was off and running.

As much as Victoria always looked forward to the agency's next big case, she couldn't wait to spend some well-deserved time relaxing with Lucas, the man she loved with every part of her being.

* * * * *

COMING SOON!

We really hope you enjoyed reading this book.
If you're looking for more romance
be sure to head to the shops when
new books are available on

Thursday 23rd October

To see which titles are coming soon, please visit
millsandboon.co.uk/nextmonth

MILLS & BOON